Continuums

Continuums

Robert Carr

To Natalie
with best wishes
Robert Carr
5 Nov 2008

mosaic press

Library and Archives Canada Cataloguing in Publication

Carr, Robert, 1945-
    Continuums / Robert Carr.

ISBN 978-0-88962-892-2

    I. Title.

PS8605.A847C65 2008   C813'.6   C2008-906136-5

Publishing by Mosaic Press, offices and warehouse at 1252 Speers Rd., units 1 & 2, Oakville, On L6L 5N9, Canada and Mosaic Press, PMB 145, 4500 Witmer Industrial Estates, Niagara Falls, NY, 14305-1386, U.S.A.

info@mosaic-press.com
Copyright © Robert Carr, 2008
ISBN 978-0-88962-892-2

Mosaic Press in Canada:
1252 Speers Road, Units 1 & 2,
Oakville, Ontario
L6L 5N9
Phone/Fax: 905-825-2130
info@mosaic-press.com

Mosaic Press in U.S.A.:
4500 Witmer Industrial Estates
PMB 145, Niagara Falls, NY
14305-1386
Phone/Fax: 1-800-387-8992
info@mosaic-press.com

www.mosaic-press.com

"My theory stands as firm as a rock; every arrow directed against it will return quickly to its archer. How do I know this? Because I have studied it from all sides for many years; because I have examined all objections which have ever been made against the infinite numbers; and above all because I have followed its roots, so to speak, to the first infallible cause of all created things."

- **George Cantor**

Acknowledgments

A first novel needs a lot of support in its gestation – especially if, as in this case, a long one – and many thanks are due.

I must start with Joe Kertes. I cannot imagine this book being published without Joe's encouragement, advice, support, patience, and humour. What began as a chance encounter between us has led to a lasting friendship.

The School for Writers at Humber College (Joe's creation) has been instrumental in moving my work forward. I have had the generous and critical advice of numerous excellent mentors and teachers. I am indebted to Antanas Sileika, now the Director of the Humber School for Writers, for his help and advice on the earlier drafts of my work, and for his constant and witty encouragement.

I owe much to Alex Schultz for his priceless editorial effort. David Lodge said somewhere that a novice writer combines modest claims for his work with obstinacy in defending his execution of it. If I did it too, this is the place to offer apologies.

Thanks are due to my agent, Margaret Hart, from HSW Literary Agency, for her relentless efforts on behalf of this book.

Howard Aster, from Mosaic Press, has been an immediate and enthusiastic supporter of Continuums. His advice has been immensely helpful. I couldn't be more grateful for all this.

I thank my family, of course. Esther, my wife and biggest fan, at all times pushing me to follow my obsession. And my children, Alexandra and Max, amused and also bemused by their father's makeover.

And finally, I thank the Canadian Space Agency, whose policies made it easier for me to decide to become a full-time writer.

To Esther, Alexandra and Max

PART I
Bucharest

Chapter 1
January 1969

Alexandra needed little sleep. It was a blessing, she thought, a gift for someone of her profession. Her husband didn't see it the same way, although in company he made light of it. "Every man needs a soft warm body to wake up to before facing the world. My wife goes to bed past midnight and gets up at four every morning. She has work to do – has to be thinking mathematics." She would try to quiet him. "There is no need, Emil. All Bucharest is aware of my sleeping habits."

He was more openly resentful of Alexandra's insistence on working in her office at the university on Sundays. She had been doing it for about a year now, ever since Ada turned three. "The only day I can sleep in," he would complain, "my only day of rest. I want to spend the day with you and Ada." If she replied, and often she chose not to, it was to remind him that it was only half a day, and that, anyway, he could look after Ada once a week, since she was doing it the rest of the time. She needed the quiet Sunday mornings in her office and he had to help her a bit. "I don't get it – you're a full professor already". "It's for me, Emil. *I* need it." "You barely sleep at night. You have the whole night and most of every day to do your math – and now Sundays as well."

The truth was that during the week Alexandra rarely had time to "think mathematics." In the early hours of the morning she marked assignments, reviewed lectures, revised papers, kept up with her prodigious professional correspondence and with the work of her assistants. Once everybody awoke, the chores caught up with her – preparing breakfast for Emil and Ada, getting Ada dressed, taking her to kindergarten. Emil helped as much as he could – in the typical male half-hearted way – but he often rushed out straight after breakfast and came home late. The one or two days a week she didn't have to go to the university – less often lately because of the many meetings and the increased administrative burden – she had to worry about bread and queue up in empty grocery stores. By the time that was over, and she never knew how long it would take, she might catch a couple of hours for her work, but by then her mind would be occupied with mundane things – what she should cook, how her mother was coping, whether she needed new shoes for Ada. Also, her in-laws needed coffee and sugar – why didn't they ask Emil? – and soap, especially soap. And what should she prepare for the usual Tuesday dinner with Mother and Leonard?

Sunday mornings were hers, entirely hers. Buses were infrequent that early, but she didn't mind the half-hour walk to the university. It stimulated her, and by the time she reached the entrance to the university building on Edgar Quinet Street, she knew exactly how she would spend the precious hours. The night porter – always grumbling and reeking of plum brandy – would switch on the dim lights leading to her office and go back to sleep. Alexandra loved the echo of her steps in the absolute silence on the stairs, her muted footfall on the worn-out carpet in the corridor, her large, high-ceilinged office, the old wooden desk with the curved metal lamp, the walls lined with books. She was overwhelmed with privileges – she was their pride, the award-winning mathematician, a candidate for the Fields medal, proof that the regime could nurture remarkable people.

Around two in the afternoon, Emil would begin to ring her. "What, still there? Don't you a have a family? A young child?" At three he'd be irate, and often she'd not pick up the phone, quickly pack up and – on getting home – claim that the bus failed to show up.

That's what she lived for, for these quiet Sunday mornings, when her mind was clear and focused and confident. And she was disappointed that morning when, around half past eight, Emil rang to tell her to expect a visit from Leonard. Her brother's call had woken him up. "I'd hoped to sleep in. Ada is up now. What's so bloody important he has to call at daybreak on Sunday? What's wrong with this brother of yours? He was rude, too."

What could Leonard want so urgently? He'd been in her office only once, last September, when he had spent several minutes in incoherent desperation crumpled in a chair. Earlier that year, the Western broadcasts about the "spring" in Prague had brought hope that things would get better. Then, late in the summer, the Soviets sent in their troops, Dubcek was removed, and the gloom returned. The first Sunday after the Soviet troops entered Prague, Leonard came to her office and began repeating to her that there was no hope. "No hope, no hope, no hope, no hope ..." He had raised a trembling finger towards her. "How could you possibly scribble equations in times like this?" He didn't stay long. Soon afterwards there were rumours about a Soviet invasion of Romania as well, although nobody understood why – there was no spring in Bucharest at all. In large demonstrations, the crowd displayed their resolve to fight. Alexandra was rounded up for a huge gathering in the Square of the Republic. The little man on the balcony far away stammered hysterically defiant words to the bewildered multitude. There were rehearsed waves of spontaneous ovations. All the Mathematics Department was there, except Aroso, of course. The sturdier ones carried portraits of the jerky, puppet-size figure on the balcony. Secretary Nicolescu – who had joined the faculty the same year as Alexandra – hoisted the largest portrait. She bumped into Leonard, who appeared to have become separated from his colleagues at the Institute of Calculations. "What a circus!" he said. "They must be shitting in their pants at Red-Army Headquarters." He looked around and greeted some of his former professors. A loud, hoarse voice, somewhere behind her, urged more fervour and began the swell of another slogan. "Very impressive!" Leonard shouted in Alexandra's ear. "Everybody's here. No, I don't see Aroso." She smiled and shouted back, "Couldn't make it. Mitzi, as usual."

Now her Sunday morning, or part of it, was a write-off. Her brother's interruption was annoying – especially today, when she had to at least outline the paper for the March workshop in Zurich. She'd been told – Nicolescu had carried the good news – that she could go. She had been to Moscow and Varna and Dresden, and a few other places, but never anywhere in the West. March wasn't far away. There weren't many weeks left. She had felt delighted, almost giddy, when she read the invitation to present a paper. Very select participation, no more than twenty or so mathematicians. Functional analysis wasn't her specialty (if she ever had one), nor was it a topic that had even held her interest particularly, but that's why the organizers wanted her. What had the invitation said? It was quite nicely worded, very flattering: " … If there are generalists in mathematics today, you, dear Professor Semeu, are among the finest. Toilers in our venerable field, we would benefit from the view of somebody younger and not mired in it. Your paper should suggest problems in functional analysis the resolution of which would likely lead to advances in other branches of mathematics …" She had some ideas, and some definite thoughts. She had already discussed them with Aroso, and the old professor had said he would likely drop in that morning for another chat. He had other matters to look after nearby and didn't mind at all. And now, Leonard. What could he possibly want that couldn't wait?

The difference in age – she was nine years his senior – meant that she had adored him as a child, and he had reciprocated, always following his Alsa wherever she went (he had had difficulty with "Alexandra," and what first came out of his mouth was Alsa, his name for her ever since). Their father's death, when Leonard was only three – old enough to see the trauma around him, without clearly understanding the reason – brought them even closer. Mrs. Jacobi was too distraught to pay much attention to Leonard, and twelve-year-old Alexandra looked after him and comforted him. If she was studying, he would quietly play in the same room. Later, when he began school, he insisted on doing his homework not far from where she did hers. She helped him with his lessons – not that he needed much help – and, best as she could, calmed his fears. When he learned how to write, he sent her brief letters, which he proudly carried to her from his corner of the room. Yes, he had been a very sweet, affectionate little brother.

As a teenager, Leonard became difficult and they had their share of arguments, but that was typical and, anyway, it didn't last long. Then she got married and moved out. She knew that he continued to admire her – he often talked about her prodigious career with unconcealed delight – and the fact that he had followed in her footsteps attested to it.

She had questioned Leonard's choice at the time. It was not enough to have a certain facility with math. Leonard definitely had that, but he needed more to become a real mathematician, a contributor, a constructor of the astonishing edifice started thousands of years earlier. To be a bricklayer – as Aroso was fond of saying. When she expressed her doubts to Leonard, he had seemed more hurt than surprised. "There's nothing else that interests me," he said. She had taught him one semester – a third-year course in complex functions – and he had been everything she expected. Competent – no, more than that, very good and quick in his responses and in his input in the class. He read extensively and was interested in the background of the problems, why they were important. He could follow and understand, but he could not create. There was no startling originality in his thought, no great ability to discern patterns – never mind create new ones. He finished the five years of university in good enough standing to avoid teaching high school, and with some support from her he began his working life at the National Institute for Calculations, recently founded to push the country into a vaguely discerned future computer age. Others would have been very happy but Leonard wasn't – he told her as much after the novelty of the first few months was over. Every morning, six days a week, he dragged himself there. He wanted be a mathematician, not a programmer. He found computers tiresome, an invitation to be mentally lazy. He had access to a Soviet clunker, slow, painful to program, and often down while waiting for the right spare part from a factory near Riga. There was also a recently arrived French computer at the institute, but all he could do was submit his deck of punched cards to the gods who ran it. The printed output could come back in a day or in a month, usually the latter. When he complained about the long turnaround, he was told he was not working on a problem of national interest. He was depressed for a while, miserable. It was, he told Alexandra, the end of his illusions. The process had been painful, because it ultimately led to the terrible recognition that he was not bright enough to be a mathematician. A true, authentic, bona fide mathematician. It was that simple, and it was hurtful. It shouldn't have taken him so long. He could finally talk about all this without much pain because he had come to a decision. "If I can't be a mathematician," he told her, "I'll be a historian of mathematics, a writer about mathematicians. It's not the real thing, I'll have only one foot in it, maybe only half a foot, but it's better than no foot at all." She had been too candid with him in her response, brutally candid, and she had regretted it ever since. "A good decision, Leonard," was all she said. A more doting sister would have whispered a few soothing phrases. She could have told him that he was a better mathematician than he was giving himself credit for, or some similar kind lie.

"Emil told me you were here," Leonard said. "You look better than ever. And so nicely dressed for a quiet Sunday morning at the office."

"Emil's boss has invited us to lunch – a late lunch – and I'm going directly from here. I've been told to look my best. Emil is not happy with you. How is Mother?"

"Well enough. I saw Professor Aroso stepping into the consignment store across the street, almost bent double under a heavy package."

"He's helping me with this paper and said he'd drop in for a chat. He should write it – not me. I asked his permission to add his name as co-author. Wouldn't think of it. It's not the first time he's done this, provide the best ideas in a paper and then refuse to take any credit."

Aroso had dismissed her request with a show of mock fear on his face, and the usual line that it would mean he might have to answer questions and provide clarifications. Well, he couldn't be bothered. They all thought he was dead anyway – dead or senile – and it was better to keep it that way.

She waited for Leonard to explain his visit. When he said nothing, she said, "Look, Leonard, I'm really busy."

"We have to talk."

"Right now? I have a lot of work. Can't it wait?"

"Give me half an hour, that's all."

"Aroso will be here any minute now."

"Pin a note on the door, Alsa. Believe me, I wouldn't disturb you if it wasn't important."

"Something wrong?"

He shook his head. "Let's go for a walk."

A good-looking boy, she thought, as he went down the stairs ahead of her, an unhappy good-looking boy. A boy of twenty-four. She had always regarded him as a boy – couldn't help it. They walked towards Cismigiu Garden. It was a cold, blustery day. A pale sun was trying to disperse low grey clouds. The snow fallen overnight made squeaking sounds under their steps. It was only inside the garden that he made the announcement.

"I'm going to try to get away, Alsa. If it works out, I won't be here this fall. I thought I'd let you know. Mother knows. You may consider doing the same thing ... I mean coming with me. With Emil and Ada, of course."

Alexandra stopped walking and he had to stop too. Suddenly hunched, gripping herself tightly to keep from shivering in the cold, she stood there looking at him. It took a long time before she answered.

"Tell me more about it."

Well, there were rumours that, for reasons unknown, possibly no reason at all, the guards at Bulgaria's border with Turkey were letting Romanian nationals cross into Turkey. It implied getting a passport with a visa for Bulgaria, but that should not be too difficult, especially for her and her family. He was planning to hitch a ride across the border into Turkey, but if the whole Semeu family chose to come as well, they could all drive in their car. Once in Istanbul, they could go to any number of countries in Western Europe on tourist visas and ask for refugee status. France seemed to be treating refugees well. Italy also. Maybe other places. Or they could consider Israel. She, especially she, would have no trouble at all – universities would do battle for her.

"And Mother?"

"They might let her go after a while and she could join us wherever we are."

"Let her go?"

"She'd free the apartment. And she'd forfeit the pension. So why would they detain her? Of course, she might choose to stay."

She took another long time before she replied. "Do you know of anybody who's got out this way? It sounds too easy. Just show up and they'll let you through? The good lads at the border will salute and point the way across?"

"I don't know anybody myself, if that's what you mean. But I've heard of somebody who had made it through this way. A friend of a friend of a friend."

"You don't know whether it works at all, do you?"

"Somebody I know well will try in a couple of months."

"You don't know. It could be just an unfounded, senseless, asinine rumour. Or a trap."

He shrugged.

"Who is this guinea-pig friend of yours?"

He shrugged again. "You know better than that, Alsa. Don't ask."

"Why don't you wait until you get the definite proof?"

"It takes three to six months to get a passport for Bulgaria, if one gets it at all. I have to apply now. I can't waste two months. This opportunity, inexplicable as it is, won't last. Two months could make a difference. Even two days. Definite proof? That's asking too much. Any success or failure we might hear about would not necessarily mean the same outcome for us. Or for me, if you decide against it. I would give it a try, anyway, even if this friend of a friend fails."

They walked in silence along the empty paths of the park. The small artificial lake on which she had skated as a child, on rusty pre-war skates, was frozen solid. A few skaters were leaving tracks through the thin layer of fresh snow not yet blown away by the wind. They had an air of determination. She remembered one spring – she may have been thirteen – falling through the ice. The water was shallow, no higher than her hips. She had dried her clothes at a friend's and their mother never found out about it.

Finally she touched his arm to make him look at her. "You are telling me that I should ruin my career, ruin my husband's career, and endanger my four-year old daughter based on rumours about a way out of the country that is both unlikely and ludicrous? Is this what you are saying? Not to mention the fact that we could easily end up in jail."

She was both angry and dismayed.

"I had to tell you, to give you a chance," Leonard said.

She shook her head. It wasn't a chance that she could reasonably take. He was telling her more for himself than for her, she thought bitterly – so that he would not feel guilty, or not too guilty. He knew she wouldn't do it – that she couldn't. By telling her about his intention and suggesting she join him, he simply wanted to get a disclaimer from her, a chit which, somehow, in the future, would absolve him of any blame for the consequences of his decision.

"Give me a chance? What chance? This is quite selfish, Leonard."

He seemed hurt. "I'm offering you and your family the same way out. The same odds. In fact, with you, the four of us, crowded in your tiny car, all of us Romanian nationals, we would look more suspicious, and the likelihood of making it through would drop considerably. I may be selfish because I am going to do it with you or without you, but I am willing to try at the lower odds nevertheless, the same odds for me and for you and your family."

"Obviously, I will not do it," she said. "It would have been better not to tell me about it."

A fat Gypsy woman crossed their path, dragging along a crying child. Farther away, near the deserted boat-rental area, two soldiers were jumping up and down to keep warm.

"Don't tell Emil about this, then," Leonard said.

They walked on some more.

"How is the paper going?" asked Leonard.

"The paper needs work. I barely have an outline. Let's turn back, I'm very cold. Never mind the paper. Good God, Leonard, this is quite a shock. What's going to happen? What's going to happen to all of us? You wouldn't reconsider would you? No, of course not." She shivered. "This is the end for us."

They were quiet the rest of the way back. She walked with heavy shoulders. In front of her building, Leonard said that he was frozen and needed a few minutes inside. When they reached her office, she collapsed in her chair. He kept his winter coat on and took a seat across from her desk. They sat speechless, looking at each other. A door slammed not far away.

"There's another thing, Alsa. I need money. Four thousand lei. I need twice that amount to buy some information. Useful information. Mother is giving me two thousand. And I can scrape together two thousand myself, if I sell a few things."

"Who gets this money, Leonard? A friend? A friend of a friend? Or a friend of a friend of a friend?"

"Don't ask, Alsa. And, please, there's no need for sarcasm."

"Ah, I'm not allowed sarcasm. Do you hear yourself? Alsa, dear sister, I am running away. In the process I will ruin your career and, very likely, your family. I also need money. And, by the by, mind the way you react to all this."

He didn't answer.

"How do you know you're not being swindled?"

"I don't."

Minutes passed with nothing said. Then he said he was sorry, but she didn't answer.

"Don't tell Emil about this," he repeated.

"If I give you the money, I have to tell Emil."

"Don't tell Emil, please. Forget about the money. I'll get the money, somehow."

After that, they were quiet again. What else was there to say? When he got up to leave, she stood up and gave him a hug. An odd thing to do, she thought. She was hugging the brother who might bring calamity to her life and her family. She was hugging him because she was frightened. Because a family stuck together even when destruction was threatened by one of its own. Because she had no other choice.

"It will turn out fine, Alsa. For all of us. I just know it."

She walked him to the stairs. On her way back she met Professor Danczay, very likely on his way to the washroom. A bit of a relic now, but still teaching one course, "Introduction to Probability," hanging on to it as if giving it up would cut the tether he had with this world. An absolute disaster as a lecturer. In her first year she had taken Danczay's course. He spoke with such a heavy Hungarian accent his lectures were impossible to follow. There was an air of mutiny among the students, who complained that they could not understand him. After the first two classes, Danczay had agreed to write practically his entire lectures on the blackboard. From that time onward he spent the two hours of his weekly class with his back to the students, hastily writing out his lecture notes, which he held in his left hand, his dark suits dusted with chalk, and mumbling to himself. This, they heard, had happened every year. The large amphitheatre was noisy, with unimpeded traffic in and out. Only the first few rows took down the notes from the blackboard. Every twenty minutes or so, Danczay would shout, "Quiet back there, or I'll throw you out," a threat he never carried out, but which preceded a trip on his part to the washroom. The students were so aggravated, they were beyond feeling sorry for Danczay's inability to make himself understood. Malicious tongues insisted that he was perfectly capable of speaking intelligible Romanian; he persisted with this charade because he had managed to master only the initial two lectures.

Danczay had always been friendly with her. He stopped Alexandra and shook her hand with both of his. "If you're looking for Aroso, he's in my office. I'll tell him you're back. You look splendid. Style and brains, both."

She mostly guessed what Danczay was saying, and it got worse when his voice suddenly dropped to a whisper. "I was talking to Aroso about this too. It's not good for us, minorities, now. Not at all. They are trying to get rid of me, you know? Retire, they say. I'm only fifty-six years old. Professor Aroso could be in danger too – he is much older than I am. I hear rumblings about the ethnic diversity of the teaching staff, that it should reflect that of the whole country. There are too many Jews teaching at the university, it's being said. And too many Hungarians. Jews, yes, there are too many – no hard feelings, I hope. But Hungarians? That's not true. Believe me, if a true mathematical ratio were imperative, they would hire more Hungarians, not try to get rid of them. You are fine, of course, you are the light of the faculty. You'd be the last Jew threatened."

He was going to add something else, then suddenly waved a salute and turned quickly away, working on his fly long before he had reached the washroom.

She walked slowly back to her office.

Chapter 2
May 1969

Professor Asuero Aroso's past had always been the subject of stories and eager gossip. Like many of his generation, Aroso must have learned quickly that the past hid many perils and that it was best to keep a tight lid on it. Only when she joined the faculty as an assistant professor did Alexandra realize how isolated Aroso was – and how he did everything to maintain this isolation. He never talked about his past. With his colleagues he shunned small talk and social occasions. His wife's lengthy affliction had given him a perfect excuse – Mitzi needed his attention. Always in a hurry to get home to Mitzi, he could also avoid the endless meetings and any political commitment.

In her student days, the most repeated Aroso stories were about the wilful waste of his mathematical genius. Aroso had been a student in Gottingen, at the most famous school of mathematics of the time. Alexandra remembered talking with her classmates about it. Their ideas about the legendary institution were based on hearsay. In their petrified little world, knowledge about anything west of them was not to be had. As a result, to them, students of mathematics and dreamers of academic glory, Gottingen had a mythic glow. They talked about Gottingen with lowered voices, with awe and reverence, but also in corners, fearing hostile ears. And Aroso, they whispered to each other, their own Aroso, had been a student in Gottingen. It was said that Aroso had been so highly thought of there that, at the end of his studies, he could have obtained a teaching position at any academic institution. All he had to do was choose. Point his finger and choose. At Gottingen, he had worked under David Hilbert, the great David Hilbert, although it was Hilbert in his declining years. Under Hilbert's approving eyes, Aroso had played the game of removing axioms of geometry and marvelling at the consequences. At the age of twenty-five, Aroso had been asked by Hilbert to return to Gottingen as an assistant professor. An unheard of honour. In the twenties, when Aroso was there, Gottingen was still considered the top mathematics school in the world. Recovered from the loss of talent in the Great War, Gottingen was enjoying its last years of fame in the twenties and early thirties before it fell quickly into irrelevancy under Hitler's racial laws. According to this prevalent Aroso story, when Aroso eventually declined Hilbert's offer, after having initially accepted, Hilbert became so angry with him that he refused to have anything to do with Aroso for the rest of his life. It was also said that Hilbert, following Aroso's snubbing, had used his name and prestige to turn other mathematicians against Aroso. This was what accounted for Aroso's lack of recognition and fame.

A colleague of Alexandra, whose father had been a student of Aroso's in the late thirties, claimed that John von Neumann had worked in Gottingen with Hilbert at the same time, and that Hilbert had considered Aroso the better mathematician. He explained to her, "No mind can rise as high as Aroso's. Nobody is with him. He is alone. Utterly alone. It wouldn't matter where he was. At the Sorbonne, or Cambridge, it wouldn't make a difference. He would be alone. Can you imagine, having nobody to talk to? He must have asked himself, What's the point? And so he waits for his end in this godforsaken place."

There was talk, also, about tormented stretches in his married life with Mitzi, whose love had shifted, it was said maliciously, like a weathercock. Many repeated with authority that Mitzi had been a stunning beauty when Aroso first met her. Mitzi, of course, had had Parkinson's for many years now.

Alexandra's student colleagues knew that she had known Aroso, and that she had studied with him since her high-school days. At the beginning, they had assailed her with questions. She disappointed them, because there wasn't much she could add or refute. Aroso had not talked to her about his earlier life. Maybe if she had asked direct questions. But she hadn't. She had been too young to be curious.

She regretted now that she knew so little about Aroso. She had glimpses of his past – it was inevitable, they had known each for almost twenty years, one puts two and two together – but that was all. Only once had he seemed willing to talk and she had caught a hint, an intimation of an earlier time. But she had felt more embarrassed about it than curious.

She had been putting the final touches to her dissertation on chromatic numbers. It had been her own choice, chromatic numbers, because although Aroso had written a couple of articles on the subject before the war, it had never been a particular interest of his and he had tried to dissuade Alexandra from her choice. He had given up, sternly amused in the face of her stubbornness. "It's a romantic choice, Alexandra," he had told her. "The beautiful name, and then the famous four-colour map problem, so simple to state and yet still unproven after more than one hundred years. All right, all right, it's a prerogative of youth to dream of glory and fame. I know, you don't have to work on the four-colour problem, and there are many other aspects, granted, but watch out, it could suck you in. And you'll be very much on your own, as I've lost touch with this field a long time ago. Yes, I'll go back and do some reading to be able to converse with you, but it's not as if I was ever actively involved in this topic myself."

He was right. It had been a romantic choice, and close to the completion of her thesis she had lost some of her enthusiasm for the topic, although she did some good work on chromatic number for orientable surfaces and Aroso had been very happy with her work.

Then, as she worked out a minor proof, she stumbled on an idea that seemed to open a very promising path of research, although with better applications in different aspects of mathematics. The thought of delaying the defence of her thesis to spend more time – a few months, at most half a year – pursuing this new idea took an urgent hold of her. She told herself that the reward, the added value to the thesis, could be huge. She became very excited and she needed to talk with Aroso. It was a Sunday afternoon and she rang his home. A busy signal. She tried a few more times – always busy. He had told her before, "Come any time you want to talk math." In the past, she had always let him know in advance that she was coming. But this one time, impatient, she took the streetcar and went to his house.

She let herself into the courtyard. The door to the small hall and the one leading to his study were both open. He was there, at his desk, sifting through a pile of photographs he had dumped out of a shoebox. Old ones, twenty years old, maybe more. He didn't seem too startled to see her, and when she began to explain, quite overwrought, the reason for her sudden arrival, he shushed her and pointed to the photographs. "Bit of bad news. Somebody who Mitzi held very dear just died. Not sure if I should tell Mitzi. Come here and look at some old photographs and help me decide what to do. Here, keep me company – just a few minutes. Then we can talk math as long as you want. Look how young we were. Look at Mitzi, look how beautiful she was. Striking, wasn't she? Oh, here it is, the picture I was searching for. And here again. It's Lavinia, Mitzi's sister-in-law, the one that just passed away. Mitzi and Lavinia were once very close. Slightly crazy, Lavinia, but everybody loved her. Oh, the things they did together, Mitzi and Lavinia! Lavinia was the instigator. Always. Well, almost always."

Mitzi – Aroso pointed her out – was wearing a *tailleur*. Alexandra couldn't see much of her face because she wore a hat with a very wide brim that hid most of it. They had such elaborate hats in those days. A hatless Lavinia looked taller than Mitzi – maybe because she was in a very tight dress. A rather long nose, yet attractive. A *belle-laide*. They had allure, the two young women, whatever that meant. A very tall and thin, and very young, Aroso grinned a few steps behind them. The threesome seemed quite happy, or at least to be having a good time. But then, everybody smiled when pictures were taken.

Aroso said an odd thing as he was putting the lid back on the old shoebox. He said he should burn them all, all the pictures. Then they talked math. They sketched the way ahead for Alexandra, weighed alternatives, decided on priorities. Even made some guesses as to what the main results would be. She made more progress that evening with Aroso than she would have in a couple of months on her own. But he didn't let her delay the thesis. He said that she had enough. It was strange. He had given her a rather hard time on the thesis, always urging her to do more. More of this, more of that. Try this, try that. And now, when she had come to him with the possibility of a major addition, he told her that she had enough. More than enough. He told her to do the research and publish it as a separate piece of work in a major international journal. Which she did, about a year later. Her first important paper. In fact, she wrote several papers out of that idea.

Alexandra had known Aroso since she was fifteen. A late starter in mathematics, she was not "discovered" earlier simply because she had excelled at all subjects in school. Nobody realized how little effort she put into math. But she had always been vaguely aware of her predisposition towards the subject. In the second (or was it third?) grade, they were taught division, and she quickly realized that some numbers were different from the others because they were not divisible by any other number. And there were many of them, although they seemed to appear less often as you counted higher. She wasn't sure how she found those special numbers, but she remembered that she went as far as 113. Her teacher told her these numbers were called prime, though there was nothing special about them. It didn't take Alexandra long to realize how wrong the teacher was – but from that point on she didn't ask her any more questions about numbers. She knew better.

In early 1954, Alexandra was in the middle of Grade Nine, the second of the four years of high school. Sternly and enigmatically, Stalin was watching every student – not for much longer – from every textbook, wall, and window. Inspired by the Soviet Union's example, a countrywide mathematics competition, a veritable Mathematics Olympiad, began to be held every year, with local winners advancing to regional tests and, eventually, the best competing for the very top honours at the national level. It must have been the second or the third time this competition was held when Alexandra was entered in it by her school. She wasn't consulted – it was assumed that she would not object to such a prestigious assignment. She was known to be very good at math, but she had always been an excellent student overall. She had an extraordinary memory and everything came easy to her. Because she was also very conscientious, following each instruction to the tiniest detail and more, she gave the impression of a hard-working, zealous student. As a result, her true gift had been masked by her overall excellence.

When the results from the local competition became known, the entire school learned that Alexandra had scored the maximum points for her grade, way above everybody else. Her mathematics teacher, Paul Storcescu, a short, walleyed, timid man, was astonished. The organizers informed him that Alexandra hadn't simply resolved all the problems and come up with the right answers – her answers and explanations showed an unusual mind, a mind that saw a myriad of connecting paths on a landscape that, to all others, seemed shapeless and barren. In many of the test problems she had provided more than one way of reaching the right answer, some strikingly original.

She stood out two months later as well, in the round for the whole city. Now, not just Paul Storcescu but the entire body of teachers at Alexandra's high school became excited – they had a definite gold medal winner in Alexandra. Because they didn't want to leave anything to chance, Paul Storcescu began to hold a weekly cramming session with Alexandra. They turned out to be useless. There wasn't much he could teach her from the material she was supposed to master, because Alexandra had already breezed through her math textbook to the very end. Not sure what else to do, Paul Storcescu gave Alexandra a first-year university book on matrices. It was a thin book, not very theoretical, more on the usefulness and practical application of matrices (a bit of a novelty in those days outside physics), and she mastered it in a couple of weeks. It was then, while Alexandra was demurely reporting to him on what she had learned and, in the process, making some poignant observations – startling for somebody so young – that Paul Storcescu first thought of Asuero Aroso.

That year, Alexandra won the countrywide competition for her grade level. Paul Storcescu had no difficulty convincing the school to enter her the following year at the highest level of the competition, even though she would be one grade lower than her competitors. Properly coached, Paul Storcescu insisted, she would win the big prize, and their school would reap increased recognition. Asuero Aroso, the greatest mathematician in Romania, Paul Storcescu told the assembled body of teachers, would be approached to coach Alexandra over the summer. Not only would she win the individual competition, but because of her, their school would win the team competition as well. He, Paul Storcescu, would talk to Asuero Aroso, whom he knew personally, and he would convince him to mentor Alexandra for the big competition.

Paul Storcescu had been a student of Aroso in the late 1930s. During the intervening years, Aroso had remembered Storcescu and had kept in touch with him, not because he had been a brilliant student, but because – this Alexandra learned later from Aroso – he had been one of the few former students who would say hello to him in the street and stop for a chat during the dark days when nobody was willing to talk to Jews, or be seen talking to Jews.

Aroso agreed with little enthusiasm to see the schoolgirl genius. "It's a nuisance to him," Paul Storcescu explained to Mrs. Jacobi in Alexandra's presence. "He's convinced that nothing will come of it. But he'll do it for my sake. He's of an older cut, and he does not believe that math prodigies come from the female half of humanity. But not to worry, Mrs. Jacobi. In half an hour your daughter will win him over."

It took Aroso only fifteen minutes to realize that he had in front of him an unusually gifted youth. He recognized, he told Alexandra years later, or believed that he recognized, himself at Alexandra's age. The same immediacy and natural ease in comprehending and connecting mathematical concepts, as if there existed indeed a mathematical universe, or a mathematical dimension to the universe, of which only a few were aware and were capable of exploring.

There was something else, something that Alexandra understood later, much later, from Aroso's words uttered during the few times he let his guard down. Alexandra had been so young and fresh and eager, and her extraordinary mind provided such instant rewards to Aroso the teacher, that he began to look forward to the weekly two-hour sessions he quickly agreed to have with her. She might have struck a chord in Aroso's heart, a chord which, however forgotten and out of tune, resonated loudly. She was in a way the child that he and Mitzi never had, the child that Mitzi had wanted. She doubted that Aroso had been heartbroken that Mitzi and he could never have children. But there she was, a ready-made, surrogate daughter, already grown up, admirable in all respects and admiring of him, and to whom, to top it all, he could teach the wonders of the arcane mathematical universe.

The rule that Aroso imposed from the very beginning was that Alexandra had to read the material by herself. Aroso was quite emphatic about it – he would only clarify things, when needed. The right books would be found. Paul Storcescu had already provided Alexandra with the textbooks for the year ahead, and Aroso had plenty of others.

They met in his office at the university. At a small table tucked in a corner, Alexandra quietly worked out the problems he gave her. She rarely had questions, and even then she waited until she had several written down on a piece of paper, in a shorthand understood only by her, before she brought them to him. She browsed through Aroso's German books and she was fascinated – it all seemed like an intricate double puzzle to her, difficult, no doubt, but eventually solvable.

During the three months of the summer, Alexandra took the streetcar to Aroso's house. Their lessons were held in a small room that seemed always dark to Alexandra. She remembered the first time she saw the two portraits hanging there. She had been a bit put off by one of them, a nude, and she did not realize, at least not immediately, that it was a painting of Mitzi. Not that she could see much – barely the contours – with all the blinds pulled down against the summer heat and only a small desk lamp on. But now and then Aroso, looking for a book or some other item, would turn on the main switch. Alexandra sat at Aroso's desk, and Aroso would wander in and out. He would sit down and talk with Alexandra for five or ten minutes, then he would disappear while Alexandra worked on her own.

At the end of their lesson they often played Ping-Pong. He always called it Ping-Pong, never table tennis. She had played a bit herself and wasn't that bad – she could keep the ball on the table and she was faster than he was. Delighted that he had found an opponent, Aroso kept repeating that he hadn't played since Mitzi had got sick, and even longer than that. The old Ping-Pong table was in the courtyard, covered by a tarpaulin of some indefinite color and age and which smelled awful. It was a bit slanted, and the net, supported by some cage-like construction on one side, was never tight enough. The surface was so chipped in places that the ball took unexpected bounces. It wrung out of Aroso cries of dismay. Worst of all were the balls. They were difficult to get, and he endlessly patched the cracked balls with acetone. Not very successfully. Ah, the curse of fragile Ping-Pong balls. Yes, he was crazy about Ping-Pong.

"Mitzi," he told Alexandra, "had been a very good Ping-Pong player, one of the best in the country in the early thirties."

That's how they ended many of their sessions, with a noisy set of Ping-Pong. Other times, just before evening fell, Aroso would walk Alexandra to the streetcar stop. On the way there, meandering through the small streets of the neighbourhood, Aroso would hold forth about mathematics.

The following school year, Alexandra duly won the very top prize at the Math Olympiad, and her school, propelled by her high scores, won the team competition. Alexandra was feted at school and beyond. In a Sunday morning radio interview, during a regular broadcast aimed at the youth of the country, Alexandra was asked about her success. How did she explain it? Alexandra wasn't an eager talker – she wouldn't improvise just to fill in a pause. When she spoke, she did it in complete sentences, expressing fully formed thoughts. If she had no answers, she was not bothered by a heavy silence, because she knew that more often than not she would eventually have an answer. But this time, when asked for an explanation of her prowess, she didn't say anything. Eventually the interviewer mentioned hard work and she quickly agreed and then added, almost as an afterthought, that she loved mathematics and that it was natural to excel at things one loved. But she knew that she was not telling the entire truth, that she had not provided the whole answer.

Alexandra had been aware for quite a while that she was exceptional. She knew already that she was not only very intelligent but also different, special. She had felt both elated and worried about it at the same time. It was one thing to be one of the best students in her class or school, as there were others who had top marks in all subjects; and it was another thing to be, in addition, uniquely gifted in one field, to see and connect things that nobody else could see and connect. It made her feel slightly alien, weary of those around her. Math formulas, fully resolved answers, often floated towards her, sometimes in colour and with an odd three-dimensional texture. Meeting Aroso had been a great relief to her. It was as if she realized, all of a sudden, that she was not the only person with "visions," that there were others, like Aroso, and that there was nothing odd or wrong about it. But she had felt instinctively that she could not say things like this during the interview, that hard work and love of mathematics were all right, but being special, being uniquely gifted, would be frowned upon.

Towards the end of the interview, she was asked if she intended to become a mathematician. She had not, she realized, given much thought to this question lately, because the answer had been known to her for a long time. There was no other possibility for her. Somehow, without being aware of how it had happened, she had found the only path in life for her, a path that had been waiting for her even before she knew of its existence. But as she was uttering these words, she felt embarrassed by her answer.

Years later, she had talked to Aroso about it. "Of course," he said, "mathematicians are preset for their profession, born for it. Encoded – that's the term genetics came up with. Musicians are the same, and so are, I think, poets. Beethoven and Mozart were preset for music. Did young Mozart ever wonder what would he do when he grew up? We are like idiot-savants who are not idiots – well, most of us aren't. We don't have a choice. We do mathematics because we have to. I've heard people talking about being attracted by the intrinsic beauty of mathematics, its poetry. That's putting the cart before the horse. The beauty and poetry of mathematics are rationalizations from those who had already stepped into the mathematical universe, and because they are already there, they are able to wonder at its beauty and talk about it.

There was another difficult question for her, at the very end of the interview: To what would she attribute her attraction to mathematics? Was it its logic and clarity? Its order and quiet certainty? She shrugged and repeated that it was natural to excel at what we liked and, vice-versa, to be attracted by things at which we excelled. Yes, maybe it was the order and clarity associated with math, and its certainty in a world that was often confusing to someone growing up. Then she laughed and said that, truth be told, she didn't find that much quiet certainty in thinking about math problems. There was logic and order and certainty in presenting the results of one's labour, true, but not in the labour itself.

It was like when her mother came home from work earlier than usual, and she, Alexandra, had to tidy up her room in a hurry by stuffing things in the cupboard or under the bed. Yes, there was apparent order in her room when her mother came in and looked around, and there was order and logic and clarity in the presentation of her math work to outsiders, but the work itself was anything but ...

After her national triumph, Alexandra still had to complete Grade Ten and finally, the year following, Grade Eleven. Only then could she think of the admission exams to university. At the beginning of her last high-school year, Alexandra announced that she would not re-enter the Math Olympiad. She was supported by Paul Storcescu, who had taken a particular pride in Alexandra's achievements and thought she would only waste her time going through it all again. Others, he said, should be given a chance to shine. The school, which had until then funded Alexandra's lessons with Aroso, promptly stopped the payments. Paul Storcescu offered to pay for further lessons himself, but Mrs. Jacobi refused, stressing that she did not consider the further tutoring of her daughter an absolute necessity. She was right, of course, but Paul Storcescu insisted that Alexandra's unique mentorship with Aroso had to continue. It was then that Aroso suggested simply that he'd continue to see Alexandra twice a month, or more often if needed, without taking any honorarium. And so, until she entered university – to study mathematics, of course – Alexandra went on seeing Aroso regularly in his faculty office. Aroso drew a plan of what Alexandra should study and in what order. He listed the books Alexandra should read. He urged her to learn German and Russian, at least enough to be able to follow a math book, as most of his math books were in German – the older ones – or in Russian. He told Alexandra that the Soviets had excellent mathematicians and fabulous textbooks and that it was a pity that his own knowledge of Russian was so rudimentary.

She had heard stories about Aroso from the very beginning. It was her mother who had supplied them at first, lunatic tales that Leonard – five or six at the time – would eat up until he became aware of Alexandra's censorious looks. At meal times Mrs. Jacobi held forth on Aroso, and

Alexandra did everything to show her impatience – rolling her eyes, frowning, making faces. Where did her mother's stories spring from? Did she just make them up, baffled and frustrated by Aroso's refusal to accept anything from her, even a dinner invitation? After Aroso began mentoring Alexandra, Mrs. Jacobi had said to him more than once, "We owe you so much, Professor. How can we ever repay you?" "It's a pleasure to teach your daughter, Mrs. Jacobi," had been his invariable reply. "You owe me nothing."

More likely, and Alexandra began to suspect this later, much later, her mother's stories were desperate attempts to keep something in common with her strange daughter who was moving swiftly away.

Aroso, according to one tale Mrs. Jacobi was very fond of, had money stashed away. There were variations over the years. It was Mitzi's money at the beginning – after all, it was common knowledge Mitzi came from a very wealthy family. In time, Mrs. Jacobi altered the source – it became Aroso's family fortune. The Arosos had been long-established merchants in Istanbul. They had arrived there from Spain, refugee guests on the Sultan's galleons. "Galleons were Spanish ships," Alexandra would observe, exasperated. Aroso's grandfather (or was it his great-grandfather? – Mrs. Jacobi wasn't sure) had studied medicine in Paris and became surgeon-general of the Turkish army during the reforms of Sultan Abdul Hamid the Second. The Sultan made sure that the surgeon's faithful service was amply rewarded. This was the tale that Leonard had liked best, he told her later, laughing, and in his mind he had filled in the details. He saw the Russian troops cutting wide swaths through the Turks, who fought bravely, but what could yataghans do against modern rifles? In the groaning silence of the battlefield afterwards, Aroso's grandfather, in doctor's whites, kneeled and, opening his surgeon kit, brought comfort to the fallen with deft, precise gestures. Moans and appeals came from all sides, and he went to them all. And behind him, in a pink turban pinned in the front with a huge diamond, followed the Sultan – a little fat man with sad, bewildered eyes – who handed the busy surgeon purses with rubies and clinking golden coins.

The wealth of the Arosos was secure in Switzerland, Mrs. Jacobi assured them, and the Professor himself had a numbered account at a bank in Bern. Moreover, a huge fortune in gold coins lay buried in a corner of his garden on Octavian Street. That was why he was still in Romania; he didn't want to give the treasure up. Who would?

Secret progeny was a theme that Mrs. Jacobi took up later. "Aroso had a daughter with another woman – no, not with his wife, Mitzi couldn't bear children – a daughter he adored. He simply didn't have the heart to part with her."

"And how do we know all this?" Alexandra would ask, mustering all the sarcasm she could manage.

"I have my ways. I keep my ears turned the right way. Paul Storcescu's wife, if you *have* to know. She knows. Aroso has been to their house many times."

After a few months, the story changed. "No, no, what daughter? Aroso had a son, a disturbed son, in an asylum, his and Mitzi's son. It was after the son's birth that Mitzi was told that she couldn't have children anymore …"

"What happened to the daughter – the out-of-wedlock one?"

"Daughter? Ah, the daughter. Who knows, maybe he had both – a son and a daughter. A son with Mitzi, though, without a doubt. Unhinged, like Mitzi. They had to give him away, but with Mitzi the way she was, who else would make sure he was looked after?"

"Mother," Alexandra would say, "this is silly. Mitzi has Parkinson's – she's not insane. And I've been to Aroso's house many times. I've seen how he lives. I've seen him borrowing money from his housekeeper."

The Semeus had a three-bedroom apartment on the fourth floor of a drab new building – very long and of an uncertain beige colour quickly disappearing under dark, humid blotches – on the Ilie Pintilie Boulevard. Getting an apartment of that size had been quite a coup, and Emil liked to talk at length about it. Mrs. Jacobi and Leonard had dinner there with Emil and Alexandra every Tuesday. Alexandra was uneasy about these dinners – her mother insisted on them, "to keep the family together, otherwise the two of you would rarely see each other" – because Emil and Leonard didn't get along. Alexandra knew that Leonard wasn't fond of Emil and that Emil felt it – or was it the other way around? They tried to hide their dislike of each other and often succeeded, helped by alcohol-induced bonhomie. Whenever he met Emil, Leonard was all smiles and slapped Emil's wide shoulders with delight. They would often drink together after these dinners, when Alexandra and her mother were clearing the table and washing the dishes. The men would often go on drinking steadily under Mrs. Jacobi's muttering distress and Alexandra's disapproving eyes. Afterwards, Mrs. Jacobi would put Ada to bed and Alexandra would retire to the spare bedroom to correct term papers or prepare a lecture. Sometimes she rejoined Emil and Leonard, hoping that her presence would inhibit the alcohol intake and maintain peace.

As the evening advanced, Emil would slowly take over the conversation entirely. He had the habit, especially after a few drinks, of answering his own questions, dismissing any interjection with a waving motion of the hand. He usually went through a dramatized version of his earlier life, with his own questions asked and then answered, even with recalled dialogue between the parties involved in the more zesty or character-building scenes. His speeches, with unexpected bursts of energy, were reminiscent of Puccini's arias. Emil always made slight changes on the earlier versions, like a fastidious playwright, ceaselessly tinkering with the text at rehearsals. The kernel remained the same: his childhood in Urja, a Transylvanian village in the foothills of the Eastern Carpathians; his rise, through sheer willpower, from a peasant family to the position of a respected medical authority. He always boasted of his poor, humble start. Alexandra knew that he was deluding himself, but found all this endearing. His father was indeed a peasant, but a well off one – still well off, as collectivization had somehow never made it up the gentle slopes to his village. And his mother had been a teacher – in a village school, granted, but nevertheless a teacher. His parents, especially his mother, had pushed Emil and his younger brother (dead of pneumonia at fourteen) toward studies. Emil had been a gifted student and became a medical doctor. He was a lung specialist, a respirologist. He told Alexandra that his brother's death had determined his choice. He was a competent doctor and a conscientious, hard-working teacher, but his research led nowhere beyond the drudgery of clinical studies. He was slowly giving up on his research since he'd been named chief of respirology. Emil had a certain inventiveness of mind, a certain ability to see connections, but these were always the more obvious ones. Even in his moments of inspiration, Emil's mind could not escape a murkiness that would never fully lift. Leonard would often stop Emil with, "Very foggy, Emil. Clarity is needed. What exactly are you saying?" "He's like a polluted industrial city surrounded by mountains," Leonard told Alexandra when she took him aside and told him to stop. "The numbing smog never gets blown away."

Emil often discussed his research problems with Alexandra. She would ask questions, offer opinions, and, almost always, after listening to one of Emil's long tirades, re-state the problem with brevity and clarity. Emil was a large, expansive man, given to shouts and outbursts, often terrorizing his staff. But not at home. Alexandra had a calming influence on him. In the last couple of years, his research had gone into snoring and sleep apnea. He worked with an applied mathematician to model the respiratory tract and the dynamics of air flow. It was, of course, very laborious, with many modelling details. Often stuck, they would ask Alexandra for help. Alexandra found all this work mundane. She was also doubtful that it would lead anywhere, but of course she helped him.

"He is exploiting you, Alsa," Leonard told her once. She had looked at him astonished. "What are you talking about? Exploiting me? He's my husband."

The discussion at that Tuesday dinner was mostly about Aroso. It was a mild May evening and they kept the windows open. The rattle of passing streetcars reached them periodically from the street below. They had stuffed peppers and – Ada's favourite desert, brought by Mrs. Jacobi – crepes filled with rose petal jam.

Alexandra had come back late from the university and put on a narrow apron over her green dress. While freshening up and quickly tying her light hair in a chignon, she had looked in the mirror. A long, exhausting day. She looked dreadful. The green irises floated in a sea of pink. And her skin had acquired a tired, greyish hue. (Was it the light?) How had George described it once, "glowing sienna" skin? She smiled. George had an enthusiastic way with words, but difficulty with colours. Nothing much left of the glow now. It seemed that her nose had lately widened at the nostrils. And her mouth – her mouth had always been too big, no question about it.

She had been late because of a meeting in the department, which had turned surprisingly nasty. Aroso, who usually skipped meetings (to hurry home and look after Mitzi), was told by the dean – Comrade Prodan – that they needed his opinion on potential candidates for joining the faculty. The discussion had lasted longer than expected, with everybody asked for an opinion. At the end, there was a sudden political attack on Aroso. It was about his receiving medication from the West for Mitzi. Secretary Nicolescu had admonished Aroso several times in the past about his continued correspondence with the West in spite of many warnings. Aroso had told Alexandra about it, but it didn't seem to worry him. He had always answered that he needed medication for Mitzi, that the medication was not available in this country, and that he consequently had to get it from the West. No harm meant, just trying to keep his wife alive. The unexpected attack at the meeting came from Professor Fraga, a good mathematician – differential geometry was his main interest – who for reasons unknown had never liked Aroso. Fraga's attack was swift and well prepared. Secretary Nicolescu appeared not to have been "in on the secret," because he seemed as astonished as the others and unsure about how to deal with the situation. Fraga stood up – middle-aged, dark, fit, with a perfectly trimmed moustache – and said that he had it on good authority that Comrade Aroso had liaisons with dangerous elements in the West. Elements hostile to the Motherland. Aroso thought it was the usual complaints about the medication and, although somewhat puzzled, explained Mitzi's needs and the unavailability of proper medication.

Fraga was prepared. "Proper medication, is it? Comrades, there is excellent medication, the best anywhere, made just east of us – in the Soviet Union. Did Comrade Aroso try to obtain any? Did he approach the appropriate authorities? No, he didn't. Grave as this is, there's worse, much worse. The person he's receiving medication from, the person he's corresponding with, is the brother of Comrade Aroso's wife, a well-known fascist, a former member of the Iron Guard. These people, I don't need to remind you, are the sworn enemies of the country. Colluding with them is unacceptable and treacherous, whatever the reason."

A heavy silence had followed, except for bodies moving uncomfortably in their chairs. Aroso became red-faced, but he managed to contain his fury, at least at the beginning. To Alexandra's astonishment, he was able to reply using the impersonal lingo appropriate to such encounters.

"Maybe Comrade Fraga could tell us how he knows that the medication is send by my brother-in-law?"

It was a mistake, of course. Aroso was no match for Fraga in situations like this. "From comrades whose job it is to be vigilant."

"Are you one of them?" asked Aroso sarcastically.

It was Fraga's turn to turn red, but he knew his way. "Do you deny that your brother-in-law is a former member of the Iron Guard?"

That was unsettling and potentially lethal. It took Aroso a while to answer, but in the end he couldn't exactly deny it. In truth, he wasn't sure. His brother-in-law had told him once, before the war, that he was not and never had been a member. As a banker, he had looked after the outside investments of the Iron Guard organization. He had taken many trips to Switzerland, and after leaving for one such trip, in early 1944, he never returned. That's all Aroso knew about his brother-in-law's politics. "I wasn't happy about it, when I found out, as you can imagine. And I had nothing to do with him until 1951, when Mitzi desperately needed Western medication. Our correspondence is strictly about the medication – what kind she needs, alternatives, these sorts of things. I'm not that fond of my brother-in-law."

Dean Prodan, who liked Aroso but was a timid man, thought fit to intervene. "We have a grave problem to address. But we should do it some other time – this is not the right meeting."

Aroso, wisely, decided that he'd had enough. He looked around him, shook his head, and said, "I have a sick wife to look after." Then he left the room.

Alexandra told the story as they ate their desserts. There were squeals of delight from little Ada, who had finished half of her desert and was transforming the other half into a wide, flat-bottom boat.

"Could anything happen to him?" Emil asked.

Alexandra didn't think so. He was too valuable in the department. Besides, he was behind Nicolescu's research. Not that Nicolescu was a dummy; he just didn't have many ideas, or didn't have the time to have many ideas.

It was Nicolescu who brought everything quickly and masterfully to a close. He thanked Comrade Fraga for raising the issue and said that Comrade Aroso still had problems with self-criticism. He said that he'd take the whole issue to a higher level and would let them know. Comrade Aroso's wife was very sick, nevertheless, he reminded them as he left the meeting room.

"Never took a course with Fraga," Leonard said. "What got into him?"

Alexandra shrugged. "Don't know. I never had much to do with him."

Mrs. Jacobi felt faint all of a sudden and went to lie down in one of the bedrooms.

"Who's helping me with the dishes?" Alexandra asked.

Emil quickly offered to put Ada to bed.

Leonard followed Alexandra into the kitchen. There was no hot water that evening, and the small kitchen was steamy from the water Alexandra had put on the stove to boil.

"I hope there is nothing seriously wrong with Mother," she said.

She washed the plates in silence. Leonard did the drying. When they finished, Leonard said, "She must have been a beauty – I mean Mitzi, in her youth. Stunning beauty. That's what everybody says."

"They do?"

"What happened, Alexandra? Why did Aroso decline Hilbert's offer? Why this wilful waste of his mathematical genius at a second rate university in a second rate city? Haven't you ever wondered? Maybe that's where Mitzi's stunning beauty comes in. Aroso, passing through Bucharest for whatever reason, simply fell for her. Smitten with love. Suddenly, and fatally, for his career."

"Whatever the truth," Alexandra shrugged, "Aroso's odd decision was my luck. Truly amazing mind, Aroso's, still swarming with ideas, and he is what, sixty-three, sixty-four? While I was working on my thesis, he and I would often spend an hour or two talking shop, and without fail he would have three or four ideas for research. Brilliant ideas. Other people might not have ideas as good in an entire lifetime in academia. He was more than generous to me. Not willing to take any credit. 'I merely point to directions. It's idle thinking. Idle thinking is easy. Exhausting a path of research is the hard work.' That's what he always said."

"Well, you saw her, Alsa. You saw Mitzi. Any traces of the past splendour?"

"What I saw were glimpses of a shaking skeleton," Alexandra said. "I don't know, Leonard," she went on. "Possibly. Mitzi may very well have been something special, considering what Aroso gave up for her."

"What exactly did he give up for her?"

"He did brilliant studies in Gottingen, there is no doubt about it. After that, well, you know all the rumours."

"But surely as his student, his favourite student and assistant, you've learned more than that."

She shook her head.

"Is Emil still with Ada?" she wondered. "Putting a child to bed takes the same amount of time as clearing the table and washing the dishes. Here is a neglected law of nature. At least the two of you aren't drinking."

"Alexandra," Leonard said, "do you think Aroso would talk to me?"

"What do you mean?"

"Would he talk to me about his life? Would he tell me his story?"

"What's this all about, Leonard?"

"Alexandra, surely there is a story here. An extraordinary one, perhaps. A man picked out by God to understand his mathematical contrivances, a man so gifted, so bursting with profound ideas – you yourself keep saying this – that he casually hands them out to his students and colleagues. And yet a man who has produced so little. His time in Gottingen must be a wonderful story too. Can you imagine, to have Hilbert ask you to come and teach beside him, at the age of twenty-five? Is there any higher peer recognition?"

"That's just a silly rumour, Leonard. Hilbert may or may not have asked him. And he has produced much more than you think. He has published less because, like Gauss, he's a perfectionist – *pauca sed matura*, few but ripe. Also, he takes leaps and expects people to leap with him. It's not so easy to understand him. His interests are also somewhat non-mainstream. Because of Mitzi, he hardly ever travels – the only time

I know he did was a few years ago to Moscow – and he publishes in Soviet journals that the West ignores or cannot read. His Russian is passable, but just, and I was told that his papers suffer because of that as well. He doesn't speak English, and his French is barely tolerable, and he can't be bothered to work with translators. There's German, of course, and there are good German journals, but he refuses to publish in German journals."

"But I heard him chattering in German. And he sprinkles his conversation with German mathematical words."

Alexandra shrugged. Aroso had told her more than once that he'd never publish in a German journal. What the Germans did, he couldn't forgive.

"Will you do it, Alsa?"

"Is this related to your recently developed interest – writing about mathematics and mathematicians?"

"Yes."

"So why don't *you* talk to him, Leonard? You took a course with him."

"I didn't do very well in his course. He's not a great lecturer, is he?"

"It depends what he teaches. His enthusiasm is gone. But I've been to some great lectures of his."

One in particular stood out vividly in her mind. Aroso taught set theory that year. Whenever he showed up in the lecture room, which was not often – there was talk of him being ill and of Mitzi taking a turn for the worse – he was clearly bored and sarcastic. Most times his assistants taught in his place. But once Alexandra listened to him give a fascinating lecture.

It was a damp March day, and the lecture hall was cold and dark. The students had complained that there was not enough light, and a maintenance man was precariously perched on a step-ladder near the blackboard and was busy with the light fixture. Aroso reached the desk in a few long strides and dropped his briefcase on it. His raincoat was wet and it took a long time to unbutton. He spread it over the desk, took off his Basque beret and an endless black scarf. He looked at the maintenance man balanced on the ladder, shrugged, and smiled at them.

He sat down in his chair, stretching his long legs, and waited for the fellow to finish his job. Aroso's body seemed endless, just like his scarf. He stared at the portraits of the leaders lined along one of the walls – dour, dull faces frozen in vigilant poses.

He must have been in a good mood, because he kept smiling throughout the wait, nodding when the light finally came on, watching the maintenance man gather his ladder and leave. She hadn't seen him in such a good mood in a long time. It was an engaging, irresistible smile, and around her a soundless cheer seemed to rise from the class in response. It struck her, then, all of a sudden, how unprepared they were to deal with a smiling face.

Aroso was still smiling when he turned towards them and inquired, "All settled?" A full smile, not just his lips, but his blue eyes as well, his entire face, even his nose and white eyebrows. He stood up and began pacing. He had lost weight, and as he paced the wide, old-fashioned trousers seemed to be bent by sticks. He said that today was the anniversary of Georg Cantor's birth and he would talk about him.

For the next two hours, mesmerized, they followed his accented Romanian. He talked about George Cantor's fight to have his radical theory of transfinite cardinal numbers accepted by his peers. The power and beauty of mathematics, Aroso told the class, had never been better illustrated than in George Cantor's work. To make his point, he needed to remind them of the hierarchy of transfinite numbers, or infinities, that Cantor had conceived and built. He was not going to get into the details of Cantor's mathematics – there wasn't enough time for that. He wanted to confine his talk to one of the conclusions Cantor had reached; namely, that there were more, far more, transcendental (or non-algebraic) numbers than algebraic numbers. A startling statement, because, at the time it was made, in 1874, only one transcendental number was known, e, proven to be transcendental by the French mathematician Charles Hermite only a year earlier. Algebraic numbers were solutions of algebraic equations with integer coefficients, and the infinity of algebraic numbers was obvious. And yet Cantor proved that transcendental numbers far *outnumbered* the algebraic ones. Remember, Aroso reminded them, delighted, that it took another eight years before the German mathematician Lindemann proved the existence of the second transcendental number, π. In a book written before the war, a historian of mathematics had the following felicitous words to describe Cantor's conclusion: "The algebraic numbers are spotted over the plane like stars against a black sky; the dense blackness is the firmament of transcendentals." Aroso wrote these words on the blackboard. "If you remember only this one thing from this lecture," he said pointing to the written words, "I have not wasted my time."

Aroso told them about Cantor's skirmishes with Kronecker, who had called Cantor a "scientific charlatan," a "corrupter of youth." He told them about Cantor's unhappiness at Halle, the lesser university where he had been stuck his entire life. He mentioned, with sarcasm in his voice, the dismissal of Cantor's theory by none other than the great Poincaré, who had called it "a grave mathematical malady." And he talked about Cantor's intermittent bouts of madness and his end in an asylum.

It was a stunning lecture. It was more than the sheer drama of the story. To them, Aroso's spellbound listeners, it was as if the tall, slightly stooped lecturer had been one of its actors, a lesser one, of course, but one nevertheless. His German accent and his use of German mathematical words (it was always *Mengelehre*, never "set theory") had contributed to the illusion. And then, the undeniable fact that Aroso had chosen a slightly dangerous topic had added to the excitement, because Cantor's theory had not been taught at the university for a long time. Lack of practical application had been the reason given, but it was known that the leading Marxists of the department had raised political concerns. Counting infinities was perceived as a dangerous branch of mathematics, very puzzling as to its interpretation, and the department had decided, a decade earlier, that it was more prudent to ignore it until a clearer signal was forthcoming from Moscow.

At the end of Aroso's lecture, there had been spontaneous cheers, and in an ironical gesture he had bowed to the class. But it was plain to all of them that he was attempting to hide his distinct pleasure.

"Please do it, Alexandra, please ask him," Leonard said. "There is nobody closer to him than you are. He loves you."

Chapter 3
September 1969

"Of course, of course, dear, come, by all means," Aroso said when Alexandra had rung him at home. "Do you remember how to get here? It's been years. Yes, it would be good to talk. Are you all right? Holding up? Well, never mind that now, I'll see you soon."

The streetcar was full. The man who stood pressed against her left shoulder and breast for a long ten minutes had had onions and wine at lunch, and she was glad to have to switch to another line in the centre of the city.

She was not all right, of course, how could she be? The last three weeks had been like a nightmare, beginning with the note from Nicolescu asking her to see him at once. They had returned home the previous day from Urja, where they had spent – something they did every summer since Ada was born – three weeks with Emil's parents.

Her in-laws had always liked her and were quite happy to look after Ada. Emil's father doted on his granddaughter and took her wherever he went. Ada loved everything in Urja except the outhouse and the dark at night. The house, the yard, and the large garden beyond, ending at the river, were a huge realm that Ada explored tirelessly. Emil's parents, especially his father, were shy and slightly overawed by the clever university professor their son had married. They let her be and tried to guess all her needs. She had no needs. Alexandra was grateful simply for the opportunity to be carefree again. She got up very early, of course, and watched the sun rising over the mountains in the east. In the clear air of the morning, the mountains seemed to bend over the village. She read on the veranda, walked the dusty lanes of the village, did some work. At night she huddled with her daughter. Ada would tuck her little body against Alexandra's chest and, before falling asleep, ask not to be left alone. Alexandra had to promise it every night. She would stay with her daughter for at least a couple of hours, touching her lightly now and then, sniffing her slightly sweaty neck, wondering at the fearful bundle safely asleep near her. Then she'd climb down, strike a match to light the oil-lamp, and, with a notebook and pencil, work on some math problem at a small table in a corner of the bedroom.

Emil had joined them for the last week. He always came for only one week – except for the first summer they went there, with Ada newly born – but Alexandra didn't mind. In fact, without Emil she could concentrate on her work. Emil told Alexandra that he and his father had had many disputes in the past and that he avoided being around him for too long. She didn't understand it – she found Emil's parents without fault – but had no interest in knowing about past conflicts. When Emil came, they took long walks, hiked a little in the nearby mountains, slept with Ada between them. It was one of the best, most relaxing summers she could remember. The sky was an endless blue. They got back to Bucharest late on Sunday, loaded with a demijohn of the local wine and other provisions from Emil's parents, Ada asleep in Alexandra's arms.

She had no premonitions about the note she found pinned on her door on Monday morning by Party Secretary Nicolescu asking her to see him "at once," although the urgency seemed odd. As she walked towards his office she didn't think of Leonard at all. They had talked only once about his plans to flee, that Sunday morning when she had been working in her office at the university. After she said no to his suggestion, and he had asked her to say nothing to Emil, that was it. Leonard chose not to talk to her anymore about his plans, and she was grateful for it. She became convinced that the less she knew, the better off she was. She hoped that, somehow, it wouldn't work out. Not that Leonard would be caught, of course not, but that he would get cold feet, or that the friend of the friend wouldn't make it across the border for some reason, or that the Bulgarian border-guards would become less agreeable and send Leonard back. Whatever. And, slowly, she began to believe that it wouldn't happen. The long-term forecast called for a damaging storm, but if she didn't turn on the radio, and if the weatherman himself did not communicate anything alarming to her, she could reasonably assume that the storm would not come. The clouds she had seen in February had somehow moved on. Life could continue as before, difficult but bearable, with little joys and little pains, with Emil and Ada, with everybody gathered at their Tuesday dinners, with her brother and husband conveniently getting drunk when it was time to clean up, with their peaceful vacations at Urja, with Ada falling asleep with her little buttocks touching her chest. And with her mathematics, of course.

That's why, when it did happen, it was so much harder. It was like being caught having done something bad or embarrassing long after the period of greatest danger had passed and all the traces, or so one believed, had disappeared.

There were three of them waiting for her, besides Nicolescu – Prodan, Fraga, and another man in a grey suit and an open-neck shirt. He was from some security organization. She didn't catch his name – Negrea, or some other colour – or the name of the organization, because she suddenly knew what it was all about and the first thing that crossed her mind was that something had happened to Leonard.

Nicolescu told her to close the door, and, after telling her who Comrade Negrea represented, asked her when she had last seen her brother. She realized she hadn't seen him for quite a while, a month, no, maybe five, even six, weeks. They had been away for three weeks. Before that, their last Tuesday dinner was cancelled, because the day before Ada had become very sick – it turned out to be a mild attack of croup, but it was quite scary – and they had taken her to the hospital and called the dinner off. And the week before that, Leonard simply hadn't shown up – but then, every so often, Leonard didn't show up at the family dinners, and it had gone almost unnoticed. Her mother had said that Leonard was away on business, somewhere in the north of Moldavia, in a town that was a railway hub. It rang no alarm, since Leonard had many times complained about the job he'd been stuck with, a huge transportation model, and that he often had to go away to gather data.

"Five or six weeks," Alexandra said. "Five weeks, I think. Why? Has something happened to him?"

"Are you sure?" Fraga asked.

Before Alexandra could answer, Comrade Negrea interjected, "Don't you see your brother every week – on Tuesday evenings – for a family dinner?"

There was no point in asking how he knew about their Tuesday dinners. She thought for a while before answering. "I've just been away for three weeks with my daughter. The week before the trip, we cancelled the dinner because Ada – that's my daughter – had been quite ill and my husband and I took her to the hospital. And the previous week he just didn't come. It's not always that he comes, you know. It makes Mother very unhappy. Please tell me what has happened to my brother."

"You tell us, Comrade Semeu. You surely know better," Comrade Negrea said.

"Let's not prolong the charade," Nicolescu said. "Your brother has run away, it seems."

"Why didn't you bring your brother's plans to the attention of the appropriate authorities?" Fraga asked. "And don't tell us he didn't talk to you about them."

She decided to stay as close to the truth as possible. Her brother had talked to her about such plans, she said, but talk was all she thought it was, silly talk about silly dreams. After all, her brother had talked about going away since he was five or six years old. She had stopped listening a long time ago. In fact, she couldn't remember the last time she had paid any attention to his announcements.

"Dreams?" Fraga's one word was full of sarcasm.

"He just wanted to know the world. At five, he was planning a trip up the Amazon River." She was improvising now, and that was dangerous. "If he did it," she went on, "if he did run away, it was out of the need for change, for adventure. Do not read a political statement into it. Leonard is still a boy. He didn't know what he was doing."

"You mean, he'll come back?"

She said she hoped so, and she knew that nobody believed her.

Prodan said he had another meeting, but he expressed the hope that the case of Comrade Semeu, who had shown unpardonable bourgeois carelessness, would be justly and swiftly addressed. Fraga shook his head as his eyes followed Prodan's retreat.

"When is the last time he talked to you about defecting?" he asked.

"He has not defected."

"When is the last time he talked to you about taking off to see the world?"

She took her time and then she shrugged. "Don't remember – could have been four, five years ago."

"Why didn't you tell us at the time?"

"There was nothing to say. As I've told you ..."

Comrade Nicolescu made a gesture to halt Alexandra, and she was grateful for it. "I think we know enough, for now, Comrade Semeu," he said.

"Needless to point out," Fraga said, "you've shown an intolerable lack of vigilance. Your brother, of course, carries with him secrets from the National Institute of Calculations. Criminal lack of vigilance. Well, we shouldn't be too surprised, given Comrade Semeu's background. Comrade Negrea, here, will want to talk to you about all this in more detail, but not now. He'll contact you."

When she went back to her office, she realized she was shaking. Sweating too, profusely. Not very ladylike. She needed to calm down. He'd done it. Leonard was gone. No question about it, he'd done it. Otherwise they wouldn't have bothered questioning her. Anyway, that's what they said: "Your brother has run away, it seems." Would they be lying to her? Could it be they were holding Leonard and now wanted to get her too? If her answers didn't match Leonard's, she was in trouble. No, they didn't have Leonard. They'd have been much more sarcastic, much more arrogant, haughty, and their questions much more detailed. Nicolescu was a dear, though. He did try to make it easier for her.

She called her mother. When Mrs. Jacobi answered, Alexandra said quickly, "I'll be at your apartment in half an hour. Don't go anywhere." She called Emil at the hospital, but he couldn't be found.

In the streetcar, she wondered how long Leonard had been

gone.

She was relieved not to meet any of the neighbours in the familiar street or on the staircase. She opened the door (she still had a key) and found her mother waiting for her all dressed and ready to go. Without saying a word to her mother, Alexandra rang Emil again, with the same result. They went out and crossed the wide boulevard. In a small park on a side street, they sat on a bench. A group of noisy boys in blue school uniforms were chasing a small rubber ball not far from them.

Mrs. Jacobi was conciliatory and apologetic, but she insisted she could not have done it any other way. Yes, at their last Tuesday family dinner, when she said that Leonard was somewhere up north, she had not told the truth, but Leonard had gone only a couple of days earlier and she hadn't known anything more. She had had strict instructions from Leonard to say not a word about his plans. By the time Alexandra left with Ada for Urja, she still had no news from Leonard. It had not been easy for her at all. Those had been twelve horrible days, before she found out that Leonard was safe. She decided not to call Alexandra in Urja. Leonard had been right – the less Alexandra and Emil knew, the more credible their story would be. Yes, Leonard was safe. He had sent a postcard with nothing written, except an address. It had been the signal agreed among the two of them that he was safely out and an indication of where he was. It was a picture of Paris, of Île de la Cité. Leonard was in Paris. Not a bad place to start a new life.

The ball hit Alexandra's thigh and fell at her feet. She threw it back towards the boys.

Mrs. Jacobi went on with her story. She had been contacted by the police the previous Monday. A nice looking policeman – she gave him coffee and a glass of cold water – had come to ask if she knew where her son was. In Bulgaria, she told him. For so long? Did she know for a fact that he was to stay for four weeks in Bulgaria? Because at the National Institute of Calculations he had put in for a two-week vacation only. She said she wasn't sure. Should she worry? she asked. Had something happened? The nice looking policeman shook his head and left.

Mrs. Jacobi seemed somewhat disappointed by the lack of dramatics in her encounter with the authorities.

Alexandra stood up. "Where are you off to?" Mrs. Jacobi asked.

"Come up and rest a bit. Or eat something."
"For God's sake, Mother, I have to find Emil."

Emil was genuinely shocked when the plainclothes policeman told
him they had reason to believe his brother-in-law was a runaway and a
traitor. In a sense, it was good he was so unprepared, so out of it, because
his shock must have appeared unfeigned. He was on his rounds – still
pleasantly mellowed by the lazy week at Urja, trying to recall things,
yelling affably with the cohort of students and residents following him
– when he was called, urgently, to the office of the party secretary. The
secretary was with a plainclothes policeman, Comrade Raducioiu.

Without wasting much time, Comrade Raducioiu asked Emil
whether he knew the whereabouts of his brother-in-law, Leonard Jacobi.
Emil shrugged – at his work, at home, he had no idea. Had something
happened? An accident? Was his brother-in-law hurt? Did Emil know,
Comrade Raducioiu went on, that his brother-in-law had travelled to
Bulgaria for a brief vacation? No, he didn't know. What was this all
about? When was the last time that he, Emil, had seen his brother-in-
law? About a month ago. Maybe more than a month. What was going
on? Emil asked again.

His brother-in-law, he was told, had disappeared. Leonard's
mother did not know where her son was. Emil said that his wife would
know – she was very close to her brother. But he regretted saying it the
moment the words came out of his mouth, because he suddenly realized
the seriousness of the matter. They had people talking to his wife at this
very moment, Emil was told ominously.

Maybe something had happened to him in Bulgaria, Emil
wondered faintly. An accident. Maybe he'd been robbed. Maybe he
was lying dead in some ditch. They shook their heads, both of them,
Comrade Raducioiu with a sneer on his face. Comrade Semeu's brother-
in-law had run away. They knew that he had crossed into Turkey. And
they also had good reason to believe that he was now in France. Yes, the
picture was quite clear, Comrade Raducioiu said.

Emil swore his innocence. The secretary kept shaking his head
and, at the very end, he promised to do whatever was necessary. Another

ominous phrase. There would be, the secretary said, repercussions, of course. They would do what they had to do. Unpardonable lack of vigilance shown by Comrade Semeu. Unpardonable.

After Comrade Raducioiu left, the secretary added, wagging a finger at Emil, that things like this were to be expected if one married into a family with a bourgeois background. Bourgeois and cosmopolitan. Emil knew what cosmopolitan meant. The secretary dismissed Emil with baleful words. Things were not looking good, the secretary said, and although he had always liked Comrade Semeu, he had to do what the party told him to do.

Alexandra heard about all this from a livid Emil. Before Emil came home she had a phone call from a Comrade Nascuta, who said he was Leonard's boss at the National Institute of Calculations. Very agitated. What kind of brother did Comrade Professor have? How could Leonard have done something like this to him? He had vouched for Leonard. He was finished. Demotion, a move out of Bucharest. With a very sick wife, incapacitated.

Emil arrived late and slightly tipsy. They went out, afraid to talk inside. They walked towards Victory Square and turned right into the neighbourhood of quiet streets named after capital cities. It was at the intersection of Roma and Oslo streets that the torrent of imputations and accusations started. Emil couldn't keep his voice down, and the few passers-by kept staring at them. She told Emil she had not known about Leonard's plans. She told him her brother had talked to her once about getting away, but she hadn't taken him seriously. (She didn't tell him that Leonard had insisted she not say anything about his plans.) After all, she argued, everybody talked about getting out, it was an endless subject, but that was it, all talk, nobody did or could do much about it. So, she told Emil, she had paid little attention to what Leonard had said to her. A half-lie or a true lie? In a way, she believed what she told Emil. In a way, in the five months that had passed since Leonard had talked to her about his plans, she had managed to convince herself that it was only wishful talk.

Emil did not believe her. In the poor light of the street-lamps she couldn't see his face that well. He wasn't shouting anymore, but his voice had a menacing sharpness. He was opening and closing his large hands, and for the first time she had a sense of physical fear near him. He was fuming. How could she pay little attention to Leonard's getaway plans? How could she "not have enough brain" to alert him to be prepared, at the very least, for the kind of encounter he had endured that day in the party secretary's office?

No, Emil didn't believe her story at all.

Asuero Aroso lived in the southeast end of the city, on Octavian Street, in a narrow bungalow built at a right angle to the cobbled road. The house was typical of all the houses in the street, built after the Great War. The rooms followed each other like compartments in a railway car. A small courtyard ran the length of the house, with a garden at the end away from the street. It had a small vegetable patch, a few hawthorn bushes, a quince tree, and an apple tree. The latter bore early apples, full of worms, which were never picked, neither from the branches nor from the ground. Jana, the peasant woman who helped around the house and looked after Mitzi, had been expressly instructed not to touch the apples or to whitewash the trunk of the tree. Aroso claimed that the smell of the slowly rotting apples helped him with his mathematics.

At the garden end of the courtyard, near the wall of the neighbouring house, an old grapevine had spread across a wooden trellis and made an oasis of shade in the heat of the day. When the warm weather came, Aroso pulled an old table and a couple of chairs under the trellis. He liked to work there, or just sit and read. He did his best work there, no doubt helped by the rotting apples. There was a small blackboard affixed to the neighbour's wall. Like Hilbert's blackboard, he told her once. Except that Hilbert liked to work standing up, pacing in front of his huge blackboard. There was a light bulb attached to the trellis and in the evening, after putting Mitzi to bed, Aroso often read there. It was under the trellis, with the grapes slowly acquiring patches of pink and purple, that Aroso and Alexandra spent many evenings the summer she had completed her dissertation. She would arrive around seven or eight o'clock, after the heat of the day had subsided, and they would talk late into the night. If it was a Friday, he would not switch on the electric light but instead brought out a candle. "My Sabbath connection," he would say, winking at her. Often, he would think his way through a mathematical problem out loud, laugh at past useless efforts, point out promising paths. There was always a connection with Gottingen. He had learned about this while reading in the famous *Lesezimmer*, or talked about that with Bernays, or with Courant, or with Lewy, a student colleague of his, or with some of the many talented Russians – Alexandrov, Schnirelman, Kolmogorov, the blind Pontryagin – passing through Gottingen in those days. He was a good storyteller and his odd accent conferred an added flavour to his stories. Somehow, the flickering candle, combined with the exotic names and places, conveyed to Alexandra a magical universe of mathematics, peopled with unusual and shadowy beings, a world of subdued glitter and fleeting revelations. She had never felt more alive, happier, more contented, more accomplished than that summer.

She didn't remember the last time she had gone to Aroso's house. To get there she would board the Number 1 streetcar in the centre of the city and ride its slow course along the banks of the brown, narrow, and often foul smelling Dimbovitsa River. The streetcar would pass the New Times Works and, soon afterwards, the slaughterhouse, where, depending on the way the wind was blowing, the stench could hit you like a blow to the belly. Thirty years earlier, in days of rabid madness, Jews picked up at random were brought to the slaughterhouse and slain like cattle. Even their corpses were not left to rest – they were hooked onto steel claws suspended from the ceiling and pulled around like pieces of meat.

She wondered whether Aroso had been living on Octavian Street in those days. Very likely.

He was glad of the company, Aroso said, when he saw her. "Oh, a bottle of white wine! Wonderful! We'll treat ourselves. Mitzi may wet her lips too. I have to be around Mitzi for a while. Jana has gone for the night. Could be a few days, even. Her brother was caught carrying fresh meat into the city and he didn't have enough money with him to bribe his way out. Big trouble. The next few days are going to be hard. You remember Jana, don't you? I don't know what I'll do without her. Oh, I'm glad you came. I have no more patience for mathematics. My mind wanders and I find myself surrounded by unhealthy and selfish thoughts. It's not good. Your company, believe me, is a relief. Mitzi will enjoy your presence, too. I think she'd like to keep us company for a while. She doesn't speak much these days, and when she does I'm not sure I know what she's saying. Jana claims she understands her, but I often doubt it."

He looked approvingly at the label on the bottle Alexandra had brought along. "Yes, maybe Mitzi would try a drop. Don't see any harm in it. For Mitzi, this is like going out. Do you mind carrying her outside? I can't do it these days, I hurt my back. She's very light, don't worry. Mitzi was very distressed the first time it was Jana and not me who carried her around. She is more used to it now. She'll let you do it."

He put the bottle of wine on the table under the trellis and motioned to Alexandra to follow him. They walked along the narrow yard and stepped into a hall with a door at either end. He opened one of them, went in, and held the door open.

"Come in, Alexandra. Mitzi, you remember Alexandra, don't you? My best student ever, and now my esteemed colleague?"

Mitzi sat gently shaking near a window that was open to the courtyard. She seemed tinier than before, thinner and more bent. Her white hair was collected in a bun at the back of her head. Her eyes were a disquieting combination of faded blue and pink. She wore a dark blue dress with long sleeves and a lot of jewellery – earrings and rings and bracelets, a gold chain, and a string of amber beads. A giant topaz brooch almost covered her narrow chest. Close to it there was a wet patch of spittle. She wore white ankle socks, the kind girls wear in elementary school, and a pair of flat, highly polished, black shoes. Mitzi's chin was wet.

A curious scent of lilac mingled with feces wafted up when Alexandra lifted Mitzi. She was quite heavy. She looked into Alexandra's eyes, and for a second Alexandra thought Mitzi was going to burst out laughing. Then her eyes became cloudy, unfocused, and a few tears began to trickle down. Alexandra carried her outside and settled her on a chair Aroso had brought out. "Now, now, Mitzi," Aroso said, wiping her eyes and chin with a handkerchief, "don't cry, please. You know that Alexandra doesn't mind. Would you like a drop of wine, Mitzi? Wet your lips, like in the old days? Sure, why not. You are my good girl, my beloved girl." He then said, turning to Alexandra, "I really don't know whether she follows anything."

Alexandra sat in one of the wooden chairs already by the table. It was an odd table, quite wide, of a faded dark green colour, and the legs didn't match. She smiled. It was what remained of the Ping-Pong table on which she and Aroso used to play when she was in high school. Aroso went into the house and quickly returned with a corkscrew and three glasses on a tray. He opened the wine and poured equal amounts in two of the glasses and hardly any at all in the third. He dipped a finger in the third glass and, with his wet finger, traced the outline of Mitzi's mouth. A slow purple tongue made a shy appearance between her lips.

They sat quietly for a long time, motionless, looking at Mitzi. Then Aroso turned towards Alexandra, leaned back, and joined his hands behind his head.

"A fleet-footed brother – Leonard, isn't it? – you've got. And quite decisive. Just like that, snap, he disappeared."

"Oh, it wasn't that sudden."

"Where is he now? What's he up to?"

"He's in Paris. As to his plans, I can only make guesses. We never talked about it. He'll probably do anything for a while. Long term, I don't know. He told me less than a year ago that he wanted to write about mathematics and mathematicians. Oddly enough, he wondered whether you'd agree to talk to him about your life. He even asked me to talk to you about it." It had been only six months since Leonard had asked her, but it seemed like six years. Reluctantly, she would have done it, if he had insisted, but he hadn't.

"My life?"

"Yes. You know, Istanbul, Gottingen, Hilbert, your perplexing decision to choose Bucharest, he's heard many stories …"

"My life? What purpose would it serve?"

The question was addressed more to himself than to Alexandra. "Well, never mind all that nonsense," he said after a while. "How are you? Are you all right?"

She looked at him and shook her head. "I'm anything but all right. I can't think clearly. I can't concentrate. I have panic attacks. It's terrible to bring my problems to you, but I have nobody else. My mother is not much help, and the few friends I have ..."

He slid her glass of wine closer to her. "Together," he said, smiling, "and with a bit of help from this amber liquid, we'll put the world right."

She told him about the Monday she found out about Leonard's disappearance and about her encounter with Nicolescu, Fraga, Dean Preda, and Comrade Negrea. He listened patiently to her story and at the end turned to Mitzi. "Did you hear this, Mitzi? Fraga. You've met his father, remember? What was his name – Miron? – something like that. Good friend of your brother and Lavinia. Always around Lavinia. A good friend of yours, too, wasn't he? This Fraga, the Fraga in Alexandra's story, is his son." He said to Alexandra, "The Fragas, my dear, were very rich before the war. With such distressing roots, young Fraga is trying to prove his political allegiance. Ah, the things we do to hang on to a job. He doesn't like Jews either, and this may add spice to his newfangled fervour. I wouldn't worry too much. They wouldn't dare touch you. You're much too good – even they know it – and too well-known. Besides, Nicolescu likes you, and Preda needs you. True, you won't be travelling for a while, and definitely not in the West. But in time ... may be in five, six years, the facts will be less fresh, less offensive, and there will be pressure from the outside to let you travel to conferences. I'm sure they'll relent. Meanwhile, hang on."

"Emil is taking it very badly. He blames me for everything. For not trying to stop Leonard, for not telling him, for destroying his career. He's been demoted, and he's very upset. He doesn't realize what he's saying. The other day he asked, 'Why was I demoted? Why weren't you demoted? I'm not his family.' Absurd, of course. He screams at me every night. Once or twice I couldn't stand it anymore and left to sleep at Mother's place. You know what he shouted after me? 'Yes, run away, flee. That's what *you people* do, isn't it?' The first time in our marriage – it really stung, I can't get it out of my mind – that he thought to remind me what horrible character we Jews have. He can't control himself, not even in front of Ada. In fact – this may sound crazy – I think he likes to scream at me and tell me how horrible and two-faced I am in front of Ada. God, poor Ada. What's she making of it? She knows that Uncle Lenny ran away. The other day she said to me, 'Uncle Lenny is bad, isn't he?' When I said that wasn't true, she said, 'Then why did he go away without saying anything? You and Daddy fight because of him. And Daddy got in trouble because of him.' Who knows what Emil tells her when I'm not there. It's madness. All I can think of is Ada. Emil … Married to him for eight years, and I thought … But Ada … I don't know what I'll do if I lose her."

"What are you talking about, my dear, how could you lose her?"

She didn't answer. How could he help her? What could he say?

How could she explain this gut wrenching fear that took possession of her? Her physical fear? Yes, in part, because Emil had the ability to shout himself into such a frenzy she thought he might hit her. Several times she thought he was very close to it. And she wouldn't stand for it, would leave him. And she'd lose Ada. But it wasn't just the physical fear. It was more than that. She felt cast loose, with no bearings. She had been tethered until now in a quiet inlet, and suddenly she was afloat on a tempestuous ocean. Her visceral fear had a constant, ominous component that has been with her since the meeting in Nicolescu's office.

She looked up and she saw him watching her. Mitzi made a soft puffing noise with her lips. Aroso rose, brought his glass to Mitzi's mouth, and she drank a bit of the wine.

"Do you manage to do any work?" Aroso asked.

"Very little. Enough for my lectures, but no real work."

He shook his head and sighed. "You cannot let this happen. You have no right to let this happen. There's nobody else I'd say such a thing to, except you."

She nodded without saying anything.

"Promise me," he said. "Besides, it would help you forget, at least from time to time. And this constant fear that you're talking about – it would disappear while working. I know it won't be easy. Right now, you don't think it's right, given the circumstances, to sit down at your desk, with a pencil and paper, and immerse yourself in work. But I know you. The moment you'll do it, you'll feel better. Because that's what you're meant for. Mathematics. Unexpected for a woman, a pretty woman especially, but that's what you are, my dear – a mathematician, first and foremost."

"A mother too."

"Of course."

She didn't say a wife. She didn't feel like one. How could that be? How could she have changed like this in a few weeks? She had loved Emil, she had no doubt about it, even though she had hesitated when Emil began to pursue her assiduously, soon after she broke up with George. It was not the same as it had been with George, she had known that from the very beginning, but in a way that was what attracted her to Emil. George had not been entirely sane. With Emil she had felt comfortable and content and safe and able to work on her math and have a child. And now ... Nothing. Only fear, and a desire to be as far from him as possible. In the last couple of weeks, she'd taken the habit, when going to bed at midnight or one o'clock as usual, of sneaking into Ada's bed, slowly, gently, so as not to awake her. And she would kiss her lightly, softly, tenderly – her tiny shoulder, her hands, her hair – before falling asleep, if she slept at all.

And yes, she was aware that this desertion of their bed only fed Emil's anger.

The telephone rang inside the house and Aroso went in. It was half past ten and the heat had subsided. Aroso took his time. She could hear his muffled voice and a word here and there. Was it German, sprinkled with Russian? The discussion was undoubtedly about mathematics. Who did he discuss mathematics with at this time? And he said he was tired of it – what did he say, he had no patience anymore? She watched Mitzi's head and upper body bob gently up and down, with perfect periodicity, like a religious Jew at prayers. She felt uncomfortable with the silence and began to tell her how privileged she had been to be her husband's student and how much she needed his support now. She needed her support too. Did she have Mitzi's support? At least sympathy? Understanding? She couldn't wish for a better listener than Mitzi, she thought – so quiet, and nodding so unceasingly in agreement. Mitzi's Parkinson's was at an advanced stage, but there were probably other things medically wrong with her. "Your husband is an extraordinary man," she said to her very loudly, trying to see if she could detect any response, however faint, even a change in her breathing pattern. Nothing. After a while she couldn't hear Aroso's voice anymore, but he stayed inside for a few more minutes. He looked tired when he finally returned.

"A call from Moscow – somebody I knew in Gottingen, way back. We talk now and then on the phone. He's older than I am and still can't think of anything else except mathematics. Especially since his wife died. He gets all excited and calls me."

She rose from her chair, slowly, and said, "Sorry for all this. Thanks for listening."

"I need your help again, my dear. I made your bed, Mitzi, with fresh sheets," he said loudly to his wife. "Alexandra and I will take you to bed now. We had a lovely evening, didn't we? Alexandra was glad to see you again. Her brother bolted out of the country a month ago. Quite a jolt for poor Alexandra. But she'll recover. You remember Alexandra, my best student ever? Of course you do."

She carried Mitzi back to the bedroom. The smell of feces was stronger. It was only when she laid her out on her bed and saw her sprawled there, incapable of rising, that she realized what a horrible and grinding daily effort Aroso was putting himself through.

"Please come any time you want to talk. Good night, my dear. Mitzi and I, like any loving couple, like to keep our bed routine private. Do let yourself out."

Chapter 4
October 1970

Dear Leonard,

What a relief to write without the fear of being read by others and without the need to weigh the meaning of every word. Unlike the first letter I sent you through Professor Natraq, this time I'll be able to keep adding to it and changing it. It will be like writing in a diary, since I know that the letter will not start its long journey towards you until I hand it over to Charles Natraq on his next visit here. I'm like a child with a new toy. It worries me a bit – this joy I have in writing to you – as it's probably a reflection of how lonely and cut off I feel.

Mother will continue to send news about Ada and Emil and me (everything is fine, and we're doing fine), and you should keep asking about us in your replies to her – otherwise they'll suspect we have other means of communication.

I'm afraid I sounded bitter in my previous letter to you, but you did ask in your letter to Mother for "exact details of the aftermath" and, while Mother was a bit puzzled by what you meant, I understood immediately. I couldn't depict to you the "exact details of the aftermath" until Charles Natraq agreed to post my letters for me. (He might, in fact, post them not from France in the future, but from a place much nearer to you, from Montreal – but more about him later.) And the aftermath was bitter – no, bitter is not the right word, the aftermath was ghastly, awful. I was in bad shape for a while, but I'm better now, recovered in a way – and by this I mean that I have adapted to the new situation. What I'm trying to say to you is that I got carried away recalling and putting down on paper the details of the first few weeks and months. Believe me, I'm not bitter – I miss you and, as always, love you.

About the family, now.

Mother has not been well – her heart, as usual. It may have taken a turn for the worse in the last couple of months or so. She is lonely. I spend as much time as I can with her, but it's not much. Sometimes I sleep at her place, when Emil's shouting becomes unbearable. While she's glad to have company, she's horrified at what's happening between Emil and me. She babysits Ada occasionally, although she doesn't have the strength for it anymore, and avoids Emil as much as she can. The Tuesday dinners have become shorter and grimmer affairs, if they happen at all. Emil often skips them under one pretext or another. Too much work, has to stay late at the hospital, visits to patients. Or meetings, the eternal meetings. Mother and Emil, who, as you know, used to get along before, are getting on each other's nerves. She can't take his badmouthing of you, which has become a Tuesday night ritual whenever Emil is there. I keep quiet and tell Mother to keep quiet. It will, I tell her, be over in a while. It has subsided a bit, but I have the feeling that he'll never get over it, never fully over, because of the setbacks his career has taken, setbacks that he attributes to you and, by association, to Mother. To me also, but Mother is easier to torment.

At the beginning, and under my devious instructions, Mother did not tell Emil that you'd been writing to her. The fiction was that you'd been writing to Dora in some codified, impersonal way – you must remember Dora, Mother's friend, the fat woman who lives in the yellow corner building with shrapnel holes everywhere – that Dora didn't mind at all, and that that was how we had brief news from you. Emil had warned us: no correspondence with you. No receiving letters, no sending letters. Under no circumstances. Too dangerous. Leonard was fine. Leonard was young. Now was not the time to take risks, and for what? He, Emil, was getting less of a cold shoulder from the comrades, he felt a thaw. He did not want to see what he had painstakingly put back together be again destroyed through some stupid sentimentality. Yes, he used those very words with Mother, "stupid sentimentality." She asked him how could he call a mother's desire to know what happened to her son stupid sentimentality. He snapped at her. She was lucky that Dora was stupid enough to allow this to happen. (The word "stupid" is now a staple in his vocabulary – everybody around him is stupid.) He told Mother that if she had been less stupid, less scheming, yes, that's how he put it, she would have been able to actually look at and talk to her son, not merely wish for a postcard.

After a few months, as you know, he relented a bit. He yielded to the argument that no letters at all back and forth would look too suspicious to the authorities, since it would mean that other ways of communication were being employed. So, reluctantly, Emil allowed Mother to send and receive brief letters from you.

I do not understand how Emil could be so mean to Mother. What did this old and frail woman do to him? It's almost as if he thinks she had deliberately pushed you to run away in order to ruin his career. Mother is now avoiding our house when Emil is around, and I am Emil's main target. Every evening I have the same rant from him. "Jews will never change. When things get difficult, they just move on. Run away. That's why they didn't have a country for thousands of years. Things are too tough? Let's move along. Pick up our bags and get going. I don't like these bastards either, but this is my country and I'm staying. Through the good and the bad. I have the fibre to stand and help things change, get better. But not Leonard, not you Jews." It is so stupid and grotesque that it is hard to argue. How he's tormenting Mother is unpardonable. I cannot make sense of it. I'm losing – no, I've lost – my feelings for him. Something else happened, too. Quite horrible. He's enraged because I'm refusing to have another child. I don't want to go into sordid details, but there were horrid scenes. I had some birth control pills – cost a fortune, and don't ask how I got them – and when those ran out I asked him to find more, or other means. Condoms, whatever. Never mind it was against the law, he was a doctor, he could find something somewhere. What was wrong with me, he screamed, why didn't I want another child? Didn't I like children? Didn't I like my daughter? He shouted this in front of Ada. In fact, he seems to prefer to do it front of Ada, because, lately, whenever the three of us are together, he tells Ada that she could have a brother or a sister – something that he knows that Ada would very much like – but that I don't want this to happen. "Mother doesn't want to give you a brother or a sister," those are the exact words.

Our life together has become very difficult. Now and then I'm dreaming of being separated, at least for a while, hoping he'll calm down, but where would I go? Back to Mother? I'd do it if I'd get Ada. But I know I'd never get Ada. So I'm staying.

He's turning my daughter against me, Leonard. Is there a bigger crime? I've heard him talking about me to her in ways that make me cringe. I can see how I am slowly losing her. You know how daughters see their fathers – no, how could you? They look up to them. Not to the mother, especially if she's always blamed, directly or indirectly, for all the problems Daddy's having. I don't know, Leonard, what the future holds. I hope … what do I hope?

At the university things have not changed much for me, at least on the surface. Travelling to the West is out of the question, of course, and even when I inquired about a potential trip to a conference in Budapest I was told not to waste my time. There is talk about a demotion – losing my full professorship under the pretext that it had been given to me much too early, a rash and unwise decision that needed review. But this would be a small price to pay, and it may not happen at all. I was lucky, Leonard, that I had published, just before your flight, two very good papers, both of them in "The Annals of Mathematics," papers that have created quite a buzz. In a way, the powers have decided to close their eyes. I was told to keep quiet about you, and, if asked, to say that you were teaching somewhere in the north of the country. Of course – I'm not sure how – everybody seems to know the truth. On the side, many tell me how lucky you are, wherever you are now. Whispering, winking. Only Aroso talks openly about it, quite delighted, almost gleeful.

Aroso has been wonderful. I went to see him several times after your flight and he has listened to my stories and laments with immense patience. I've become more attached to him than ever. He's the only one I can talk to about you, and about me and Emil and the difficulties I'm having at home, and about my worries with Ada. Can you picture it? Can you see Aroso listening to this melodrama? Yet he does it, with great kindness. "You're the daughter we never had," he said to me one evening when I was blabbering out excuses for keeping him up late with silly stories about marital distress. "Isn't that so, Mitzi? Isn't she like a daughter to us? Besides, what's a bit of marital distress to us. We're old hands at it, aren't we?" We were in Mitzi's bedroom

– well, their bedroom – when he said that, because, you see, whenever Mitzi is in reasonable shape he wants her to participate, somehow, in my visit. Mitzi, of course, was as absent, as unresponsive as ever.

About Charles Natraq.

Professor Charles Natraq. I knew him vaguely – he was at the workshop in Zurich, the first and last time I was allowed to travel to the West. An excellent mathematician, with a high reputation in topology and analytic number theory. Especially the latter, lately. Many publications, top journals, respected. He teaches in Paris, or near Paris, at the Institut des Hautes Études Scientifiques. There was a European workshop on number theory six weeks ago near Bucharest, at Snagov. Not a big participation, it turned out, but good people came, and Charles Natraq was one of them. The university has a house at Snagov, big enough to accommodate such a gathering. I've been there before. A large villa of a former patrician, close to the lake, lovely in the early fall – a quiet retreat for brainy mathematicians. I was glad to be away from Emil, although I was missing Ada. I presented a paper on Dirichlet series (one of my rare forays in the area) and talked to many of the participants. And I talked to Charles Natraq. He had presented a paper too, a very good one – in the sense that it raised intriguing questions. I thought I had a way to answer one of the questions, and I mentioned it to him during a break. We had a good chat at lunch on the second day of the conference and we talked about the possibility of writing a paper together. Probably nothing would have come out of it – you know how it is, Leonard, we always talk about collaboration, but it rarely goes beyond talk and intentions. Mathematics is often a solitary game and East-West collaborations are quite rare. He seemed very keen, though. It was he who suggested the common paper. In fact, he suggested a series of papers, even a book. He sounded very enthusiastic. I wasn't sure I wanted to spend too much time in number theory. It reminded me a bit of chromatic numbers, with an even larger list of old unsolved problems and the danger of being sucked in. (You know what I mean – the old quest to solve once and for all the distribution of prime numbers, or Fermat's last theorem, or Goldbach's conjectures, weak and strong, the twin-prime conjecture, whatever, with or without the help of analysis.) I tried to moderate the whole thing. I said that a whole series of papers – never mind a book – was a huge undertaking and that it would be best to write one paper and see how it worked out. I also pointed out to him that my interest in analytic number theory could at best be described as lukewarm and that my knowledge mirrored my enthusiasm. He dismissed that by saying that a fresh, untainted mind, new – or relatively new – to the topic, was best.

As we were finishing lunch, he said that he would definitely put down some thoughts on paper the moment he got back to Montreal and had a few quiet days, and then mail them to me. You'll understand, Leonard, that my heart jumped. I told him I thought that he was French and living in Paris. He said he did live in Paris much of the year, but he was actually Canadian, French Canadian, and for three months every year, or almost every year, he taught a course at the Université de Montreal. In fact, he said, soon after his return to Paris he would being flying to Montreal for a few days.

I didn't return to the afternoon session that day, although one of the presenters was Aroso and I wouldn't have missed listening to him under normal circumstances. But that afternoon I had to think, Leonard, think quickly, because a way of communicating with you was now possible. Would I dare to ask Charles Natraq to take a letter for you and mail it to you from Paris? You two could even meet, I told myself, as on the map Toronto and Montreal seemed very close. And, even more important, his taking a trip back to Bucharest, and bringing a letter from you, would be a distinct possibility if we were to write a paper together. I scolded myself for sounding doubtful about collaborating on a series. To work together on a whole series of papers, or a book, he'd have to travel to Bucharest quite often, since I couldn't travel to Paris. A way to properly correspond with you was right there, under my nose, and I, idiot that I was, had pushed it away.

At dinner that evening I sat with Aroso, an East German, and an Austrian. The three of them were happily chatting away in German, Aroso regaling them with Gottingen stories. I caught the name of Hilbert and Einstein and I gathered it had something to do with Hilbert's interest in general relativity. I tried, but couldn't pay attention to them. My German is very poor anyway. I kept thinking of you and me, and of Charles Natraq as a potential go-between. Would I dare ask him to do it? Would he do it? What if he was a Communist sympathizer? Was that a foolish fear? On the other hand, there were so many of them among the French. Hold it, I told myself, he's not French, he's Canadian. Were there fellow travellers among Canadians? And, anyway, just being a Communist sympathizer didn't necessarily mean telling on my wicked schemes.

While I was having these thoughts, I kept looking at Charles Natraq. I was unaware I was doing it, but I was trying to guess what kind of person he was, how he would react to my unusual request. Charles Natraq's best feature, by the way, is his eyes – thoughtful and kind. Average height, slightly plump, and with a wild crown of curly white hair. He told me later that his hair became wholly white only last year, as a result of a very nasty divorce. He maintained also that his rotundity – that's what he called it – was acquired during the same period. "It's an outrage," he laughed, "mathematicians are not supposed to be fat." Anyway, I had a good view of him from where I sat, even if he was several tables away. He was half-turned my way and in animated conversation. For whatever reason – he must have felt my eyes on him – he would look towards me from time to time. The first time, he waved, and I nodded and smiled, acknowledging his wave. The second time, he caught me looking at him, and I think I blushed. I felt rather foolish – as if I were back in the seventh grade. I couldn't help it, though, couldn't stop studying him. Aroso noticed it and said to me in Romanian, "Staring into the fourth dimension, my dear, or at a good-looking mathematician?" I shook my head, smiled, and said that the likelihood of seeing either one was similarly small. I apologized for my non-participation. Aroso laughed and translated my slight on male mathematicians. There were screams of indignation, of course, and I had to participate in the silly banter that followed. As we left the table, I caught Charles Natraq looking at me again.

I retired after dinner. I still didn't know what to do. In the morning, I woke up very early, must have been six o'clock, and went out for a walk on a gravel path along the lakeshore. There was a heavy fog on the lake which spread out over the path. And then I heard steps coming fast behind me. I turned around and saw Charles Natraq marching towards me, almost running, in a blazing-red jogging suit and thick-soled running shoes. I have to say he looked slightly ridiculous. He was red in the face and puffing. What people do to lose weight, he joked. He went into a long explanation, physics and all, about why running on gravel wasn't easy. It removed one's dignity. We laughed and exchanged pleasantries. Yes, he was an early riser, as I seemed to be. Then he suddenly said that he had come out this morning hoping to catch me – he had seen me from his window walking down to the lake. He wanted to talk to me. It was at that moment that I decided to do it, to ask for his help. Why? Probably because he looked so ridiculous. A plump mathematician who got up at six in the morning to pursue a damsel in distress along a foggy path – no, there weren't any mean bones under that running outfit. I told him that his decision to follow me was quite fortunate, because I also wanted to talk to him. We argued for a while as to who should be the first, and the lady won. And it was a good thing I did – as you'll see.

I told him about you and me, and Mother, and about you fleeing, and about the impossibility of communicating openly with you. I also told him about Emil and about how he was making everything so much more difficult. I told him that you lived in Canada, in Toronto, which had made me think of asking for his – a Canadian's – help. I told him that it would be entirely understandable if he refused and that I hoped that, were he to do so, it would not affect any professional collaboration we might have. It was fortunate, in a way, that I didn't have time to rehearse any of this. I think I was natural, direct, somewhat skeptical of the outcome, somewhat resigned. He told me later that it was a compelling and moving advocacy. If it was, it wasn't needed, because he agreed immediately, without the slightest hesitation. He said it was nothing, no burden at all. He'd be delighted to help.

And that was that, Leonard. It explains my previous letter and this second one, via Professor Charles Natraq, citizen of Canada, resident of Paris and Montreal. As I already wrote to you, but it bears repeating, please respond through him and only through him. He will come to Bucharest in a month or two and will bring your letter.

This letter must be the world's longest. I should end it, but you'll be curious to know what Charles Natraq wanted to tell me that early morning on the foggy shores of Lake Snagov. When I asked him, after profusely thanking him for agreeing to help us, he hesitated. He said that in light of what I had just told him it wasn't relevant anymore, in fact it was outright ridiculous. I assumed he was joking – what could my brother and I, and our inability to write to each other, have to do with what he wanted to say to me? I pressed him, and in the end he relented. I had the feeling he was glad I pressed him. He said he couldn't fail to notice that, at dinner the night before, I kept looking at him. It had given him heart to try to talk to me – he meant, of course, about things other than mathematics. Because, he told me, he had always noticed me, looked at me and admired me, but until that evening he had felt that his high regard for me was not reciprocated. And now he realized that what he had taken as encouragement, as hope, was in fact the product of very sensible

– admirable, no doubt, but very practical – reasons and sentiments. Which
he understood very well. All this said in a very touching way.

There you are, Leonard, you have it all.

You're wondering, probably, what has happened to your sister. Who
is this person, writing verbose confessional letters? Who is this person who
does not mind at all writing to you so many pages?

Take care. Hugs, many hugs. Mother and I, and Ada, miss you.

Alexandra – Alsa.

PS: Leonard dear, why Canada? What made you suddenly leave
France and cross the ocean? Please write at length. Your letter – the one
that Charles brought with him, the first bona fide letter from you – was
disappointingly short on information about you. What I want to know is
how you're doing, what's your state of soul and mind, what your plans are.
Among the many questions I have – are you or aren't you in graduate school?
No, it's not good enough for an aspiring writer.

How lucky they were to have found Charles Natraq, to be finally able
to write without fear, without afterthought. A minute taste of another
world, in a way. She had written her first letter at Snagov, the very day
(or night, to be precise) of her talk with the puffing and panting Charles
Natraq. Until Charles, Alexandra's news to Leonard had been recast in
Mrs. Jacobi's childish handwriting and expressed as if Mrs. Jacobi were
conveying news about her daughter and her family. Things were fine,
Alexandra was fine, and so were Emil and Ada. Mrs. Jacobi wrote about
the courses that Alexandra was teaching at the university – a way for
Alexandra to inform Leonard that her position was not affected by his
flight. And she always added that Emil was still upset with her, with
Mrs. Jacobi, for her lack of vigilance – a sentence that Emil insisted must
appear in each letter from his mother-in-law, for the eyes that would read
the letter before Leonard's, and for the subsequent report. Alexandra
had found the idea grotesque, humiliating, but decided not to argue, and
Mrs. Jacobi merely shrugged.

She wondered why she hadn't thought of this before – sending a letter out to Leonard through one of the visiting mathematicians from the West. Besides the embarrassment of having to ask, or the lack of trust, it was the inability to get news back from Leonard. This was the important connection, from Leonard to her, more than from her to Leonard. Charles as a mail hub seemed to offer a solution, at least for now. She wasn't exactly sure how things were going to end up with Charles. One month after the workshop at Snagov, he had come back and spent three days in Bucharest, ostensibly to discuss their work on the future paper – papers, he kept insisting, and then a book – but also because he was attracted to her. He didn't try to hide it, but he didn't press her either, because, he told her, he realized that Alexandra was at a disadvantage – a troubled marriage (he had guessed more than Alexandra had told him), his help to her in communicating with her brother, the very fact that he was the enviable Westerner in her drab, dreary existence. He had not used these words, he had been quite delicate about it, saying that Alexandra seemed at a crossroads and didn't need added complications and pressure, but that he wanted to help in whatever way he could. For this unexpected gentleness and tact, she was grateful. More than grateful – could that be? A sort of silly giddiness took hold of her in his presence – her rotund Cupid with his curly white hair. No doubt that her initial feelings were both an amused and bemused curiosity. She couldn't forget his scarlet face that morning, the way it almost matched the colour of the three-striped Adidas jogging suit, a dishevelled, dutiful, unnatural jogger, trying to fulfil the demands of both his body and his heart. But was that all? Nothing else?

On his last evening in Bucharest, Charles took Alexandra and Emil out to dinner. It took a while to convince Emil to join them – "Why do you need me? You'll talk shop all the time" – and he arrived late and was taciturn throughout, although quite handy in convincing a sulking waitress that being more helpful would result in a better tip. He warmed up a little with the second bottle of wine and showed some curiosity about Canada, but his French was poor, and after a while he gave up any pretence of being interested. Alexandra had been quiet, too, uneasy with the sulking Emil and aware of Charles's feelings towards her, and so it was left to Charles to do most of the talking (which prompted Emil's bitter remark, back in their apartment, "Have you ever seen a Frenchman unable to fill a silence? They can talk for hours about bed sheets hung up to dry"), and he did, first with stories about French politics – De Gaulle, Pompidou – and then, mainly, about his life. He was born in Quebec City, the capital of the Canadian province of Quebec, and with this came a crash course in Canadian geography that left both Alexandra and Emil thoroughly confused. His studies in Montreal, then Yale, his parents, both high-school teachers (his father also of mathematics), recently retired and looking for a house near the ocean, in New Brunswick (where his father was from), with his mother quite appalled initially by the idea but slowly getting used to it. It all seemed unreal to Alexandra – the exotic names, Bouctouche, the Northumberland Strait, the ocean, retiring and buying another house. Then came an instalment of Canadian history, about Acadians, the descendents of French settlers in the Maritime provinces, and their harsh luck. He talked about his siblings, two sisters and a brother. One of his sisters, married, with three children, was a professor of French literature at the Université de Montréal. Yes, the same university he was teaching at when he was not in France. He talked at length about Montreal. In the end, Charles talking about Montreal and Canada and his family saved the evening. And Toronto, where Leonard lived? Not a nice city, not at all. Ugly, spread out like a cowpat, and with the same character, didn't have Montreal's chic, *savoir-vivre*, not a place he would choose, not one decent restaurant. Probably larger than Montreal, he wasn't sure. Then, sipping Greek brandy, Charles talked about political violence – so foreign to Canada – sparked by Quebec nationalists. By whom? Nationalists, those who think a sovereign Quebec would be better off. There were bombs, political kidnappings, one man had been killed as a result. Recently. Where, in Toronto? No, no, in Montreal. Anyway, it was quieting down, now, and she shouldn't worry about Leonard. Emil laughed, and Alexandra assured Charles that she was not unduly worried about Leonard.

At the end of his brief trip in October, Charles had told Alexandra he wouldn't be able to travel back to Bucharest until late January and, after that, only in May or June. He had found their direct exchange of ideas invigorating, exciting, and he hoped that their mathematical collaboration would not suffer too much through the slow crossing of letters – Alexandra had already warned him that her correspondence would be read carefully by vigilant eyes and might take weeks to reach him. Alexandra had nodded at this without saying anything, merely thinking that it would be months before she had news from Leonard again, but now, only several days after Charles's departure, she found herself thinking of him often.

Was she in love with Charles? Could that be? Or was it simply that he was the only pocket of air she could breathe in? Did it matter what it was, as long as it kept her breathing? The ship was going down and she was trapped, the water almost to the ceiling. When she was with Charles, it was as if she had managed to find an air pocket and fill her lungs. But was this love?

The only reference she had was George. With Emil she had found steadiness (well, anybody would be like a rock, compared to George), she had found sanity and a certain predictability, or monotony, that she didn't mind at all, but not love. She knew this now.

She had been on the rebound after George, although it had been her decision to end it. She had been distraught when she had taken that decision, angry with him, unable to understand that madness, that cheerful desire to self-destruct, but now when she thought of him, it was mainly with a smile, the indulgent smile of adults who remember the things they've done as youngsters, with that satisfaction that they've had their crazy days and got away with it. She smiled when she thought of George's outrageous clothes, especially his ties and hats, in a world in which colourful ties and hats, anything that set you apart, were dangerous.

"George," she would tease him, "you look like a clown, like a magician. All you need is a cape. Every time I look at you I expect you to make people levitate."

"And you shouldn't be surprised when it happens, my dear. Because it will one day. I'm just apprenticing."

Under his influence, she began to add some colour to her clothes, to match her hair, her skin, her eyes. It was his contribution, his gift to her, and, although for a while she had laughed at his attempts to "improve her," she relented once their affair became serious. He told her she was beautiful, that she had a radiant, luminous beauty. Who could resist such words? She began to spend more time in front of the mirror and found a modicum of truth in George's words. She had met him at a party, one of the few she had gone to as a student. It was during her last year, and she had been dragged along by Lily, who was quite difficult to resist – both the tidal wave of words and her physical presence. The large, red-haired, irreverent Lily, on her way to becoming a teacher, had been in high school with Alexandra. They had lost touch with each other during university – she was in another city – and met again, by chance, a few weeks before the party where she saw George for the first time. She and Lily had coffee together, talked – that is, mainly Lily talked – and had a good time reminiscing about high-school days. They promised to see each other again. Three weeks later, Alexandra succumbed to the whirlwind and went to the party where George's whereabouts – George was in high spirits, jumping from group to group – could easily be discerned. "That's the good thing about George," said Lily, who had confessed to Alexandra that a couple of years earlier she had had an affair with him, "you always know where he is in a crowd." "What happened? Why did you split up?" "Oh, Alexandra, it's so obvious. We're both loud, forceful. We both wanted to have it our way. We fought too much. And his great failure, his 'tragedy,' as he calls it, got on my nerves."

George's tragedy was that he had come from a family of doctors – his father, his uncle, his older brother and his sister, all doctors – and George had taken it for granted that he'd become one, too. He failed his entrance examination, and the family had to pull strings to get him out of starting his army service that fall. He tried and he failed again the following year. When he came back after the compulsory two years in the army, he thought of trying again but realized that he was less prepared then ever and instead wrote the entrance exams for pharmacy. He'd made it, but just.

George had already grinned his way through the required five years of study when Alexandra first met him. Now he was finding out what it meant to be a working pharmacist. He was still seething with anger at the incompetents in charge of the medical Mafia who were denying him his birthright. And not just medicine, but surgery, like his older brother and his father. "Look at these hands," he'd say to Alexandra.

"Have you ever seen such powerful yet such fine hands? What do you think they were made for?" "To caress me?" "You, dear idiot, all you understand is math. How would you recognize the perfect hands for surgery?"

George's hands were powerful and fine. Small too, like his feet, ridiculously small for such a big body. He was tall, and so wide you didn't immediately realize his height. George would have been a menacing presence were it not for his smile, a constant, happy, insouciant smile, even when he talked about the conspiracy to thwart him. George's face was always cheerful, a pleasant shock in a city where faces were homogeneously gloomy. A large, lively, beguiling man, with the beginning of a bare patch on the front of his head, a nose blunted at the tip, a neck concealed by shoulder muscles. They were together for almost two years, Alexandra and George. Two years unlike anything she'd experienced, or would experience again. Her two crazy years. Crazy by her standards, not George's.

After five years of pharmaceutical studies, "only one step away from medicine," as he kept telling everybody, George found work in the medical lab of a new and already crumbling hospital in the southern outskirts of Bucharest. After a few months of getting used to his new surroundings, George adopted the habit of staying late in the lab. With a stethoscope around his neck, he visited the sick in his white coat and talked to them.

"Never told them I was a doctor," he said to Alexandra, "but they all think I am. I have a wonderful bedside manner – I inquire about their family, I tell them jokes. Alexandra, they're so grateful they'd eat out of my hand. Especially the peasants. Nobody takes an interest in them. Nobody talks to them. Nobody explains to them what ails them or what they're doing to them. What a horror show. The lack of medication is appalling – but there isn't much one can do about it. But to treat them like this, with utter disregard … And the diagnostics. God, half of them are wrong, or the medication isn't right. Alexandra, I know more than these so-called doctors ever knew. I've read all the books. And yet I'm not allowed to practice."

George's medical dreams turned into a comical nightmare. He began to make house-calls. Alexandra didn't know how he picked his patients – possibly ones discharged from the hospital he was working at. Alexandra learned about George's new venture from a friend of his, who quickly clammed up when he realized he shouldn't have told her. George knew that she – prejudiced, ordinary, conventional – wouldn't approve. It surprised Alexandra that the impostor wasn't caught. When she confronted him, he laughed. That's when Alexandra realized that she should get away from him. But then – to her horror – she found herself pregnant. George asked his brother, the surgeon, to do the abortion. George, in fact, offered to do it himself. Alexandra lost it. "Are you out of your mind? Are you demented?" "Why, what's the big deal?" the would-be surgeon wondered. "I've seen it done. I've assisted my brother a dozen times. A little scraping, a little blood, it's all over in twenty minutes. The only problem is finding pain-killers."

George's brother did the abortion in Alexandra's house, on the large oak dining-room table, with the centre leaf inserted for added space, while Mrs. Jacobi was away visiting a friend at the other end of the city. They counted on four hours, enough to do the whole procedure and erase all traces. With luck, when her mother came home, Alexandra would be safely in bed. A good night's sleep was all a young body needed. George assisted.

Alexandra was lucky, because George's brother had brought enough pain-killers for her to barely feel anything. In one hour it was all over, and by eight o'clock she was in her bed pumped up with sleeping pills and more pain-killers. George was delighted by the happy outcome. He was even more delighted by the technical perfection of his brother's procedure, by its simplicity. He talked about it at length and declared himself hooked. He had already been hooked, it turned out. Alexandra later realized that by the time George had suggested to her that he could carry out the abortion himself, he had already done a few.

Not long after, Alexandra stopped seeing George. He had been more puzzled than hurt, and for a while he followed Alexandra around, struggling to understand what had happened. After she began going out with Emil Semeu, George stopped her one day as she was coming out of the university. He was wearing a black raincoat, a black narrow-brimmed hat, and a yellow silk *foulard* knotted on the outside. There was no small talk. "Is it because he's got a medical diploma? I know it for a fact that

Emil Semeu is a peasant, Alexandra, a common, unmitigated peasant. A bore. Hitched to him is like riding in a train through the desert. There is nothing but sand. With me, it's mountains and breathtaking gorges. How could you?" "With you, it's a roller-coaster, and I don't have the heart for it. George, he's sane, and you're crazy. It's as simple as that. Outside mathematics, I'm ordinary and conventional, I'm afraid. Your words. That's all there is to it. He's not boring, he's sane. He's sane, and you're crazy." George laughed at that and went away.

Chapter 5
February 1971

Charles came back to Bucharest for a four-day working visit in early February. Alexandra had looked forward to his return, but she attributed her anticipation to the pleasure of working together. For their collaboration was, to Alexandra's surprise, not only fruitful, but also very agreeable. They had already submitted one paper – a further development of one of the results from Alexandra's Snagov paper on Dirichlet series – and were working on a second one. In one of her letters to Charles, and using her strength in complex analysis, Alexandra proposed a couple of ways to advance the proof of the Riemann zeta-hypothesis, and Charles suggested they should write a paper on major problems in analytic number theory. The days that Charles would spend in Bucharest were to be dedicated to that – to thinking about where the analytic number theory should be in the next twenty years or so, what were the most important problems to attack. Of course, the Riemann hypothesis was one of them, but wasn't the obsessive preoccupation with the minutia of the distribution of prime numbers somewhat detrimental to progress elsewhere? This, according to Charles, was a question they should pose and try to answer. They should also try to assess which of the problems were more likely to be resolved sooner rather than later

Alexandra had been initially rather reluctant. She thought she was, by temperament, more inclined to resolve problems than to define them, but Charles had been adamant in his correspondence that there was great value in such a paper, and slowly she was beginning to warm up to this view. It wasn't the idea that she minded at first – after all, what could be more attractive than speculating for a few days, letting your mind float in pleasant company, with another keen mind as a catalyst – but she wondered whether this newly found pleasure in posing problems as opposed to trying to solve them had something to do with age. Was she, at thirty-four, getting a bit old for the supreme effort required to resolve a difficult problem? Was it Hardy, in his memoirs, who said that mathematics was a young man's game? She had always thought, and Aroso had too, that defining problems was the territory of weary veterans who had lost their sharpness. Aroso called it "retirement mathematics." "That's what I've been doing," Aroso told Alexandra once when she had expressed admiration for this ability of his to define almost at will research problems and paths, "for the past twenty years or so: define problems and programs. Retirement mathematics, ha! Mind you, it has its usefulness. Your intuition – your mathematics wisdom, if you wish – is honed by age. It helps you avoid wrong turns." No, it couldn't be her age, thirty-four was still young, thirty-four was the peak. She had never felt stronger, more sure of herself, than now. And Charles? Charles was seven years her senior. Was he tempted by "retirement mathematics"?

Charles landed late on Saturday and called her house once he got to the hotel. Emil made a sour face as he passed her the phone. "Ah, your co-author cum admirer is here." She told Charles to come to her office the following morning, as early as he could – as usual, she would be there from five o'clock.

He came at six, confessing he couldn't sleep at all. "I had to see you. I'm like an *ecolier*," he said, blushing, and kissed her. She didn't exactly return his kiss, but didn't protest either. She had been somewhat surprised by it, although she expected it to happen eventually. Alexandra wondered whether a tacit understanding was established between them at that moment, by that awkward kiss at six o'clock in the morning, that theirs was more than a mathematical collaboration. What on earth was she doing?

They weren't sure what to say to each other for a while, and then

Charles took an envelope from his coat, handed it to her and announced triumphantly, "I saw him." She knew immediately who he meant. "You went to see Leonard! Oh, this is very kind, very generous."

He talked at length about Leonard that morning, and they didn't touch their work until several hours later, after he had promised her that he'd come to dinner that night and repeat all the stories for the benefit of her mother. She called Mrs. Jacobi and asked her to cook something, anything, and have it ready to bring over, because there was news, first-hand news, from Leonard, to be heard around their dinner table that evening. And then she called Emil to let him know that she had invited Charles Natraq to eat with them.

"Start without me. I don't know when I'll get home. I promised a colleague of mine that I'd have a drink with him. His wife is leaving him and he's a wreck." He sounded as if he was improvising.

"Please try to be home early, Emil."

Dear Alsa,

Good Professor Natraq – yes, imagine my surprise – brought me your letter today. He's visiting a colleague in Toronto, and he called the department here on the chance that I'd be around. I was. In fact, I had been at my desk reading about rotation groups – I'll tell you why later – when he got through to me. After a few confusing moments, he suggested lunch. We've just finished it – a long and copious lunch the kind of which I haven't had in a long time. He paid, of course. I don't think he enjoyed the fare as much as I did, but anything halfway decent tastes heavenly to me after months of cafeteria poisoning.

We talked a lot about you. What's going on, Alsa? Could it be that the famous mathematician, married and with a child, and approaching middle age, is entertaining romantic thoughts? Because he's head over heels about you, no doubt about it – he didn't try to hide it, either. He said he could not go back to Bucharest, back to you, without meeting me first. He had to learn and register everything about me, the smallest detail, so that he could report later to you, one of the most astute minds he had ever encountered. The way to my sister's heart, one way at least, he declared candidly, was to be able to talk to her about me. He could not be hasty, he had to get to the core of things. I was subjected to a friendly but detailed inquisition. He had heard you complaining about how little you knew about me, and he saw an excellent opportunity *pour gagner des bons points* with you. I even had to take him back to my residence, to let him see how I lived.

He's taller than I expected, *ton* Charles. I don't know why I formed the image of a short, chubby man. A bit portly, he is, yes, but it almost adds to his charm. Maybe the large crown of curly white hair makes him seem taller. He has an easy, pleasant smile, and he's very straight, very candid. He said he's in love with you, deeply in love. Wow!

It was a long lunch, about three hours, and as he kept pouring wine into my glass, I became quite garrulous. He knows all about my life here, about my plans, my aspirations. I'm almost tempted to make this a short letter, as he now can tell you much more than I could possibly write. Charles, the message-carrier, is the true letter. He has it all in his brain, all you have to do is pick it.

Yes, a wet lunch for me. He didn't drink much, at most two glasses, claiming he had a long afternoon and evening of work ahead of him. We agreed that I'd write to you this evening, and that tomorrow morning, on his way to the airport, he'd drop by and pick up the letter. So here I am, writing, pleasantly smashed and tempted to have a nap. But no naps for dedicated letter-writers. I have instructions from Charles to cover some specific points. I'll try.

First, details about the getaway.

Hopeless. Too long for a letter. I told Charles the story and he'll convey it to you.

Why did I leave France? How could anyone leave beautiful Paris?

Again too long. I'm not sure Charles understands either, although we talked about it. We'll have to leave this for our reunion.

Why Canada?

Here, Alsa dear, I'm a bit at a loss. But once you decide to leave Europe, the choices are rather limited. There was Israel, but it felt too small, too self-involved with its endless problems with its neighbours (even after their huge victory not long ago). I felt the state would make (for good reasons) too many demands on me, and the last thing I wanted was to live in a place where you were not left to be. Just be.

Australia? Too far. USA? Yes, a possibility, but somehow my heart was not in it. Too in-your-face, too boisterous, too much noise. That left Canada.

Do I like Toronto?

I have an ambivalent view of the city. My first impression was of a cold and desolate city of mediocre, careless, slap-down architecture. It was an impression I have not been able to shake off. You see, I arrived in the winter – well, it was March, but it was cold and windy, and the piled-up snow was old and dirty. I landed late on a Saturday night and spent the first night at the Ford Hotel – a rather dubious place, downtown, near the bus station, recommended to me by a tired immigration official at the airport. Next morning, a blustery grey Sunday, well below zero and with a few tormented snowflakes, I walked through the city following a map that the wind was trying to tear away. My hands froze. The view I took of Toronto on that first day was of a dull, deserted city, punished for its graceless mien by inclement weather. By the time I decided to turn back I was hungry and shivering. I needed to be careful with the money I had, and I looked for a café or anything open where I could get a sandwich. As I looked around I imagined the sound of my teeth biting into a crunchy baguette. What would it be with? Jambon, salami, fromage? There seemed to be few restaurants or stores, and all the ones I saw were closed. It began to dawn on me that I had been spoiled by my months in Paris. Near the hotel, I decided to go into the bus station, hoping to find something to eat there. A small cafeteria was open, and I bought two triangular sandwiches, wrapped in cellophane. Ham and cheese, I was told. I ran back to the warmth of my hotel room. In the elevator, I unwrapped the sandwiches and took a bite. The bread was cold, musty, and slightly sweet. The cheese was a strident yellow, almost orange. In my room, I sat in the armchair and finished both sandwiches. I noticed the water as I was looking for the dustbin to drop the cellophane wrap. The toilet bowl was leaking, and a stream of water had made its way to the bedroom, and likely to the room below. I went downstairs to ask for another room, since I didn't trust my ability to explain what was wrong on the telephone. At the reception desk, a tall black man smiled throughout my story and, after telling an unseen Lisa to mind the desk, followed me back to my room. In the elevator, he kept smiling at me and humming a tune. He cast a pensive look at the flow of water, said, "Cool, man," and, brandishing a set of keys, told me to follow him. In a few

minutes I was moved into an identical room, one floor above, in which I had
a few hours of despair.

Now, in the summer, Toronto is quite pleasant. It can get hot and
humid, but it doesn't bother me. The summer Toronto is startlingly sunny
and green, and under that green all its sins disappear. Had I arrived in the
summer, I am sure that my immediate impression would have been different.
To me, Toronto is two cities. A grey, dreary one in the winter. An affable,
slyly alluring, very green, sunny one in the summer.

The winter one is the true face. The green mask of the summer is just
that, a beautiful mask. Yearly make-up.

My studies and my plans for the future. I was told by Charles, in
almost threatening terms, that I was not to skimp here.

I came to Toronto because my inquiries about pursuing graduate
studies in mathematics, with emphasis on, as I put it in my awkward
application letters, "the trends and history of mathematics," had received the
most promising reply from the University of Toronto. Professor M.L.Walker
(Murray Lannard, I found out later) wrote to say that he was interested
in my application, although it was an unusual one. It was not often that
they had students inclined towards the history of mathematics, students (and
here he quoted my pretentious words in the application letter) "intrigued by
mathematical fame, prestige, and recognition, and by what it often seems is
their unsuitable distribution." He continued by writing that graduate studies
strictly in the history of mathematics were uncommon at the University of
Toronto. There was one such course given at the University of Toronto each
year. Nevertheless, he would be willing to supervise my unusual interest. He
suggested that courses related to the foundations of mathematics, such as set
theory, topology, algebra, would, by their very nature, be most suitable. I
could, he continued, take these courses – graduate level, of course – and then
do a survey paper which could be "bent" towards a historical perspective.
He also wrote that he gathered from my letter that English was not my first
language and that I should also enrol in English writing courses. That, he
wrote, was imperative if I was serious about making a career in writing about
mathematics.

The acceptance to the program was of course based on undergraduate
marks and letters of recommendation, three of them, to be precise, from my
former school, supporting my application to the program. In my response to

Professor Walker's letter, I decried the impossibility of ever obtaining letters of recommendation, given my sudden and unsanctioned departure. Could an exception be made, I asked, in my unusual case?

Professor Walker's reply came quickly. Alas, he could not think how my admission would go through without adequate proof of academic achievement. The best he could recommend, given my special situation, was for me to take at least two graduate courses as a tentatively admitted student. If, at the end of the term, I had proved that I belonged, then I would become fully admitted in the graduate program. The courses taken could count towards my degree. But there could be no question of financial support during this probationary period. I would have to support myself, and also pay for the courses.

I met Murray Walker a few days after I arrived. Friendly, tall and solid, with poetic longish hair, wearing a short-sleeve shirt without a tie, he did not strike me as the most typical mathematician. In time, I learned that he was from Nova Scotia (a Canadian province on the Atlantic coast) and had come to the University of Toronto four years earlier. We agreed quickly on the two probationary courses I would take, starting in September. If I did well, he would be able to support me financially throughout my graduate stay – very likely paying me as a teaching assistant. He advised me to use the time till September to perfect my English, to speak it at every opportunity. "Read in English. Read a lot and, yes, watch television. Television, is bad for people who know English, but it's excellent for those who don't. It might not be a bad idea, either, to get a temporary or a part-time job." His office was very small, much smaller than yours. I told him briefly about my getaway and how I ended up in Toronto. I had the feeling that Murray Walker viewed my place of origin as a wellspring of odd characters not entirely reliable or stable, and that I was a somewhat restless soul. He confessed that he had no idea what the Communists where up to these days, and that he had no time or desire to find out. As there was, at that point, a threatening long pause, I told him about you, that you were my sister. Now, that changed the atmosphere a bit. He was quite familiar with some of your work and papers and seemed relieved when he realized you were my sister. "I'm confident you will be a great addition to our group. The mathematics gene often dwells in the same family."

I did get a job. I drove a taxi part-time for an outfit called Metro-Cab. I worked once or twice a week, in ten-hour shifts. I don't think I've ever been so magnificently incompetent at anything. Perfectly inadequate. This is something not easily achieved, perfect inadequacy. I paid for the fuel and I kept the tips and half of the fares. I made about a dollar an hour. With tips. I lasted three months. Through another graduate student, I found another job in the east end of the city, in a yard near the railway lines, moving merchandise from railway cars into trucks and vice-versa. Any kind of merchandise, from furniture to toys to refrigerators, TVs, nails, shingles, aluminium window frames, lumber. It met my needs. Like driving the cab, you could call in anytime you wanted to work. There was always work. Well paid. I made three dollars an hour. Heavy physical work, but well paid.

I did well in the two courses I took – in fact, I did very well. I was accepted in the graduate program and, with Murray Walker's support, I became a teaching assistant. It was enough to keep me going. In early January, only two weeks ago, I moved to the Graduate Student Residence, a rundown redbrick building at the fringes of the university. The windows of my room look down on a small, unpaved parking lot and, a bit further south, three tennis courts. I might take up tennis.

I'm getting hungry – how can I be hungry after the lunch I had? – and this letter is too long. One more thing, though, related to plans – the topic of my thesis. I've just about made up my mind to do something around Olinde Rodrigues. Who, on earth, is Olinde Rodrigues? you'll ask – no you won't, with your amazing memory you probably remember his formula for Legendre polynomials. It was at a lecture by a visiting British mathematician that I first heard of him. The topic was rotation groups, and I went to it both because it was a cold, rainy November afternoon, and because the note announcing the lecture mentioned a historical treatment. Although I had some difficulty following it, the lecturer turned out to be a dispenser of delightful arcane bits, one of those being Olinde Rodrigues – a French banker and mathematician whose work on rotations never received the proper credit. A Jew, the lecturer added, whose family had been chased out of Spain during the time of Isabella and Ferdinand.

I thought immediately of Aroso, of course. The proper credit. And his ancestors being refugees from the same place and era, except that they boarded the Sultan's boats instead of crossing the Pyrenees. After the lecture I asked the speaker if he could tell me more about Olinde Rodrigues. He smiled and shook his head. "Afraid not. Very little is known about him, it seems."

Somebody else asked him another question, more to the point of the lecture, and then several people surrounding him got into the discussion and I left. But I left with Olinde Rodrigues in mind.

I spent much of the next few days seeking out anything about Olinde Rodrigues and his work. I browsed through dusty books and old bound journals. His relatively meagre mathematical output was of manageable complexity – I could understand it. But the fact that very little was known and published about him could be both a blessing and a curse to a researcher. More likely the latter, for somebody in my situation.

So, Olinde Rodrigues it is, and if you know anything about him – doubtful, maybe Aroso? – do let me know. I told Charles about my choice. He shook his head in doubt, but said that he'd try to help me. After all, if there is any material about Olinde Rodrigues, it should be in France.

This is it, Alsa. Many hugs.

Leonard

Chapter 6
September 1973 - April 1974

Life with Emil was not pleasant, but Alexandra told herself they had reached an acceptable plateau of unpleasantness, a modus vivendi. They saw each other as little as possible. They took turns with Ada, and seldom were both of them with her together. Alexandra was sure Ada felt it. Once, prompted by Alexandra, the three of them went to a movie. Ada had a startled reaction, "Oh, Daddy is coming too?" When Alexandra suggested the same a couple of weeks later, Emil told her bluntly that he didn't think it was a good idea. "Why fool her that we're a family?" Without Ada, the two of them were like neighbours, polite and indifferent. They talked briefly about divorce or separation, but it remained just talk.

Alexandra couldn't explain to herself why Emil hadn't put in the papers for a divorce. She dismissed the thought that, like herself, he was afraid of losing Ada. Not because she didn't think he loved Ada as much as she did, but because her affair with Charles gave him enough ammunition for a quick divorce and custody of Ada. Why then? Why did he hesitate? Was it because a divorce would be frowned upon at the hospital, where his career was taking an upward swing again? Or was it because he just wanted to make her miserable?

Emil travelled a lot, especially to Timisoara, where, he said, good research in respirology was being carried out. She was told by a colleague of Emil she met at the bus station one afternoon that he had somebody there. She got further details in an anonymous letter mailed to her from Timisoara. It described Emil's involvement with a young woman, a medical doctor specializing in sleeping disorders.

Yes, it seemed likely. She had heard him on the phone talking about sleep apnea. She didn't care.

She was working harder than ever. Her work with Charles had proved fruitful beyond expectations. They worked together very well, Charles and she. Whenever Charles was in Bucharest, they had long talks with Aroso – a bit awkward, because Aroso's French was laughable, and she often needed to act as an interpreter. Aroso had not kept up with developments in number theory in many years. This ignorant freshness, combined with his uncanny understanding of the underlying structure of all mathematics, made him come up with very useful ideas. Charles was overwhelmed, astounded by Aroso. They proposed to Aroso that he be made the third author of the series of papers, but Aroso declined.

The papers they wrote – there were six of them in relatively quick succession – were very well received. The fourth paper proposed a whole set of problems and ways of attacking some of them, and while they joked that it was "retirement mathematics" with Aroso, who had been a significant contributor to it and had reluctantly agreed to be a co-author, in the fifth and sixth paper they did resolve one of the problems put forward in their previous paper and made good progress towards the solution of another one. Other papers began to refer to the Semeu-Natraq-Aroso program, or, because it was more brief, the Semeu program, which Alexandra thought unfair but found a guilty joy in.

The book was taking shape, and they began to wonder whether they had material for two books. They already had a publisher in France, and Charles had written to her that an American publisher had approached him about a translation.

Charles's kindness and support were her crutch, her supporting scaffold, and she told him so. Where would he find, he smiled, another beautiful woman, strikingly beautiful, with whom he could talk about the Ravenel conjectures or elliptic cohomologies? He loved her. He didn't mind waiting for her to decide what was best for her. His patience was endless, he assured her, and he was convinced that she also loved him, in her wounded way, which was good enough for him.

Her love for him was complicated and worried. She felt particularly so the rare times they made love, always at his hotel (not far from the university) and always hurried, and she stepped into the hotel lobby and strode quickly towards the elevators, without daring to look anywhere but straight ahead, convinced that everybody stared at her. It was a wounded love – how right Charles was – undemanding and hopeless. Hopeless in the sense that there were no events to look forward to, no future. A resigned, day to day, take-it-as-it-comes love. She was glad to see him, glad when he was there with her, but when he was away she didn't pine for him, and, while she thought about him, it was more in the context of their common work. Perhaps it was the only kind of love she was still capable of.

Charles came again at the end of August for a week-long visit. He arrived from a conference in Barcelona, where an official letter was signed by all the participants – all except those from the Communist countries – asking the Romanian authorities to allow Professor Semeu to travel abroad. Frequent, direct contact with peers, said the letter, "was invaluable to a mathematician, like the oxygen in the air we breathe."

"I know who was behind all this," she laughed.

"You have no idea how valued your work is. It took no convincing at all. Yes, I drafted the letter, but after the conference chairman read it to the gathering on the very first day, there was spontaneous clapping in support. It is quite unique, my dear. You know very well that these meetings are hardly ever political."

Emil had gone to Timisoara, and Ada was at Urja with her grandparents. Alexandra had been there with her for a week but came back to Bucharest for Charles's visit. For the first time since she had known Charles, she was more or less free, unbound by obligations or fears. They took long walks in the city, and Charles began to find in it a quaint charm. A lover of architecture, especially of what he termed French Neoclassical – abundant in Paris, to his delight, but not often found in Montreal – Charles delighted in discovering such buildings or features and in pointing them out to Alexandra. He thought the university building was a perfect example – roofs with mansards and small round corner towers, jutting window sills, shallow balconies, and its endless carved frieze – and they walked around it whenever they left her office. He also loved the broad boulevards lined with trees and was appalled by the socialist drab of the new apartment and office blocks and the ubiquitous dirt and grime.

She let herself relax, and for several days she had a taste of what her life could be.

They took the train to Brasov and spent a few hours in the mountain-surrounded medieval city before returning, exhausted. A well-dressed man, who was asleep in the first-class compartment when they climbed in, woke up around Sinaia and promptly proceeded to throw up. He apologized profusely, "Too much to drink at my son's wedding," but the stench chased them out of the compartment.

"He seemed very polite," Charles laughed after a few minutes.

"He was."

"And genuinely sorry."

"He definitely was. He asked for the forgiveness of the Comrade Foreigner."

"That's me?"

"Of course."

"After all, one is allowed to drink at a wedding."

"Especially a son's wedding."

"In fact, one is expected."

"To get drunk?"

"He didn't count on the ride. Don't you find it a bit jerky?"

"A bit, yes. And too many turns."

"Poor man, I feel sorry for him."

"Me too."

"Do you think we upset him? He seemed very distressed when we took off."

"It wasn't personal."

They spent the rest of the trip in the passageway, looking out in silence through the darkening window, Alexandra leaning slightly into Charles.

They went one evening to Aroso's house, where Jana cooked a feast. They ate outside, under the leafy trellis, with Mitzi properly dressed and absently nodding in the most comfortable chair, her tremors of an alarming amplitude. A pleasant smell of quince surprised Alexandra, until Jana told her that earlier she had made quince jam. Alexandra couldn't remember having had such a pleasant, relaxed dinner in a long time. As night fell, Jana brought candles to the table. It became very quiet, and the men's voices acquired a deep, comforting quality. Aroso reminisced about Russian mathematicians in his Gottingen days (with the help of frequent translations from Alexandra), and Charles told them how he got to the Institute des Hautes Études Scientifiques. And they talked math, of course, about their common work.

They had quite a lot to drink, especially Charles, who rarely had more than a glass of wine. When Jana carried Mitzi to bed, Alexandra said it was time to go, but Charles protested that they should all have another glass. He then whispered to Aroso that he was winning the battle, as Alexandra was slowly joining the queen's side – an allusion to Gauss's observation that number theory was the queen of mathematics. Alexandra smiled and shook here head. "I heard you, Charles. I don't know if you're right. I wouldn't trumpet victory yet. I know I've said yes, and I'm writing papers in the field, but I'm having second thoughts."

"Damn these second thoughts," Aroso said.

"I don't know ... I'm wary of embarking fully on number theory, analytic or otherwise. All these old, unsolved problems that suck you in. So simple to state, so hard to solve. And then there is the black hole of prime numbers. There's no escape from the Riemann hypothesis. It's like being on Devil's Island, you're a convict for life. Is there freedom from it, from this obsession with the distribution of prime numbers. It's like a drug, the convicts are addicted. They're all oddballs, anyway."

Charles chuckled. "I've heard of a mathematician sleeping with his wife only on those days of the month whose dates were prime numbers. He said he felt unworthy on composite days, and wouldn't let his wife approach him. Unworthy or impure."

Aroso laughed, too. "More joy in the early part of the month. That's an apocryphal story, though. I heard a similar one while I was in Gottingen, about a celibate mathematician who'd share his bed with his housekeeper – young and pretty it seems – only on two days of the month, the sixth and the twenty-eighth. Because only these two dates were perfect numbers."

"Perfect dates," Alexandra said.

"Maybe she wasn't young and pretty," Charles said. "Maybe it was because she wasn't young and pretty that he came up with this condition."

"Why," Aroso said, "is the distribution of primes so messy? It just doesn't fit the elegance of other laws of nature. And yet, is there anything more basic and important than the prime numbers? They are the basis of all numbers, and numbers are the fabric all the laws of the universe. We accept the simplicity of $E = mc^2$ as natural, and also as an intuitive confirmation of what our logic has told us to be true, but when it comes to the flow of prime numbers, we have only approximations. Aesthetically unappealing, too, these approximations. Complex, ugly. What did Hardy say? 'Beauty is the first test; there is no permanent place for ugly mathematics.' We might discover and prove the exact law of prime number distribution, but, based on what we already know, it would fail Hardy's test."

"It's odd," Alexandra said, "how the simplest of problems, problems that, when stated, are understood by the average layman, are so intractable. And when they are solved, if they are solved, there are often hundreds of pages – proofs so large that it needs committees meeting for years to decide if they are correct or not. No wonder they are talking about using computers in proofs. We can't even prove that every even number is the sum of two primes. Is there a simpler problem to state than Goldbach's conjecture? Oh, I don't know … 2,300 years ago, Euclid needed a few lines to prove that the number of primes is infinite. Today, we can't prove in hundreds of pages that there is, or isn't, an infinite number of pairs of prime twins. Why? Doesn't seem to be that different. And yet, it must be."

The next day, Lily came from Tirgu-Jiu, brazenly declaring that she had to at last meet Charles, that Alexandra had hidden him away from her long enough. "I rang the school to say I had an attack of gout and I needed a couple of days to recover. A doctor friend will sign the authorization."

"You're a bit young for gout, you know," Alexandra laughed when she heard. "Women don't often get gout, either. Suspicious, if you asked me."

"But very handy. I could have an attack of gout anytime."

Charles took them out to dinner at a restaurant near the lake, a place where they could enjoy a cooling breeze. There, he was cross-examined ruthlessly by Lily, whose French was very good, much better than Alexandra's. Lily, who was wearing her best dress – the latest fashion in Tirgu-Jiu, she told Alexandra, chuckling – and had gone to the hairdresser that morning, declared, "in case Charles doesn't realize," that she was looking her ravishing best for the occasion. Lily had a lot to drink, and by the time dessert arrived she had begun to giggle at everything Charles said. "Lily, you're tipsy, and flirting with Charles," Alexandra laughed as they walked away from the restaurant. "True on both counts," Lily said and then began to cry. "I can't help it, I'm a flirt. But I love you both. I love you, Charles. And I especially love you, Alexandra. She's very special, Charles. Be nice to her. I'm crying because I see the two of you happy. Yes, you have a limitless potential for happiness. Alexandra, you are the luckiest and the silliest of women."

She went on crying for a while. Alexandra took her arm while Charles kept a few steps behind, not knowing what to do. "Don't worry about me," Lily sobbed, "it will pass. I don't know what's got into me – probably envy. It's the thought of Tirgu-Jiu and of my love prospects there. There is a mine engineer who's courting me and whose idea of a good time is … oh, you don't want to know. And Radu, the geography teacher at my school, short, sweet, a bit stupid, married with two children and afraid of his wife. We fuck in silence, with grim determination, as if to prove to ourselves that … Oh, dear, what am I saying? Don't repeat any of this to Charles. I'm babbling. It's all drivel. I'll be fine, I'm fine."

Mitzi died, quite suddenly, a few days after Charles left. She had lived for so long, against such medical odds, that Aroso had begun to fear he'd die before her and there'd be nobody to take care of her. Aroso had retired at the end of the academic year, and a wit in the faculty observed that Mitzi had waited to make sure Aroso had all the time for her before

she booked her passage beyond. Alexandra called Emil, who was still
in Timisoara, but Emil told her he wouldn't be home for another week.
She went to the funeral with her mother, who, although very frail herself,
insisted on coming. "I won't be long myself," Mrs. Jacobi said. "Better
scout the setup."

"Mother, please."

"We'll go to your father's place afterwards. I have a few things to
tell him."

"That you won't be long?"

"Oh, he knows that already."

Mitzi's wish, written in a strangely worded will more than twenty
years earlier, had been to be buried beside Aroso, "so that Asuero cares
for me in the afterlife as well." That meant burial in a Jewish cemetery.

That is how Mitzi became Jewish post-mortem, very quickly, the
day following her death, after Aroso cried his heart out and emptied
his wallet ("for the good of the congregation, it will help so many poor
families") in front of several old, sad-looking men with wrinkled noses
and watery red eyes. This was Aroso's own description of the synagogue
elders. He told Alexandra the story on the telephone as he was explaining
to her the funeral arrangements. "I was their carbon copy," he laughed,
"just taller. Scaled up in one axis. They couldn't refuse me."

They agreed, but her burial had to be conducted very early in
the morning, almost at daybreak. There was only a handful of people
at the cemetery. A second cousin of Mitzi's came. Most of her relatives,
incensed and disbelieving that it was Mitzi's wish, refused to come to a
Jewish cemetery, and Aroso had nobody. With so few people, Alexandra
was happy that her mother had insisted on coming along. Danczay, who
had retired a year before Aroso, was there. Two other former colleagues
from the faculty came. Jana, Mitzi's caretaker and factotum in the Aroso
household, was there, and so were Jana's brother and his wife. Alexandra
wondered whether they were the providers of the food that Aroso told
her would be laid on at his place after the funeral. Several of Aroso's
neighbours came, probably out of curiosity to see a Jewish cemetery.

It had rained through the night, and although the rain had
stopped, the sky was grey and low. Fog trailed lazily on the ground, and
near the rectangular hole, steamy black earth was piled up. It seemed to

Alexandra, surveying the small knot of people in the drifting fog, that they were taking part in a burial at sea, paying their respects on the deck of a ship, the rabbi just a chaplain in disguise.

It was a quick ceremony. Nobody had time to ask awkward questions about the recently converted. Alexandra was moved when Aroso, in an unexpectedly sure voice, said the "kaddish" with the rabbi. When that was done, they lined up to cover Mitzi's coffin with shovels of earth.

After the funeral, she took her mother to Mr. Jacobi's stone, only a couple of rows over from Mitzi. Though her mother still went there regularly, it had been years since Alexandra had come with her, maybe as many as ten. The grave was well kept, and when Alexandra said so, Mrs. Jacobi complained that it cost a fortune. Her mother stood there for about ten minutes, very thin – she had lost a lot of weight lately – and bent, and Alexandra, who stood a few steps back, had the impression that she was humming. They didn't speak afterwards except that Mrs. Jacobi asked to be taken home.

Jana, her brother, and her brother's wife were with Aroso when Alexandra arrived at his house on Octavian Street. A couple, neighbours of Aroso who had been at the cemetery earlier, were there too, quiet, old, withered. Aroso, who told Alexandra when he saw her that it had been a long time since he'd been in the house without Mitzi, was drinking plum brandy brought by Jana's brother. He was sitting on a low stool, his back against the wall, his long legs stretched out in front of him. Everybody was drinking with him, but it was obvious Aroso had had a head-start. Alexandra had a glass of white wine to which she added some water. There were slices of salami, feta cheese, tomatoes, black bread, and green onions, all quietly set on a side table by Jana. There were stuffed vine-leaves in a tomato sauce, and some roasted chicken for those with a heartier appetite, although nobody was touching the food.

"I'm going to sit for seven days," Aroso said to the gathering, smiling at Alexandra. It was as if he'd waited for her to arrive before he began his speech. "An odd shiva, an odd shiva, indeed. We might be amiss by a dietary rule or two, and the departed was not Jewish during her term on this earth, but our hearts are in it. I don't even know what we are supposed to do. I know we are allowed to drink. Are we allowed to eat? Alexandra? We must be. No wise rabbinical rule, tested thousands of years, would give the green light to drinking on an empty stomach."

She told him, yes, as far as she knew, food and drink and reminiscing about the departed were allowed and recommended.

Aroso talked about Mitzi. Their marriage, he said, had been an agony for both of them, but possibly more for Mitzi than for him, because he had been the one who had loved, and she had been the one who couldn't. She had viewed Parkinson's, she told him, shortly after she was diagnosed, as a punishment for what she had done to him. He laughed. What nonsense. The trouble with Mitzi was that she was a good, upright soul – a rare commodity in that part of the world. From 1940, Aroso told them, his eyes slowly becoming watery, he had not been allowed to teach anymore. No Jewish mathematics to corrupt young, inchoate Romanian brains. He had some money saved, and it lasted him for a while. He became a recluse, or more reclusive than he already was. His few friends, former colleagues, acquaintances, all avoided him. The hatred of Jews had received official commendation, and it was freely and zestfully displayed. Romanians had a natural streak of *schadenfreude*, Aroso laughed. Those who bothered to talk to him, did so only to let him know that the Jews were getting what they deserved, that they had only themselves to blame. Slowly, horror stories began to trickle through to him as well. He became aware of – maybe not fully aware, but who could have imagined such savagery? – what was happening to Jews in other parts of Romania and in Europe. There were several calls for the Jews of Bucharest to gather at certain locations and times, with light luggage. Miraculously, nothing happened, the orders were always countermanded at the last moment. Every time the orders to gather Jews were rescinded, there were wild rumours that the Jews had paid large sums of money to Antonescu's government. For almost four years, he had kept a brown suitcase packed with warm clothes near the door. The worst part, he said, was the lack of hope. There was none. Until 1942, it was hard to entertain even a glimmer of hope. Those who had not lived through those years could not understand how bleak it was. No hope whatsoever. Aroso thought of ending it all by hanging himself. He said he had an uncle who hanged himself, an uncle he had loved very much. He was ready to emulate his uncle. It was Mitzi who saved him.

From what Alexandra understood – Aroso had drunk quite a lot of plum brandy by the time he got to this part of the story, and he was almost whispering, as if he was talking to himself – Mitzi came back to stay with him in early 1941. And she never left again. She stayed with him through the rest of the war, never letting him out of her sight. She stopped seeing friends who refused to have anything to do with the Jew Aroso. She didn't do it because she loved him – Aroso was quietly sobbing now – oh, he was quite aware of that. He was quite aware that she had stopped loving him many years ago. He did not know why she did what she did. No, he did know, but couldn't exactly put it in words without sounding trite. They lived on her money. She rarely went out. If her friends wanted to see her, she insisted that they come to their house. To Aroso's house. To make him, Aroso, Aroso the Jew, feel less isolated, less useless, less nothing.

Jana gave Aroso a huge handkerchief, and he wiped his eyes and blew his nose loudly. He put the handkerchief in his pocket and then took it out again and repeated the operation.

That was the eulogy, Alexandra thought, Mitzi's eulogy.

But he began again, still whispering, then, clearing his throat, suddenly more audible. The first symptoms of Parkinson's had appeared as early as 1945. It was rare at such a young age and in a woman. He thought it had started that early, but diagnosis was very difficult. In Mitzi's case, it progressed quite slowly, but ten years later, the need for medication had become quite acute. There was no medication in Romania. Luckily, her brother began sending medication from Canada. This brother had sent medication until the very end, for fifteen or sixteen years. He had written to him, Aroso said, to let him know of Mitzi's death and to stop sending the medication. He made sure to let his brother-in-law know that, according to her last wishes, she had been put to rest in a Jewish cemetery. He said he wished he could see his face when he read that. In fact, the medication may not have helped at all. It had reduced her discomfort, but only for a while. In the long run, it made everything a long drawn-out misery. There was a time when Mitzi had refused to take the medication. Would a quick death, even with a lot of discomfort, have been a more satisfactory end, more humane, less painful to both Mitzi and those taking care of her? Aroso was crying again, quietly, as if he had no strength for anything louder. He cried and sipped plum brandy. He didn't know whether he was crying, he said, for Mitzi, for his hardships with Mitzi, for fear of his own turn soon, or for some other reason.

That was grim reminiscing. There was silence in the room. Jana and her sister stood up to clear a few things and bring new plates that still nobody touched. They had to manoeuvre around Aroso's legs. He was silent now, motionless, and for a moment or two Alexandra feared that he had fainted. Then a muffled snoring sound reached her. Jana went to him and shook him gently. He got up unsteadily and said that he needed a nap.

"I won't be long. Give me ten minutes. There's much to talk about and drink, yet."

She stayed a bit longer, overwhelmed and unable to move, and then went home.

In the evening, Aroso rang and asked her to come to his house. He had just woken up. His voice had a pleading, tremulous sound, like a child awakened in the darkness and begging for his parents to come to his room. She called her mother and asked her to come and babysit Ada.

Only Jana was at Aroso's house, and she was keeping herself busy in the kitchen. Aroso was in the same clothes he'd been wearing earlier, now crumpled, which meant that he had slept in them. Only the tie had disappeared. Aroso frowned and tapped his finger against his forehead. He mumbled he had got up with a headache and had something to eat. He was drinking plum brandy again, or had been; a half-empty glass was beside him. He said he wasn't used to plum brandy, but he could see how he could grow fond of it. At that, he attempted a half-hearted smile.

They sat in his little office, the one with the portraits of Mitzi, he at his desk and Alexandra on a small uncomfortable chair. Aroso's eyes were bloodshot, his white hair tousled, and his head was leaning on one side, as if his neck no longer had the strength to support its weight. He said that somebody had just brought over a bottle of wine – that's what woke him up, the doorbell. With some difficulty, he stood up and announced that he was going to open the bottle. He came back after a short while with a glass for Alexandra.

He didn't understand why he was so overcome by Mitzi's death,

he told her. It was not as if he had not expected it. He had been preparing
for her death for years. He had had plenty of time to siphon off, to drain,
all the sorrow. Plenty of opportunity, he said, trying to smile. Physically,
he had felt exhausted, and there had been many times he wished she was
gone. He should feel relief, not sorrow, he said and pointed an accusing
finger at Alexandra, as if she was the one injecting grief in his veins.

 Mitzi had not been a good wife, he said suddenly – almost
defiantly – after a short pause. A good companion, yes, when she was
around, but not a good wife. She had been a terrible wife, in fact. She
had left him for other men. Did Alexandra know that? She shrugged,
to convey polite uncertainty. After this unexpected confession, he had
a good slug of plum brandy and motioned to her to drink up her wine.
Yes, she had, he went on. Several times. He had been young and naïve,
and he had resented Mitzi's behaviour. He had been jealous, yes, quite
jealous, although the passage of time had dulled the painful memories
of those days. All he remembered was anxiety and a depressing feeling
of inadequacy. He then said something that startled her. Because of her,
because of Mitzi, he had lost the best, the most creative, years of his life,
his mathematical life. He had been in his early thirties, twenty-nine or
thirty, when she left him for the first time. He had just done some good
work, some excellent work, even extraordinary … There had been one
piece of work in particular … And it was then, at the very moment that
he had been so exhilarated with his discoveries, that Mitzi chose to leave
him, to elope. He had not tried to find out where and to whom Mitzi
had gone. In time, quite quickly in fact, people had told him. They had
been quite eager to let him know. He had brooded alone. He had been
very unhappy. Fate, the gods of mathematics, had conspired to provide
him with the solitude demanded by good work. And instead of taking
advantage of her having walked out on him, instead of carrying on with
his research, he, the fool, had found he couldn't apply himself. He could
not stop thinking of Mitzi. He tried, once he was free, unencumbered,
but it wasn't much good. His mind would not cooperate – it had been
restless, always coming back to Mitzi. Exactly when he had needed to
concentrate the most, exactly when he had needed to bring his wonderful
work to fruition, to acceptance.

 He talked more about Mitzi, about his lost years, his best

years, his wasted, excellent, work. He began to cry again. It was a long evening. Jana came in several times. Finally, shortly after eleven o'clock, she announced that the professor was very tired and had to go to bed. She was looking at Alexandra as she said it, but she was addressing Aroso. Alexandra was grateful to her. Aroso didn't move from his chair. As Alexandra was leaving, he asked her to come to his house as often as she could during the next few days. It would be, he said, an immense succour to him. He realized that it was a selfish imposition. His parting words were similar to the first ones he'd said to her when she arrived. He confessed that Mitzi's death, as much as he was prepared for it, and as much as it had freed him, had depressed him more than he had expected and in a strange kind of way. "We don't know ourselves even after a lifetime of self-study," he said, smiling sadly. As she left, she repeated to herself that he had nobody else except her. Not a soul. Frightening.

She went whenever she could. He spent the next six days in his backyard, sitting under the shade of the vine. He sat there taking small sips of plum brandy. Jana sat with him, but whenever Alexandra showed up she would disappear. In the afternoon of the last day of shiva, it rained, and she found him in an old raincoat with an umbrella fixed to the trellis above his head by wires. He had not shaved and looked quite awful. But he smiled happily and waved to her and shouted to Jana, who was somewhere in the house, to bring another umbrella for his esteemed colleague. To her surprise, he wanted to talk math. His mind was as sharp as ever.

Mrs. Jacobi had her first heart attack two weeks later. They took her to the hospital where Emil worked, and she was well looked after. Dr. Gimbau, a heart specialist at the hospital, talked to Alexandra in his small office the day after her mother was admitted. She had known Dr. Gimbau through Emil – an older, kind man with a large wrinkled nose and very long fingers which always seemed to pick invisible lint from his white coat.

"We'll have to see what happens, my dear. It was not a minor heart attack, yet she is recovering well. There was damage done, but the exact nature and extent of it can't be determined until she's a bit better and able undergo some intrusive checks. If I had to guess, and, at my age, my guesses are quite good, I'd say she needs a bypass. Not an easy operation for someone of her years, especially with the inadequate equipment we have here. I suggest you talk to Emil about the pros and cons. You should talk to your mother as well. Ultimately, the decision should be hers, but you and she should know that it will be dangerous."

When she tried to talk to Mrs. Jacobi about it, three days later, she was much too weak, and Alexandra decided to postpone the discussion for later. She could barely hear what her mother was whispering to her.

"I miss him."

"Who?"

"Leonard."

"Of course, mother."

"Go to him."

"What?"

"Go to him ...'

"You know that's not possible."

She thought she heard her saying, "Oh, why don't you lie to me," but she wasn't sure. Why, indeed, wasn't she lying to her?

Mrs. Jacobi died several days later. Alexandra rang Leonard's number, after she asked for Emil's permission. She tried several days in a row, but there was never an answer and she gave up, wondering whether she had the wrong number. In a letter Alexandra prepared for Leonard, to be collected by Charles on his return to Bucharest, she wrote that their mother had died of "heartache disguised as a heart attack." She put in few other details, saying just that it was sudden and, in a way, for the best, "as Mother had very little strength left in her." She felt very low when she wrote the letter.

Leonard got married in November. Alexandra found out about it in early January, when Charles arrived for a few days and brought two letters from Leonard – a very long letter written two weeks after the wedding, when he was yet unaware of Mrs. Jacobi's death, and a shorter one, written in late December, in which he wrote mainly about their mother.

Monica, his wife – he wrote in the first letter – was lovely, tall, with long legs and a beautiful figure. He was deeply in love with her – had been deeply in love with her for a long time. She was older than he was by a couple of years, had been married before, and, unlike him, knew what she wanted. She was not, however, very much in love with him, but he hoped that, in time, this would not be too much of a drawback. Although she admitted that she had "a good time with him" (heartbreakingly dismissive, Leonard commented), she hadn't been ready to marry again. Leonard owed his good luck to an accident – Monica got pregnant and wouldn't consider an abortion.

Monica was rich, or her parents were. She was the junior partner in a small law firm – a *boutique* firm, that's how they were quaintly called. The senior partner, a Mr. Carragher, had done some work for Monica's father. Mr. Carragher was told soon after Monica divorced her first husband, a playboy endodontist, that much more work would come his way if he took Monica in, and he did. Leonard had met him – a sardonic, withered old man, who kept talking of retirement, a bit of a crook – and quite liked him.

Erwin Goren, Monica's father, owned a trucking company in Kingston, a city in Ontario east of Toronto. Leonard had done some schedule optimization – after all, he'd done a lot of similar work at the Institute of Calculations in Bucharest – for Mr. Goren's fleet, and that's how he had met Monica.

Monica and I got married on a windy November day. "It's not the baby," Monica had joked when she finally agreed to marry me. "I'm marrying you simply because my mother dislikes you." Edna, that's Monica's mother, was beside herself. She barely addressed any words to me. My religious indifference, indeed my amazement that anybody could be religious, is seen by Edna as a moral fault, much like dishonesty or stealing. Edna is convinced that my Communist indoctrination has removed a dimension – the religious one – from the space in which we all develop and evolve, and as a result I am inadequate, a cripple, in some way. The fact that I was bringing no chips to the marital table disturbed her, too, but this was something for Erwin (that's Monica's father) to look into – Erwin and his lawyers. There were two things that stopped Edna from coming out straight against my marrying Monica. The first was that Monica insisted on keeping the child. The second was that

Edna had been a great supporter of Monica's first husband and was reluctant to further interfere. She was convinced that Monica was getting into another disastrous marriage, this time foreseeable.

Erwin was harder to read. I think he took the whole thing as a business disappointment. Monica had disappointed him much like a long-trusted business partner whom you couldn't help but like. Unlike his wife, Erwin does not think of me as a bad sort, only as an odd, unfocused, purposeless, unsuitable partner for his daughter. But he loves his daughter too much and is too shrewd to voice his objections. His lawyer presented me with a pre-nuptial agreement. A pre-nup. I signed, barely looking at it. I'm becoming fond of telling anybody who cares to listen that I signed a pre-nup. I love the word. Pre-nup. I love both its sound and the certain sophistication that goes with it. Not everybody has a pre-nun. I was worth a pre-nup. No, Monica was worth a pre-nup.

The wedding was a muted affair, from what I was told. To me, it was quite elaborate. While plans were being made, the Gorens announced that they would invite just close family. Monica invited only a few friends and Mr. Carragher. Mr. Carragher is an old curmudgeon who can be quite entertaining when it's in his interest.

A fair crowd gathered in the Gorens' mansion, and a rabbi performed a long and tiresome service. I felt out of place at my own wedding. I could truly say that there were few faces I knew. Most people were complete strangers and, I felt, hostile towards me. Monica confirmed my suspicion that most of the relatives invited were from her mother's side.

My party was an improvised team, put together for this one event only. My supervisor, Murray Walker, and his wife, and two colleagues from graduate school – Fred, or Freddy, the Egyptologist (guess what he's studying), who had a room in my suite at the student residence, and Wolfgang Kleist, a German who's studying with Murray Walker for his Ph.D. I invited Kleist with some trepidation, but I was desperate. I also invited the department secretary, Elma, who brought along her husband and their two children and thus doubled the number of my party. I didn't know Elma very well – a friendly hello in the corridors, a message for Professor X, "Have you finished your thesis?" – so she was a bit startled by my invitation, but she sportingly accepted.

I wrote to Charles Natraq in Paris, inviting him to the wedding as well, and asking him to tell you about it at the first opportunity. Charles regretted that he could not come, but he sent us a wedding present, a small crayon and watercolour sketch. In time, he wrote in his card, it might turn out to be quite valuable, if a friend of his was to be believed. Like good wine that needs maturing. If not, he hoped that we would enjoy it anyway. He had loved it the moment he had first seen it. Let me describe it – two naked women are black-pencilled in supine positions, with angular yet vigorous thighs and breasts. Their faces have worldly smiles. The colours are very simple – yellow, pink, and green.

At the wedding, I met (or re-met, but they all blur into a few archetypal family members) Monica's cousins and nephews and nieces and aunts and more cousins and uncles. I finally met Rhomo, Monica's older brother, an amiable and tired-looking man, and his wife Grace. Rhomo (what kind of name is this?), eight years older than Monica, and a successful heart surgeon in Ottawa, resembles his sister. The two seemed very fond of each other. Grace was elegant, thin, good-looking and very English. That explained somewhat the rare appearances of Rhomo and his wife at the Gorens' house. Grace's father, who happened to be visiting his daughter for a few days, was at the wedding, too, keeping close to the bar and looking incredulously around him. I thought he came straight out of a Galsworthy novel, just for our wedding. In one of his rare forays away from the bar, he offered his best wishes to me and then added, "'Best wishes' are the only honest words. In my view, and I was married three times, marriage is a dog. Utter nonsense. But don't lose heart. Try your best. Hope for the best. Your wife is lovely. Where did you say you hail from, Mr. Jacobi?" "Romania, the cradle of democracy." He looked suspiciously at me and headed back to the bar.

I had a lot to drink, too, Alsa. Towards the end I was introducing Freddy the Egyptologist as my cousin from Rochester, New York. Monica looked lovely, in a long, dark-green dress made for the occasion. It displayed a generous portion of her breasts, which, at four months pregnant, had a mouth-watering embonpoint. She looked happy. I hoped she was happy. I was.

Alsa, tell Mother a sugar-coated version of my marriage. I got married a few months earlier, my wife adores me, my in-laws love me. She doesn't need to worry about me more than she already does.

The child, I'm sure you, and especially Mother, would want to know, *is due in April. Monica is ecstatic about her pregnancy. She's going to be a doting, wonderful mother. As for the rest, we'll see …*

Enough with boring family matters. I have other news.

In September, after several interviews, I got a job. I thought I should have a job before getting married. Yes, I'm a respectable man, a family man, a man that goes to work in the morning and gets paid for it. I'm employed in a bank. It has a grand name, the Canadian Imperial Bank of Commerce. Murray Walker was so glad to be rid of me that he swore to open an account there. I was assigned to a team doing economics modelling. We develop large and tiresome mathematical models, run what-if scenarios in powerful mainframes, and help economists make foolish predictions.

And yes, hurray, I defended my thesis successfully at the end of October. The questions and comments were all on the mathematics. I had the distinct feeling that nobody read my attempt at a biography of Olinde Rodrigues and the controversial claims I made there about his contribution to mathematics. If Olinde Rodrigues had been undeservedly ignored, it was not a pressing issue to those who judged my thesis. …

There were a couple more pages, but Alexandra put the letter back in her briefcase to finish it the following day in her office. Such news! So many things had happened to Leonard. Married, with a child soon, his degree completed and in a new job. And all so fast. That's what happened when the channels of communication were opened only briefly. And he'd kept his pursuit of his new wife to himself. He'd probably thought it wouldn't amount to anything, if she read properly between the lines. A Jewish girl, too. Their mother's prophecy had turned out to be right. Mrs Jacobi was distressed when Alexandra had married Emil – he wasn't a Jew, and there would be trouble. She had warned her about George, too, but marriage to George was never discussed, and, in addition, Mrs. Jacobi had found George a real mensch, a goy mensch, but a mensch. She had no such illusions about Emil. "You'll see," she told Alexandra just before she got married, "Leonard is going to marry a Jewish woman. Much smarter than his sister. Not as brainy, but much smarter."

Chapter 7
March - April 1976

Whenever she thought of her marital status, Alexandra was at a loss. So, when Lily asked her to describe it, Alexandra quickly acknowledged that she wasn't sure. "Not that I haven't given it a lot of thought," she hastened to add.

"Let's look at this together, then," Lily said. "In fact, let me tell you how I see it."

Lily, who was spending a few days with Alexandra, had just got up, and they were sipping tea at the dining room table, half of which served as Alexandra's desk when she worked at home. There was eagerness in Lily's voice and a hint of merriment. She was in her nightgown, a large tousled woman still smelling of morning sweat.

"Officially married, with a nine-year-old daughter — nine or ten — and having an affair with a French professor…"

"Canadian."

"Having an affair with a whatever-nationality professor. Mind you, a rarely consummated affair because of the correspondent living in a different country, and the annoying fact that you are married and still living with your husband. The said husband who, it seems, has a mistress in Timisoara — are you sure about this?"

"Quite sure. And quite relieved, to tell you the truth …"

"And who also has minor affairs with nurses at work – no, don't shake your head, we all know what hospitals are like, especially for a handsome doctor who tells everybody that he's not getting along with his deceitful wife. I'd go for him, too, if you were not my friend. How do you do it? How do both of you do it? What do the two of you talk about? I grant you, last night Emil was quite charming, but, then, I was around, and he enjoys my silly jokes and stories, and it was I who did most of the talking the whole evening. But what happens when the two of you are alone? What did you two talk about this morning, for example?"

"Nothing much."

"Details."

"I made tea, and he had a slice of bread and jam. He said he might be able to get some coffee – a patient of his had promised him. He told me about this patient, a high-level technocrat in the Ministry of Heavy Industry who is often in the West. I told him that I was working at home today, that I had no lectures or meetings, and that later, whenever you got up, we'd go out for a walk. And that, if he was going to work late, maybe the three of us, you, Ada, and I, would go to see a movie. I also told him that Ada's teacher had called again to complain about her – how disruptive and uncontrollable she's being, and that it can't continue like this and what are we going to do about it. It was civilized up to this point, and then … then he said that Ada is only taking after her uncontrollable mother, and as long as this continues in our household … Well, nothing much was said after that, and then he left."

"Does this happen every morning?"

"No, Ada's teacher has been calling about once or twice a month."

"You know what I mean."

"Yes, I know what you mean. It happens often enough. But there are days when it doesn't happen, and we don't insult each other, and we talk about work, and we talk and laugh with Ada. We also keep a good façade when we are with friends. Emil has a lot of friends – he's good at making and keeping friends – and we just go on."

"Do you still sleep with him?"

"Lily!"

"Do you still sleep with him?"

"Now and then. Not often."

"What's 'not often'?"

"Lily, please."

"Come on, Alexandra, out with it. Why be vague?"

"It depends."

"Well?"

"Maybe once a month."

"What does it depend on?"

"I don't know, his mood, my mood."

"But more often his mood?"

"Yes."

"Do you ever start things?"

"Never. Sometimes I say no. Often I say no. Maybe not so often … Oh, Lily, let's stop this."

"How do you do it?"

"Lily, don't be a child. There isn't much to it, and you know it."

"You mean, he says nasty things to you, sometimes he's very close to hitting you, insults you and your race – you've told me so – and the next thing that happens is that you're between the sheets together?"

"It never happens if we have a fight. Lily, it's easier and simpler like this."

"Ah, easier and simpler."

"Yes."

"Why don't you stop sleeping with him? Why don't you leave him?"

"Because I'm a coward. Because I'm afraid of the consequences. Because I don't want to have another reason for fights. Because there are only two things that matter to me at this time – Ada, and having the peace of mind to continue with my work. If we divorce, I'd lose both. I'd clearly lose Ada, and with that any peace of mind."

"What does Charles say about this?"

"About what?"

"Well, first, about you still sleeping with Emil. About you refusing to divorce."

"He's not happy. But he understands."

"He understands what, exactly?"

"My fear of losing Ada."

"Has Charles asked you to leave Emil? To divorce Emil and
marry him? He could, you know, in time, get you out of here."

"Yes, he's asked me to leave Emil. He asked me to marry him. He
told me about the wonderful career I could have in the West. He told me
that we could get Ada, eventually."

"And?"

"You see, I didn't believe we could get Ada. That's the crux of the
matter. Lily, I'm exhausted. Let's stop this."

On her way to Aroso's house, Alexandra thought about Lily's visit and
their discussion. She also thought about Charles. He had asked her
again last fall to divorce Emil and marry him. Or elope, if she hadn't
the strength for the battle of a divorce. "Elope? What do you mean?"
He told her that the pressure exerted by mathematicians in the West
to let her travel was beginning to bear fruit. He reminded her about
the forthcoming conference in Stockholm, where they had two papers.
There was an outcry among mathematicians that one of the authors,
one who had made such a substantial contribution, was not allowed to
participate and influence the discussions. Charles had heard that the
Romanian authorities might have relented, and that if she applied she'd
be allowed to go. And once out … She had shaken her head. Charles had
been dismayed by her answer and remained quiet for a while. At the very
least, would she consider going? To the conference, to Stockholm, then
back to Bucharest? That way, they could have a few days to themselves,
like the wonderful week when Emil was away and Ada was with her
grandparents. She had said no again, and she said it with such vehemence
that Charles was taken aback. She tried to explain to him that she had
already put a lot of thought into it – not necessarily Stockholm, but an
opportunity like it – and had decided she couldn't go, even if allowed,
because, once out, the temptation not to come back would be irresistible.
Staying put, she wouldn't know what she was missing, she could only
surmise – and that, she could resist. Her explanation didn't convince
him, and he looked at her in despair. "What do you expect me to do,
Alexandra? It's been already, what, five years? How long do you expect

me to wait?"

It had been a very warm April, and they were sitting outside, under the familiar trellis. Jana had left minutes earlier, shouting she won't be late. She had stayed with Aroso after Mitzi's death, although she had always talked about going to live with her brother and sister-in-law once she was no longer needed by Mitzi. "I've changed my mind," she told Alexandra not long after Mitzi's death. "What would be the point? They don't have much space there, at my brother's house, and there is plenty of space here. Besides, who'd take care of the professor? I know that the professor can't pay like before, with the retirement pension only, but I don't need much. There isn't a lot to do now, anyway. I'm kind of retired too."

'There is a mathematics congress in Rome next year," Alexandra said to Aroso, "one of those huge gatherings where everybody shows up. Charles and other mathematicians prodded by him – although he tells me that not much convincing was needed – have put political pressure to lift the ban on my international travel. He is well connected, Charles, and the French had made some discreet but firm demands, it seems. It's very possible I'll be allowed to go. On top of this, the institute where Charles teaches has invited me to spend two weeks there after Rome – it's somewhere near Paris."

Aroso was nodding at her, a sort of encouragement, almost as if he knew what she wanted to say and how difficult it was to say it.

"I might not come back," Alexandra added.

"Might?"

"It's a good chance – if they let me out, that is – that I won't go to France at all, but directly to Canada from Rome. Charles thinks it's better that way, so the French government won't be too embarrassed. That's why Charles didn't want to involve the Canadian government at all."

"Might?" he repeated.

"I don't know what to do. There was an opportunity for something similar in Stockholm this year. I was told that if I applied they'd let me go. I didn't apply. I didn't want to be tempted. It upset Charles terribly."

He kept nodding without saying anything.

"What should I do?" she asked.

"You want my advice? Not a good idea. It's up to you, my dear – never mind anybody's opinion."

"Surely you have an opinion."

"I couldn't advise you."

"I can't think of anybody more suited."

"Me? You can't think of anybody more suited than me?"

Was he playing stupid or did he really not see it? "You chose to be buried here," she said, "at an obscure university in a dusty and forgotten city, at a time when you had quite a future ahead of you. Yet because you loved your wife, because you were devoted to her, you put her ahead of your career and chose Bucharest. I'm not even sure why I'm asking for your opinion, since the answer is right there, in your deeds."

"That's what you think happened?"

"It didn't?"

There was no answer. Aroso seemed lost in thought. When Alexandra began to say something after a minute or two of silence, he raised his long right arm as if to stop her. He stood up and began pacing. After a while he sat down again.

"It wasn't that simple, Alexandra, it wasn't that clear cut. I couldn't tell you about it in a few minutes. It would take me hours, days. I don't know … maybe …"

"I'm a good listener."

"Alexandra, if you really want to know what I think, here it is: Get out of this country, run at the first opportunity, without looking back. Go. Like a dog let loose, like a bullet out of a rifle. Don't think, because there is nothing to consider. Don't look so horrified. You wanted my opinion; I've given it to you. Ah, you want reasons. Why? Look at me – old, white haired, wrinkled, don't you think I've gathered enough wisdom? You just said that I went through a similar dilemma, so why question my advice?"

He threw up his thin arms, dismayed by her demands, her incomprehension. "Very well, reasons. You don't love your husband. You're having an affair – or I think you are. The only reason you're still with your husband is your daughter. From what you're telling me, your daughter is already estranged from you. Well, get out. Once out, try to persuade your husband and your daughter to join you, if you must. It will take a while, a few years, but eventually it can happen, especially if money is involved. The lure of the West will convince your husband to join you. And with him, your daughter. Once he joins you out there, you could decide on a divorce or you could have another go at life with him. Why not? Don't shake your head. At least you'd have a chance for a civilized separation. A chance at getting your daughter back. While staying here ..."

He stopped for a moment, lost in thought. "But that's not the main reason you should go. You should go because your mathematics would be much better over there. Other considerations are of second order."

"You preach what you didn't do."

"My dear, you don't know what I did or didn't do."

"And yet ..."

"I don't understand you. It's almost as if you want me to tell you to stay."

She didn't reply.

The telephone began to ring. It startled Alexandra. She thought it was a signal to her, some subtle message that she failed to interpret. It rang for a long time, but Aroso didn't move, and then it stopped. In the silence that followed, Alexandra heard Aroso wheezing, as if struggling for breath. She asked him if there was anything wrong. Nothing but old age, he laughed – old lungs, old heart. Bit of bronchitis, too, it seemed.

"All right, I'll tell you what, my dear – and this might be the best for both of us. I'm going to tell you what happened to me, the whole story of how I ended up here. It's not going to be easy, and it might take several visits. I'm curious myself to see how I explain certain things. Maybe I should put it in writing. A thoughtful sequence of facts and arguments. There's merit in that method, but there's also the danger that I'll end up thinking what a ridiculous being I am. Once committed to paper, the stupidity of it would be too obvious, too striking – it would stare at me from the page and not go away. No, too dangerous. I'd rather tell the story. That way, I'll have your company more often, and we'll laugh together at my folly. And in the end, after you have listened to it all, you'll make your decision. It's a deal? It will be a verbal, fleeting *apologia pro sua vita*. Or is it *mea vita*? We need to hurry, though – senility beckons."

Chapter 8
January 1976

They sat quietly for a long time under the trellis. Alexandra could see a few bunches of grapes, the fruit small and of a strident green. The sun was down, somewhere to the left of the house. A streetcar on Splaiul Unirii came to a screechy halt. They took sips from the wine she had brought with her and which Aroso had uncorked earlier and poured into two glasses. She found the wine slightly sweet, pleasant, and, in spite of the long trip, still cool. Aroso put his glass down on the table and smiled at her. He said that together they would turn the soil in the untended garden of his past. He felt, he added, like a gardener who had neglected his patch for many years and was now asked to re-sow the plants that used to grow there.

"I was raised, as you probably know, in Istanbul. The Ottoman Empire was still around – Abdul Hamid was the Sultan. There were only two more sultans after him, both with brief reigns. Although many reforms were introduced during Abdul Hamid's reign, including a new constitution, the empire was disintegrating. Istanbul had a million inhabitants, of which about three percent were Jews. My father was one of them, an ignorant man wrapped in Talmudic lore. It was an effective disguise – coupled with fatherly authority – and I did not see through it for a long time. Behind the biblical genuflections hid a stubborn man with a petty mind. His universe was small. His commerce – he was a middleman in the grain business – and his synagogue were all that he needed and all that he recognized. He had his family, of course, my mother, my sister, and me, but I think he went about acquiring a wife and having children in a mechanical sort of way, like brushing his teeth. God told him to acquire a wife and have children – boys, preferably – and he did it to please God. If anybody had told him that making his wife happy, or at least smile from time to time, might please God also, he would have dismissed the thought with an impatient shrug. He was a short, thick man who wore the traditional Ottoman caftan until he died. A good-looking man, with a face that seemed both kind and thoughtful, but he was neither. He was suspicious of the new ways. He was suspicious of anything that had not sprung out of a rabbi's mind. He disliked people who did not share his views or who were not like him. In Istanbul, especially in Istanbul, that meant that he disliked everybody. He disliked the Greeks, because the Greeks hated the Jews; he hated the Armenians, because the Armenians pushed the Jews out of many businesses; he despised the Turks, because, according to him, the Turks had 'lost their fire,' whatever that meant. His dislikes fuelled his discourse, always in Ladino, at the dinner table. He did not want anything else spoken in his house.

"He had plans ready-made for me. At the end of my schooling I was to work with him and for him. My sister and I never felt he had any warmth towards us, a feeling which, as children, was only vaguely understood. Mother was more affectionate, but her natural warmth was always undermined by Father's admonishments that she was spoiling us. Mother was a tall woman, taller than Father by half a foot. I inherited from her my height and my stooping posture. My face looks very much like hers. But what gave me, as a man, a passable face, had made her hard to look at. She was, or considered herself to be, an old maid when she consented to marry Father, and had feared she would never marry. She was a Dacosta, but that would not mean anything to you. The Dacostas had been, for many years, a leading family in the Jewish community in Istanbul. One of the richest also, and, during my childhood at least, one of the least traditional. They had not approved of Father and suspected him of dowry hunting. With time, they liked him less and less. The feeling was reciprocated. By the time I became aware of all these undercurrents,

Father had stopped going to their house. It was an arrangement that suited everybody. When Mother, my sister, and I visited the Dacostas, we could enjoy their big, comfortable home, the unrestrained laughter of my cousins, the kindness of my mother's family without being inhibited by his presence."

He rose, went into the house, and returned quickly with a photograph.

"The Dacostas. 1909. Well, some of them. I have no pictures of my parents. My father would not let our picture be taken."

What struck her was how recent the photo seemed. Yet it was almost seventy years old. It had been taken outside on a cold day, because, although there were leaves on the surrounding trees, everybody in the picture was wearing wool overcoats. They were all dressed in fashionable, European clothes. The women wore headscarves, and Alexandra could see that under their coats they had ankle-length dresses. The men looked tall and sported moustaches. There were fifteen or twenty Dacostas, half of them children.

"Several times during the summer, the Dacostas would rent a large *kayik*, a boat with a rowing crew, and everybody would embark on a nautical expedition that lasted the whole day. Mother, my sister, and I would sometimes join them. The busy Golden Horn was avoided, and the *kayik* would proceed quickly north of the Dolmabahce palace towards the less crowded waters of the Bosphorus. It was a picnic on the water. The steep banks of the Bosphorus with the beautiful *yalis*, the waterside villas of the very rich, would slide gently by. In the early afternoon, the heat at its peak, the younger children would fall asleep and even the adults would lower their voices. I never slept. Uncle Elias, one of my mother's brothers, had a beautiful, slightly husky voice, and would sometimes sing *romanceros* in a soft and dreamy way. I liked sitting beside him, listening to the old Castilian words of lament and despair. The only accompanying noises were the swish of the water displaced by the oars, the creaking of the wood, the occasional cry of a seabird. It was a quiet and peaceful universe that slowly glided by us. The hills on both sides, green, with red patches of roofs, now and then a *yali*, the blue sky punctured by minarets like arrows. Food was, of course, very important, and large quantities were brought aboard under the watchful eyes of

Uncle Elias, who was in charge of these expeditions. Uncle Elias was full of jokes and his pockets full of candies, and the children adored him. But I knew even then that he was not respected by the adult family members. Poor Uncle Elias. I remember wishing that my father were like him. Elias made sure that the passengers were supplied with *pilaf*, roasted lamb, chicken with walnuts and paprika, fish stuffed with currants, onion, and pine nuts, several dishes of aubergines. We had *halva*, *lukum*, and other sweets, and fruit juice. But my favourite was a treat not brought with us. It came from one of the many fishing boats crowding the small harbours along the Bosphorus, which, equipped with stoves, would sell fish caught on the spot and fried, with slices of black bread and raw onions. Uncle Elias and I were the only ones who shared a taste for such vulgar fare, and I had to make sure I had left enough room for it. Uncle Elias was picky about his fish, and would drive the *kayik*'s owner crazy by insisting he manoeuvre alongside his favourite fishing boat, the one at which he was always greeted with enthusiastic cheers by Fazil Numat. With his hooked nose and a dark, wrinkled face, and a loose-fitting blue blouse and equally loose strawberry-red trousers, Fazil Numat, the owner of the fishing boat, looked like a pirate in a touring operetta company. Fazil knew exactly what my uncle wanted, and he would tell his son Ismet to throw a fish on the stove the moment he noticed our *kayik* approaching. It was Ismet, my age or slightly older, naked to the waist and sun-baked, who would clean the fish with a few sure strokes, and then turn it and swirl it on the frying pan according to some definite science while uncle Elias and Fazil Numat caught up with each other with loud palaver."

Aroso was quiet for a while. "Elias Dacosta hanged himself while I was in Gottingen. Nobody would talk about it. 'Money trouble' was the only explanation Mother gave when she mentioned uncle Elias's demise in one of her letters. A shame to the family."

"Was he married?"

"When he died? No. He had been married once, but the marriage lasted less than a year and there were no children. There were all kind of rumours about him, but you know how children are – I didn't understand half of what I heard, and I heard very little."

"We lived in Pera," Aroso went on, "across the Golden Horn from the old city, in a modern apartment that came as Mother's dowry.

My father grew up in Haskoy, a Jewish district on the same shore not far from Pera. He would have liked to move back to Haskoy, back to what he was used to and approved of. Mother, supported by the Dacostas, opposed him quietly and stubbornly. As usual in these disputes, Father had to give in to the Dacostas' will. The Dacostas helped my father, for Mother's sake, in his commerce. In the battle between religious or moral principles and economic consequences, the latter had the upper hand, but Father had his revenge by making Mother's life miserable. Mother lived in terror of my father and would go against his will only on the rare occasions when she thought it was in our – the children's – interest, and only with the full support of the Dacosta clan. She would never dare say a word at the dinner table when my father spoke disparagingly about the Dacostas' modern ways or about her inability to bring us up properly. None of this affected me much. I was a self-sufficient, dreamy child, with a strong imagination in which I spent much of my time. I felt confined, but I did not rebel. Or not openly. The idea that we are shackled by our births, by our parents, to a predictable and monotonous future was something that I understood and accepted early. I had a non-rebellious but wondering mind. I wondered how different my life would have been if I'd been born to different parents. It was interesting and endless. The answer was easy, for example, if I wondered what life would be like if Uncle Elias were my father. That was obvious – I would have been like one of my cousins, speaking French and wearing a sailor suit. With Uncle Elias, it would always have been cheerful around the dinner table. It was more complicated when I imagined I was Ismet's brother. Under that variation, I saw myself spending many hours cleaning fish with Ismet's sharp knife, expertly disembowelling each one and tossing it nonchalantly on the stove under the admiring eyes of customers. Even Ismet would look impressed. With the little boat heaving up and down on the waves, I'd never missed a step, a toss, or a turn. And I was forever inundated with the glorious smell of fried fish. For some strange reason, I never considered the actual, concrete activity of catching fish. I knew, of course, that there was more to this game of the imagination. I had to take the bad with the good, the hardships with the pleasures. I had to assume, logically, that as Ismet's brother I would have stopped going to school already; that I would not have my own, fresh-smelling room and clean clothes laid out for me; that every day, summoned by the *turkito's* wail, I would go to the mosque with Ismet and Fazil Numat. Also, Ismet and I might only have been half-brothers, because once I heard Fazil Numat complaining to my uncle that it was difficult to keep two wives."

Aroso stopped, looked at Alexandra, and laughed. "I'm drifting away. That's not what you're interested in, I know, but I can't help it. All right, to the main story now. The *gymnasium* – yes. It was a miracle that Father allowed me to enter the German *gymnasium*. It was a decision he came to regret. He kept repeating that by allowing me to attend the *gymnasium* he had brought too much modernity into his family. He had sent me there against his better judgement. Mother, who saw all my Dacosta cousins channelled through the French *lycée*, had beseeched him for months. In the end, he agreed to the *gymansium* more to spite the Dacostas than anything else. I knew German, because I grew up with a German nanny, hired also to spite the Dacostas. The Dacosta children all had French nannies and chirped away in French all the time. Unwittingly, my father was keeping up with the events, since German was heard with increased frequency in Istanbul and on the Grand Rue du Pera.

"The name of the school was the German School, or something like that, but we all called it the *gymnasium* in my time, as did our teachers, all of whom were German. The school had been around for a few decades, but it had been extended to include the high school forms only a few years before I entered it.

"Dr. Eric Jansen was one of my mathematics teachers in the *gymnasium*. It was the year before graduation. We called him Doktor Jansen. Herr Doktor Jansen. There I was, just turned seventeen, brought up in the most conventional and narrow way, probably a total bore and also very shy. And I met this remarkable man, who would have had no time for me at all except that he found out, rather quickly, that I had this extraordinary ability to do mathematics. Eric Jansen must have been forty-five or fifty years old at the time. Of medium height, wiry, and upright, he had a completely bald head and a neat moustache, turning grey. He believed in physical fitness and swam the waters of the Bosphorus from early spring to late fall. He also belonged to some sort of boxing club and often showed up with cuts or bruises on his face. His nose was beginning to get bulbous, and while his affection for *raki* may have contributed, I think that at his age he was mainly on the receiving end in his boxing bouts. At the *gymnasium*, mathematics was taken seriously. Doktor Jansen taught us both analysis and geometry. In the former, we spent the first months doing combinatorial analysis, a somewhat arid topic, as you well know, which he tried valiantly to make more exciting. Spine tingling, he called it. Contemplating a beautiful result at the blackboard, he would often turn to us and say, 'Don't you find this spine-tingling, you sand brains?' He did not think much of us. 'Dandelion heads' was another insult. He loaded us with homework. One morning, about a month into the first term, there were the usual groans and protests as he was listing on the blackboard the homework we had to do for the very next day. He turned to us and said, 'Too much? Very well. Can you figure out a geometric interpretation for the combination of ... say, eight objects taken three at a time. Unordered combinations. If one of you can figure it out, then nobody has to do any homework for tomorrow.' That day, we had Doktor Jansen for the next class also, geometry. During the break, I suddenly came up with a geometric interpretation. It came to me as if served on a platter by a waiter, with no particular effort by me. As Jansen came in for the next class, I raised my hand and announced that I had a geometric interpretation. After a few screams of joy, a deadly silence fell over the class."

Aroso had another sip of wine.

"What did you tell him?" Alexandra asked.

"Ah," Aroso said, clearly happy that she had asked, "you are curious, aren't you? Well, I told him that a geometric equivalent would be the volume of a pyramid having as its base a right-angle triangle. The height of the pyramid could be 8, while the short sides of the base triangle were 6 and 7. Alexandra, I was shy and gangly and awkward in those days. Yet I heard myself explaining the solution with a clarity and confidence that makes me proud even now, thinking back after so many years."

"And Jansen's reaction?"

"He said that I had not supplied the answer he had in mind, but nonetheless it was a good answer. I became an instant class hero. And, believe me, my dear, Herr Doktor Eric Jansen was surprised. I wasn't.

You see, by that time I knew I had a knack for mathematics. How did I know? To begin with, the math classes were by far the easiest for me. I never had to work in them. I was slightly bored and often irritated by the slow pace at which it was taught. I would do my homework in minutes, often with mistakes due to inattention. Also, about a year earlier, I must have been sixteen at the time, I chanced upon a book on algebra. It was a university-level book. One of my Dacosta older cousins must have used it. I remember reading it and understanding it. I was somewhat astonished. Not only did I understand it, I could do most of the exercises. I didn't tell anybody about this. I thought it a bit freakish. Anyway, mathematics had no great standing in our household. Religion, Hebrew, the Talmud, and my father's commerce were things of import. Getting my older sister married, also. Not mathematics. To my father, mathematics meant adding and subtracting. He had no inkling that there was more to it than that. When I first told him about my desire to study mathematics, he was genuinely puzzled. 'More study? What for? How many ways can you add two numbers?' My father could barely do his business arithmetic and avoided fractions. He could not avoid percentages, but he felt he was on shaky ground with them and would sweat heavily. No question, the math gene skipped at least one generation.

"I grew up respecting and, without realizing it, avoiding my father. A few months after I met Eric Jansen, I knew that my father was a conventional man, quite limited, with petty worries and hatreds. I continued to avoid him, but this time deliberately. He became irrelevant to me, and he knew it. It hurt him. It hurt his pride, I think, more than his feelings. He blamed it all on the German *gymnasium*. I blossomed there, but I wonder whether I would have done so well without Eric Jansen.

"That year, the year I had Eric Jansen as a teacher, I became so taken with mathematics that often it kept me awake at night. I had math fever. I would lie in bed, late at night, sometimes reading it, more often just thinking it. At dawn, I would open my bedroom window and watch the sun creeping up and painting an orange path towards me along the dark waters of the Golden Horn. Mist would rise from the water, and I'd hear the call to prayer from minarets across the city. I was taken to a play once, I might have been five or six years old, another of Mother's radical ideas frowned upon by my father. I remember the music at the beginning, and then seeing the curtain slowly rising and the stage lights coming on in a blinding flood. Similar, I thought, was the view from my bedroom window: a very large stage bounded by two continents, the muezzins – hidden from sight, like the orchestra – providing the music, the mist rising like a curtain, and the sun furnishing the stage lights. I loved that view from my bedroom window. I would rehearse, sitting at the window, the things I would say to Dr. Jansen that day to impress him. I would repeat in my mind the theorems I had learned, the insights I had thought of, the difficult problems I had solved.

"In long walks with me along the streets of Istanbul, up and down the hills, but holding as close as possible to the shore, because he liked to look at the water, Eric Jansen held forth on mathematics. He told me about the birth of non-Euclidean geometry and the revolution it had created. It was the romantic story that attracted me also, more than the revolutionary idea put forward by Lobachevsky. I imagined Lobachevsky, at his obscure university in the old Tartar city of Kazan, working out his odd geometry in which there is more than one parallel to a line through a point. I heard him talking himself into admitting, while walking lonely through Kazan's narrow streets – same as Istanbul's, I imagined, but full of snow – that the sum of angles in a triangle is less than two straight angles. I had difficulty tracing mental triangles on a trumpet-like surface, as Eric had advised me, but the two-dimensional geometry on a sphere, the simplest example of Riemannian non-Euclidean geometry, I understood immediately. Even more romantic was the thought of Bolyai, the Hungarian who had independently discovered the same thing as Lobachevsky but, alas, published a few months too late to be given any credit. I felt terribly sorry for him, as did Eric. At least Riemann, as Eric was fond of repeating, had a few other tricks in him. Not Bolyai.

"Because he loved Istanbul, Eric Jansen's roving lectures were as much about the city as about mathematics. He was overwhelmed by the city, by its past, by its diverse people, by its geography, by its buried and latent cruelty. The biggest city in the world for much more than a thousand years, he was fond of reminding me. 'Look around you,' he would say. 'Wherever you end up, whatever cities you will see, there will be nothing like this.' He would stop on the Galata Bridge and point out to me the multitude of the busy crowd. Turks and Greeks, of course, they were the most numerous, but also Armenians, Jews, Circassians, Serbs, blacks (don't forget, he would say, that Pushkin's great-grandfather was an Ethiopian slave bought in Istanbul by the Russian ambassador), Wallachians, Albanians, Bulgarians, Arabs. And Westerners, of course. We took long walks along the narrow lanes of Istanbul. The narrower they were, the more Eric liked them. He would laugh like a child at the names of the streets: the Alley of the Chicken that Cannot Fly, the Street of Ibrahim of Black Hell, the Avenue of the Bushy Beard, the Street of a Thousand Earthquakes. Equally delightful to him were the names of the many winds of the Bosphorus, which he claimed he could identify on our walks. He taught them to me, repeating their Turkish names several times, and even running drills to make sure I had learned them by heart. *Huzun Firtinasi* , the Agreeable Wind; *Kozkavuram Firtinasi*, the Wind of Roasting Walnuts; *Carkdonumu*, the Wind of the Turning Windmills; *Koc Katimi*, the Wind of the Mating Ram. As well as their names, I had to learn their seasons.

"Eric Jansen was an eccentric, and to me he was a godsend. He may not have had a spectacular professional career – he got by mainly on the strength of his enthusiasm and ability to teach – but he was a Gottingen graduate, and it was he who told my parents that I must go there. He spent hours talking to my father, trying to convince him that not to let me go would be against the wishes of any god one would choose. 'A talent like your son's,' Eric Jansen said to my father, 'is clearly no accident, but a gift from God. Not to cultivate this talent would be against His intentions. Otherwise, why would He have bothered conferring such gift?' It would have been a powerful argument for such a religious man as my father, except that Father never understood the gift I had. In the end, he gave in and promised to send me to Gottingen only after Mother threatened to ask for the Dacostas' help and I threatened to side with them. Eric had already written to some of his former professors and colleagues about the young prodigy he had found in the most unexpected place and that they should watch for my application.

"I did not have Eric Jansen as a teacher in my last year at the *gymnasium*. That summer, he disappeared without a trace. I was terribly hurt. How could he leave, just like that, without saying goodbye? I am sure now that he died, probably violently, somewhere in Turkey, or further east. He was reckless. In Gottingen, when several years later I inquired about him, there were a few stories about his student years, mostly about his habit of punching his opponents instead of crossing swords with them. There were rumours that he was homosexual. Never laid a hand on me. I was so naïve in those days that were he to make any advances, I would have remained blissfully unaware, anyway. Did he die violently in a lover's quarrel, or in one of the many male brothels in Istanbul? Or did he die somewhere in Iraq, or Afganistan, places he told me he liked to travel to in the summer?"

Aroso fell silent and then he rose.

"I'm afraid we will have to stop here," he said. "I wonder where Jana is – she's been gone since noon."

Chapter 9
January 1976

In early July, Charles came to Bucharest for a few days to work with Alexandra on the outline of the book. It led to the first serious disagreement between them. Alexandra wanted the book built strictly around their six papers, possibly starting with the fourth paper, the one outlining the program for future work. The papers would be expanded, of course, but she felt that the only new material should be connecting commentaries between the papers. The book would be addressed to researches in the field, to specialists.

Charles saw a much larger book, a treatise on number theory. Obviously, their latest work and their program would be incorporated in it, but he had in mind a book for a wider audience – one that could serve as a textbook for advanced courses in the subject. Charles admitted it would take much longer to write it, but, he argued, it would have a much bigger impact if the serious student – future researchers and professors – "grew up" with the book and the program included in it. He even talked, although guardedly, so as not to drive her off, of covering not only the analytic approach but also all modern developments in algebraic, geometric, combinatorial and computational number theory. After all, their program paper made incursions in these areas as well.

They began the argument in her office, and after a while Alexandra said that a walk would do them good. They went to the

Cismigiu Garden.

Alexandra was afraid that the effort to write such a book would be too exacting and they would have too little time for research. The "big book" could wait. But Charles was adamant. "Besides," he added, "it would allow me to spend more time with you. Everybody understands how much work there is in writing a treatise."

That's when she decided to tell him. "That may not be necessary, now, Charles. I'm going to Rome, to the congress. That is, if they let me. And –"

He leapt in, surprised, but delighted. "They will, I'm sure. Oh, we'll have such a good time, you'll see."

"And not coming back. Please, let me finish. I think I've made up my mind. You've said that Université de Montreal has an open offer for me. I'll take it, whatever the terms are. Now, Charles … Maybe *almost* made up my mind is a better description. Because I'm still not completely sure … and I could change my mind anytime. Can you put up with this? I know it's not fair to you, but I can't do it any other way."

He was overwhelmed and, at first, unable to speak. Of course, of course, whatever she said. It didn't matter, he'd do anything. Yes, he would begin making inquiries to find the best way, the fastest way, for her to be accepted as an immigrant in Canada. Maybe a work permit to start with … whatever. He took her hands into his and held them.

She pushed him back, gently. "I don't think it's a good idea to show too much affection so close to the university. It's strange, all getaway announcements in our family are made in this place. Leonard told me about his plans to flee here, in this garden, as well. It was a cold winter day, though. Oh, never mind … I'm talking nonsense."

She became aware that these might be her last months in Bucharest. It was a beautiful summer, with hardly any rain. She took long aimless walks through the dusty city – often with Ada at first, but mostly by herself – knowing that, if she left, she would not return to it for a long time and trying to imprint it in her memory. She could not make up her mind whether the city was truly beautiful or only had some minor charm, the kind often attached to slow decay, a settling into seediness. She had the foolish notion that, aware of her intentions, the city had already turned its back on her, that her inability to make up her mind about it, or even to fix it in her mind, was caused by some naughty trick played on her by an irascible city spirit. She took her walks in the late evening, to avoid the heat, and often without knowing where she was going. They were a long goodbye to the city, a lengthy process of abandoning a failing connection. It was as if the sutures of a badly mended union were coming apart. She had no feelings for her fellow citizens. If anything, it was a bewildered aversion, the kind she felt in the inevitable rupture with Emil.

Back from her walks, she'd give Ada sudden, avid hugs. She told her that she loved her more than anything in the world. She felt that Ada was annoyed by her behaviour, by the long, inexplicable absences, the sudden and suffocating hugs, her declarations of love.

Aroso's story moved both forth and back in time. He was clearly enjoying his reminiscences in Alexandra's company, and he seemed to relish the utter lack of order his stories followed. He let himself go, his disorderly ramblings somehow kept coherent by his storytelling gift, a unifying melancholy irony, and Alexandra's interest. It was only in the last couple of weeks that Aroso finally began reminiscing about Gottingen, about how he and Ovid Lovinescu, Mitzi's brother, became friends there. Ovid had arrived in Gottingen at the same time as Aroso, and had rooms in the same *pension*. Gottingen quickly brought Eric Jansen back into the story, because Eric Jansen had been a student there as well, at the turn of the century. But Aroso's story was like a river in the flatlands which flows along for ten miles only to end up half a mile from where it started. From Eric Jansen, Aroso went back to Istanbul. He recounted what had happened to each of his Dacosta relatives after the war. The First World War, of course. She received a lesson on the occupation of Istanbul by the Entente forces. Alexandra learned about the Turkish-Greek war, the route of the invading Greek army and Attaturk's revolution. Aroso told her how he once saw Ismet Pasha, later Inonu, Attaturk's right hand. It was the spring of 1923, in Istanbul, when he had gone back for his father's funeral. Inonu, surrounded by similarly dressed officers, had a long heavy military coat, shiny boots, a tall Astrakhan hat and a long sabre hanging on his left hip.

On another visit, Aroso had wasted one whole hour on suppositions about the financial ruin and suicide of his uncle Elias. He had never found out the real story behind it, but he had his own theory, based on speculation, which he shared enthusiastically with Alexandra. Then Aroso went back to Ovid Lovinescu, his brother-in-law. Ovid's father had sent him to do his studies in Germany. It didn't matter what he studied, Ovid's father told him, or where, as long as he learned the language and got a degree.

As he was talking about Ovid, Aroso suddenly skipped a few years and began to talk about the summer vacation he spent, towards the end of his studies, in Bucharest with Ovid and the Lovinescu family. It was the summer he had first met Mitzi. She had been very young then, only seventeen. He had – this was the cliché Aroso himself used – fallen head over heels in love with her the moment he saw her. For two hours, Alexandra learned about what Mitzi had worn and on what occasions, and about the witty things she had said that summer. She had the suspicion that much of the story around Mitzi was apocryphal, or exaggerated – after all, Aroso himself had told Alexandra that when he settled in Bucharest after he married Mitzi he hardly spoke any Romanian. It wasn't that he was inventing stories to dazzle or impress Alexandra; more likely, he had reconstructed a past that became, as years went by, more and more marvellous. Towards the end he mentioned the endless Ping-Pong battles he fought with Mitzi, one set after another, one match after another. That was his luck, Aroso believed. There was no need for much communication. The Lovinescus had acquired a Ping-Pong table two years earlier. This very table, Aroso added, pointing a forefinger downwards. Well, half of it, anyway. To Mitzi's distress, she had been the only one who'd loved to play. Aroso happened to have played a bit in Gottingen, and he thanked his lucky stars that he had. He became Mitzi's willing slave-opponent …

Alexandra tried to bring him back to Gottingen, where he had briefly wandered that evening, but suddenly his mood changed and he began talking about Mitzi's father. George Lovinescu had been a well-known lawyer and landowner, with solid connections and interests in banking circles. For a brief time he had been a minister in one of the many governments they had in those days. An early supporter of the Iron Guard, he had not been fond of Jews. He had disliked Aroso from the very beginning. George Lovinescu died in 1931, of a sudden stroke, but not before he had brought his son Ovid to share his views and become a supporter of the Iron Guard.

Towards the end of July, Alexandra travelled with Ada to Urja, where she rested for a few days. She left Ada with her grandparents for the remainder of the summer, and took the train back to work on her Rome paper. She went to see Aroso the day after her return. When she reached his house, Aroso was talking at the gate with a short, bald man holding a battered briefcase. Aroso motioned her in and joined her in the courtyard soon afterward. He looked pale and feverish. "I'm not feeling well," he said. "That was the doctor, and Jana has gone to the pharmacy. It's going to take her a while, since not many pharmacies are open at this hour. Look, dear, I have to rest a little, maybe I'll feel better after a bit. Do you mind waiting? I'll tell you what. If you get bored, go into my study and pick up a book to browse through. You know where it is."

She sat under the trellis for a while and then she went into Aroso's study. Although it wasn't dark yet, she switched on the lights. The room was tinier than she remembered. It had always seemed small to her, probably because of the gigantic desk it contained, which was so large she thought it must have been brought into the room in pieces and put back together once inside. She had never asked Aroso how that desk and made it in, or about its odd shape. The desk was at the only window in the room, which looked onto the courtyard. Through the partially closed jalousies, she could see the table under the trellis. The odd thing about the desk, a rather fine piece of dark wood, was that one corner was cut clean off, as if by a giant guillotine, well before the two sides met at the usual right angle. Of course, without the chopped-off corner, you could not open or close the door to that room. On the wall opposite the window, and continuing for about half a meter along the adjacent walls, were built-in bookshelves. Before she could reach for any of the books, Alexandra was stopped, not for the first time, by the sight of two large paintings hanging on the wall opposite the door. She was in fact quite familiar with them, although she had never asked Aroso about their history. The first one, entitled *Mitzi with Colourful Hat* (the title was clearly inscribed in black letters low in the left-hand corner; the painter's name was there as well, very short but unreadable), was a head-and-shoulders portrait of Mitzi wearing a hat, with a wide brim, of dark green, almost black, material finished with a gilded edge. The hat had magnificent plumage, red and blue, striking and voluminous. Mitzi's dress was the same dark colour as the hat and fastened high up with large buttons. A necklace of white, nearly transparent flowers was tightly wrapped about her neck in a delicate jabot. Mitzi was outside. The background sky was blue-green, like a tropical sea. It was sunset, because farther away, near the horizon, there were clouds turned yellowish and pink. Golden hills, with brown dark patches, luscious and post-harvest melancholic, supported the sky. Mitzi's hair was golden brown, with a distinct tinge of red, and seemed almost a part of the hat's ornamentation. Her eyes were immense and sad, almost resigned. Resigned to what? To a long sitting, to sharing the life of a mathematician, to a soul unhappy and in shreds? Alexandra loved the painting, the heavy, thick application of the oils, but she wondered if she would have liked it as much if its subject were not a familiar figure.

The second painting, clearly by the same artist, was a beach scene. There was no title, nor was there a signature, but there was an unmistakable resemblance between the naked young woman on the beach and the one in the plumed hat. Mitzi was sitting on a white towel, almost three-quarters turned away. Her face looked back towards the painter. Her legs were crossed under to one side, and on the other side an outstretched arm, hand anchored on the sand and only partially visible, provided the required balance. The Mitzi on the beach looked younger than the Mitzi in the colourful hat, but it may only have been because of the softer, more diffuse colours of the second painting. Mitzi's hair, in some disarray because of the sea breeze, was much lighter here, possibly the effect of the sunny outdoors, but the red tinges were obvious in this painting as well. There were patches of pink on Mitzi's back, buttocks, and thighs, an artifice imparting the sensation of exhausting heat. The whole painting was a luminous combination of yellows. The paralyzing power of the sun, stamping a golden tinge on the sea itself, was what struck her most about the painting, together with Mitzi's large, unsmiling eyes, and the lazy vigour of the young, nude body.

She heard the gate being slammed, then Jana's steps, then voices from the other room, across the little hall, as if Aroso and Jana were having an argument. He joined her in his study, a few minutes later. "It seems," Aroso told her, "that I'm too weak to tell silly stories. I've been ordered to rest. The doctor fears pneumonia, which, he claims, at my age is bad news."

"It's fine," she said. "Of course, you need to rest. I've had a good time looking again at the two paintings. You know, that nude of Mitzi had me very embarrassed when, as a fourteen- or fifteen-year-old, I dutifully did my math in this room that first summer."

While he walked her out, wheezing a bit, he told her that the two paintings were done more or less at the same time, some two years after he and Mitzi had been married. He also said that he almost sold one of them, one winter years ago, when a pipe froze and then burst, making a big mess in the house. It needed urgent fixing, but in the end he didn't have to sell. Luckily, Jana's brother – an unexpected source – lent him the money to mend the pipe.

Chapter 10
August 1976

It was pneumonia, and although diagnosed early, it left Aroso very weak. Alexandra didn't see him again until late August. He was waiting for her under the trellis when she arrived. He had a cardigan on, although it was quite warm. As usual, he made happy noises at the bottle of wine she brought along. "Do you mind going into the kitchen and bringing out two glasses and the corkscrew? You'll have to open the bottle, too. I don't have much strength today."

She went into the kitchen and poured herself a large glass of water, which she gulped voraciously. She had walked from the centre of the city to Aroso's house – for some reason she had felt that she needed the long walk – along the endless Mircea Voda street, and then through small side streets, and it had left her very thirsty. She found two glasses and the corkscrew and brought them with her to the table. The light outside had begun to dim. She opened the bottle and poured wine in the two glasses. Aroso looked tired and aged. He seemed unfocused, almost as if wondering what she was doing there – in his yard, under the grapevine – and it took him a while to begin. She asked him to tell her about Gottingen.

"Gottingen was a small university town surrounded by woody hills – probably still is – very pretty, a post-card town, with red-tile roofs and half-timbered houses, some hundreds of years old, and the appropriate number of churches and taverns. There was a walled inner town, and the university started there at first, on Wilhelmsplatz. The top of the old town walls had been transformed into a circular park lane, a promenade, with shady trees on one side and the former moat, overgrown with bushes, on the other. 'Walking the wall' – that's what the locals called it – was a favourite activity of the citizens of Gottingen on beautiful days and often a pleasant way to get to where you wanted to go.

"Slowly, the university grew and spread out past the old city walls. The Mathematics Institute was just south of the city walls, on Bunsenstrasse. A large unattractive building, utilitarian – there was very little money around when it was built – looked like a military barracks slapped down quickly out of necessity. I left Gottingen soon after it was built. Richard Courant did it – he took over Klein's position as director of the Mathematics Institute – with part of the money coming from an American foundation. At the time I arrived there – early twenties – mathematics at Gottingen had miraculously recovered after the Great War. Some of the best young minds from all over the world were coming to Gottingen again. Our place, Pensione Huber, was on Munchhausenstrasse, outside the city walls. It was not an established *pension*. Frau Huber was a young widow. Her husband had taught zoology at the university. He had been an assistant professor, *Extraordinarius*, they call it, when he died from an infection. Quite young, mid-thirties. 'From dissection. He dissected anything that had stopped moving,' Frau Huber would say, laughing. 'Sometimes, at the dinner table, holding the carving knife above the roast, he looked with such scientific longing at me. Oh, he was such a wonderful man. I miss him so.' Frau Huber had been very much in love with her husband, or so everybody said, and had decided not to remarry. She was left with little after her husband's death, and what she got from the university was barely enough. She supplemented her income by keeping lodgers. She took only male lodgers, never more than four, often students. During that first year, besides Ovid and me, there was a retired judge who seemed to resent young people (we were all guilty of something, his disapproving gaze suggested), and a clerk at City Hall, a timid man in his forties, whose wife had had enough of him and told him to go away. Frau Huber's help, Rosa, was from a nearby village. Rosa had a small, pleasant, pink face. She was a hefty young woman, with heavy breasts and thighs. She had a respiratory affliction, probably asthma, and breathed heavily walking up the stairs. Rosa adored Frau Huber, who was very kind to her. In spite of her loss, Frau Huber was quite a cheerful presence, and I think I was mildly in love with her. Rumour had it that she would sometimes tiptoe her way into a lodger's room in the middle of the night and smother any astonishment with the warmth of her body. I dreamt of her visits, although I was prudishly disapproving of them. Ovid claimed to have been visited by Frau Huber – not once, but twice – but I thought he was lying, in spite of the details he was eager to reveal, and which I refused to hear. And then, one night, towards the end of that academic year, it actually happened. I was awakened in the middle of the night by the soft squeak of the door. It slowly closed, and I knew she was in, tiptoeing her way towards me. I was overcome by an acute attack of shyness. I felt awkward, yet overwhelmingly happy. I wished her trip towards my bed would last forever. And then I became aware of the asthmatic breathing. She sat on the bed and after a few seconds lay down on it and moved towards me. She was soft and sweaty and her words were soft, too. 'It's me, little Rosa. Make love to me, Herr Aroso.'"

He stopped and laughed. It was a full-hearted laugh that ended in a series of coughs. The sun was almost gone, fiery pink patches marking its getaway. "Rosa's breasts had that colour," Aroso said, pointing west. He was laughing and coughing again. He took a small sip of the wine and stood up. "Are you hungry? I'll ask Jana to bring out a few morsels. This wine is quite bad."

He went into the house, taking small, measured steps, as if he were walking on ice. The dark fell with the usual suddenness. It was the best time, now, with the heat gone and the growing quiet. A dog, probably next door, was wailing softly. The lights were on in Mitzi's bedroom – why did she still call it Mitzi's? – and in the kitchen. She heard doors opening and closing a couple of times, and then sounds of dishes from the kitchen. After a while, Jana came out from the kitchen with an oil lamp and a tray. "The light bulb is gone. The Professor has been trying to buy one for several days," she said.

Jana unloaded the tray with efficient, unhurried movements. Cheese, butter, half a loaf of black bread, and a massive breadknife with the two sides of its wooden handle secured together by string. A blue plate held several tomatoes and a green pepper. There were slices of salami and a few olives on another plate. Jana placed everything on the table, and also two empty plates and cutlery. Her shadow on the neighbour's wall made gigantic, flickering, surgical thrusts.

"This is quite a feast, Jana."

"My brother brought a few fresh things this morning. See that the Professor eats something. He hardly eats at all these days, and the doctor said he needs to eat well."

Jana went away. Alexandra cut herself a slice of bread, spread some butter over it, picked up a tomato, and began to slice it on her plate. Aroso came back. "Don't you find," he said, pointing to her plate, "that the taste of tomatoes depends on the way you slice them? Random cuts are best. Avoid parallel slices."

"Tell me about Hilbert," Alexandra said.

"Hilbert. Everybody wants to know about Hilbert. I don't have much to say, I fear. Hilbert was old. Nominally, my studies were with him, but it was Paul Bernays, his personal assistant for many years, who supervised my work. Richard Courant took an interest in my work also, because of some overlap with his research. Hilbert must have been – what? – sixty-five or sixty-six years old when I finished my required eight semesters. That was in 1928. No, it was Bernays. It was only on paper that I was Hilbert's student. It was very prestigious to have Hilbert's name associated with you. And Bernays had no official position with the university.

"Ah, Alexandra, what days. I had a brief period – brief? one year almost – when I was not a nice person to be around. I was insolent, impertinent, downright rude. Nobody, I thought, was like me, nobody had my gifts. I reached that conclusion at the end of my first year. These were talented people, my dear, I don't need to tell you, those who came to study mathematics in Gottingen. Fools did not come to Gottingen's Mathematics Institute. And yet, even among them, I knew I had more than they had. Without trying much, I shone and astonished. I felt anointed. It's a powerful wine, this superior feeling, Alexandra, you know it as well as I do. Terribly intoxicating. It goes quickly to your head. I had an unusually quick mind, and I had little patience with lecturers who got stuck in the middle of a theorem. I once behaved with stupendous arrogance towards Hilbert himself. It was in my second year. Hilbert had never been very quick, and as he grew old he would stumble quite often. Bernays, of course, was always there, but if he pointed the way out too quickly Hilbert would get upset. Bernays knew exactly when and how to jump in without bruising Hilbert's ego. I was too impatient once, during a long pause, with Hilbert lost and Bernays waiting for the right time to vault in, and I suggested, in an incredibly impertinent way, that 'maybe Herr Bernays could continue.' Hilbert feigned that he did not hear me. A few minutes later Bernays took over. Maybe Hilbert did not hear me, but the entire class did and fell into a deadly silence. After the lecture, Bernays took me aside and chewed me out. 'You are very lucky he did not hear you,' he said to me.

"My observations during lectures and a paper I wrote caught Hilbert's attention. The paper was on integral equations, and it was a slight generalization of one of Hilbert's results in that field. When John Neumann came to visit later that year, I found myself invited to dinner to the Hilberts. Bernays was there, of course, and so was Lothar Nordheim, Hilbert's physics assistant. Nordheim left early. John Neumann had a quick mind, he was famous for it, but I felt his equal, at the very least. Of course, I did not know at that time that he would become the famous von Neumann. All I knew was that he was in Berlin and that he was Hungarian, bright, and very young. I must have been in particularly good form that evening. I had large gaps in my mathematical knowledge, but what I had learned I knew well and it was always quickly retrieved. What impressed them was my ability to quickly see similarities between different aspects of mathematics and, based on them, to predict promising paths to take. I've always had this ability. In my career, because of this almost clairvoyant gift, I rarely forked to an unfruitful path of research. When you impress such a select audience, Alexandra, it's hard not to feel arrogant. I calmed down in my third year, though. By the time I reached my fourth year, a few people even began to like me.

"The Hilberts lived on Wilhelm Weber Strasse. It began just outside the city walls, near the Botanical Gardens. It was a nice, quiet street, with large stately houses and with the highest concentration of famous mathematicians anywhere in the world. The Kleins lived on the same street, in the first or second house from the Botanical Gardens. Never met him, Klein. He had been retired for quite a while and was not well. He died the year after I arrived in Gottingen.

"Hilbert's house was further down the street, past a large church. The Courants were there too, on the same side of the street, in a large, imposing house that had been Carl Runge's.

"I don't remember much about the Hilberts' house. I was there only a few times. A yellow-brick house, I think. Quite large. Hilbert had a working office outdoors, with a huge blackboard nailed to his neighbour's wall, all under a glass roof so he could work during rain."

"Much like your setup here," Alexandra suggested.

Aroso laughed. "Much more modest, my setup. He had space. He liked to pace, not sit at a table.

"Although he held no teaching position, Bernays received a small sum from the university as a concession to Hilbert. He supplemented his income with the meagre fees he collected from the few students who attended his lectures. Bernays was already thirty-six, not that young, when I arrived in Gottingen. He had no means to support a family, but I never heard him complaining. Hilbert did not like his assistants and collaborators burdened by other duties, especially a family, and exploited them mercilessly. Marriage meant dismissal.

"I don't think Bernays got the recognition he deserved. He did all the work. From 1912 or so, preoccupied with physics, Hilbert had done hardly any mathematics, anyway. It was Bernays who supervised us, Hilbert's students working towards a doctoral degree. I may have had seven or eight meetings with Hilbert in the two years of work on my doctorate. And Bernays was always there, of course. The meetings with Hilbert had an established format. First, Bernays would explain the thrust of my recent work to the old man. Then it was my turn to talk about my work, but no more than ten or fifteen minutes. At most. Hilbert would nod, smile, ask a few questions – good questions, mind you – and I was off."

"What happened to Bernays? Did he finally get a position in Gottingen?"

"Oh, he went back to Switzerland. I think he's still alive. I kept in touch with him for several years. Yes, he left Gottingen in '33 or '34, when all the Jews left. So many of them. Gottingen was finished. Richard Courant, Bernays, Edmund Landau, Emmy Noether. The two Nobel Prize winners from the Physics Institute, Max Born and James Franck. They all went to America, except Bernays. It was Courant, in fact, who asked me to stay in Gottingen. He could not offer me a position – for that, patience was required, but he could find some modest funding which would allow me to work with him, the same way Bernays worked with Hilbert. This, Alexandra, believe me, was quite an offer. Positions, I knew, did not open up unless an incumbent professor retired, or died. Or moved to some other university. But people rarely moved away from Gottingen. Hilbert had had offers from Berlin several times and didn't move. There were no funds for additional positions. Money was scarce. Germany was still not fully recovered from the war and the economic crisis was at its peak. But Courant could do it. He could definitely get the miserly amount required. Courant had a knack for getting funds."

"Flattered as I was," he continued, "I told Courant I needed a month to make up my mind. I had several other offers. The University of Turin had promised me a position of Assistant Professor within a year of my arrival. And the University of Maryland had offered me a teaching position in Baltimore. America had never appealed to me, I don't know why, but the offer from Turin was very tempting. Turin had a solid mathematical tradition and Peano was there.

"I needed to know, though, where I stood with Mitzi. I had seen Mitzi again, two years earlier, in 1929. Ovid Lovinescu, Mitzi's brother, had gone back to Romania in 1928. He was making his way up as a banker, no doubt helped by his father's connections. He had invited me again to spend a few summer weeks with him. I went and stayed with him at Ulmata, the Lovinescus' family estate. It was in the foothills of the southern Carpathians, a two-hour train ride west from the main line going to Brasov through the mountains. Beautiful place. Good hosts, the Lovinescus, and fond of visitors. It was quite a large place and it was swarming with guests. There were many young people and many army officers. There was another brother, Tudor, the eldest of the children. Tudor was an army officer, a captain at that time, if I remember correctly.

His wife, Lavinia, was a spirited young woman who liked men and sought their company in an unrestrained way. Lavinia was wild, and only moderately attractive. Everybody was in love with her, though, including the women whose husbands lusted after her. Tudor was not exactly faithful, either. It may seem strange, but the two of them – Lavinia and Tudor – were quite devoted to each other. Lavinia lost her bearings when Tudor was sent to the Danube–Black Sea canal in the early fifties. But that's another story. That summer, Lavinia discovered Mitzi, who'd just turned nineteen. She found in Mitzi, Lavinia used to say, a kindred spirit. Mitzi was darker, more complicated, Lavinia said to everybody, but essentially a kindred spirit. In time, I had to agree that she was right. Mitzi's men, it turned out, were fewer, and she went to them with a sardonic determination, devoid of any illusion, then dropped them with ease and indifference. But that was later. What they had in common, that summer, was a lot of laughter and an inability to take anything seriously. 'Here are the pompous and the grave,' they would often say, laughing, when breaking into a group of men.

"Ovid, who had the habit of making extravagant claims, would introduce me as 'one of the few geniuses of today's mathematics.' He would also invariably add, 'A charmer, and a most amusing man.' Of course, as I barely managed a word or two in Romanian, he was hardly going to be contradicted. Mitzi was nineteen and thought the world of Ovid. She did not fall in love with me; she fell in love with Ovid's description of me.

"I left after ten days, when a telegram came from Istanbul telling me that Mother was very sick. When I left, I told Ovid that I was in love with Mitzi. Ovid assured me that Mitzi liked me, too. No, he had never discussed it with her, but he knew. A brother knew. Anyway, he would do everything in his power to keep me in her mind. He advised me to write to her. In Istanbul, Mother was dying. She went quietly, as if afraid to make too much fuss, just the way her life had been. I watched her die and thought of Mitzi. I wrote to Mitzi, first from Istanbul, then from Gottingen for the following two years. I wrote polite, boring letters, in which I awkwardly expressed my love. She answered that she was not indifferent to my appeal and that Ovid often talked about me. Her letters were brief and rushed, which I attributed to her youth.

"After Courant made me the offer to stay in Gottingen as his personal assistant, I went back to Romania intent on marrying Mitzi. Ovid's signals were becoming less encouraging, and his father, George Lovinescu, had been very much against Mitzi's marrying a Jew, genius or no genius. Later I found out that George Lovinescu had pushed Ovid into the fascist circles with which he was closely connected. My luck was that George Lovinescu died, of a sudden stroke, in the early weeks of 1931. I proposed, and to my delight and astonishment Mitzi accepted. I was as smitten as ever. I was like a puppy. If there was to be mathematics in my life, it was to be on terms that suited Mitzi. Mitzi was not willing to live abroad. Of course, the wealthy Lovinescus had a wonderful life in Romania. Gottingen was out of the question. Baltimore was not even given a thought. She did consider Turin, for a while. She may have gone with me to Rome or Paris, maybe Berlin, or some other glamorous city, but I had no such offers. I don't think she thought much about what her life would be as the wife of a mathematician teaching at some university, but I believe she had the instinct to recognize that it was not for her. Too lonely and too quiet. So, the solution was Bucharest. 'All my family and friends are here,' she said. 'I need them.' She agreed to marry me only if we settled in Bucharest. I was lucky again, because that year, in spite of the economic crises, the mathematics department at the University of Bucharest had a new position created from a recent endowment. And, during the summer, one of the assistant professors went suddenly mystic and joined a monastery. I applied for a position. I had several papers already published and solid credentials. I had already had offers from two reputable institutions. Courant and Bernays had sent letters of recommendation. It was generous of Courant to do it. I'll always acknowledge this. But it may have been that, seeing the Nazis' steady rise to power, he'd become doubtful about his earlier offer. So I was offered a position at the University of Bucharest. Like her husband, Mitzi's mother had been against the marriage, but in the end she gave in, concerned about Mitzi, who went into one of her 'moods' whenever the suitability of my forthcoming visit was discussed. Because, you see, Mitzi was damaged goods. She was manic-depressive, with the periods of depression getting slowly but steadily longer. This is a modern diagnosis, of course. In those days, we didn't really know what it was. It was accepted that Mitzi was special, and very sensitive. And it was also accepted that Mitzi was often too active and tried to do too much, and it was only natural that, now and then, for a few days, at most a week or two, she had to rest. She was to be left alone and have all her whims met. This happened, I was told, three or four times a year. I'd never seen any of these 'moods' in the brief periods I was around Mitzi before we got married. Frankly, it didn't matter to me. I was going to take care of her.

"We were married in November 1931. Two months earlier, I had started teaching. I taught only one course that year, on the Cantorian set theory. I wanted to learn it, and what better way than to teach it. I gave the course in German. I had only three students, and one of them dropped out after the first month. My mind was more with Mitzi than with mathematics. At the university I was told to learn Romanian by the next year and that I'd have to teach three courses the following year, all in Romanian, to make up. It was all fine with me. I could work hard. I could teach three subjects. There would be little time for research, of course, in the following year, unless I slept less. But I was young and could do it. With Mitzi, I was going to learn Romanian fast. Until then, our conversations had been in German. Mitzi spoke a rudimentary version of it, acquired as a child from a Fraulein Mina, who had spent four years with the Lovinescus looking after Mitzi. Fraulein Mina had to leave when Mitzi's mother found out that her husband and Mina touched each other under the table. Mitzi was six years old at the time, and her German remained at a childish level. It gave our conversation a certain charm. It also hid my inability to make small talk and be amusing.

"Was our marriage a mistake? Very likely. Do I regret it? On most days, my answer would be no. Well, you would say, this is either quite a paradox whose subtlety I cannot follow, or Aroso has lost his mind. But, Alexandra, how does one judge these things? Is it at all possible? We do not live multiple parallel lives within the same environment, like rats in a controlled experiment. No rat-watching scientist is looking at the maze of my life and comparing it with other lives I could have lived had I made different decisions.

"Let's do it now. Let's take lab rat 'Aroso 2' and place him in Gottingen, having accepted Courant's offer. Quickly, in a year or two, he would have joined the exodus to America. It would have been the same story with 'Aroso 3,' the one that chose to go to Turin, although he would have had a greater chance, if not prescient enough, of ending up in one of Hitler's gas chambers. But in the end they probably would have all landed in the place 'Aroso 4' had already gone to directly – a university in America. This assumes, of course, that I could have obtained a visa for America. Not that obvious, given the difficulties Jews had at that time getting into America. We are lucky, Alexandra, that we don't have to follow too many alternatives, and thus the problem is tractable. What next? Marry, have children, go to faculty teas? Sorry, no teas, cocktails in America. With some luck, no, even without luck, I would have got a job in some major American university. A very satisfying professional life, I grant you. The banal happiness of a carefree existence. The middle-class, middle-risk existence, soul-killing in its predictability."

"But that was what you wanted, wasn't it, to use the talent God gave you? Yes, a quiet existence with a paper and pencil in front of you. That's what mathematicians do. The adventure is all in the mind. And, anyway, once in America, you could have gone gold-digging or robbing banks. There is a good tradition there in these non-banal activities." She was really worked-up and she wanted to understand. "Do you think your life here is any less banal and predictable? It's the same, it's not less banal just because it's hard to buy a loaf of bread. It's the same, it's not less banal just because the dear comrades are watching your every step."

She stopped to gather her thoughts and then went on. "Didn't you tell me I should get out – like a bullet out of a gun – because my work would be better served? Why does that apply to me if it didn't to you? And what about fame? With your mind, at a decent university, you would have become a famous name."

"My dear, I'm telling you what I thought then. Didn't I say to you, before I began to recount all this ancient history, didn't I predict that I'd end up looking silly, looking ridiculous? As to fame, I don't know of many mathematicians of fame. Even a short-lived and misunderstood fame, which is the only one a mathematician could aspire to while alive. Strictly speaking, yes, professionally, my output, my contribution to mathematics, would have been more solid had I stayed in the West. I grant you that. And from that point of view, I have some regrets. Because, at least in theory, remaining here led to the stunting of my development and to a rather modest output in the one field in which I definitely had more than generous talent."

He remained quiet, most likely contemplating one of the parallel lives he had dismissed a few moments earlier. She took several sips of wine in quick succession, emptying her glass. She was still thirsty. She should get some water. A third of the bottle was gone, and Aroso had hardly touched his glass. He stood up and went into the house.

A noisy band of amorous crickets was filling the silence with a monotonous chant. From the street she heard a faint sound of laughter. As its source approached, it turned out to be sobs. She heard words spoken in anger by a man. A quick shuffling of steps, then a slap, then louder sobbing and wailing. Then she could see them, in the dimly lit street, he gripping her arm and poised to strike again as he pulled her, she trying to get away. He hit her again, and then they were out of sight, the wailing becoming muffled, until once more the only sound was the sound of the tireless crickets. Now, that was a woman who regretted her choices. When he finally stops hitting her, thought Alexandra, when at last he falls into his bed and into a drunken stupor, she will continue to sob softly and wonder about the paths she might have taken. Wonder and despair. Would Alexandra also, years from now, question the choice she was about to make? Everybody did, sooner or later. If one was lucky, one questioned and wondered. The unlucky ones, well, they despaired, they bitterly despaired and resented.

She heard the toilet being flushed. It was late. When Aroso came back out, she stood up and said that she needed to go. He nodded. He was tired, too. She took a few steps towards the gate, then she returned and kissed her old professor on the cheek.

Startled, he chuckled, "Good night, my dear."

Chapter 11
September 1976

The oil lamp was already lit, although there was still light outside. Aroso had pointed at it and said he still hadn't managed to find electric bulbs.

"And marrying Mitzi?" Alexandra asked, once they settled. She asked her question softly, almost whispering, trying to conceal its annoying directness. On her way to Aroso's house, she had wondered how to bring him back to where they were the last time they talked. And there was something he had said the evening of Mitzi's funeral, when she had come back to keep him company, at his heart-rending request, something that had stayed in her mind. But she could never be sure where Aroso's memory would take him, and she needed his answers. "You said, once, that some extraordinary work of yours … oh, I don't know, was not completed because of her … Of course, if it's too painful … It's just that …"

It took him a long time to answer. "Ah, Mitzi, yes. Of course, with Mitzi things got rather difficult. She was complicated and made people's lives complicated. And unpredictable. At times she made my life miserable. The first year of our married life, though, was bliss. We were always together. It was a whirlwind life. The one course I taught did not take much of my time. I was spending, on average, two hours a day working on it and another two learning Romanian and reading mathematics in

Romanian to acquaint myself with the proper mathematical terms. I even began a rough translation of Cantor's *Beitrage* – his work on transfinite sets. The rest of the day belonged to Mitzi, and Mitzi made sure that we were very busy. We were asked everywhere and went everywhere. We were even invited to the palace – twice, in fact. These were very large receptions, of course, but it was still a palace reception. We were invited because, first, she was beautiful, Alexandra, she was breathtaking; second, because she was a Lovinescu, with a myriad of friends and relations; third, because there was a certain curiosity about me. Ovid – and Mitzi also – with his penchant for expanding on a potentially good story, had touted my genius everywhere, though I also sensed in this an eagerness to explain why his sister had married a Jew.

"We travelled a lot that year. We went away at the smallest pretext. The Black Sea, Sinaia, Ulmata. We were everywhere, and Mitzi was the soul of everything. Mitzi and Lavinia. Whatever Mitzi did that year, she did it with me or with my complicity. She always looked at me to make sure I was amused and I was included in the good time. When she was dancing with somebody else, and held tighter than appropriate, she would wink at me and pull a face to look like she was choking. It was a blessed time. I was happy and, I think, Mitzi was happy too. During that first year, Mitzi did not have any of her 'moods.' Maybe once only, but very short. She got pregnant, but had a miscarriage. For several days afterwards she did not talk and did not want to see anybody. It was a normal reaction, I thought. She recovered quickly and we were on our merry rounds again.

"In September of 1932, I started teaching again, this time more than a full load. I became, suddenly, very busy. I worked long hours. I had many students. I had administrative duties. Preparing lectures in Romanian took a lot of effort. I also held a seminar on ideals, again because I was interested to learn about the topic. And a research idea took hold of me, an idea which held a lot of promise. Its source had been the course I had given the previous year, on Cantor's theory of transfinite cardinal numbers. At the beginning, Mitzi stayed home with me. She would bring a book and curl up in an armchair in the room where I was working. Then she decided she would learn how to cook properly so as to feed her genius an appropriate diet. 'What's appropriate food for geniuses?' she asked. In answer to the challenge, she served up some odd combinations, often difficult to swallow. We laughed a lot and frequently ended up going to a restaurant. But she quickly got bored of this, too. She went visiting her friends, went to dinners and parties without me. Lavinia was often with her, and where there was Lavinia, there were always eager men around. I didn't mind. I needed to concentrate, and for that I needed solitude. In December of that year, Mitzi had a long bout of depression, three weeks, the longest she'd ever had. Then, in February, another one, shorter, but darker. She shut herself in our bedroom and did not want me there at all. I was worried. I talked to Ovid. After several days, she came out of it and, laughingly, told me that suicide had crossed her mind. Out to parties again, and then, when the snow melted, driving up to Ulmata, where she stayed for two months. Lavinia, who was an avid rider, got it into her head to teach Mitzi riding. 'It will do her good to get away and have something to do besides watching you scribble on paper,' Lavinia said to me just before they took off in Lavinia's roadster. 'You ought to spend more time with your wife. You can't keep her in your study, for ever. She is a diamond. She needs to be shown off. I'm not sure you two marrying was such a good thing.' Off they went, and I thought it was a good idea, for both of us. I promised Mitzi that I would join her the moment I had some free time. But I did not have any free time in the next two months. I spent more and more hours on my research. I thought I was closing in on a major breakthrough, but I needed to give it my fullest concentration. That's why I kept postponing going up to Ulmata. Every week, I telegraphed Mitzi to give her my love and explain the need to stay at home and work. I told her that she would be very proud of me if it all panned out as I envisaged. I told her that I would be a famous man, and she the wife of a famous man.

"It was while Mitzi was away at Ulmata that I first heard the rumours that she might be involved with another man. The university year had ended, and I still postponed my departure. With more time on my hands, my research had taken full hold of me, and I felt the rush of vain pride and excitement. Mathematical immortality was staring me in the face with each new advance I made.

"One evening, I was working late at the university. Around ten o'clock, tired but reluctant to end what had been a very fruitful day, I realized I'd had hardly anything to eat. I ended up having dinner at an outdoor restaurant not far from the university. While I scribbled on a piece of paper, I chewed absentmindedly what was put in front of me. There were only a few other tables taken. A very noisy group of nine or ten people was gathered around two tables pulled together and loaded with empty bottles. A young man, an army officer, stood up, amidst protests, came towards my table, and collapsed in the empty chair across from me. He greeted me very politely. He was tight. I did not recognize him immediately, but then, when he introduced himself and mentioned Tudor, I made the connection. He had been a guest at Ulmata the previous summer. All I remembered about him was that he had spent much of his time around Mitzi, had seemed somewhat in awe of her, and of the Lovinescus, and that he had a ready, infectious laugh. 'Captain Tolescu,' he said, searching for equilibrium on the chair, 'Horea Tolescu. A friend and colleague of your brother-in-law, Tudor. We met last summer.' I nodded and lied that I remembered him very well. He was in Bucharest, he said, recently transferred to the Ministry of War. 'A promotion?' I asked. 'Yes, you could look at it as a promotion. Definitely a promotion.' In fact, he was just celebrating the transfer with a group of friends. Would I mind joining them? It would make him very happy, as he had great respect for both me and Mrs. Aroso. I declined. I told him that I was tired after a long day of work. I also told him that I was closing in on solving a very important mathematical problem. 'I would be bad company. I'm too wrapped up in it. As you can see,' and I waved my hand over the piece of paper in front of me, 'I can't let go even as I eat. I am a few feet from striking gold. Can't possibly think or talk about anything else.' I carried on like this for a while. Why? Why was I bothering to say all this to an army captain I hardly knew, who was quite tipsy, and who looked at me in bemusement? 'How is Mrs. Aroso?' he asked. 'I saw her several weeks ago at Ulmata.' I told him I was supposed to join her there, that this important problem had kept me in Bucharest for a while, but that I'd join her as soon as I could. He got up, with some difficulty. It was clear he was searching for the right words. It turned out it wasn't only the wine that kept him wondering how to say what he wanted to say, but also the delicate nature of the message. 'Yes, I'm sure, Professor, that you'll end up finding whatever you are looking for. In the end, we all do,

sooner or later. But can't it wait a bit? What's the hurry? What's a week
or two, what's a month or two? Would the world be any different if the
square root had been discovered a few months later? While in our life, a
week or two – what am I saying? – a few days, can change a lot. If I were
you, I'd drop everything and join Mrs. Aroso at Ulmata immediately.
When I last saw her, she was much too amused by the company. Much
too amused. It's not a good sign, without her husband around. I only
want to help.' He gave me a salute, shrugged, and returned to his friends.
After a few seconds of silence, there was renewed laughter at his table.
It was only then that I understood the meaning of his words. I think I
turned red. I expected his guests to turn around and look at me. But it
didn't happen, and slowly I calmed down. They were probably laughing
at something completely different.

"That night, I sent a telegraph to Ulmata. I told Mitzi I'd be
arriving the very next day. I took the train the next morning. At Campina, I
switched to a local train, which seemed to stop everywhere for no reason.
I swore out loud in exasperation, and an old man in my compartment
nodded with approval. 'It stops at every tree, like a dog pissing.' The train
stopped for half a minute some seven kilometres from Ulmata. There
was a dirt road, with level-crossing gates on each side. There was no
station, only the gatekeeper's house. It was a tiny house with no sign on
it, and a small garden enclosed by a short white-painted fence. They had
sent a horse cart for me from Ulmata. The driver was chatting with the
gatekeeper's wife, while two little girls were looking at the horse.

"We arrived in the early afternoon, covered with dust. It had not
rained in a while. I found Mitzi in bed, not speaking, and everybody
around quite concerned. She had fallen off her horse that morning.
There was a young doctor among the many guests, and he took me aside.
'Val Rimnic,' he said. 'I am a doctor. She has suffered a concussion. She
has to rest and, especially, not move. I wouldn't be too concerned right
now. These things happen, and ninety-nine times out of a hundred there
is a full recovery within a day or two. You have time to become concerned
if she does not fully recover in a few days. Then we would have to take
her to a hospital.' That evening, she did not recognize me, or anybody, for
that matter, but the next morning she felt better. Three days later, against
the advice of Dr. Rimnic, she was back in the saddle.

"Once she recovered from her fall, Mitzi seemed happy to see me. There were the usual army officers around, five or six of them, including one of Lavinia's brothers-in-law. It was no wonder, then, that at Ulmata, riding seemed a regular cavalry manoeuvre. I did not have any interest in horses. I saw neither Ovid nor Tudor around. Ovid had left several days before my arrival, Mitzi told me. There were a few other young men and women, besides Dr. Rimnic, none of whom seemed to have definite plans for their lives. The army officers all looked alike to me. In the evening, they dressed in their fancy uniforms and were quite formal before the booze got the better of them. Then, they became loud, quarrelsome, and ready to chase skirts with absolute effrontery. They did not know what to make of me, and, since my Romanian had remained somewhat trying, they ignored me. I tried to figure out who was after Mitzi, but I couldn't. My mind remained half-tuned to the mathematical problem I was wrestling with. During the day, there were long riding treks in which just about everybody participated. I never went along, but I sometimes met them at some pre-arranged point midday. I would be taken there in the horse cart, loaded with food and drinks. Mitzi's mother drove it one day. She was an odd woman, with sudden volleys of words, but quiet most of the time. She was busy with running Ulmata and with the unending cohort of guests. She rarely left the place, even during winter. She was the only one who had genuinely tried to find out what kept me so busy. What would keep me away, what would generate such commitment? I did my best to explain, sitting beside her in the horse cart that day, although I knew it was useless. She said nothing after I finished my convoluted and ridiculous justification. She looked briefly at me and shook her head. The air was sweet and hot at noon. The mountains seemed very close. One or two peaks had tiny snow-caps, like pointed white yarmulkes. They conveyed timeless wisdom. They watched me and told me that, undoubtedly, I was a fool.

"Mitzi seemed happy. She laughed a lot and tried to get me involved. But it was obvious that my presence hindered the general merriment and that she knew I felt uneasy and restless. I still could not figure out who it was that Tolescu had meant. Was he not there? After a while, I gave up and assumed that he had been talking nonsense. I left after ten days. Mizti was to join me at the end of July and we would drive, with Lavinia and whoever was free, to the Black Sea for two weeks.

"I went back eager to return to my mathematics, but apprehensive. I began to fear that we were less compatible than I thought, that may be George Lovinescu had been right, for the wrong reasons, to oppose our marriage.

"I did not go to the Black Sea. Ovid went with Mitzi and Lavinia. Ovid was working in a bank, but it seemed that he could take off whenever he wanted. Tudor was to join them later. I promised I'd join them in mid-August. Ovid, when I told him this, pointed to my head and made his usual homage to my genius, but it was obvious that he considered my decision strange. So did Lavinia, who announced that she was convinced I was less smart than everybody said, and that, anyway, whatever smarts I had were obsessive and very limited. Mitzi shrugged and kissed me on the cheek.

"One year later, in the fall of 1934, Mitzi told me she was leaving me. We had come back from Ulmata at the end of August. She had spent the whole summer there, and I had joined her for the last two weeks of August. It was in the evening, and I was preparing a lecture for the next day, in that very room, right there, when she came in dressed to go out and announced quietly that she was going to leave me. For the last month or two I had been floating on a sea of happiness mixed with some wonder and a tinge of doubt. I had finally resolved the problem I had struggled with for two and a half years, but the result had been somewhat startling, and I was a little afraid I had made a mistake. In spite of the doubts, I had a feeling of extraordinary achievement. I already saw my name being mentioned with the best of them, Poincare, Hilbert, Klein, Peano … I had told Mitzi several days earlier about the wonderful future awaiting me, and she had seemed genuinely happy for me. For us, I thought. When she came into my room to give me this news, she had a small suitcase with her. She had already called a cab, she said. 'It's better for both of us. I would end up hating you, and I don't want that. I'll send for more of my things later.' I begged her to stay. I told her that now I had finished this important work, we would have more time together. I told her I loved her. I told her that things would be different. 'I know you love me, Asuero,' she said. 'I know you mean it, but I doubt that things would be different in the future.' 'I'll wait for you,' I pleaded. 'When you're ready, please come back.' She laughed and kissed me on the cheek. 'Maybe if we had met later, when we were older, we would have had a better chance.' And she left."

Aroso's last few sentences were whispered. They sat in silence for a minute or two.

"What time is it?" he asked.

Alexandra looked at her wristwatch – it was a few minutes before eleven. The regular streetcar runs ended at midnight. The night runs came at hourly intervals. "What happened next?"

"She was gone almost two years to the day. She came back in September of 1936 and stayed with me for seven or eight months. Left again after we had a horrible fight, the only time I ever screamed at her. Came back after five months, in February or March of 1937. Stayed for slightly more than a year and left again. She came back in January 1941 and stayed for good."

It was quickly compressed by Aroso in a few words, yet there must have been so much drama, so much torment. All this while he was in his thirties, the best, most creative years one had.

"You've not told me anything about the big mathematical problem you solved," she said.

He laughed and waved his hands as if to say what was the point, and then his laugh turned into a series of dry coughs. When he recovered, he said, "Oh, dear," before continuing, barely audibly, "Have you made up your mind?"

"My mind?" she asked, startled.

"Yes. Have you reached a decision?"

"No, not yet," she said softly. "I told Charles the last time I saw him that, yes, I'll defect in Rome, at the congress early next year, but I'm having second thoughts. I don't know. I just don't know what to do."

"So Charles doesn't know yet that you're reconsidering."

"No. Though I did warn him I could change my mind. In a couple of weeks, he'll be here for a few days. There's a small gathering in Vienna in November, just a short two-day session, and Charles and I have a paper there. Charles told me to ask for permission to travel to Vienna. He thought it would be a good idea to test the system – give them an opportunity to say no. It would make them feel better, powerful, according to him. Maybe get it out of their system. I don't see how he's suddenly so knowledgeable. I didn't do it, though."

Aroso remained quiet for a while, then he got up and disappeared into the house. When he came back, after a long time, he was carrying a large faded blue envelope. "Have a look inside while I make some coffee."

The envelope was not sealed. She took out forty or so yellowish sheets of paper, covered on both sides with words and mathematical symbols. The writing was very careful, small and orderly, in violet ink. It was in German. She saw David Hilbert's name on the first page. The mathematical symbolism was only vaguely familiar (was it obsolete?). She recognized the letter "aleph", and this symbol, of the cardinality of infinite sets, shed a small light on the topic. She looked for Cantor's name, and there it was, several times, Georg Cantor. But otherwise she couldn't make much of the content of the work – her German was too weak, and the light from the oil lamp was poor. There were hardly any corrections, so it must have been a carefully transcribed copy, probably made from a working copy already in good shape. On the first page, at the very top, there was a date, December 28, 1934. She put the sheets carefully back in the envelope.

"What is it?" she asked, pointing to the envelope, when Aroso came back with a coffeepot and two small cups. He poured the coffee, and she took a sip. It was hot, lip burning, and bitter.

"I'm afraid we've run out of sugar. It will keep us awake, though. It's a double jolt to our system, both the bitter taste and the caffeine." From the breast pocket of his shirt, he fished out the small remnants of a cigar carefully wrapped in cellophane. He unwrapped it, releasing an awful stench, and lit it with a shaky hand. He was delaying his answer with the skill of a veteran actor who knew that the audience was holding its breath. "What you see here, Alexandra, is the proof of the consistency of Cantor's continuum hypothesis. I even went as far as to conjecture the independence of the continuum hypothesis. I did not prove it, but I sketched the path of a potential proof, albeit lengthy and arduous. Done by me, Asuero Aroso, between 1931 and 1934, six years before Godel published his famous findings, and thirty years before Paul Cohen's independence proof." He did not say any more. He knew he did not have to. He was looking intently at her, though, with mildly amused eyes, proud of the stunned silence that his words had caused.

She knew enough about the topic to be stunned. It wasn't an area of mathematics Alexandra was familiar with, but she was aware of some of the history around it. Alexandra liked to wonder about the strange realm of infinite sets, and she and Leonard had talked about it many times during the Tuesday dinners, before Emil had drunk enough to dominate the conversation. Georg Cantor was the one who, almost a century earlier, had brought about the transformation of the infinite, the infinitely large that is, from a useful name, hiding uncharted territory, into a mathematical entity which could be characterized and, in a relative way, measured. He had showed that there was more than one kind of infinitely large set, hence more than one kind of infinity. Cantor had assigned the symbol $\aleph_0$ to the size of the infinite set of natural numbers, and reserved $\aleph_1$, $\aleph_2$, $\aleph_3$, and so forth, to denote the size of infinite sets with increasingly higher number of elements. He called these $\aleph$ numbers, quite appropriately, transfinite; that is, above or beyond infinite. Because a cardinal number expressed size, as opposed to order, the transfinite numbers were also called the cardinal numbers, or the cardinality, of the respective infinite sets. Cantor proved that there were as many even natural numbers as there were natural numbers. He proved that there were as many integer numbers (positive and negative) or rational numbers as there were natural numbers. To his surprise, he proved that there were as many rational numbers as there were natural numbers. The size of all these sets was the same, $\aleph_0$. They had the same cardinality. He called these sets numerable, because they could be numbered along – or with – the natural numbers. To these findings, he soon added more startling ones. First, he showed that there were more real numbers than natural ones. This was to be expected. He also showed that there were as many real numbers between 0 and 1 as between −10,000 and +1,000,000, or any interval however large. Even more startling, he proved that there were as many real numbers on a line as on a plane or a volume.

Real numbers were also called the "continuum." Cantor called the size of the set of real numbers, or the continuum, c. The small letter c. Not an $\aleph$. Not yet. It was a temporary, interim, notation, because Cantor was not sure whether c was $\aleph_1$ or $\aleph_2$ or $\aleph_3$, or even higher. He thought he could find an answer to this question rather quickly, but it proved harder than he expected. Meanwhile, he continued his work. The algebra of transfinite numbers was unusual also. $\aleph_0 \times \aleph_0$, for example, was $\aleph_0$ again. He also proved that $2^{\aleph_0} = c$, a theorem of such arcane beauty that it left Alexandra breathless. But however hard he tried, Cantor could not find the place of c in the sequence of increasing $\aleph$ transfinite numbers. He eventually conjectured that $\aleph_1 = c$; in other words, there were no other transfinite numbers between $\aleph_0$ and c. This conjecture of Cantor's became known as the continuum hypothesis. Cantor's astonishing results and the new mathematics of infinities, by themselves, would have made this problem famous. But there was one more development that added to the fame of this problem. In 1900, in his invited address to the International Congress of Mathematicians, in Paris, David Hilbert listed a set of twenty-three mathematical problems whose resolution, he claimed, would significantly extend the boundaries of mathematical knowledge. And first among the listed problems, and thus considered by some as the number one mathematical problem of the time, was the continuum hypothesis, or, as Hilbert called it in his address, "Cantor's problem of the cardinal number of the continuum." There was more to this story. An answer, but not the final answer, to the cardinality of the continuum was given in 1940, by the Czech-German mathematician Kurt Godel. Godel was, at the time of his discovery, at the Institute of Advanced Studies in Princeton. He had left Europe because he was going to be conscripted into the German army, and after the war, like many others, he chose to stay in America. Godel showed that, taken as a postulate, the continuum hypothesis was consistent with the other postulates of the set theory; that is, it did not lead to any contradictions. The final statement on the cardinality of the continuum was made in 1963 by Paul Cohen, a young mathematician at Stanford University. Cohen's findings were unexpected (although now, it turns out, they were unexpected to all but Asuero Aroso). It was not possible to prove or disprove the continuum hypothesis. Either position, taken as axioms, led to consistent, non-contradictory theories of infinite sets. Just as Euclid's statement in two-dimensional geometry about lines through a point parallel with another line eventually led to several kinds of geometry, the continuum hypothesis led to more than one theory of infinite sets. The

Cantorian set theory accepted the validity of the continuum hypothesis, while the non-Cantorian set theory rejected it. Cohen was awarded the Fields Medal for his discovery four years later, at the International Congress of Mathematicians in Moscow. In fact, Aroso had been there, in Moscow, at the congress.

Lacking words, Alexandra whistled softly. "Why Godel, then? Why is the credit given to him?" she asked.

Aroso puffed several times from his foul cigar stub. Then he decided it needed another match. Finally, he said, "I never published this. Never sent it to a journal."

"What?"

"Never submitted it. In fact, you are the only person I've ever shown this to."

What was he saying? She looked at Aroso, or what she could see of him in the weak light of the oil lamp. He sat contemplating the tip of his malodorous cigar, quietly, as if he had just told her he'd neglected to return a library book due a week earlier.

"I don't understand. Why? Surely it was not because of modesty. Please, don't tell me you despise worldly acclaim." She'd forgotten herself and was almost screaming at him.

He shrugged, "It's late, Alexandra."

"You have to tell me."

He remained silent for a long time, and she thought she had overstepped a boundary. Then he finally answered, "I am not sure that the explanation is simple. To start with, I was not sure, myself, of my results. I had doubts, fears of being ridiculed. It was the first time since I was seventeen and decided to be a mathematician that I doubted myself. It may be that losing Mitzi had not added to my self-esteem. Several times I drafted letters to Bernays in Switzerland, and every time I destroyed them. First, it was the fear of being laughed at, yes. But then, after a while, a silly fear of being robbed also. Look at it from my point of view. Buried in an obscure city, at a second rate university, with a name barely known several years earlier and quickly forgotten since, I would be unable to stop Bernays, or others with whom he would talk about my findings, from presenting my work as their own. I know, I know, it sounds silly – this was me many years ago. And it was not just the resolution of the continuum hypothesis. To do it, I had to follow a barely trodden path. There were many new intermediate results, and a somewhat different way of looking at problems dealing with the foundations of mathematics. I think the fear of being ridiculed slowly transformed itself into a paranoiac fear of being outmanoeuvred by my cannier colleagues in the more established universities. So, I gave myself five years. It wasn't that crazy, Alexandra. The problem had not been solved in sixty years (since Cantor first posed it) – the likelihood of it being solved soon was small. I told myself that every year during these five years I would continue to look at it and see if there were any flaws. I told myself that I would publish the results as soon as I felt certain about them. And that at the end of the five years I would publish them even if my fears had not subsided."

He stopped and yawned again. Alexandra looked at her watch. It was close to one o'clock. He's an old man, she thought, and this is not adding to his strength.

"I can't keep my eyes open, my dear. I've got to make this brief. In 1939, of course, the war started. I thought again of sending the paper to Bernays. I even had a new letter written – you'll find it, there, in the envelope. But in the end I did not send it. The war and all its fears and worries had taken over. You would agree that, viewed that way, the continuum hypothesis is a somewhat irrelevant topic. In 1940 Godel published his results. I did not know about it. It was only in 1945, at the end of the war, that I found out about his findings, which mirrored mine exactly, although the path he followed was somewhat different."

"You were in Moscow, I think."

"In Moscow?"

"At the congress, in 1967."

"Ah, yes."

"And?"

"Weren't you there?"

"No, Ada was sick and I stayed home with her."

He sighed. "Are you asking me what I felt, when Paul Cohen was basking in all the adulation and glory for his magnificent completion of the road opened by Godel, with Godel there, sharing it all with young Cohen?"

"Yes."

He stood up. "No more," he said. "I can't do this at my age. I hope this is not just a story for you, but a parable from which to learn. It's the only reason this silly story is not dying with me. Anyway … We'll get back to this, but now I'm too tired. There is so much more to say. Maybe …"

He flicked his hands in a hopeless gesture, shrugged, and then patted the sides of her shoulders with his hands. A hybrid between a polite send-off and a hug.

"It's very late, you know. Wouldn't you rather sleep here? We could set up a bed for you."

"I'll be all right. Don't worry."

He arranged the coffeepot and cups on the tray. He put the lamp on the tray also, and started walking carefully with it toward the house. The large blue envelope containing his manuscript and the letter to Bernays was left on the table. There was light enough, from the stars and the moon and from the street lights, to see it clearly.

"I'm taking the envelope with me," she said.

Aroso kept walking, as if he hadn't heard.

"I'm taking the envelope with me." This time she shouted. She didn't want there to be any misunderstanding.

Aroso was close to the door. He did not say anything. He held the tray with one hand against his body, ready to open the door with the other. Without turning, he raised his free hand, a salute and a mute acknowledgement of her message. He opened the door and went inside.

Chapter 12
September 1976 - February 1977

In retrospect, it was a terrible idea, and she should have listened to her first instinct. The day before had been Ada's eleventh birthday, and as usual they had many of her friends over. Too many. Alexandra had queued up for butter, ham, some cheese. She was lucky to get a few oranges. She made a cake, and she made sandwiches – against Emil's advice that there was no point in preparing them, since they'd all end up on the floor. He was right. Not just the on the floor, but the walls, too. She made the mistake of serving the sandwiches in the living room, and now there were several greasy marks everywhere. Three adults, and still the children were hard to control.

Ada, she feared, had been the main culprit. She ordered everybody around. She was the one who started the food fight. She was excited, of course, but she was almost uncontrollable. Emil had to shake her and scream at her before she finally settled down. Alexandra was becoming convinced that this was not just a phase, that Ada was a difficult child. She was not doing well at all in school. When she was with Emil and Alexandra, she was uncommunicative and defiant. When she was around other children, she was wild and disruptive and overbearing.

No, the birthday party had not been pleasant. She was embarrassed to let Charles see such behaviour. He'd been in Bucharest

– well, still was, leaving in a few hours – for a three-day working visit. They continued to work very well together, thanks to Charles, since she was a bundle of nerves and anxiety. As usual, they met in her office at the university and took long walks in the Cismigiu Garden. The evening of Ada's birthday was his last, and he wanted to spend it with Alexandra. She told him it wasn't possible, that it was Ada's birthday, and then, seeing his miserable face and without thinking, she had invited him to join them. His gift to Ada had been a lovely pleated skirt and matching blouse, which he must have brought with him. She had probably told him, at some point, about Ada's birthday, and he had remembered it. Ada, as she could have guessed, paid scant attention to the beautiful clothes brought by Charles. Emil, on the other hand, had a coarse reaction. "Ah, a gift from the rich West. Corrupting us with their gold, is he?" He made the remark in Romanian, and Charles didn't understand it, but it was unpleasant anyway, and Ada heard him. In fact, Alexandra was sure his remark was meant as much for Ada as for her.

Emil was becoming more impossible than ever. He was incensed when he heard that she had invited Charles to Ada's birthday party. It was the first time that he asked her outright if she was having an affair with Charles. He had made allusions before, in a half-joking, half-serious way, testing the water before plunging.

They were having arguments almost daily. The latest was about her spending a few hours, here and there, with Aroso, trying to get him out of his devouring loneliness. It was absolute lunacy; he had never minded Aroso before. She got Aroso to come for dinner at their place, as a compromise. It didn't work out. Emil quickly got bored with their mathematical chatter and gossip about the department – Aroso was always curious to hear the latest gossip – though they both made an effort on this occasion, for Emil's sake, to keep it to a minimum. Emil said to her afterwards that he had not liked the way Aroso had been looking at him throughout the evening. He felt Aroso was mocking him. And he had another odd accusation: the only reason she was nice to Aroso was because he was Jewish. And Jews, it was well known, had to help each other. He pointed out to her that there were many old people in Bucharest and – thank God – most of them were not Jews. Why not be nice to them? She didn't argue, of course. There would have been no point.

She caught herself trying to imagine her future life. She kept a map of the world in a desk drawer, and she often peeked at the large purple patch on the North American continent. It didn't tell her much. She wasn't that surprised that she couldn't imagine Canada's geography – Charles had told her not to try, since the country was too large and its landscapes too varied – or her future life with Charles and her relationship with his family. She couldn't even picture taking a walk with Monica and Matt, her little nephew she had never seen. She wondered whether this inability of hers was a grim premonition, and she ended her letters to Leonard pleading with him to give her a better sense of his life with Monica and their child, send photos, relieve her nagging feeling that all was not well between her brother and his wife.

Towards the end of September she spent a whole afternoon with Aroso. It was a sunny day, and she managed to get him out of the house. He asked about Leonard, which was rare. "How is the smart brother? A lousy mathematician, but a smart boy."

Aroso was declining. He was frail, thinner than ever, bent. He tired quickly and needed many stops. His hands were shaking. His biggest trouble was buttons, he said. He hated buttons.

To Alexandra, it was obvious that he had given up. She had to drag him outside. Once out, he enjoyed it, and he was, as always, excellent company. "If we are going somewhere," he said, "let's go to the park. The big park." They took a cab to Aviators' Square and then walked towards Herastrau Park. The rosebushes were still in flower, and he bent often, awkwardly, to smell them. "I'd like to fill in my lungs with their fragrance and then hold my breath. Wouldn't be a bad way to go, if one could do it." He made jokes of his morbid thoughts, laughing whenever he uttered them, but there was no doubt that death preoccupied him. "It's time for me to go," he kept saying. "I've lived well past the average age of a law-abiding Romanian male. Done my duty. Mitzi is gone. Mathematics – well my mind is not there anymore."

She was not sure what he meant by that. He could still astonish her with the clarity and the scope of his thoughts. Only earlier that month, when Charles had been in the city, she and Charles had visited him and they had talked shop. They talked about the Riemann Zeta function, and about a few of their ideas in analytic number theory. He told them that he found their discussions about mathematics very pleasant, stimulating. "But the thrill, the curiosity, the impatience, have all gone. Math is still with me, but not with the same intensity. Like a shallow river, with clear waters. Beautiful to look at, to admire, from the bank. If somebody held my hand, I'd wet my feet. But I have no desire to wade in on my own."

During their visit, Aroso told her, again, and quite forcefully, to get out, to leave the country, the first time he did this in Charles's presence. They were sitting in the courtyard, under the trellis, with the vine leafs beginning to turn colour, and Alexandra could see hints of purple on some of the grapes. It was the early afternoon, and the heat of the previous days had subsided. Jana brought out coffee, and Charles, a lover of the Turkish method of preparation, was making appreciative sounds. It was after he finished his coffee and had turned his cup upside down that Charles told them about the breakthrough in the four-colour map conjecture. In America, at the University of Illinois, two professors had found a proof of it. He had just learned about this before he flew to Bucharest.

"It's a theorem now, not a conjecture anymore – if the proof holds up under peer scrutiny. I've heard classes were cut short and there was much rejoicing when the word about the breakthrough got around, but there was less enthusiasm later when it was learned that computers were used. About a thousand hours of computing on three machines. Appen and Haken – the two researchers – have shown that all possible map variations on a plane can be reduced to some fifteen hundred cases. Then they used computers to check each of them – in other words, to try to paint them with only four colours. The check was positive, and thus the theorem was demonstrated. Of course, the checking could have been done by hand – that is, by mathematicians – but it was simply too time-consuming to check each individual case this way, so they used computers. People are unhappy, though. It's a controversial proof. No, unhappy is not the word – people are uncomfortable. Some say the computer might have goofed. Others that the proof, if true, provides no insights. There is talk about lack of elegance and beauty. A brute-force proof, getting at it with a two-by-four. Paul Erdos had declared it not from the Book – not from God's Book."

"Is it that, though," Aroso said, after they were quiet for a while, "or is it uneasiness that computers are beginning to play a larger and larger role in this paper-and-pencil-only profession of ours? After all, we accept large primes generated or checked by computers. They do Marsenne prime number searches, from what I understand, and nobody seems to worry that much about computers making a mistake. We resolve equations with computers, and we accept the result without much worry. We build airplanes and fly in them. No, it's an end of an era – even if, from what I gather, it was in the drudge aspects of the proof that computers were used and not directly in the proof itself. It has been a matter of pride for all of us, this romantic view that we can do math anywhere, with only pencil and paper. It's a bittersweet success."

Aroso looked at both his guests in turn, before adding, as if Alexandra was not there, "Alexandra's thesis was on chromatic numbers. I remember the arguments we had, and how I tried to have her switch to another topic. Hmm ... No, the romance is over. Unless things have suddenly changed – Alexandra would tell me if they had – there isn't much computing power available to mathematicians here. Finding zeros for the Riemann Zeta function is a job for a computer if there ever was one. The whole Riemann problem may be solvable only with the aid of computers. You need proper tools nowadays, more and more. Alexandra should do math where these tools are available. The best mathematical minds have always clustered wherever the best tools and conditions are made available. Not that she necessarily would use these new tools; she's quite wonderful with a pencil and paper, but she needs to be where advances are made, to dip into the creative energy of the group and to exchange ideas."

Although Alexandra was not looking at Charles, she felt that, towards the end of Aroso's little monologue, he was staring at her.

"I'm not sure mathematics nowadays is a solitary pursuit anymore," Aroso said, shaking his head. "Another romantic myth exploded. Maybe it never was."

For a while they rested on a bench, pleased to have found one in the shade. Aroso was wearing a suit. It was quite warm for the end of September, but he refused to take his jacket off. He wasn't too warm, he said. Past a certain age, he claimed, there was no such thing as too warm. They made their way slowly to the restaurant overlooking the lake to have something to eat. It was four o'clock, and only a few tables were taken. They had cucumber salad and cheese and bread. They drank spritzers and enjoyed the silence of the warm afternoon and the blue-green lake and the shadowy trees. There were a few lazy boats near the island.

A couple walked past them and sat down three or four tables away from theirs. The man was short – a little, lithe man. She was petite too, and quite animated, although Alexandra couldn't hear exactly what she was carrying on about. The couple ordered a full meal, but it was he who ate most of it, as she was busy haranguing him. Alexandra could make out the question "Why?" uttered several times, probably marking the end of each charge. The short man was facing away from them, but it was obvious he wasn't saying much. He shrugged a lot and continued eating.

Aroso nudged his head towards their table. "It's the main question, though, isn't it? Why do we do the things we do? She's asking him the impossible question. He has enough sense to eat and not try answering."

"The quiet man," Aroso went on, "looks exactly like Courant." The man had glasses and short hair brushed back.

"The mathematician?"

"I saw the Courants at a restaurant once, also sitting several tables away, and, like this couple here, Courant's wife was very animated while he was quiet and nodding. It was not easy to keep Courant quiet, by the way."

"Richard Courant, who had asked you stay in Gottingen as his assistant and you had refused. I can't get over that decision of yours."

He turned and smiled at her. "Well, my dear, it wasn't as silly as it sounds now. Leaving aside my feelings for Mitzi, Courant wasn't sure whether he could secure an official position at the Institute or if he had to fund me as a personal assistant. Whichever way, the pay was quite small, a paltry amount in fact. Well, yes, Courant wanted me to stay in Gottingen, he had told me so. But he also told me – he was a master of ambiguous statements – that there was an opinion that there were already too many Jews at Gottingen, in the math and sciences anyway, and that he was under pressure, especially as a Jew, to counter this opinion. What do you want, my dear, it was 1930 or 1931. Hitler was only a couple of years away. So, with Mitzi and all these, my decision to decline Courant's ambiguous offer was not that silly. Besides, I had this romantic, no, not romantic, arrogant, yes, very arrogant notion that I could do good math, brilliant math, math that would startle the world, anywhere – at the foothills of the Himalayas or in a forest in Madagascar.

He stopped and looked at her, and then added, and she was sure it was for her benefit, "I was wrong, of course."

When they walked back from the restaurant, Aroso asked her to put her arm in his. "It makes me more stable," he laughed. "Also, it feels good to walk arm in arm with a beautiful woman. At my age, I'm allowed to say silly things. Mitzi and I often took long walks like this, arm in arm, especially in our first years. And even later, before she got sick. Whenever she came back to me, she'd appear with no warning – she always kept her key and I never changed the locks – her coat and luggage near the door, ready to go again in case I told her I didn't want her back. She'd look at me, smile, and softly say the same first words every time: 'Should we go out for a long walk?' She liked to walk the streets of Bucharest, look at houses and people. She preferred the quiet little streets. We'd often walk to Lavinia's house in the evening. Lavinia and Tudor lived on Rosetti Street, a big, beautiful house with many servants. It was always open house at their place. It took us almost an hour to get there. I'd stay for half an hour, an hour at most, then take a cab back home and do some work. Mitzi often stayed past midnight."

Alexandra asked him what they talked about during those long walks. The question came out sounding a little awkward, as if she were asking whether he and Mitzi had anything in common at all. He was somewhat surprised. "It was mainly Mitzi who talked. Oh, about everything and nothing. She was quite bright, you know, and often very amusing, especially when she talked about her family and friends. Gossip, a lot of gossip, of course. Who was sleeping with whom, the latest fights

and reconciliations. The latest plays. Ah, yes, the theatre. How could
I forget? Mitzi was a theatre-lover. We saw a lot of plays. She'd often
see the same play several times. For a while, she toyed with the idea of
getting into it, becoming an actress. She even took lessons, private lessons
from a friend of hers, an actress. She's still around, her former teacher, a
rabid Iron-Guard supporter in those days, now an admired Artist of the
People. Party member, of course. Yes, she took lessons for almost a year,
and then all of a sudden she gave it up. She said she realized she had no
talent, but I'm not sure that was the reason. Many of Mitzi's friends were
"in" the theatre, or around it. Mitzi was around it. She'd get involved in
a play, especially if her friends were involved, from the early stages of a
production, and she'd often help – practical things, you know, making
sure this or that happened, that the costumes were ready in time, that
actor X, known for his long nights, showed up at rehearsals on time
and was not too tired or drunk. Yes, she talked a lot about the theatre,
what her friends were doing, how she was helping, the latest gossip, what
actress had slept with what director or writer to get a shot at a good role.
She even read the plays of young, aspiring writers for various producers
and directors she knew, busy people who didn't have enough time. They
trusted her judgment ..."

Aroso slept in the cab on the trip back – mouth open, head askew
and bobbing with the jolts of the cab, his knees so sharply pointed they
seemed to be breaking through his trousers. When they got to his house,
he had great difficulty climbing out. He was very lucky, she thought, to
have Jana.

"You had a sister," Alexandra said. "Are you not in touch with
her?"

It took him a few moments to gather his thoughts. "My sister?
Long gone, my dear. Married a very religious man – chosen by our father,
of course. I barely knew him, it happened while I was in Gottingen. She
was appalled when she heard I was marrying outside the faith, and in
a church, and she had nothing more to do with me. I don't know if it
was she or her husband ... I didn't care much at the time. Such are the
brainless young. She had a daughter – she gave birth with great difficulty
– a year or two before I got married myself. The doctors advised her not
to have other children. She got pregnant again, much later, and she died

in childbirth. The child too. It would have been a boy – I heard it from one of my Dacosta cousins who I kept in touch with until the war."

He sighed and shrugged. "I probably have a niece, somewhere. Don't go away, I have something for you."

Back after a few minutes, he handed her a small brown-paper parcel. His notebooks, he said, his math notebooks. He had not looked at them in years. Some of the notes were in German, but less and less towards the end. He was certain she'd find some good ideas in them. She tried to talk him out of it, but he wouldn't listen. Giving her his notes made him feel better. "If you find you have no patience to decipher them, give them to your assistants. They'll extract whatever is worth extracting. Take them, my dear. Believe me, you'll find one or two useful things in these notes. Besides, it helps me clear out and close another drawer. An orderly departure, you understand."

Aroso's pneumonia returned a month later. He was bedridden for several weeks. He refused to go to the hospital, claiming that Jana would take better care of him at home. In the end, the antibiotics worked, but for a couple of weeks it was touch and go. Alexandra brought him flowers one evening. Aroso was emaciated, lying helplessly in the same bed Mitzi had occupied not many years earlier. Jana brought a vase, and Aroso watched Alexandra arrange the flowers. His breathing had an ominous whistle.

"Flowers? What kind? Can't see that well. I don't see any colours. Is it possible – grey flowers? Put them on the windowsill, please. I'll see the colours tomorrow morning, in the natural light. If I live that long."

Alexandra shook her head. "Don't talk like this, please."

"It's all right, dear. I just hope it won't be much of a struggle. I wonder if there's any interest in math up there. Not that I intend to do any – I don't want to chase Mitzi away again – but I can't stop wondering."

He paused to catch his breath, but his pale skin stretched in a smile.

"Do you think there is more than one heaven?" he asked.

"More than one?"

"I heard a lecture last year about the possibility, in fact the likelihood, of there being more than one universe. The 'multiverse,' the lecturer called it. Now, is there a common heaven, or does each universe have its own heaven? To put it in mathematical terms: Is God an invariant of the multiverse? And another query, closely related: Would the math of each universe be different? Is math an invariant of the multiverse? You want my opinion? I think the math of each universe is different. Otherwise, what would differentiate them?"

When he recovered, his doctor told him to spend at least a month in a sanatorium. It was somewhere in the mountains, he told her, his weak voice sounding very excited on the phone. Emil laughed when Alexandra told him about it. "Who's his doctor? They're going to kill him." She considered ringing him and telling him about Emil's warning, but thought better of it. He had sounded so eager to go. Aroso told Alexandra that he would call her when he got back. After the New Year she heard from others that he was back in the city. She rang him. He answered, and seemed glad to talk to her. But he wasn't feeling well, he told her. He tired very quickly. He said he'd call her back.

He didn't. She called again, several days later. This time, it was Jana who answered. The Professor was feeling very weak, couldn't come to the phone. When Alexandra asked whether she could visit him, Jana said he was seeing nobody.

He died in February.

There were fewer people at his funeral even than at Mitzi's. Nicolescu showed up, together with another former colleague. Danczay had disappeared, the others couldn't be bothered. Two of his former students were there, and somebody from the Soviet embassy, a cultural attaché of some sort, with a huge crown of flowers from the Steklov Institute in Moscow. She knew he had kept in touch to the very end with several Soviet mathematicians, probably the ones he had met in Gottingen in the twenties. For some reason he had hit it off with the Soviet visitors in Gottingen and had stayed in touch with them.

He was buried beside Mitzi. Jana found a rabbi who performed the service. A short, stocky man, with narrow eyes and a moustache that made him look like a disguised Tartar. The rabbi was in a hurry and kept looking at his watch. The day was sunny and windless, and a few mysterious snowflakes fell gently over them. There was nobody to say Kaddish with the rabbi and he sped through it. The cultural attaché seemed quite bewildered by the smallness of the gathering and the perfunctory service. As they walked away, Jana told Alexandra that Aroso had left all he had to her, to Jana, including the house. "There are gold coins in the garden," Alexandra said.

PART II
Montreal

Chapter 13
March 1977

The plane was half-empty and the flight attendants pampered them. Charles asked for champagne, to celebrate the start of their new life.

     Alexandra had listened to the first paper in one of the early morning sessions. In the almost deserted room, the speaker, a Swedish mathematician she knew of from papers he had published – and who turned out to be much younger than she had thought – joked that that was his usual luck: his turn always came early in the morning when everybody was asleep. At the end she had asked a question and nodded at the enthusiastic answer – although she didn't really follow it – and then she slipped out of the room and out of the hotel with only her purse hanging from her shoulder. She was wearing her olive-coloured dress with the dark green jacket that had seen better days and a scarf loosely thrown around her neck, but she felt chilly as she made her way slowly to the side of the hotel. "Just walk as if you were out for a leisurely stroll to refresh your mind after so much tiring mathematics," Charles had advised her with a stern, professional look on his face, and that made her laugh. She thought of her raincoat left in the hotel room with all her luggage. Once she turned the corner, she stopped the first available cab that passed, said "Fiumicino," and got in without daring to look whether she had been followed. Not likely, anyway. After the lavish Italian food and quantities of good wine at the reception the previous evening, she had seen very few early risers that morning. During the reception she had kept looking at Nicolescu, who was at a table nearby, and the two mathematicians from Iasi, further away to her right, one of them quite unknown to her, and they all seemed to partake fully and merrily in the feast.

She prayed throughout the drive that Charles would be at the airport as agreed, waiting for her at the entrance to the departures hall. The trip turned out to be unexpectedly long, or so it seemed to her. If Charles wasn't there, she wouldn't have enough money to pay for the cab. But he was there. Not registered at the congress, he had flown in the evening before and had checked in at a hotel near the airport. They had not seen each other since they made their plans, in January, during what they hoped would be their last walk in the Cismigiu Garden for a very long time. And they had agreed that they would not call each other unless something happened that required a change of plans.

Charles's suit was rumpled, his tie loose (eventually placed in his pocket), and he seemed to have lost weight. A whiff of alcohol reached her when they furtively embraced once inside the terminal. He confessed that he had had a few drinks overnight. "I was afraid that you'd change your mind at the last minute. I couldn't sleep. It's a relief to see you."

The flight attendant, a young, oversized, good-looking woman, leaned towards them and asked if they wanted more champagne. "Newlyweds?" she smiled. "Did I hear something about celebrating the start of a life together?"

"All this champagne is putting me to sleep," Charles said. "But pour away, why not."

The flight was very smooth. Were it not for the drone of the engines, she would have had no clue of the speed at which they were being whisked away from Rome. With this flight, her decision became irreversible, unless the plane suddenly looped back to Rome. It wasn't just a flight to another country or continent, it was more like a spaceship hurtling to a new world from where there could be no return. Her agony of indecision was over, and as a result, or maybe because the tense morning had tired her out, she felt relieved. It was a relief without illusions and of short duration – she knew it would soon be replaced with the agony of waiting for Ada. And, worst of all, if things did not work out, the agony over the choice she had made.

She tried again to imagine her future – to contemplate this parallel life, much as Aroso had done when he talked to her about his decision – and again, as many times before, nothing came of it. "If you don't think about the future, you cannot have one." Where had she read this? What was it, this refusal of her mind to venture beyond a reunion with Leonard? Somehow, the paths Aroso might have taken were easier to imagine. His marriage with Mitzi had been childless – that was a simplifying factor.

What she had not tried, or not tried as thoroughly as she might, was an analysis of her decision. Why had she done this? Was it the unbearable life with Emil? Her love – if that's what it was – for Charles? Or her fear of losing Charles? (Were they the same thing?) Had she simply succumbed to the better prospects in the West for her, as a mathematician? And to the lure of an easier, much easier, life? Or was it the realization that she had lost the battle with Emil for Ada's heart, and that her only chance back to Ada was the shock of her departure and her reappearance in a completely new light?

She felt the slow onset of tears. Please, not again. What she should have done was calculate the odds that she wouldn't be able to bring out Ada. But whenever she had reached this logical step, her mind had refused to go any further. It was futile, it was not possible to work out the odds. Her imagination retreated whenever there loomed the vaguest thought that the chances were too small. And she had convinced herself, by letting this happen, that she'd get Ada out no matter what. But now, in the plane carrying her away from Rome, from Ada, she knew that her less-than-honest analysis was a voluntary delusion.

She looked at Charles, who was nodding off. "The paramour, the knight she had eloped with, fell asleep soon after they began their journey," she whispered to him, but he didn't hear her. Turbulent air shook the plane for a few seconds, then the ride became smooth again. She said the rest to Charles silently. "But the horse knew the way and carried them along."

She looked up when she realized that someone was speaking to her. The flight attendant asked if she should stretch out her husband's seat. She understood what she was after only when Charles body became almost supine. Alexandra had questioned Charles's extravagant decision to get first class tickets – he had joked that he wanted to corrupt her – but now she realized he needed this more than she did. She hadn't slept much the night before either, but then she had always been able to get by with very little sleep. Poor, dear Charles, what had he got himself into? – well, not now, it had been seven years already.

She thought of Ada, and wondered whether she would ever understand her sudden disappearance. How terrible and brief the parting from her had been at the railway station – a hug and a few kisses, with Emil watching them. Not enough kisses, and a short-lived hug, transitory, fleeting, with almost no recollection, no feel. When she kissed Ada, Alexandra had buried her face in her daughter's slender neck and shoulder, avid to smell her, to retain her scent for a long time – and now it was gone, or almost gone. She should have kept on kissing her. She had come apart there at the station, while bending down and hugging Ada. That was when she began to cry. Did Emil guess that she wouldn't be back? When she was whispering to Ada, kissing her squirming face, "Remember, Mommy loves you, loves you very much," she had heard him sneer, "Yes, Ada, and keep those words with you. Keep them for a long time, those beautiful words. Mommy is clever with words. Words and numbers." She had the feeling Emil knew she wouldn't return. Could it be – was it wishful thinking? – that he wanted her out, so that later they, he and Ada, could re-join her wherever she ended up? But if that were the case, why hadn't he talked to her about it? Maybe he had guessed her plans only there, at the station.

She began to cry again. She had become so weepy in the last couple of years. A guilt-ridden sniveller. A good mother would not be flying with her lover to a far continent, leaving her daughter behind her. Obviously not a good wife, but that she could explain. A good daughter? Yes, she was (had been) a good daughter, and a good sister. And she had remained a good mathematician, too, to Lily's wonderment. Lily's affair with the geography teacher had become quite serious, and she didn't know what to do. "He has a wife who'd make his life miserable if he divorced," she had told Alexandra the last time they met, "a wife who threatened to throw boiling water all over me if she saw my face around her husband again. And he has two small children, one quite sick, and the doctors don't know what's wrong with him. Do I need all this? I don't know what to do, I can't sleep, I can't work. And my work is not like yours; after so many years of teaching the same crap I'm an automaton. But I can't work. I find myself addressing the class and not knowing what I'm supposed to be saying. Good Lord, Alexandra, how do you do it? With so much trouble around you – a lover, a sour marriage, a difficult daughter – how do you do it? How do you turn out one paper after another – and great papers at that?"

A faint noise came from her right – a delicate snoring from Charles. Did knights snore? She had never heard him snore before, but then they had rarely slept through the night together. The flight attendant leaned over Charles's sleeping body, startling her. "Are you all right, Madame?" She looked motherly. Alexandra realized it was her tears that had caught her attention.

"Ah, yes, I'm all right. Quite all right."

"Are you in pain? Is there anything I can do?"

"No, no, I'm fine. I just thought of somebody dear I lost recently. I do this easily. I'm a sobbing champion. I have endless reserves of tears."

This was embarrassing. She should pull herself together.

Charles opened his eyes, smiled at her and touched her arm. He straightened his chair and picked up the newspaper he had tucked in the seat pocket in front of him. After a few seconds, he began to shake his head. "Never a dull moment in the politics of your new country, my dear. A month ago, in the early hours of the morning, our premier (our provincial premier, that is), who had spent the evening at a friend's house, drove over a poor bastard lying in the street. No alcohol tests were performed on the premier after the accident, so the question of whether he was drunk or slightly inebriated would never be answered officially. And now – this is the latest surprise – now it turns out that his mistress was with him in the car."

"I knew I was going to the right country."

"As if he didn't have enough to keep him busy."

"Did you vote for him?"

"I didn't vote at all the last time; I was away. But he's too radical for me. The Parti Quebecois – his party – is after separation. 'Secession.' They want to take Quebec out of Canada."

"What for?"

"What for? Oh, dear, where do I start? There are many opinions about it. The simplest one is that, you know, the French, the English ... they don't get along that well. We – the French, that is – have a lot of stored up anger because of what we had lost and how we were treated ..."

"Can you? Can they?"

He shrugged. "Separate? Probably not – too messy – but one never knows."

"If they separate, would they close the borders?"

"Close the borders? What for? What do you mean?"

There was nothing to worry about, then, she thought. "Oh, never mind."

"My sister Gislaine is a separatist. A hardened one, in fact. And so is her husband, although he's much too busy with his practice to have much time for it. Gislaine and Hugue are 'into politics' and very well connected. They helped arrange for your sudden admission as an immigrant. They're very, very curious to meet you. Especially Gislaine. Her older daughter, Isabelle, doubts you exist. She told her mother she could not believe that boring Uncle Charles had charmed a married woman in exotic Romania and made her elope with him."

He looked up from his newspaper and added, "Alexandra dear, you're crying again."

"It's all this talk about separation," Alexandra said.

Gislaine taught French literature at the university, Charles had told Alexandra. He also told her that Gislaine and Hugue Lortie lived in Outremont, not far from his own apartment. It was why he had chosen that neighbourhood of Montreal when he separated from his former wife; Gislaine could keep an eye on his place whenever he was away. It was also convenient – close to the Université de Montreal. Alexandra found Outremont on the map, near Mont Royal and a winding street called Chemin de la Côte Ste Catherine. The Chemin de la Côte Ste Catherine, Alexandra read in the guidebook Charles had given her when they took their seats, was, in fact, a wide road "curving around at the feet of the mountain that was so defining of the island-city of Montreal." The guidebook called Outremont the French counterpart of the English-speaking Westmount neighbourhood, each on either side of the mountain, an allegorical illustration of the divide between the French and English. It also reported that the mysterious Iroquois village of Hochelaga, visited by Jacques Cartier in 1535 and later vanished without a trace, may have been in that very Outremont district. Jacques Cartier, Alexandra read, was sent by the French King François I to find gold and other riches, just as his lifelong enemy, Emperor Charles V, had done further south. Cartier travelled to Quebec three times and caused a sensation when he brought back to Europe the captured Iroquois chief Donnacona and his two sons.

To Alexandra, it all seemed unreal, almost as if, like a child in need of calming down, she'd been given a book of fantastic tales of voyages. Fearless explorers in the fifteen hundreds advancing up the St Lawrence River seeking open waters westward to the Indies; Mikmaq and Iroquois warriors; settlements that mysteriously disappeared; the city of Montreal that was built on an island, had a mountain in the middle of it, and was made up of villages with an implausible mixture of Indian, English, and French names.

"Gislaine de Hochelaga?" she asked Charles.

"I recommend Gislaine."

"My in-laws, Hugue and Gislaine Lortie de Hochelaga. I like the sound of it."

There were many names to remember, but by now, gradually putting together the stories she had heard from Charles, Alexandra had formed a good idea of his family landscape. The questions she asked Charles were mere clarifications, like minor touches added to a sketch already fully outlined. The Lortie children, to start with. Pierre, twenty-eight, a lawyer like his father, encouraged by Gislaine towards a political career. Isabelle, twenty-two, close to pursuing graduate studies – literature, what else. Anne-Marie, nineteen, a reluctant student.

"What's Isabelle like?"

"Lovely."

"And?"

"She was delightful as a child. The truth is, I don't really know what she's like now. She's hardly ever there. Whenever I visit my sister and I do happen to find her there, it's a quick peck – so good to see you, Uncle Charles – and out she goes. She doesn't find me that interesting."

"And Hugue? Hugue Lortie? Tell me about him."

"A lawyer."

"That's it?"

"I should have said a successful lawyer. Like all successful lawyers, he talks only about himself and his work. I exaggerate, of course."

"And Gislaine? What's Gislaine like?"

"Gislaine is intense, and very efficient. Very clever. Has no time for small talk."

Then there was Charles's younger sister, Lysiane (Lisette), living with somebody named Ray, of undetermined occupation, on an island on the West Coast. She had a child from a previous marriage – a girl, already married and settled in the United States.

It took two hours to process Alexandra at Dorval, in spite of the special treatment Charles was assured she was receiving. He applied relentless pressure and grumbled at all the declarations he had to sign, insisting, exasperated, that he had already done it. Alexandra's only annoyance was born from her desire to call Leonard. She had not dared phone him from Rome, not even from Fiumicino, although Charles had laughed at her fears.

With the formalities over, and after Alexandra had shaken hands with a tired woman immigration officer who told her "*Bienvenue au Canada*," they ran to the nearest public phone. It was already four in the afternoon. Charles dialled Leonard's number and handed her the receiver, saying it was unlikely they'd be home yet. He was right, there was no answer.

They took a cab from the airport. The day turned out to be sunny and surprisingly warm. It had snowed heavily two days earlier, the driver said. There was fresh snow everywhere, still hanging on the branches of the trees. It gave the streets of Outremont that afternoon the joyous air of a village transported from a children's book, its houses made of coloured sugar and cream, now melting away. The cab stopped in front of a very large red-brick corner house with limestone arches above the windows and above an imposing main entrance. Charles told the driver to go around the corner. There was a secondary entrance on the adjoining street, with its own number clumsily painted on by hand.

Charles paid the driver and, with a large key, opened the door. "This house," he said, "was built in the early nineteen hundreds for a wealthy man named Berthiaume Forchon – yes, 'Berthiaume,' a picturesque first name – who had made his money shipping goods along the St Lawrence River. It was built to his specifications. He didn't spend much time here – his wife and children did, though – because he found it too far from the river and the port of Montreal, where his business was. I've heard all this from the current owner, Mme Lamoureux, a lonely old widow and a grandniece – or maybe great-grandniece – of Berthiaume. She lives in the main part of the house. There were rumours of a mistress as well, or mistresses, and Berthiaume may have stayed away from the house in Outremont for that reason. Who knows? It makes for a good story. The house has had major surgery twice – the last time some ten years ago, when it was divided into two apartments."

Charles told Alexandra he had moved into his, smaller, apartment seven or eight years earlier, shortly after his divorce. There were two bedrooms and an office upstairs, and a dining room and a living room on the first floor. Also a large, modern kitchen. Climbing the wooden staircase, Alexandra listened to the soft creaks, and she found the sounds soothing and reassuring. The wainscoting and the wooden floor, dark and covered sparsely with a few Persian carpets, gave the apartment warmth. There were bookshelves and books everywhere, and furniture that looked expensive and fragile. It was clearly a home without children, with everything in its proper place. It had a feeling of graceful and thoughtful living.

"A beautiful apartment, with nobody living in it."

"No, no, I'm here several months of the year. Much more now, with you here, you'll see. Gislaine uses it when I'm not in Montreal and she needs quiet time away from the family. Less and less now, with the children gone or almost gone. She has a key, by the way. And now you."

"It's almost six. Let's call Leonard again. How do I do it?"

Gislaine looked very much like Charles – a thinner, smaller version of him, with the same curly, almost white, hair and the same round face. Her hair was cut short – "to keep control over it" – and there was a purposeful directness in everything she did and said.

"Finally!" she said to Alexandra, kissing her when they came in. "Poor Charles has been pining for you for so many years. My older daughter – Isabelle, she'll be here soon – didn't think you existed. Even pictures of you didn't convince her. 'So what?' she said. 'Anybody can take pictures of anybody.' You look better than the photos of you Charles brought, I have to say. I'm beginning to understand his perseverance. You're dazzling, my dear. *Eblouissante*. But your eyes are very red. A beauty with red eyes."

All the Lorties came, intrigued by the unexpected arrival, including Pierre, who had moved out years earlier, and Anne-Marie, who flew in from Quebec City, where she was studying. They didn't try to hide their guarded curiosity, but never asked her about Ada or Emil, and Alexandra understood quickly that Charles had coached them well and she didn't have to worry about weeping all of a sudden. They asked about Romania, about life under the Communist regime, pronounced with difficulty Ceausescu's name – practically the only thing they knew about her country. And why should they know more, Alexandra wondered. To her relief, the conversation soon shifted to René Lévesque and his latest mishap. They talked about Edgar Trottier, the homeless man struck by the premier's car, about Corinne Côté – his secretary and more – who was with him when it happened, about Yves Michaud, the friend and political sidekick in whose apartment the premier had spent the evening of the fatal drive. Alexandra learned that the premier had been separated from his wife for a while. Pierre said he'd heard from reliable sources that the premier would soon marry his secretary. Everybody seemed to agree that the press was making too much of the incident, especially the anglophone press, which was unwilling to let go of a juicy story.

Alexandra could follow most of the discussion and only lost

them when they spoke too quickly or slid into the intimate abbreviations and slang every family uses. Isabelle, who sat beside her at the dinner table, translated or explained whenever the information being exchanged became too local or idiomatic, and Charles, now and then, would warn them to stay within the more beaten paths of the language. "I need to learn this, Charles," Alexandra whispered to him. "It's good for me." But in spite of her efforts, her mind was slipping away, and she was glad not to be the centre of attention. She occasionally caught a probing stare – the same scrutiny Chief Donnacona must have attracted. No, no, that was an exaggeration, a poor comparison. She was more like – except with Charles, of course – a half-welcome intruder, like Elijah suddenly showing up at the Passover dinner. "What if he comes?" she remembered asking her father on one such evening. While he was alive, they had kept the tradition. It was a couple of years after the war, she must have been eight or nine, probably the first Seder in her family they had felt able to relax, and there were more people around the table than the other times, and more noise and laughter. Her father, in particular, had had many glasses of wine, and he had talked and laughed a lot. "What if he comes?" Alexandra had suddenly asked. "Who?" "Elijah, what if he comes?" "He'll have a glass with us," her father had said, puzzled. "Do we want him? Do we want him to show up?" she had asked. Her father's eyebrows had arched, a sign that he had not understood her, but she didn't persist, she did not explain to him that she feared Elijah would spoil everything, that they were quite happy the way they were, that there was no need for anybody else.

Gislaine probably saw that Alexandra's mind was elsewhere and asked about the arrangements she had made with the university. Alexandra shrugged and smiled and looked at Charles, who said that the terms were still being discussed. Very likely Alexandra would teach one graduate course and also lead one seminar on a topic of her choice. And, of course, there would be the graduate students she'd slowly acquire and have to supervise. "That's all?" Gislaine asked. "I'm green with envy. I never understood why our teaching load in the arts is so much heavier. What's there to discuss, Alexandra? Take it. It's a great offer."

"It's an all-right offer," Charles said. "Alexandra is very special, very much in demand. She could get an offer from a famous university in the States with hardly any teaching load. And here, they want her to teach an undergraduate class as well – for one year only – because two professors are going on sabbatical and they're a bit short. This is the last thing to settle. I'm trying to convince them that Alexandra should be allowed time to do research, that the university would get much more out of her that way."

It was only on Friday night that Leonard picked up the phone. It took him a while to realize who was at the other end. Still in English, he finally mumbled, "Alsa? It's you? Good God! Alexandra? I can't believe it." Then, switching to Romanian, "Where are you? Montreal? How come? When?"

Yes, she was in Montreal. She had been trying to get in touch with him since she'd flown in several days earlier from Rome. Then she told him about her decision not to return. She tried to keep it short – they'd have time later – but he kept interrupting her. Yes, he had heard right, she was not returning. She would be teaching at the Université de Montreal. Everything was settled. Charles Natraq had arranged it all. He'd done everything. He was with her now, in Montreal, helping her through the first few days, although he would be flying to Paris on Sunday evening since he had to lecture on Tuesday. She had applied for landed immigrant status. Charles had it all prepared in advance for her. She would, of course, ask Emil to join her, together with Ada. She realized that this could take time. She would buy their way out. She would be paid well, very well, by the university. Yes, she would have the money to get them out. Even if it took a lot of money, because she would be able to borrow.

"Alsa, where exactly are you?"

She gave him the address.

"Alsa, this is wonderful. I'm stunned. I'm ... Why didn't Charles let me know in advance about your decision? Was it on the spur of the moment? I'm coming right away. I'm off to the railway station right now. I'll take the train. I'm pretty sure there's an overnight sleeper. I'll see you early tomorrow. I'll stay over the weekend. You did the right thing, Alsa. Absolutely the right thing. Without a doubt. I can't wait to see you."

Had he changed? Yes, he had. Well, it had been more than seven years. He had gained weight. He looked more solid, more substantial, somehow. His eyes were sad and tired – probably hadn't slept much on the train. And wrinkles around his eyes, at his age? Close to thirty-two now. A constant smile, although a touch sad. This was new – he hadn't smiled much back home. Back home? This was home now for him – and for her, too. Better get used to it.

She stared at him, laughing, "Let me look at you first." Then she hugged him. It felt good to hug this troublesome brother, this boy who was not a boy anymore. She did not let go for a long time.

They sat beside each other on a sofa and she held Leonard's hand.

"You've changed," she said.

"You haven't. Maybe a bit. Your eyes are very red."

"Tell me about you. Tell me about your family. Do you have pictures?"

No, he hadn't brought any pictures. Hadn't thought of it in the rush. Monica was away at her parents with Matt. She was fine. They were going through a rough patch right now. Matt was a dear, of course. Yes, he should have brought pictures.

"That's all? That's all you have to say about your son?"

"So far he's shown no special talent for mathematics. Crawls into our bed in the morning. Sometimes in the middle of the night. He's still not fully toilet trained. Minor accidents, here and there. Brown hair, brown eyes." He shrugged. "Oh, one thing is remarkable about him. He hardly ever cries."

"Do you adore him?"

"I love him, of course."

"Tell me about Monica. What do you mean a rough patch? Minor differences – all couples have them, sooner or later – or more serious than that? Talk, Leonard, talk."

He looked bemused at her. "You've changed too. You never had any patience for such things. The Alexandra that I knew would get the information she needed as quickly as possible – with just the essential details. Where did this need for talk, for mundane details, come from? I'll talk, don't worry, I'll talk. About Monica, well, we may not be together for much longer. We are having difficulties – the rough patch may be more than a patch. I'll tell you everything later, more than you'll want to hear. But first tell me about Ada and Emil. And about you and Charles. That's the way it should be, Alsa. First, the basic items of news. Then, slightly more detail – on the state of my marriage, for example. Finally, in due course, all the tiresome minutiae. Oh, Alsa, it's so good to see you."

She heard the front door slam, and Charles came in, brandishing a shopping bag like a prize. "Ah, the long-lost brother has arrived! Fresh croissants and baguettes. Yes, Montreal remains a civilized place, in spite of the English – and the test is whether you can find croissants and baguettes within a ten-minute walk. You can. This bag is the proof. How are you, Leonard? You look more mature, more solid. Robust. Isn't it wonderful to have your sister here, in Montreal?"

He shook Leonard's hand and said, stepping towards the kitchen, "I'll leave the two of you alone. I'm sure you still have many things to tell each other."

"There's no need, Charles," said Alexandra. "There are no state secrets here. Besides, the secrets are in the details. And the details come later, according to Leonard's theory of siblings' reunions. Like peeling the layers of an onion, not everything at once, and definitely no details at the first layer, which is where we are right now."

"I'll make some coffee and then we'll sit down and have breakfast. I can't stay long. I have a meeting with Professor O'Shea. Claude O'Shea is the chair of the Math Department, Alexandra, I think I told you. You'll meet him tomorrow; the O'Sheas have invited us for lunch. Leonard, I'm sure they wouldn't mind if you came along. She's a wonderful cook – it's worth it. Claude would like to get me here full time. Now that you are in Montreal, my dear, I think I'll be more receptive. We'll also talk about your terms. He's been away this last week, and I'd like to settle everything, if possible, before I fly back to France. I also have a few errands. I'll call in the afternoon and we'll have dinner together. We'll go out. Somewhere glamorous. My treat. Your sister needs distractions, Leonard, she needs amusements."

He left with his bakery victuals to prepare breakfast. Leonard watched him go, then turned back to Alexandra. She read many unspoken questions in his look and she pre-empted them warily. "Charles has been wonderful. Don't know what I'd do without him. An angel. In difficult times, angels appear, if one is lucky. That's the basic report, to follow your theory. Details later. Don't ask me now, Leonard."

He put his arm around her shoulders and held her tight for a while, and then stood up and began to pace.

"How is your work?" he asked.

"I've done some very good work. This enforced isolation has been good – to a point. I've published a lot, and in good journals. At least they didn't stop me from submitting papers. Professionally, I've done very well in the last six or seven years. Working with Charles has allowed me to break the isolation. Yes, I did very good work. At a personal level, it has been a steady decline since you left. Perhaps the two never go together. The last years have been very difficult."

There were clinks of dishes in the kitchen and Charles appeared with a large tray, croissants on a plate, slices of baguette, jam, and gigantic bowls of café au lait. He set the tray on a coffee table and lowered himself into an armchair beside the sofa. He looked tired too.

"I don't know if I have time to eat. Five more minutes and I'm gone. Your sister, Leonard, continues to astonish the world. The small world of mathematics, of course. She could have gone to any university. Her choice. Stanford, Yale, Columbia. Anywhere in Europe, even stuffy Cambridge. They all wanted her. They all offered positions. She chose the Université de Montreal because of the language, because she wanted to put some distance between herself and Bucharest, and because of you. Not hungry, Leonard?"

Alexandra smiled and said, "Surely my choice had something to do with you as well, Charles."

Leonard sat down and shook his head. "Well, I have to hand it to you, Alsa. I would never have thought you'd be able to get Emil to go along with this. What did you use? A magic potion?"

She didn't answer immediately. She looked at Leonard and sighed, then glanced at Charles, who nodded slightly.

"Emil didn't know about this, Leonard," she said, softly but clearly. "I didn't tell him."

"Will he agree to join you? Do you want him to, first of all?"

"I don't know, Leonard, I don't know. What am I saying? I want my daughter. Oh, Leonard, it's been only five days, and I miss her terribly. Without Emil, I doubt I'll get my daughter. There's your answer."

"In the end, were you separated?"

"I must run, now," said Charles, getting up. "Your sister, Leonard, is very tired. And stressed. The last thing she needs now, please believe me, is a cross-examination from her brother. Give her some time. She will tell you all when she is ready. And when she sorts things out herself."

"It's all right, Charles. Sooner or later I'll have to face these questions. And sooner is probably better."

"There is no rush," Charles said. "You don't have to decide anything now. Whatever you think or do now, its complete opposite in a week would not change anything. Got to go. I'll call."

"Where were you, Leonard, by the way? We kept ringing you?"

"Oh, it was work."

"No, I want details. I want a glimpse of how you live and work."

"I was in Ottawa – much closer to Montreal, by the way, than Toronto – for a three-day workshop on economics modelling. I went without much enthusiasm, but I was told to go and pay attention. It seems I needed it for my professional development. For two and a half days, we listened to and learned from luminaries of economics. We heard the latest on trends, fallacies, new theories, and on our duty to harness the ever-increasing power of computers. We had, we were informed, such extraordinary tools at our disposal that it was only our limitations that prevented us from being able to forecast with outlandish precision our economic and financial future."

"Invited speakers?"

"Yes, all of them. Heavy-rimmed glasses, long titles and credentials, associated with prestigious universities or think tanks. One of them, whisked in late for a forty-minute speech, then immediately out because of an another engagement for which he was already late – apologies for not being able to entertain our questions – was a Nobel laureate. Although his message was quite abstruse – in fact, I had the distinct feeling he may have got his speeches mixed up, the one he made to us being in fact originally meant for his previous or his next engagement – his talk was full of bonhomie and good humour, almost as if he were saying to us, his delighted audience, 'Look how nice and funny and learned I am, and I don't mind talking to you at all, although I have a Nobel prize and my time is very precious.'"

"And Monica? Matt?"

"Monica has been with Matt in Kingston for the whole week – that's where her parents live. She was planning to come home this morning. I called the Gorens' home, just after I talked to you. Edna answered the phone and quickly passed me on to Monica without even bothering to ask how I was doing. Before I could say anything, Monica reported that Matt had used the word 'extraordinary' in a sentence. 'Extraordinary,' I replied, was in the air. I told her about your extraordinary and unexpected arrival in Montreal and that I planned to spend the weekend with you. Monica said she was very happy for me and, yes, it was fine by her. She added that she was curious to meet the genius sister. There you are. We do try to talk to each other as if everything were all right, although we both know that nothing is further from the truth. She had left to spend a few days in Kingston to 'think things over, because, believe me, Leonard, we can't continue like this.' Her words. Our marriage, Alsa, is hurtling towards non-existence. We fight a lot, and often I'm not sure what about. It's not a good sign when the fighting is for the sake of it."

"I wrote that long article about Olinde Rodrigues, Alsa, in *Mathematical Archives*, three years ago. Do you remember it? I've sent it to you through Charles. Charles was of immense help, by the way. Anyway, I was quite proud my article. It had a few unorthodox things in it. I put it bluntly that the inventor of quaternions was Olinde Rodrigues, not Sir William Rowan Hamilton, however romantic the story about Hamilton carving some formula on a bridge, in front of his wife, after years of relentless search."

"Of course I remember it. And I liked it very much. I recall thinking at the time that I didn't know anything about Olinde Rodrigues. Almost anything. Rodrigues's formula for Legendre polynomials."

"Exactly. And fundamental work on rotations, a contribution that everybody seemed to ignore. I was trying in my paper to bring attention to this ignored part of his work. Well, the paper wasn't very well received. It may very well have been that the writing was awful. I wrote most of it in 1973, but somebody did help me with the writing, so it couldn't have been that bad. Anyway, it got some nasty reviews. Some unpleasant letters from England and Ireland. I remember one by heart, its venom has etched it in my brain. 'It is easy to see, by reading the article, that the writer has only a cursory familiarity with both the English language and with mathematics,' was one line that hurt, both because it contained some truth, and also because it was quite unfair, since the case I made did not depend at all on a thorough understanding of mathematics. Here is another sample, it goes something like this: 'Mr. Leonard Jacobi, a newcomer to this field, attempts to remove with one poorly written paper in *Mathematical Archives* the reward of fifteen years of hard work from Sir William Rowan Hamilton. And, what do you know, an obscure French banker and hobby mathematician deserves the glory. We are amazed that the editors of *Mathematical Archives* would publish such ridiculous material.' Ah, well. On top of that, in France it was ignored altogether. The country of Olinde Rodrigues. It was a good paper, maybe not that well written, but the content was right. Murray Walker, my former supervisor, liked it. Anyway, the important thing is that it was published. I also wrote a more popular and much briefer version of it for an American popular science magazine. This shorter version hid under the silly title of 'Are Quaternions Back in Fashion?' a title I hated. I played down the strong case for the recognition of Olinde Rodrigues as the first and true discoverer of quaternions. For a few dollars, I made Hamilton and Rodrigues co-inventors of the quaternions, although it is quite obvious that Rodrigues invented the quaternions years ahead of Hamilton's near-the-bridge epiphany."

He stood up and picked up the tray. "Sit, sit, I'll clear this. You didn't touch your coffee. Should I leave it here?"

She shook her head and followed him into the kitchen. He found detergent under the sink and washed the cups and the plates.

She watched him doing it, and then emptying the dishwasher. She had looked on as Charles loaded it and started the wash cycle, but she had kept away from the mysterious contraption. Leonard, though, seemed to know his way around it.

"You're quite handy in a kitchen, aren't you?"

"It's probably just as well."

"What do you mean?"

He turned towards her. "Things aren't working out with Monica and me. It's not likely that we're going to stay together."

"Why?"

"Oh, I don't know, we are getting on each other's nerves. I more on her nerves, than she on mine. I don't think she loves me, it's as simple as that. I don't think she ever did. Yes, she did like me, in the sense that she suffered me without distress, but … She finds marriage constraining, stifling. She told me that after her first marriage failed – she had been married before – she began to think of it as an absurd undertaking. Too much drudgery and imposition, too many adjustments and compromises – and for what? Having children was the only reason she could think of that made some sense – some *sense*, mind you! When she met me, Monica was in the process of sorting these thoughts out. And she found herself pregnant. She went through with it because she wanted the child, and because she did not want to embarrass her parents. Yes, she kind of liked me and hoped for the best. It just didn't work out. It's not a tragedy, Alsa. Yes, I'd like our marriage to work, but … I knew from the beginning, when we got married, that of the two of us I was the one who loved. She tried. She gave it an honest try, dear Monica. Such is life … And we love Matt, and we'll make sure that he won't be affected by whatever happens. No, it's not a tragedy, Alsa. Minor bourgeois hiccups."

"That's it?"

"Other things, of course. We may not have much in common. We don't share the same interests and ambitions. She is annoyed by what she perceives to be a certain lack of enterprise, of ambition, of wanting advancement. No, this sounds too crude – her way of putting it was that I refused to take 'steps on the ladder of life.' Her expression, not mine. At the beginning, she had found my interest in Olinde Rodrigues refreshing, kind of endearing – after all, you don't meet people interested in the lives of dead and forgotten mathematicians every day. But she thought it was a once-only fantasy or fling, and a means to get my degree. Yes, she could understand that, but then it was time for me to grow up, to do and pursue more grownup things. We had long discussions about it, especially after Matt was born. I told her that researching the life and work of Olinde Rodrigues turned out to be quite captivating and that I'd continue to look for similar subjects. I even told her that that I might confine myself, at least at the beginning, to more obscure mathematicians – the many that did excellent work but somehow remained obscure, unknown or not as well known as they deserved to be. Like Olinde Rodrigues. Or Asuero Aroso. I told her about Aroso, about the many stories circulating around him back in Romania. I told her that I felt there was a story there – but that, as you know, nothing came of it. The more I talked to her about what I wanted to do, the more upset – no, irritated – she became. She did not understand my interest in the lives of dead people. Why would one scour the past of an obscure mathematician? What for? Wouldn't it make more sense, she said to me, to do things that would profit my career, so that all of us, and Matt in particular, would benefit? She did have a point. Writing about Olinde Rodriguez or any other mathematician was, in her view, a waste of time. As was writing about mathematics. She was appalled by the idea that this was what I wanted to do for the rest of my life.

"Our marriage, Alsa, is infected with the virus of incomprehension. There is no medication. We belong to different worlds. Sets with no union. I spend my time writing about Olinde Rodrigues and wondering about others unjustly forgotten, instead of grasping at the extraordinary opportunity which my marriage with her is. Yes, she did like me in some way, but after a few years it's not about romance and a good time, but about being serious, about accumulation and pecking order, about steps on the ladder of life. It's only a matter of time before we separate."

"What does the future hold, Leonard?"

"Monica and I will separate. We need to. For one year or sixteen months, I don't remember how long it takes. Then we can divorce, claiming incompatibility. Or get back together, although I doubt it."

"Is there any chance that you and Monica would stay together?"

He shook his head.

Chapter 14
March 1977

Charles called to say he would not be able to join them for lunch, and then gave precise instructions where to meet for dinner. Leonard made cheese sandwiches with the remains of the baguette. He found a kettle and tea-bags and, in the fridge, a lemon not fully desiccated. He boiled water, put a few slices of lemon on a small plate, and prepared the tea. Alexandra leaned against the wall near the large kitchen window, her arms folded across her chest. She watched him quietly throughout the entire preparation. Now and then she looked out the window into a backyard of pristine whiteness and several snow-laden firs.

They had their tea and sandwiches in the kitchen, not talking much but smiling at each other, and then went out for a walk. The milder temperatures of the previous days were gone, replaced by a grey and windy cold. Tiny snowflakes fought their way to the ground. A few streets away, they crossed a small park, white and deserted. In the middle of the park there was a monument dedicated to the locals fallen during the First World War. A woman and a child walked quickly past them. The child, a girl in a red coat with a huge hood, was crying and trying to keep up with the woman, who was walking a few steps ahead and constantly turning to look back.

"Just like the walk we took in the Cismigiu Garden, when I first told you I was planning to flee," Leonard said.

"And I'm just as cold," Alexandra said, "let's go back." She laughed after a short while. "You know, my life can be divided into two parts – before that walk and after."

They met Charles that evening for dinner in a large restaurant with a broad staircase leading to an upper level. The food was delicious. Waiters with black vests and long white aprons moved about quietly and efficiently. Leonard said it reminded him of Paris, not that he could afford such an exquisite restaurant when he was there. Charles touched Alexandra's hand and said that he hoped they would spend the summer together in Paris. He looked forward to showing her the city. Paris, Charles and Leonard agreed, was simply the most beautiful city in the world.

Towards the end of the meal, Alexandra told them the story of Aroso's unheralded discovery.

Both Charles and Leonard were quiet for a long time after she ended her story.

"What did you do with the blue envelope?" Leonard finally asked.

"It's here, together with his notebooks – several of them. Hard to decipher, though. Some of them are from his Gottingen days."

"Here? I thought you left everything behind, that you took off with nothing but your purse."

"Charles brought them over several months ago."

"I'm afraid they are still in Paris," Charles said.

"I wonder …" Leonard said and then fell quiet.

Back in the apartment, Alexandra and Leonard watched Charles kindle the fire while he muttered that that room was always cold. Then they sat in front of the incipient flames, Charles and Leonard with glasses of cognac in their hands. A couch and two armchairs were set in a semi-circle around the fireplace. It was the third time, already, she was ending her day in that small sitting room, in front of the fire with Charles. She liked the room. How quickly one developed habits. It was a very pleasant place during the day as well, with light coming in through the large French window leading to a snow-covered lawn gently sloping down. Near the window, a miniature tree, with gnarled, silvery, multiple trunks, and long, narrow leaves, grew out of a yellow urn. A small walnut table and two delicate chairs were pushed against the wall opposite the fireplace. "My sister's taste," Charles had told her. "Only anorexics are allowed to sit in these chairs." He told her Gislaine had picked the paintings in the room, too. A large rural landscape over the mantelpiece, a fiddler, a still life. The same artist, a Frenchman who settled in Quebec after the '67 World Exhibition, a friend of Gislaine.

After a while, Charles yawned, and said he'd had a full day. Was Alexandra warm enough? He was going to get more logs for the fire, then go to bed.

"He treats me as if I'm made of crystal," Alexandra said after Charles had gone. "I'm unusually jumpy and sensitive these days, I have to admit. This whole thing is like a fairytale opera, with the music written by a brooding, suicidal composer. The Ada theme keeps recurring and the joyous passages are rare. I'm the capricious, fickle princess, slightly unstable. This house, so beautiful, is my castle. Charles is the angel guardian. Yesterday morning it snowed for many hours, and I sat here, in this beautiful room, pleasantly warm, surrounded by tasteful objects. It was so still. I kept looking out the window, looking at the large flakes slowly falling, the neighbours walking up and down the street and stopping for brief chats, at the snow-clearing trucks, the children walking back from school. It was peaceful and tranquil and orderly, and I felt I was a trespasser, a fraud who didn't belong, an impostor with fake credentials."

She was crying now, the tears coming freely. "You've never seen me crying, have you? I've become an expert. Charles calls me Miss Lacrimath. Last evening he made a game of it. With a dictionary he identified the many ways of shedding tears available to me. Should I cry? Should I weep? Sob? Snivel? Whimper? Howl? Wail? Whine? Quite comforting to have chosen a country whose language – no, languages – are so descriptive of my state.

"Yes, I'm easy with the tears and altogether a sad and jittery person. Lily – you remember my friend Lily, don't you – marvels that

I've been able to work so well, that I produce so much, in spite of my circumstances. She sounds almost as if I should feel guilty. The thing is, Leonard, I manage to keep the math away from my unhappiness. Often, I will it that way – I tell myself to think about this or that problem, and it works. But most of the time it is the math that shuts the unhappiness out, that protects me, that keeps me sane. I'm happy that I've managed to do such good work. After all, that's what I am, a mathematician, who happens to be a mother and a wife ... a bad wife, with a lover. And a terrible mother."

They didn't say anything for a while, and she was grateful to Leonard when he began talking about his plans. "I'm thinking of writing something about Aroso, Alsa. What do you think? With the notes of his you brought out and this fascinating story of his unacknowledged discovery. A long paper, maybe even a thin book. Yes, more likely a thin book, if I could get a publisher interested. I've thought of Aroso often. He's typical of the kind of mathematical figure I'm attracted to, I think. And now ... what a story, Alsa, what a story. You know, about a year ago, I wrote an impression of Aroso as a student of his. Not that good. You may be able to help me a bit there. Maybe the book should not be very mathematical ... no, of course not. It would be about his life, his choices, his discovery and the way he kept it quiet. His life with Mitzi. His life during the war. His childhood in Istanbul. No, maybe that's too ambitious. It would take too long. Maybe later I'd have a second go – the definitive biography of Asuero Aroso, but not now. It would have to have some math in it, after all, he was a mathematician – and for this I'd need your help also. Not now, when you settle down. I'd like to keep the math to a minimum. Yes, more likely a thin book. I'd see how things turned out. It's too bad I can't travel to Bucharest to gather more material and to talk to other people who knew him and worked with him. I'd like to travel to Istanbul and Gottingen. There may still be traces of him in these places, although I don't have much hope. It would be interesting to see how the world of mathematics reacted to such a book. To the claim that I'd make in it that Aroso deserves the glory, or at least a share of it, now bestowed on Godel and Cohen, for the resolution of the Cantor's conjecture."

"I'll tell you how they'd react, Leonard. With lofty outrage and irony. If they reacted at all. But most likely your book, or paper, together with your outrageous thesis, would be ignored. I don't mean to discourage you. On the contrary, I think your idea of writing a book about Aroso is wonderful. Useful, too, and I'm not saying that to make you feel good, either. But don't assume that your book would suddenly make Aroso a recognized name among mathematicians. Maybe the kind of name tossed out by a few specialists and lovers of esoterica – like Bolyay – but even that I doubt."

"Let's get some sleep, it's past midnight, Alsa."

"You go. I'll stay for a while. I think I'm going to cry a little bit more ... Better to do it here, without disturbing Charles."

"Should I stay? Keep you company?"

"No, no, I'll be all right. I don't mind being alone. Not at all."

Chapter 15
March 1978 - April 1978

In March, Leonard rang Alexandra to remind her that a year had passed since her arrival. "How did you celebrate it? Has it been a good year? Have you adapted to the materialist corruption of the West?"

"Oh, Leonard, there was no celebration. I'll do that when Ada gets here. Besides, Charles was away. Gislaine took me to lunch the other day, at the Faculty Club. Isabelle came too. They are comfortable enough with me now to ask uncomfortable questions, such as what's happening with Ada. I did my usual crying, although this happens less and less. I was very discreet. I'd say it was a delicate snivel, like a bad cold. Poor women, they don't know what to make of me. I think they like me – especially Isabelle, who feels very protective and calls me often to find out if I need anything. But I confuse them; they don't know what to make of this Romanian Jewess who doesn't go to Synagogue, cries all the time, and prefers to be alone.

"And you?" she asked. "How are *you* doing?"

Three months earlier, Leonard had called her and announced, "This is it, I've moved out." He had moved into a small two-bedroom apartment in the Yonge and Eglinton area. It took a fair slice out of his monthly income, but it was functional, and close to the subway. He had bought a bed for Matt as well as himself. "You should visit me," he told her, "you can sleep in Matt's room when he's not here. I've got a table with six chairs from a friend at work who won't need them for a while. I have two comfortable armchairs I'm very fond of, and a TV set." There hadn't been much acrimony over his departure; he and Monica had been glad to put some distance between them. "We agreed quickly on everything. Boringly civilized. There wasn't much to divide, anyway. Most of the furniture was Monica's, and she kept it."

He had sounded all right, then. She had tried, since, to find out his true state of mind. She was annoyed with herself by her prying, but she couldn't help it. How did he find living by himself again? Was he sad? Lonely? Did he have friends? Many friends? Did he go out? Did he go out on dates? How was Matt taking the separation? Did he mind spending the weekends with his dad, in his small apartment? What did Matt do or say lately?

Leonard's answers were often monosyllabic, building up to protest. "Never mind about me, and my state of mind, Alsa. I'm fine. Matt is fine too. The weekends here are a bit baffling to him, but he never complains. I don't want to talk about me. I'll send you a letter one of these days. A long letter with all the details."

It was the same this time. Towards the end she asked Leonard if he was writing anything? Did he begin his book about Aroso?

"Yes, I did begin it," Leonard said. "I have an outline and some recollections about him written down. You know, kind of student snapshots; how did the students see him, new students, fully new to him. I'm trying to remember my colleagues' reactions to him. I may need your help here and there, Alsa. Not now, later."

When she put the phone down, she found herself saying aloud, "Yes, a year already." Maybe she should draw a line and do some additions, report like a good accountant on her decision and her life thereafter.

What column should she do first? The easy one, the professional column. Nothing to complain or worry about there. She had continued her work with Charles, of course much easier now, and had even begun to think of some work in an area new to her, one she had been getting into because of the seminar she was running at the university and which turned out to be attended by very good people.

As to the course she was required to give, she had struggled with the language a bit, for a couple of lectures, but had since become quite comfortable and hardly ever looked at her lecture notes anymore. Her teaching load was lighter than it had been in Bucharest, but the main difference was that she spent time on lecture notes now. In Bucharest, she had needed only to jot down a brief outline, bullets to remind her of the logical order of the ideas. Her prodigious memory did the rest, and she never hesitated unless she veered in pursuit of a sudden new thought. She used to do it quite often; it was the only time she found teaching exhilarating. Her mind was fully taxed, and she would talk, she had been told by colleagues who sometimes came to her lectures, as if in a trance, as if re-transmitting thoughts received from elsewhere. At such moments, she was told, she looked through, not at, her audience. Some of her students had complained about her sudden forays into the unknown, and she had understood why. The lack of books made the class notes very important, and following her sudden thoughts while neglecting the basic material was not helpful. She had kept doing it, albeit not as much as she would have liked, because she enjoyed doing it, and because she believed it was a useful demonstration to her students of the working of a mathematical mind.

Here, she wrote everything down, not only because she had to hand out lecture notes, but also because she had been worried about stumbling for words. Lately, however, she had become quite comfortable with the language, and, knowing that she had given the students her lecture notes anyway, she began again to move away – more often that she ever did in Bucharest – from what she had planned to tell her students. She would say to the class, "Oh, well, you can find all this in the handouts – let's pursue this interesting idea that just crossed my mind. It should be enjoyable, don't you think? Assume we remove this constraint ..." She asked for suggestions from the class, and reasoned through unknown territory hoping to carry the students along with her. She told them that this was the exciting part of mathematics, these sudden journeys in the unknown. She was lucky, because she had a good class, about a dozen of them. Her impromptu excursions quickly became the talk of the students and then of the department, and, just as in Bucharest, her colleagues began to come and listen to her, hoping she'd have one of her unplanned departures from the lecture.

The seminar was quite informal. Claude O'Shea had wanted her to do it in Number Theory or in Complex Analysis, but she had balked at the idea. She told him she'd rather do it on a subject she was less familiar with, so it would be as useful to her as to the other participants. She proposed advanced topics on Lie theory, and, after some discussion in the department, it was approved. The seminar started with three students and a young professor, Pierre Azelmaid, who also wanted to learn more about the topic. At their first meeting, she told them that they'll learn together, and that she wasn't much ahead of them. Years earlier, she had read a rather good book on Lie algebras, but it was an old one, from the late fifties or early sixties, and she told them she was sure there had been many advances since in this rather fashionable field.

During the first three seminars, she gave them a quick summary of what she knew, all of which was from the book. Afterwards, each of the seminars was run by one of the participants, Alexandra included, and centred on an interesting paper, or group of papers, or idea they had and wanted to discuss. Another professor joined them about a month after the start, and one of the students dropped out. They often held the seminar over lunch, at a Moroccan restaurant that was only a ten-minute drive from their building. Pierre Azelmaid drove the five of them in a large, battered American sedan. He knew the restaurant owner, a friend of his parents, and they were treated royally, allowed to linger long after all the lunch clientele had disappeared and preparation for the evening had started. Pierre's parents were Moroccan Jews who had left Morocco after the Suez War. They had been in France for a while and eventually settled in Montreal. The lunch consisted of a huge number of appetizers assembled by the owner and, depending on the topic and the general mood, it would stretch well beyond the seminar's prescribed two hours.

One of the seminar participants, Jérôme Lacroix, was her first graduate student. He was not selected by Alexandra, but "given" to her by O'Shea. Dean O'Shea told her, when he had approached her with his request, that Jérôme had been one of the most promising students they ever had in the department. He had started working on his Ph.D. several years before Alexandra's arrival, got into trouble with his supervisor – arrogance on both sides, the dean had shrugged – and then into more serious trouble of a personal nature. Police trouble. Neither Claude O'Shea nor Jérôme tried to hide it from her – he had spent more than a year in jail. He had since reappeared, on parole, and was readmitted in the doctoral program. Since his topic was Number Theory, did she mind, as a personal favour to him – he was vaguely related to the young man – being his supervisor? O'Shea kept saying that in his many years at the university they'd never had a more gifted math student.

Jérôme was unique all right. Not tall, with small dark eyes and a long, ugly cut under his lower lip, he would sit motionless for minutes at a time and then, unexpectedly, make a sudden move with his hands or head. It was a bit unsettling, and for a while, until she got used to it, Alexandra thought his sudden movement meant he was going to say something, and she'd wait for him to talk. Most of the time he had no intention of saying anything. And when he did talk, his words were also sudden and rapid and unexpected, jerky triumphs of the mind. He was not easy to follow, both because he had a strong local accent and because he was a heavy user of foul language.

She learned Jérôme's story from him one afternoon when they lingered even longer than usual at the restaurant to talk about his progress on his thesis. All the others had left, and Jérôme had had a few beers. He wanted to set the record straight. He knew that there were wild stories about him, and that certain professors and students didn't want anything to do with him. Did she mind if he told her what happened? No, she didn't mind, she told him, but it wasn't necessary. It was for him, Jérôme said.

He came from a poor and violent background – a "fucked-up family," he said. His stepfather started as a construction worker but for many years now had worked for the union. Aldo – his name was Aldo Moratti – was a mean, violent bastard. Jérôme didn't know who his real father was, and he didn't think his mother knew, either. She had married Aldo when Jérôme was twelve years old. Aldo beat them regularly, both him and his mother. No, not only when he was drunk, although he was drunk quite often, and drink didn't improve his mood. In a couple of years, Jérôme began to stand up to him, and this only increased his stepfather's rage. "I'm not big, as you can see, but I'm fast. And I'm quite handy in a fight," he said, matter-of-factly, "handy in the sense of using everything at hand. With Aldo, I would grab whatever happened to be around me. Chairs, pieces of wood, stones, even a knife if there was one within reach. I had to, because the fucker was very big."

Jérôme was still in high school when he left home. He had odd jobs and lived in a derelict basement room rented to him by a cousin of his mother. He was still there, as a matter of fact. Good, poor people, and a bit simple. They kept the room for him while he was in jail. His rent was next to nothing. He got involved with a few wrong people, bad people, and had some minor troubles with the police. "Minor shit, you understand? Stupid things. Joyriding, bit of drug dealing – I had to make a living." Several times, he had been very close to quitting high school. It was only math that had kept him relatively sane and on the right side, barely, of the law. He was a terrible student otherwise. He just made it through – every year advancing only after his math teachers convinced the other teachers to close their eyes and pass him. Finally, in university, he was able to study math alone.

Soon after he left home, his mother got pregnant. "She had me at eighteen, my brother at thirty-five. My mother is a cow, a stupid fucking cow. Why does she stay with Aldo? I told her to leave him and come and stay with me. She wouldn't. Why did she have a child with him? To divert the beatings she got from Aldo to my little brother?" Jérôme became quite attached to his half-brother, Mario, and because of him he'd go and see his mother once in a while, always when Aldo was away. When Mario grew up a bit, Jérôme began to take him to movies, to the zoo, or simply walked with him, Mario straddling his shoulders whenever he got tired. Mario was a timid boy. "Aldo, the fucking brute, began to treat him – his own child, dammit, his own fucking child – the way he had treated me. I could tell by Mario's terrorized look whenever his father's name was mentioned. I felt it, yes, I could feel it. The thing was, Mario was much younger and more frail than I had ever been. That's how the big trouble began, the big fuck-up."

He had gone home (he laughed at calling it "home,") on a Sunday afternoon to see his little brother – not his mother, he's given up on the cow a long time ago – maybe take him to a movie. Aldo wasn't there, only his mother and Mario. Mario was shivering in a corner, with two broken fingers and an ugly cut above his left eye. Jérôme feared it might

even become infected. Mario's hand was swollen. Jerome took Mario's
shirt off and there were bruises all over his little body. He didn't have
to ask what had happened, only when. Friday night – Aldo had come
home drunk. Jerome snapped, but still he remained calm. Yes, he always
could do that. He could become very angry, yet at the same time remain
in control, because he knew immediately what he had to do. Most people
lost it because they didn't know what to do and they panicked. But he
knew. Oh, yes, he knew. He called a cab and gave his mother money
to take Mario to emergency. Go, he said, and stay with him until he's
looked after properly. He couldn't go with them because he was busy
that afternoon.

He waited for Aldo for several hours. It got dark and he didn't
turn on the light. When Aldo finally came home, Jérôme sprang on him
with a bottle, broke it on his head, and cut into Aldo's big fat body with
whatever was left in his hand. He left some ugly marks – even on his
puffy face. Aldo lost a lot of blood, but he didn't die, although Jérôme
left without calling an ambulance. Somehow, Aldo managed to get help.
He was in hospital for a month, fat, fucking Aldo. And Jérôme spent
eighteen months in prison for aggravated assault and battery. The judge
was understanding, but couldn't let him go free. After all, he almost killed
a man. He was lucky, too, because the police knew already about Aldo's
violence – they'd come to the house many times after getting calls from
neighbours who heard yelling and screaming. That's what she was good
at, the cow. Screaming. Well, it was better than nothing.

In the reunion-with-Ada column, all Alexandra had was one big zero.
Her first attempts to bring over her family, or at least her daughter,
were less successful than even the very cautious predictions she had
received on that matter from everybody, including Jean (Ion) Revescu,
a somewhat shady Montrealer she had hired to expedite her case. Jean
Revescu supplemented his income by acting as an intermediary between
the Romanian authorities and private individuals in delicate cases such
as hers. She got in touch with an immigration lawyer as well, and Charles
was calling on all his connections in both Canada and France for help, but
she believed that if a relatively quick and happy conclusion was possible,

it would be through the services of Jean Revescu. Revescu had done this kind of thing before. He had a track record, and Alexandra had met a family, right there in Montreal, reunited by Revescu. Revescu travelled five or six times a year to Romania – he imported ceramics, glassware, and undrinkable wine to Canada – and thus could plead her case directly, in situ. He was an importer and a problem solver – that's what he told Alexandra in his thickly carpeted office a few subway stops from the university. She didn't like him, but that increased her trust in him, because she believed that unsavoury people dealt best with unsavoury problems in unsavoury countries. A tall, well-preserved man, Revescu moved with the stealth of an aging predator. His speech was soft and grave, but then the matters he dealt with – and this was a statement his whole body and demeanour made – were grave. Photographs behind his desk showed him in hunting gear, talking with others dressed similarly or posing by a couple of dead wild boars, and Alexandra recognized among the people holding rifles the prime minister of Romania. She was not disturbed by it, quite the contrary.

Revescu had told Alexandra that it would likely take a long time, two or three years, possibly more, before she could hope to reunite with her family, although he would do his best, of course, to achieve it as quickly as possible. He had promised he would leave no stone unturned. Alexandra had also been impressed by the considerable amount of money he had asked for up front, and by the sum to be handed to him at the happy conclusion of the case, which was twice as much again. Charles was a bit more skeptical. It was, he told her, like eating at a restaurant, or consuming a bottle of wine – the more one was charged, the better one believed it was. Revescu also added, as one of his conditions, the right to terminate the agreement any time after three years. He had to do this, he explained, in order to protect himself against working for nothing in long, hopeless cases. The immigration lawyer had asked for a retainer as well, but it was a much more modest amount, and Alexandra had been disappointed.

Revescu soon brought disturbing, but not unexpected, news. Emil Semeu – who refused even to see him – was in the process of getting a quick divorce and full custody of Ada. This was almost automatic, given the crime that Alexandra had committed. Alexandra was advised not to fight it, both by Revescu and her immigration lawyer, who consulted a family lawyer who had dealt with a similar case before (although it wasn't clear to Alexandra whether the case had been in Romania or in Hungary, because the city of Budapest was mentioned). It would be a waste of her money, and it would only strengthen the animosity Emil Semeu felt for her now. She would be wiser instead to add to the "buy-out" funds she was setting aside. Let time lessen Emil's wrath. Her hope, her only hope, she was told, was that, in time, he would mellow.

The next day, she rang Leonard and told him the news brought by Revescu.

"It was to be expected," Leonard said.

"I know. I'm trying to tell myself the same thing."

"Well, it's true."

"I know that hoping for a quick reunion with Ada is utterly unrealistic, but I can't help it. There are days I regret my decision to leave, although reason tells me otherwise."

"What does Charles say?"

"'I'll soon be able to marry you' – that's what he said. I just talked to him. I'm spending a fortune on long-distance calls. Of course, he also said the same thing you did – it was to be expected. But he was quite happy with the news, and didn't try to hide it."

"Are you going to?"

"Marry him? I don't care, Leonard. I will, if he wants it. It's not high on my list of priorities."

"You should. He adores you, Alsa."

"When he's here, Charles is as wonderful as ever. Next year he will lecture more at the Université de Montreal and I might give some lectures in Europe. That way I'll feel less lonely, but I'm afraid that I'm drowning poor Charles in my sorrow. A week ago we were out at a restaurant with another couple. At the other end of the room, a woman my age was having dinner with a girl of Ada's age, clearly her daughter. They were talking and laughing. I couldn't take my eyes of them. It was all right for a while – my lack of participation in conversations, my odd behaviour in general, is always discreetly explained and magnanimously excused – but then I started crying. Quite awful. Quite a scene."

Not that Leonard was doing much better than she was. Alexandra had been quite distressed by the news that Leonard and Monica had separated – she thought it was enough *she* had a broken family. And she liked Monica. She had liked her from the very first time they met, a month after Alexandra had landed in Montreal, when Charles and she had driven to Toronto and Monica had them for dinner. Also there that evening were Leonard's former supervisor, Murray Walker, and his wife. Alexandra realized that Leonard had invited them for her, because Murray Walker was a mathematician, but also because it helped hide the awkwardness of a marriage on its last legs.

No, Leonard did not sound very cheerful on the phone. She tried to make him talk, but he said he had to go out and would call her the next day. He didn't, so she called him, thinking, as the phone rang and rang, that they were a fine pair of depressed siblings. She tried the entire evening. Leonard finally answered around half past ten, and he was tipsy. It made him chatty and lyrical, and Alexandra for once felt indebted to the effects of alcohol.

"It's been a long time since I felt so down, Alsa, dear. That's all you need, more melancholy, but you wanted to know how I was. A difficult and lonely winter and spring."

"Is it the separation?"

"Nothing is more depressing than early April in Toronto. Days of dull sky with brief outbursts of cold sunshine, and dirty mounds of snow slowly melting and revealing unsavoury detritus. Matt pointed out to me only the other day, on one of our walks, the shrivelled body of a dead raccoon."

Alexandra laughed. "You know, I've yet to see one. Never seen a raccoon, dead or alive."

"Marriage, Alsa, dear, is like snow – blinding white and fresh at the beginning, grey, almost black, and quickly melting at the end, and revealing decaying corpses."

"That's quite inspired, Leonard."

"Truth is, I had a few drinks."

"And Matt? How is he?"

"I spend lonely weekends with Matt in the apartment. We take long walks, for him at least, in all directions from the Yonge and Eglinton station. For some reason, Matt finds the idea of his dad as a former cab driver fascinating, an adventure to be recreated. I don't know what goes through his mind, but when I told him once that the walk we had just taken traced a route I took with a fare, a trip which stayed in my mind because of the gigantic tip I collected, he became extremely excited. So, most weekends we take at least one walk along one of my cab routes. Matt is a quiet boy, and not given to much chatter, but he asks very precise questions. 'Did you turn here, at this very corner?' 'Yes, I slowed down and turned right here.' 'Why did you slow down? Weren't you in a hurry?' 'If you don't slow down, the centrifugal force pushes you off the curve.'"

"What did he say?"

"He accepted the explanation, but centrifugal force became a person in his mind. Not a feared one, but one of naughty and curious habits, who pushed people off if they didn't slow down at turns."

"Matt's wonderful. Very special."

"He's learned all the cabs. The Metros, the ABCs, the Diamonds. He obviously thinks that the Metros are the finest, since, after all, his dad had a glorious stint with them. Sometimes we take short cab rides. We sit in the front seat, with Matt on my lap, his face beaming with pleasure. He insists on flagging down only Metro cabs, and invariably tells the driver about his father's past."

"How has he reacted to the fact that Mom and Dad aren't together anymore?"

"He finds the quiet weekends spent with me, in an apartment devoid of toys, quite puzzling. It is clear he prefers his mother's place – our former place. He calls it home, and rightly so. 'How long before I go home, Dad?' Poor little guy, he never cries, puts on a good face, and, when prodded, he doesn't mind giving me an affectionate hug. He calls it a *fectionate* hug. 'Matt, give Daddy a hug.' 'A fectionate hug?' 'Yes, Matt, a fectionate hug. They are the best.'"

"So, what else do you do with him? I mean, beside retracing famous cab trips.'

"Last Sunday we froze at the zoo. We also go to children's shows and, ah, yes, we take art lessons together on Saturday mornings from a good-looking young woman with heavy rimmed glasses which, for some reason, make her more attractive. There are eight of us in the class, held in the basement of a small church, four adults and four children, and we all learn how to dip our palms in paint and then make marks on white or dark blue cardboard."

"The adults as well?"

"Of course, although I don't think the teacher with glasses expects to find a late bloomer among us. She makes no comments on the adults' artwork, but she explodes with enthusiasm every time one of the children manages anything other than a splotch. Her demonstration on how to dip a palm in paint seems highly sensual to me, but then I'm the only father there, and I haven't slept with a woman in quite a while. Matt does his dipping dutifully, but he's clearly not as taken by it as he is by our cab-emulating walks. I think I'm the main reason we're going to all eight palm-dipping sessions. I'm going to ask her out after the last session, although I have a feeling she's either married or has a boyfriend."

"Wedding ring?"

"No, she has no wedding ring."

In late April, Alexandra added Jacobi, her maiden name, to her last name. She became, and henceforth introduced herself as, Alexandra Jacobi-Semeu, and it was clear in her mind that she'd soon drop the Semeu altogether. She couldn't do it instantly; she was too widely known and had too many papers authored as Alexandra Semeu.

Chapter 16
July 1978

In early July, Leonard rang her and, in a triumphant voice, announced that he had found him.

"Found who?"

"Ovid."

"Ovid?"

"Yes, Ovid, Ovid Lovinescu, Aroso's brother-in-law, who else?"

She recalled that on the very first weekend after she arrived in Montreal, she had mentioned to Leonard, matter-of-factly, like a piece of curious but inconsequential information, that Mitzi's brother had sent medication for her throughout her illness, and that he had sent it from Canada. It would have been Ovid, of course. Was he still alive? they had wondered. And where in Canada? There was a good chance he would be living in Montreal or Toronto, although Alexandra had said that the name of the place was not one of the big cities, which she would have recognized. But maybe, Leonard said, he lived in one of the many suburbs, like Lachine in Montreal, or Scarborough in Toronto. Montreal was the more likely place, as it had been Canada's only really big and glamorous city when Mitzi's brother had arrived, in the mid- to late-forties. "

How did you find him in the end?"

"The telephone book, how else?"

Leonard told her the whole story. He had continued to scribble notes for his book about Aroso. A week ago, he suddenly remembered Ovid. It was little effort to look in the Toronto telephone book, and there he was, O. Lovinescu. Ovid. Leonard was certain. After all, there were not many first names starting with an "O." He called. Nobody answered. He tried a few more times over the next couple of days. He was about to give up when Ovid himself picked up the phone. Obligingly, he grandly announced, "Ovid Lovinescu's residence. Ovid speaking." Leonard told him his name, the fact that he had left Romania almost ten years earlier, that he was one of his brother-in-law's former students. He also told Ovid that he was a great admirer of his remarkable brother-in-law and that he would like to pay him a visit and talk. Or, if he, Mr. Lovinescu preferred, they could meet elsewhere, in a restaurant for example.

"Talk? What about?"

Flustered, Leonard told him that his sister, Alexandra, also a former student of Professor Aroso and a famous mathematician in her own right, now teaching at the Université de Montreal, had worked closely with Professor Aroso and had seen him not long before his death. She had been at Aroso's funeral. She had been at Mr. Lovinescu's sister's funeral as well. Aroso had been shaken by Mitzi's death and had talked at length about her. Mr. Lovinescu, Leonard suggested, might be interested to hear all about it.

His answer was blunt, but not unfriendly in tone. "What for? It's done. Almost two years already since Aroso died, and I've lost track of how many since Mitzi passed away. Four? Five? Besides, I've already had all the grim details. More than I care to know."

But Leonard was determined not to give up without a fight. "Look, Mr. Lovinescu, I dabble in writing stories about mathematics and mathematicians. Putter about. Nothing very serious, but an article of mine about the French mathematician Olinde Rodrigues has been printed in a specialty journal. I'm interested in the work and life of mathematicians. I believe that your brother-in-law was an extraordinary mathematician. I'd like to write something about him. I have some papers of his – he gave them to my sister before he died. He talked to her about his life at length. My sister told me all she knew about your brother-in-law. I wonder whether you could add to the picture I have of him and of his life."

"I left Romania in '44. I doubt I have any information you don't already have."

"Whatever you have, it would help me."

"Wouldn't a trip to Bucharest solve your problem? I'm sure you'll find there much more about Aroso that I could ever tell you."

"There are not many people in Bucharest, alive and willing to talk, who knew Aroso before the war. Besides, going back is not an alternative at all. The authorities didn't like the way I left."

That seemed to soften Ovid's resistance. "What's your name again?"

He told him. Ovid asked for his address. His sister's name. Her address. His phone number, at home and at the office. His sister's phone numbers. Finally, he said, "All right, Mr. Jacobi, come up a week from today, next Wednesday. Make it about eight o'clock. Bring your sister with you. No sister, no visit. And tell her to bring some proof that she is a mathematics professor in Montreal."

Ovid had given him an address in Etobicoke, a suburb of Toronto.

"You're coming down, aren't you, Alsa?"

"Wednesday? I don't know, Leonard. I'm meeting Revescu Thursday morning."

"Any news?"

"No. He asks me to his office once a month to tell me there is no progress and why there is no progress."

"Alsa, you have to come. He won't talk to me without you. Take the sleeper back to Montreal."

The truth was that she was curious to meet Ovid. No, to find out more about Aroso's past. And to meet Ovid, too – Mitzi's brother.

Then early on Wednesday morning, Leonard called her and said she'd have to go by herself. He sounded awful.

"I'm sick. It's some flu virus or food poisoning. I had a horrible night – kept throwing up. I have fever, quite high. You must go, Alsa, you must go to see Ovid. Get a tape recorder, some secretary must have one. Borrow it and tape him. It's very important to me, Alsa. You're the best of sisters."

"Leonard, you sound awful. I should come and look after you, not visit Ovid Lovinescu."

"Don't worry about me. I'm fine. I will be fine, that is. Anyway, Clara is with me."

"Who?"

"Clara."

"The palm-dipping teacher?"

He laughed, "I wish. No, she teaches English, not palm-dipping. She's the mother of a schoolmate of Matt. Divorced. Our children's friendship and our divorced status gave us things to talk about."

"Tell me about her."

"Clara's chatty. She grinds her teeth at night, sleeps in heavy cotton nightgowns. She has delightful freckles in her most intimate areas. She plays second violin in a quartet that meets and rehearses once a week in her house. Clara is invariably harassed for her inability to count. They have a nickname for her, "five-in-four," because of her habit of counting five beats in a four-beat bar. They also joke that the quartet sounds good only from several rooms away, in fact the farther the better."

"Leonard, she sounds delightful."

Outside Union Station in Toronto, she climbed in a cab and gave the driver the address. "Etobicoke," she said. "Is it far?" The driver shook his head.

When Ovid opened the front door – she assumed it was Ovid – his first words, in Romanian, were, "I expected two of you. You must be the sister, the mathematician."

She explained what happened.

"I checked you out. Both of you."

"Checked us out?"

He motioned her in. He told her that he had used a friend of his, a private detective, to confirm their story. It checked out. His worry was that a newspaper or some Jewish organization was trying to look into his past. There were rumours, he was sure she'd heard them, that he had been a supporter of the Iron Guard. He was not keen to have people dig into his past at a time when he needed all his energy, or whatever was left of it, to deal with his old age and a wife who, recently and quite suddenly, had been diagnosed with lung cancer and was undergoing radiation therapy.

"Lung cancer. Imagine that! Never smoked a cigarette in her life. They call it aggressive radiation therapy. It's an ominous qualifier, wouldn't you say? Don't like the sound of it. No, not at all. I didn't tell Mariska they were aggressive towards her body. No, I didn't."

Alexandra pushed an envelope towards Ovid. "Some proof of my employment. And a picture of me and Aroso."

Ovid waved away the papers. "No need. I said I checked you both. I'll have a look at the picture, though."

It was a split-level house, fairly large. They sat in the backyard, at a glass table, not far from a kidney-shaped pool with a sea of flowers behind it. There were flowers near the table, too, a row of tall pinkish-red clusters.

"Those are phlox. Easiest to grow. My wife must have planted these twenty years ago. First flowers we planted in this garden. We should replace them. They lose their vigour in time. But these are still looking good, don't you think? Mariska's hobby is flowers. She's Dutch. The Dutch like flowers. That's what she keeps saying, but I don't know. I've been to Holland many times, and I saw no proof of this particular affection towards flowers. Well, maybe the silly things they do with tulips. Now that I'm retired, I work in the garden too. It gets into you. I've been doing nothing else since she's been in the hospital. That's all she worries about, her flowers. Can you imagine, in her condition? She calls me on the phone and I have to describe to her, in exact detail, the condition of each flower. Then she gives me instructions on what to do next."

He fell silent, surveying his wife's flower kingdom, now dependent on him.

"There is a golf course beyond the fence. Do you golf?"

Alexandra shook her head, laughing.

"A pity. Women golf these days too, you know. Best thing for retirement. Golf. Mariska was a good golfer. Is. I golf, but not lately. Not since my wife went to the hospital. The garden takes too much time. And I don't have the heart, somehow. I guess we'll have to give up the house. I'm seventy-three and my wife is seventy-five. And now with this treatment ... What exactly do you want from me, Mrs. Jacobi? Not a Romanian name, is it?"

"Probably a Jewish name."

"I forget myself. A drink? I'm going to have a beer."

"A glass of water, if possible."

"Possible, possible, why wouldn't it be possible? Of course."

Ovid went into the house – a short man shrunk by age and worries, wearing a rather rumpled short-sleeve light blue shirt, brown shorts, skinny legs, making unsure tiny steps in brown shoes and socks of the same colour – and came back with two Molson bottles and two glasses. One glass had water in it.

"In case you change your mind," he said, raising the second bottle.

She didn't think he looked much like Mitzi. It was difficult to say with old people anyway, especially if not the same sex.

Alexandra had brought with her a copy of Leonard's article about Olinde Rodrigues. She handed it to Ovid and said she was there on her brother's behalf, that her brother would like to write something similar about Aroso, only of a much larger scope. Maybe, if he could find a publisher, write a monograph. There was enough drama and achievement in the life of his brother-in-law to warrant a monograph. Her brother could not go back to Romania to find out more about Aroso because he had left without the blessing of the authorities. The monograph was going to put less emphasis on Aroso's mathematical achievements since her brother was more interested in Aroso's life, and how his life and the choices he made affected his mathematical work and output. Any light Ovid could throw on Aroso's life, any detail, however insignificant, about him or about those close to him (like his sister Mitzi), would be very helpful to Leonard.

Ovid nodded, but the unhurried, almost torpid signals he made with his head, and the doubtful sounds emanating from his throat told Alexandra that his understanding of the purpose of her visit remained vague. She repeated what she'd said earlier. Ovid kept nodding. Alexandra asked him whether he had anything against her taping the conversation. Ovid thought for a while, and then decided that he did not like the idea.

She took out a small notebook and a pen and showed it to Ovid. He shrugged, as if to say, yes, go ahead.

The trouble was, Alexandra realized quickly, Ovid had difficulty telling a coherent story. He had difficulty remembering things. He jumped from one thing to another, without, at least to her, obvious connections. Aroso had done this too, but you could always follow him. Aroso would be driven in a new direction by an allusion, by a name, by an idle thought of a lazy evening, in a kind of Proustian meandering. She may have resented it as a method, but it was difficult not to succumb to its charm. But Ovid's talk was not easy to follow and often didn't make sense. Writing things down while trying to make sense of what he was saying made it worse.

Ovid felt his story was not going well. He stopped, embarrassed, and apologized. He said that since his retirement he had not used his mind much and it showed. He had not talked to anybody in a long time, except with his wife and his wife's doctors. "It doesn't take much brain to follow the wife's instructions and dig here and there," he laughed.

Alexandra suggested that maybe the better way to proceed was for her to ask questions and for him to answer as best as he could.

"What did you call him?"

"Who?"

"Aroso. What did you call him? You didn't call him Aroso, did you? You must have called him, in the family, by his first name, Asuero."

"Yes, Asuero. Mitzi always called him that. She liked it. She said that 'Asuero' invoked unexplainable powers and arts, like Aroso's arcane mathematics."

"Do you have any letters? Either from your sister or from Aroso himself?"

"No, I'm afraid I don't."

"Not one?"

"Well, my sister stopped writing in '51 or '52. It's a quarter-century since – even more. I don't usually keep letters, and even if I had, I likely dumped them twenty years ago when we moved here."

"And from Aroso?" Alexandra asked.

He looked with suspicion at her. "From Aroso? He didn't tell you?"

She shrugged, "Tell me what?"

"Aroso and I didn't speak to each other. Not since, oh, 1938 or maybe '39. He refused to talk to me. It was my association with the Iron Guard. I can't blame him, especially in light of what happened afterwards. You know, Mrs. Jacobi, I wasn't exactly a member of the Guard. Never joined it. What I did was look after some of the financial aspects of the Guard. What do you want, I was a banker."

"Look, Mr. Lovinescu," Alexandra said, "it's Aroso I'm interested in. I'm interested in your past only inasmuch as it's connected with Aroso's. There is no need to justify your actions or associations to me."

"Aroso never wrote to me. After Mitzi couldn't write anymore, I had news about her and Aroso only indirectly, through Lavinia's letters. My sister-in-law. Until 1960, when she suddenly died."

"What did she die of?"

"Oh, I could only guess. Sadness, loneliness, misery, cold, all of these. I'm sure there was a good medical cause on the death certificate, but I trust my hunches. I tried to help her as much as I could. My brother, Tudor, died in 1952, working on the canal. The Danube–Black Sea canal. He was arrested in '48 or '49. Lavinia saw him only once after he was arrested."

He took a sip of his beer and looked at the bottle. "Last time I saw Tudor was in the summer of 1942. He was a colonel at the time. He was back from the front for a fortnight, and I had a beer with him. It was somewhere outdoors, in Bucharest, near one of the lakes. I don't remember which one. Tudor went back to his infantry division, at that time about a hundred kilometres northwest of Stalingrad. He was by far the smartest of us. Wasted in the army. It was Father who forced him into it. Poor Tudor. He survived Stalingrad, the Russian offensive of November, survived the Russian POW camps, came back – a ghost – in 1946 and was re-arrested and sent to hard labour on the canal two years later. He didn't have much luck, did he?"

She wondered how Ovid had managed to avoid the war. "What was Aroso like? I mean, at family gatherings, with friends, in society? What did people think of him?"

Ovid gathered his thoughts for a while. It was obviously an effort. The gap between his bushy eyebrows wrinkled dramatically. He frowned like a young child in a classroom who, while not knowing the answer to the teacher's question, is keen to show he is hard at work on it.

"It's difficult for me to say how others saw Aroso. You know why? Because I'd known him as a student. He and I even had adjacent rooms at a *pension* in Gottingen. What was the name? Oh … I don't remember. There isn't much I remember. We were friends, good friends, and we had a common language, we could talk to each other in German. The others, and I presume that included Mitzi, saw him from a different perspective. To them, he was an exotic figure. Mathematics was exotic. And he was a genius. I told anybody who cared to hear that he was a genius. I just repeated what I had been told in Gottingen. Having a genius as a friend was rather nice, wouldn't you agree? Made you more worthwhile, by association.

"I liked spending time with Aroso. We had the shared experience of Gottingen, our student days and pranks, the *pension*, several years in close proximity at an age when friendships are easily built, our love for Mitzi. The others? Our friends, society? It's not everyday that one meets a mathematician of genius. You don't just bump into them, do you? And, if you do, what do you talk to them about? What did the others have to say to Aroso, or he to them? They had hardly anything in common. Come to think of it, even language was a divide. It took a year for his Romanian to become functional, and it still remained a struggle, a strain on the conversation. It was many years before he learned the nuances of the language to the extent that he was able to say things that were amusing or interesting. Amusing and interesting from society's point of view, of course. From the point of view of our frivolous friends and acquaintances. He didn't have it, anyway. He didn't have that gift, or desire, or need to be at the centre of a gathering, to amuse, to charm, to be diverting. He was clearly not interested, in any case. He was usually quiet, kind of in his own world, and everybody assumed he was floating somewhere, in his realm of mathematics. He would talk occasionally, if he was asked a question, or when he wanted to find out about something or someone. He found, I think, Romanian society and the country puzzling but often not worth his time. When he did talk, his words seemed to be meant mainly for Mitzi. You're sure you don't want a beer. Wine? A liqueur?"

"I'm fine, thanks."

He brought out two more bottles.

"I guess I won't be working in the garden tonight. What was I talking about? Oh, yes. After a while, after the novelty wore off, people began to avoid Aroso or just ignored him. He was quite happy about it. I mean, being left to himself."

"Why would Mitzi fall in love with him?"

"Ha. That's an impossible question. Maybe it was just infatuation. There was no question that she was quite taken with him, but was it love? What is love? There you are, you're shrugging. He was a good-looking young man, though. You didn't know that? Oh, yes, he was. Very tall, slim, high forehead, longish hair, genius-wild, many years before Einstein made it fashionable. Come to think of it, he did look a bit like an elongated Einstein, wouldn't you say? And he had a lot of confidence in himself, bordering on arrogance. His look and demeanour conveyed that clearly, and later, much later, his discourse as well. Women like arrogance, don't they, Mrs. Jacobi? There you are, that's why she married him: he was enigmatic, the mysterious stranger, handsome and arrogant. It's probably as good, and silly, an explanation as any other."

"And him being a Jew?" Alexandra asked.

"To Mitzi, it didn't matter then. It didn't matter later. It didn't matter to me, either. I liked Aroso, always liked him. My parents, on the other hand, were very opposed to the marriage. My father went into a rage every time the possibility was mentioned. He was so opposed, he refused to talk about it. But he died, and so the main impediment disappeared. Tudor wasn't happy about his future brother-in-law, either, but wasn't very vocal. Mother never said much about the whole thing, and in the end did not oppose their union, which was strange, because she was no Jew-lover. What did you expect, Mrs. Jacobi? Those were the times. And in that part of the world, and you know this as well as I do, anti-Semitism is a national pastime. It's not only the Jews. They hate anybody at all different."

Ovid stood up and walked into the house. After a while, Alexandra heard a toilet being flushed, and the sound brought back the summer evenings she had spent with Aroso. An embarrassingly prosaic link she had hit upon, she thought. Ovid switched on some lights inside the house and one outside, on the wall near the table. It was getting dark.

When Ovid sat down again, he was back to his brother. "Funny thing
is, I didn't even know where Stalingrad was. It was, at that time, a name
that meant nothing. It was Tudor who told me it was a sleepy industrial
town on the Volga, whose only claim to glory was that it had the name
of the monster. They chose the front held by the Romanian divisions.
The Asian hordes went thorough them as if through melted cheese.
Thousands of tanks against a few guns. They just ran over them. Three
and a half years in a Russian POW camp. Can you imagine the horror,
Mrs. Jacobi?"

There were a few answers crowding on Alexandra's tongue, but
that was not why she was there. "Why do you think Aroso chose to stay
in Romania?" she asked.

"After the war?"

"Yes, after the war. Many left as soon as it ended."

"Oh, I don't know. It's such a long time, Mrs. Jacobi, such a long
time. I'd say that it was Mitzi who didn't want to leave. Don't forget, also,
that life was not very comfortable anywhere after the war. Well, maybe
here, on this continent. Later, once Mitzi became very sick, it was too
difficult to move with somebody so incapacitated."

"And before the war?"

"Because of Mitzi, without a doubt. Aroso loved her and was
willing to wait to get her back. And he did get her back. In a way, because
of us, because of the Iron Guard, strange as this may seem to you. And
then her sickness ensured that she would stay with him forever."

"What do you mean?"

"Mitzi went back to Aroso several times. She was unhappy with
him, unhappy without him. She was difficult, depressed, guilt-ridden,
but then marrying Aroso had been a mistake. In '39 or '40, she told me
she would never go back to him, that they were incompatible, that they
did nothing but hurt each other and were better off separated. And
yet, in January 1941, she went back to him and they stayed together
afterwards. During the events of January 1941. Do you know what I'm
talking about?"

"I think so. Go on, please."

"The Iron Guard tried to take control of the country. There
was an attempted coup. Relatively quickly and easily put down. But for

several days there were excesses, horrible excesses, committed against the Jews. Jews picked up at random were killed on the spot or dragged to the Bucharest slaughterhouse and killed there. Aroso's house, on Octavian Street, was not far from the slaughterhouse. Mitzi got word about what was happening. She went berserk. She tried to call me to make sure nothing would happen to Aroso. To ask me to use my influence. The thing is, I was not in Bucharest at that time. I was in Switzerland on business for the bank, and for myself, as I was trying to move some funds out of the country in case things took a turn for the worst. So her frantic messages didn't reach me. I don't know how much influence I would have had, anyway. I looked after the Guard's banking interests; I didn't know any of the thugs who were going after Jews, and my intervention, had I been able to intervene, would have led to nothing or been too late. And furthermore, the attacks on the Jews were random, and as a result were very difficult to control. Anyway, as I said, Mitzi's frantic messages didn't reach me. She didn't have anybody else to approach. She had always despised the Iron Guard (we had numerous arguments about it), and consequently she had nobody to call on for help. So she decided to go and stay with Aroso. First of all, to get him to lie low. To hide him. And, if need be, to defend him or even share his fate. I know this sounds melodramatic, but you had to know Mitzi, to understand this. I don't know whether she would have done it, but, believe me, that was her intention. Well, it turned out there was no need for any heroics. Some Jews from Morilor, which runs parallel with Octavian Street, were picked up, but none from their street. Not from Octavian.

"Aroso was happy to see her, of course. I don't know exactly when and how he figured out why Mitzi had come to stay with him that winter, but he did eventually, because he talked to Lavinia about it. Mitzi always maintained she had simply returned to her lawful husband. She stayed with him, through thick and thin, through the war, worried every time he was sent to forced labour, worried he would get sick or be taken away. Anyway, you know that Bucharest Jews, with the exception of those killed in January 1941, all got through the war.

"We all thought Mitzi would leave Aroso after the war. But she didn't. Oh, she still had affairs, brief and meaningless, but she never left him again. Aroso was not happy about her flings, of course, but he still loved her. Her support during the war affected him considerably. He felt bound to take care of her, see her through her moods, her depressions, her follies. That was before she came down with Parkinson's. At the end of 1945, I remember, she was depressed for three months, during which time she didn't utter a word. One doctor even suggested she might have to be committed. She was in bad shape. Nobody could diagnose what was wrong. So, immediately after the war, when it was still relatively easy to leave, Aroso stayed to look after her. She got slightly better, and then she came down with Parkinson's. And that made Aroso even more determined to take care of her. This, Mrs. Jacobi, was quite a commitment. He had no illusions about Parkinson's. He knew it was there to stay, and was only going to get worse. From what Lavinia wrote to me, he remained absolutely devoted to Mitzi.

"I wrote many letters to Aroso after Mitzi became too sick to write. He answered only once, a very brief letter. In it, he wrote that Mitzi and he were very grateful for the medication I was sending, that it was very helpful to Mitzi, but that I should stop writing to them, because Mitzi couldn't answer and he wouldn't. So, until her death, in 1957, it was Lavinia who kept me informed about what was happening. For the last ... what, twenty years or so, I learned about Mitzi and Aroso through hearsay from others. When Mitzi died, I received another brief note from Aroso telling me what had happened and that I was not to send medication anymore."

The garden had been in darkness for quite a while now. Ovid got up and flicked a switch near the door to the house. A path of light was instantly created beyond the pool, amidst the sea of flowers that followed its convex side.

"Would you like some coffee? Real coffee, not the crap they drink here."

"Please, if you'll have some," Alexandra said.

"Yes, I'll have some."

"Do you remember their house in Octavian Street, Mr. Lovinescu?" Alexandra asked. "How long were Mitzi and Aroso there?"

He began to nod slowly, several times, as if this repetitious agreement helped him remember places and people from the past. After a while he said, "When I think of them, in Bucharest, that's the house that comes to mind, nothing else. I think they lived in that house from the very beginning, but I'm not certain. Aroso didn't want to live in a more expensive neighbourhood. Silly pride. He said he didn't have the money for anything else. As if he had the money for that house. It was bought with Mitzi's money. But he insisted he would pay back the whole amount in due time."

"Did he?"

"Who knows, Mrs. Jacobi? It was Mitzi's money, not mine. Probably. The houses in that area were not expensive. Near the Lemaitre Works and the slaughterhouse. A colleague of Aroso at the university had talked him into it. This colleague, another struggling academic trying to make ends meet, had bought a house there. The city had just built a streetcar line to the centre of the city, so there was transportation to the university. The thing is, with Mitzi's money they could have lived anywhere in a comfortable apartment. But Aroso refused. Mitzi was unhappy on Octavian Street. She didn't like the neighbourhood. She got away from there as often as she could. It wasn't Aroso's best decision. You see, Mrs. Jacobi, when it came to making Mitzi happy, Aroso never had the right ideas. He took good care of her once she got sick, he knew how to do that, but he didn't know how to make her happy. He just couldn't figure out what made a woman like Mitzi happy. I'll make the coffee."

It was very quiet now, with only a faint swish of traffic. Alexandra watched him through the window in the lit kitchen. He made Turkish coffee in a proper pot – small, with a long handle, the top, with a spout, slightly narrower than the bottom. The enamel, she noticed later when he brought the pot out, was appropriately chipped in places. The process was lengthy and interrupted by worried pauses, as if he'd suddenly forgotten something he had done his entire life. He had the coffee ready with the pot on a tray, together with two small cups, when the telephone rang. He put the tray down and picked up the receiver of a wall-mounted phone near the kitchen door. He talked for a long time, and as he talked his body seemed to become smaller and more hunched. He hung up, stood motionless for a while, then disappeared into another room. When he came back, he was holding a tall green bottle. He placed it on the tray, from a cabinet took out two shot glasses and set them on the tray as well, and brought everything out. He poured the coffee into the small cups.

The coffee was bittersweet.

"Sorry it's cold," he said. "I had a call from the hospital, from my wife. She didn't have a good day at all today. It's unexpected, because early this morning, when I went to check on her just before her radiation session, she was feeling fine – quite fine, in fact. I'm going to have something stronger. Would you join me?"

She declined, and she added, "I'm sorry. She'll feel better tomorrow, I'm sure."

He didn't bother to answer. He drank his coffee quickly, in two gulps, then poured himself a shot from the tall green bottle.

"Mr. Lovinescu," Alexandra said, "there were two paintings of Mitzi in Aroso's study on Octavian Street. One of them was called *Mitzi with Colourful Hat*. There was a signature, a short name, but I couldn't make it out. It was a head-and-shoulders portrait of Mitzi wearing a large hat with a dark-green brim and wondrous plumage. In contrast to the hat, Mitzi looked very serious, somewhat resigned. There were hills in the background and, far away, clouds turning pink. The other painting had no title or signature and may not have been fully finished. It showed Mitzi, nude, at the beach, sitting on a towel. She had her back to the painter, although her head was turned towards him. In this painting too, Mitzi's large eyes were serious, and sadly questioning. Do you remember them? They seemed to have been painted by the same artist. Do you know who that was?"

Ovid's face again showed a visible effort to remember. Alexandra was touched by his willingness, by his obvious labour – after all, she was asking about things that happened more than forty years before. Would she do any better as his age? She doubted Ovid would come up with anything.

"Do you do puzzles, Mrs. Jacobi?"

"Puzzles? No, I don't."

"Mariska is very much into puzzles. Flowers and puzzles. She buys gigantic jigsaw puzzles, and it takes her weeks, sometimes months, to complete them. My memory is like one of those large puzzles from which many pieces have disappeared. And other pieces are in duplicate or triplicate, at least in shape, while the images are all different and hardly connect at all. That's the hardest part – what to do with these triplicate pieces? Which ones fit? They all fit, in some way, but which ones are the true ones? I think I know about the paintings, at least about the one on the beach, but there are so many pieces missing, and there are so many multiples. Very yellow, the whole canvas, wasn't it? Very sunny – an explosion of sun. That's all you see, the beach, the sea, and the sky – and Mitzi, of course. She didn't pose on the beach, Mitzi, if I recall. It was just transplanted there. Transpainted – is there such a word? Ionel Groza was the name of the painter. You've said Aroso had this painting hanging in his study?"

"He did."

"Hmm … They lived at the end of the world, you know? Why did they choose to live there? Poor Mitzi. She went with him, to live in that awful suburb. What she had to put up with. Our mother was right, you know, the two of them should never have married. Not suited to each other. I didn't go that often to their house on Octavian Street, but that painting I would have noticed. Mitzi had it with her when she was living apart from Aroso. I saw it many times, but never around Aroso. I wouldn't have thought Aroso would keep it in his study. It did not have happy connotations for him."

Ovid's face lit up in a big smile, and he tapped his wrinkled knees with satisfaction, clearly happy with his ability to come up with the recollection. "Hey, I'm not that decrepit, after all. Yes, I remember. You know why? You know why I remember? For two reasons. It had been the first time I had a fight with Aroso. Quite a disagreement. I told him a few harsh words. It was about Mitzi, of course. How he did not deserve her. How she had every right to look for life and fun elsewhere. Yes, it was the summer of '33. That's the summer I got entangled with Maria, which was the other reason I remembered the painting, the whole set-up. '33 or '34. Aroso had worked the whole winter and spring, continuing into the early part of the summer, on some mathematical idea. I don't know what, never understood a word of what he was doing, but he seemed quite taken by it. He had no time for anything else. What was Mitzi going to do? In fact, Aroso had encouraged Mitzi to go out, meet people."

The ringing of a telephone reached them, and Ovid hurried back into the house with small, unsteady steps. Alexandra heard a sound, a high-pitched grunt, faint but definite, and, looking in the direction it had come from, she saw a cat coming towards her along a path ending near the neighbour's fence. It was a ginger cat, with a fluffy tail, extremely fat and unconcerned. This visit of hers was taking longer than expected. Why all this effort to find out about two paintings of Mitzi, about the sordid affairs in Mitzi's life? Sordid? Why had she assumed that? Sordid was the verdict of time and of critics. To Mitzi and her beaus, the affairs, as they unfolded, may have been anything but sordid. Oddly, the feeling one got was that Mitzi had all these affairs with a sad and heavy heart. Why have affairs, though, if that was the case? What was the point? Was it this impression of a sad and heavy heart that made one think of her affairs as sordid? Was this cat fat or pregnant? Could a cat be that fat? No, she was probably pregnant. After a sordid affair. Cats always had sordid affairs. That was why they always look sad. Cats had sad and heavy hearts and had sordid affairs and got pregnant.

Ovid came back and said a friend of theirs had called for the latest news about Mariska. He sat down and patted the cat, which had relocated itself at Ovid's feet. "Hi, Motram. Odd name for a cat. It's the neighbour's. A tomcat. A fixed tomcat. Quite a good size, isn't he? Very, very fat. Mariska's been a prime contributor to his shape, feeding him whenever he comes about. And he comes about quite a lot. Motram has great difficulties jumping the fence these days. Fat and old."

"I wonder, Mrs. Jacobi," Ovid continued, "I wonder if Aroso was really so disturbed by the idea of Mitzi having affairs. He loved her, and didn't want to lose her, but Mitzi having a life of her own, even if that entailed an affair or two, might not have been so disturbing to him. Maybe at the beginning, but after a while … You know why? Think about it. It was the only way he had enough time to do his work and not lose her completely. You're raising your eyebrows, Mrs. Jacobi. You shouldn't. Is it dismay or disbelief? I think this is what happened.

"Mitzi, Lavinia, and I went to the Black Sea that August. Aroso was supposed to join us, but at the last moment he changed his mind, because he had work or was close to a big discovery or whatever. Well, we went, and it was there that I became aware of Mitzi's liaison. With Ionel Groza, the man who painted those two paintings. We had rented a villa, quite a large one, and had a few friends with us, including Ionel Groza and his wife, Maria. Were they married at that time or just together?

Doesn't matter. Who else was there? Val Rimnic, the doctor, was there, together with his wife; a journalist whose name escapes me; others who came and went. Mitzi and Ionel had known each other casually, and they were casually fond of each other. That summer they had time, much more time, together. I remember seeing them talking and laughing for hours. Ionel had his moments of posing as a brooding artist, but mostly he forgot about it and was quite entertaining. He had ideas, he thought of amusing things to do. He wasn't the most amusing man, but his sudden enthusiasms were contagious. He was fond of practical jokes, and so were Mitzi and Lavinia. We were a merry group. There were always new faces coming and going, young people laughing, beautiful young people. Mitzi loved it, loved the people and the jokes and the dances and the screams, and the dips in the sea at night, and the food and the wine … Ah, it was a good summer, Mrs. Jacobi, a wonderful summer, probably the best. A time without worries, when we were young. I've never seen the sea so blue as I saw it that summer. The Black Sea, as you remember, was not often blue, but that summer it was calm and blue, almost greenish, like a tropical lagoon you'd see in a movie. I might be the only one left alive.

"Yes, I remember that summer very well. You know why? Maria. I was pursuing Maria, and I was only too happy to see Ionel busy in other quarters. Ah, to be young and in love. The girls looked delightful. Mitzi and Maria were stunning. Lavinia also, entertaining and making sure everybody was busy and seduced. I don't know who had the idea. We were watching the three of them – Maria, Mitzi, and Lavinia – walking towards the water, young, graceful, careless, laughing, looking back to make sure they were admired, when somebody said – I don't remember who – that it was too bad this sublime image would quickly fade away and eventually we'd have nothing to remember our youth and the beauty of the girls. Hire a photographer, somebody suggested. But no, photos would not do justice, and, besides, they always get lost. That's when we all agreed that Groza should paint them. From there, to the suggestion of painting them nude – and I think it was Ionel who suggested that – was only one small step and, when the girls returned, it didn't take much to convince them, either. Lavinia agreed at once, Maria with a shrug – she'd posed nude for Ionel many times already – and Mitzi, well Mitzi wasn't sure, that's why her portrait is with her back to the painter. Nothing came of the group rendering, because Groza couldn't find a way to place them such that he was happy with the arrangement, or he lost interest, or whatever. But he did Mitzi's portrait separately, and Maria's. Lavinia's too, likely, but I don't recall seeing it. I bought Maria's painting from him. I kept it until I left Romania. Ah, Maria was devilishly attractive. I can still smell her. She did play hard to get for a while, but when she saw that Ionel had eyes only for Mitzi, well, she responded to my supplications. She either did it to get back at him or his behaviour was the awaited green light. Did I care? Not a bit. To this day … I must be quite drunk. My wife is very sick, dying, and I love her dearly, and here I am reminiscing fondly about Maria's thighs."

Alexandra wasn't that interested in Maria's legs and Ovid's fascination with them. "So Mitzi's affair with Ionel Groza started there?"

"Yes."

"Was this Mitzi's first affair?"

"Mrs. Jacobi, how would I know? Maybe. Definitely not the last one."

And then he asked something that made her think that he was still quite with it. "Does it matter, Mrs. Jacobi? For the monograph – or whatever you or your brother are writing – does it really matter whether it was or wasn't the first of Mitzi's many affairs?"

Alexandra smiled and asked, "What kind of person was Ionel Groza?"

"As I said, full of enthusiasms, with ups and downs in mood, more ups. When up, often reckless. When down, he expected us all to commiserate with him for the pain in his artist's soul. As a painter, he took himself very seriously, struck the right poses, talked the right jargon. I didn't like him that much, but he was a good painter."

"And Mitzi fell for him. She dumped Aroso and went to live with Ionel Groza, right?"

"Yes, but she didn't leave Aroso until the following summer or fall. I don't think she made the decision that lightly, and I think Aroso was much to blame, but, eventually, it was bound to happen … They were too different, and Mitzi would have left him anyway, but it would have taken longer."

"What happened to Ionel Groza?"

"Mitzi left him in a year or two. Groza became involved with the Iron Guard. We drifted apart. Well, I was never a friend of his, and my affair with his wife made our relationship awkward. I learned what had happened to him only because I kept in touch with Maria, who, when Mitzi left Groza, went back to him. Filled the vacant spot, which was hers before. Groza was killed in '41, during Antonescu's reprisals. I've heard that he was bludgeoned to death."

"How did Mitzi's portrait get into Aroso's studio?" Alexandra asked.

"I presume Mitzi had it with her when she returned to him. It was a beautiful portrait. I could see how it ended up in Aroso's studio."

"You said you had a fight, the first fight with Aroso. What was it about?"

"About Mitzi. It was when we got back from the Black Sea. He had promised to join us, as I said, for a week or two, but he didn't. I might have felt a bit guilty about what had happened between Ionel and Mitzi, on my watch, in a way with my blessing. Not that Mitzi would have cared about my opinion one way or another. I told Aroso that he would lose Mitzi, that he had probably lost her already, and that he had only his stupid self to blame. I might have said a few harsh words and he took offence. You know how it is, one unpleasant truth leads to another and before you know it ... You're sure you don't want anything to drink?"

"No thanks. It's late and I should be going. Many thanks, Mr. Lovinescu, I'm very grateful to you ... My best to your wife."

"Don't go yet. Let me show you the flowers. Mariska would be angry with me if I let you go without showing you our flowers."

"Another time, Mr. Lovinescu. You must be very tired. I have to catch the night train back to Montreal. Could you order a cab, please?"

"Humour an old man, Mrs. Jacobi. Please. I'll have something nice to report to my wife tomorrow when I visit her. And you won't leave me too abruptly with all these memories and the thought of my wife dying."

Chapter 17
January 1980

Jean Revescu did not manage to get Ada out of Romania within the three years he estimated it would take. He had kept Alexandra informed with quarterly reports meticulously prepared, typed, and enclosed in large dark blue envelopes, hand-delivered by Revescu's secretary, Gala, a perfumed beauty who seemed to find Alexandra wherever she happened to be. A golden crown and "OMNIA" – the name of Jean Revescu's firm – in discrete letters underneath occupied the upper left corner of each envelope. Revescu's business card, also dark blue with gold lettering, was always attached to each report, together with a sheet instructing the "dear client" to destroy the report or, "at the very least, place it in a secure location. Our business and your interests are best served through full and complete discretion." Charles thought the whole thing childish. "A grown man playing spy games, Alexandra. Who is this M. Revescu? What hole did he crawl out of? And what's that crown doing there?" After a while, Alexandra began to hide the reports from him.

Revescu's reports had a section called Engagements – not more than a few paragraphs summarizing what "the Organization," as he called his office, had done for her in the three months since the last report. The other section of the report, by far the longest, under the heading Expenses, was filled with useless minutiae, or so it seemed to

Alexandra. There were, of course, the numerous flights to Bucharest, a major component of the expenses. The travel cost was shared when the trip was not undertaken uniquely on Mme Jacobi's behalf (the term used was "trip with multiple objectives"). Then there were the accommodation and dining expenses of the agents and of Revescu himself. "Agent" was Revescu's term, and Alexandra's agents were identified as Agent A, B, or C. This had prompted Charles to ask, "Are these agents inside already, or parachuted in?" And then there were entertainment expenses – theatre and concert tickets, meals for two or more at various restaurants, fishing or hunting trips. There were also pursuits of a more delicate nature, labelled "companionship" expenses. Finally, items out of the ordinary came under the category of "special/non-recurring expenses." Included here were mainly presents and outright bribes offered to various security and ministry officials and bribes to hospital officials. "Why bribe hospital officials?" Charles had wondered. "In case he gets wounded?" And Alexandra wondered why "companionship" expenses were not considered special, but classed instead in the same category as ordinary entertainment.

Yes, she could see the silly side of it, and she felt embarrassed at her reliance on Revescu. He was almost like a drug everybody disapproved of but one she needed to keep going.

Leonard had been doubtful about Revescu from the very beginning. He willingly admitted to Alexandra that his skepticism was related to his personal dislike of the man. Leonard had gone along once with Alexandra to meet Revescu and had been taken aback by his unctuousness, his pompous, orotund manner of speaking. "Alsa, get rid of him. He's a crook. An East European nightmare, with sinister Balkan touches. In his office I had the feeling I was back in Romania." But Alexandra wouldn't hear of it. Besides, the lawyer she had retained for the same objective (who, in all fairness, had never seen much reason for hope) had not achieved anything either.

Then, on a Thursday in May, Alexandra was summoned to a meeting with Revescu. Summoned was not the right word – Revescu asked her to join him for lunch at his favourite Romanian restaurant – but to Alexandra it felt like a summons, because of the language in which it was made and because it had been three years since her first meeting with Revescu and she remembered the time limit he had put then on his efforts on her behalf. It felt like a summons also because Revescu had insisted that they meet for lunch. They had important things to discuss, he told her, delicate things, and not necessarily agreeable, and the congenial atmosphere of the restaurant would make the whole thing easier. This sinister preamble had filled her with anxiety, and she was trembling by the time she was shown to Revescu's table in the small restaurant.

Revescu solicitously stood up to kiss her hand and pull her chair out for her. He wore a light beige suit with a blue open-neck shirt revealing a colourful cravat. He has, she thought bitterly, the kind of style one begrudgingly and suspiciously admired. Very good at kissing hands and holding chairs, but it had not crossed his mind that his refusal to say anything more than a few enigmatic words to her before the meeting was heartless.

Alexandra was too paralyzed by fear to ask any direct questions, and Revescu took his time. He told Alexandra that she looked lovely, that she had in her the quintessence of the true Romanian beauty. He said that Alexandra reminded him – not in any one feature, but on the whole, and that's where quintessence came in – of his beloved wife, alas gone to the realm beyond. "Ah, the beauty of Romanian women is very special – there are weightless, spiritual features that cannot be captured and described."

With that out of the way, he began a discussion with the owner of the restaurant, who had waited politely a few feet away until Revescu acknowledged his presence, whereupon he had approached the table and expressed his "enormous joy and pleasure in greeting such a distinguished patron." To Alexandra's relief, it took little time to decide what to have – the owner had emphatically advised they order the braised spring chicken with garlic. "It's real *poussin*," he said, looking at Alexandra, "and the season is almost over. These ones, from a late hatch I've got from a friend, are the very last I have. The garlic sauce is very light and not offensive for other appointments." There, he and Revescu smiled at each other, but then Revescu recovered and quickly mentioned that Professor Jacobi probably had lectures that afternoon and the owner departed with the hope of seeing her often in his restaurant.

Alexandra couldn't take it anymore. "If we could start, Mr. Revescu. It so happens I do have to meet one of my students this afternoon."

Revescu said, "Of course, of course," but then proceeded to tell her that the restaurant owner, M. Dragoi, an engineer in earlier days, had jumped ship – literally jumped from one – at night, somewhere on the Aegean, on seeing lights nearby on land. The lights turned out to be a passing ship, but luckily M. Dragoi was a good swimmer. Even luckier, at daybreak he could see the shore. "I reunited his family – brought over Mme Dragoi and their two children. It's Mme Dragoi who does the delightful cooking you'll have a taste of today."

M. Dragoi returned with an ice bucket in which a bottle of wine was already opened, a white linen napkin wrapped around the neck. Revescu went on, "I have my favourite wine here – from the old country, of course – so I don't have to order it. This white is delicious, peaches and yellow plums. You must have a taste of it." He took a few sips, interspersed with lip-smacking noises, and wouldn't start before Alexandra had a sip and declared her delight at it as well.

"It's been more than three years, Mme Jacobi," Jean Revescu began – these were the dreaded words – "three years of trying, of unsparing endeavours on your behalf. In my opinion, and I say this with a heavy heart, it's useless to continue our efforts – no, please, let me finish. Hear me out. Emil Semeu, your former husband, will not hear about letting Ada go, not even under government pressure. The Romanian government, not surprisingly, wants your dollars, Mme Jacobi. Under your instructions, I went as far as to triple the usual price. I offered thirty thousand dollars, and hinted that fifty or even a hundred thousand might be possible if they held out. This was, of course, very late in the game, when I realized that my best chance was to incite their greed. But they said they can't force him, they can't force Mr. Semeu to sign the papers. They also made the usual – ha, ha, both amusing and nauseating – this-is-a-free-country speech.

"I have done all I can. Whenever I have approached him, your former husband has refused to talk to me. I sent him a letter – no, I sent him many letters. I offered him money – a lot, as per your instructions. Nothing. I stopped him in the street. When he found out who I was, he walked away without saying a word. I talked to his neighbours, with his colleagues at the hospital, with officials at the Ministry of Health. All very discreet, you understand, very understated, trying to make him change his mind. The hope was, Mme Jacobi, that if a colleague, over a meal and a glass of beer, offered opinions of a certain kind, it would help your case. And with a little of your money and with a lot of careful direction, many of his acquaintances and friends, some very new acquaintances, in fact – ha, let me boast a bit – offered opinions very much according to your wishes, Mme Jacobi. Nothing worked. He wouldn't budge."

He paused, then went on, "At this time, Mme Jacobi, your best course is to wait until Ada turns eighteen and is legally allowed to make up her own mind. We have reached the delicate point, Mme Jacobi, when I have to discontinue my services. I cannot continue to serve you on the terms we set three years ago. I feel it is my duty to advise you to stop your efforts to achieve a family reunification for two or three years; that is, until your daughter is eighteen. We can resume our efforts at that time. I am convinced that this is the best course."

Alexandra froze. She couldn't contemplate three years with absolutely no hope. Better a doubtful, forlorn hope than no hope at all. She needed Revescu's quarterly reports, however ridiculous they were, she needed the feeble but always present hope that Emil would change his mind and let Ada join her. She told Revescu that he should not stop, that he could not stop. She told him she had to have some glimmer of hope, some expectations, however unrealistic they were. She begged him. She told him to name his conditions, but that stopping was not an option she could consider at all.

The *poussin* arrived, brought by both M. and Mme Dragoi – or at least Alexandra assumed she was Mme Dragoi, because Revescu, after bringing his nose near the plate uncovered in front of him and sniffing noisily, pronounced her the best chef in Montreal. Happy laughter cascaded down the full chest of the sweaty and happy Mme Dragoi who had also brought a lettuce salad and golden dilled potatoes in separate bowls.

"Eat, eat, Mme Jacobi," Revescu urged. "This is divine. Nectar of the Gods. Mme Dragoi's ancestors must have apprenticed on Mount Olympus."

But Alexandra couldn't touch anything, although she took a few leaves of lettuce on her plate. She watched Revescu enjoying his meal, really going at it with delicate gluttony. He was a noisy eater, and Alexandra had the definite impression that he was chewing the bird's tender bones.

With little of the *poussin* left on his plate, and with a sigh of both worry and satisfaction, Revescu said, "Mme Jacobi, there is another problem as well. Even if Ada were free to come, what makes you think she would want to do so? Come and live with you. Or visit you."

She immediately knew there was something behind Revescu's question, that this was not an idle query. She took a long breath and asked him what, exactly, he meant, since she was fairly sure that, if she could, Ada would join her.

"Oh, I don't know. The thing is … I wouldn't be so certain, Mme Jacobi. Maybe the best is to tell you exactly what happened. Elena Semeu, you do know this already, is the current Mme Semeu. She is, of course, Ada's stepmother. I met her last month for the first time. Lovely woman. Not, of course, of the class of the first Mme Semeu, far from it, but a good woman. A lot of common sense. Life has never been easy over there, or at least not for a long time, I don't have to tell you this, Mme Jacobi, but now it's getting worse. I offered the new Mme Semeu, on your behalf, twenty thousand dollars if she could convince her husband to change his mind. Twenty thousand dollars would be a fortune for her. Would settle her for life. She literally began to tremble when I mentioned the sum. Of course, she would have to spend it hush-hush, in trickles, but I presume she would be able to buy all the dresses, shoes, or jewellery a woman dreams of. She wanted the money badly. She told me that outright, without trying to hide it. But she also told me something startling, Mme Jacobi, something that, if true, would change everything. She told me that even if her husband, Ada's father, changed his mind and agreed to let her go, Ada would refuse to leave. According to the current Mme Semeu – and Mme Jacobi, please take this with a grain of salt – well, according to her, Ada is … she's not keen on joining you. She, it seems, well … she, Ada, does not want to have anything to do with you. She does not seem to be … a … very fond of you. Mme Semeu claims that Ada has said that if she were ever forced to join you, she would simply run away before she had to leave.

"It appears also, Mme Jacobi, that Ada is already beyond reach, or half-gone anyway. Ada, according to Mme Semeu, has not been an easy stepdaughter. Not been an easy child to begin with. Yes. Mme Semeu believes that Ada had always been a difficult child. Ada is hostile to her stepmother, in spite of the best efforts of Mme Semeu. Ada has been wild and uncontrollable. Always. From the very beginning. That's Mme Semeu's story, of course, I'm just repeating her words. But if we were to speculate, Mme Jacobi, if we were to ride the wave of easy psychology so fashionable today, we could say, and this is what Mme Semeu said, that Ada, already abandoned and betrayed by her mother, is afraid that her father would do the same."

"Mr. Revescu, please do not …"

"No, no, of course I do not believe this, Mme Jacobi, there is no need to argue and disturb yourself, nor do I believe that M. Semeu, Ada's father, your former husband, would do such a dastardly thing. I'm just repeating what Mme Semeu said, and what might be going through your daughter's mind. Did you know that Ada now has two small stepbrothers? You knew about one? Yes, the second one arrived less than a year ago. Ada feels threatened. She feels edged out. Anyway, it really does not matter why, our understanding of such things is, of course, at best imperfect, but the fact is that much of Ada's life is now on the street. I mean, and again, this is Mme Semeu talking, there are nights when she does not come home at all."

She wanted to shout at him to stop, but she knew that she had to hear it all. Listening to Revescu's story was like receiving repeated blows to the head, yet she was powerless to protect herself from the onslaught.

"I saw her. I saw Ada, your daughter. The current Mme Semeu pointed her out to me. On the street, not far from their home, with an alarming, menacing looking group her age or older. I tried to talk to her. I was alone, since, once she pointed Ada to me, Mme Semeu had hastily retreated. She might be a bit afraid of her. I tried to talk to Ada. I told her that her mother, her real mother, thinks a lot about her, misses her and wants her to go to Canada. And that she had sent her a few things. She laughed and then used a few choice sentences. Chiefly, she told me to go away. She used much ruder words, which I won't repeat. And she threatened that if I ever returned, her friends – with her assistance – would break my ribs. Yes, quite distressing. She seems capable of it, too. Quite a fierce girl, I'd say. She is, what, fifteen, going on sixteen? According to the current Mme Semeu, she has failed twice in school already. And, again according to Mme Semeu, Ada had had a self-induced miscarriage several months earlier."

She stood up and ran to the washroom. Inside, she leaned against the wall and cried. After a while, she tore off some toilet paper and, looking in the mirror over the sink, tried to repair the damage as well as she could. When she went back, Revescu stood up and moved her chair for her. A dessert plate with traces of brown syrup lay empty on his side of the table.

"I know it's very distressing for you, Mme Jacobi, but I feel I have to tell you all this before you decide on the course to take. I have to be frank with you. If I were to continue my efforts, and I would do it, but reluctantly, it would cost you a fair amount, and probably for nothing. It's your decision, of course. Would you have dessert? No? You're absolutely right. Wouldn't do justice to Mme Dragoi's talents. I keep promising myself that one day I'll come here and have only desserts. What's the point of having dessert when your belly is already pleasantly full?"

She rang Leonard that evening, but there was no answer. She thought of calling Charles, then realized it was too late. She rang Isabelle, but when she heard her voice she put the phone down. She went out for a walk and then, back home, she began trying Leonard every half-hour. He picked up the phone close to midnight. He sounded annoyed and tipsy. He tried to say something, but she told him to stay on the line no matter what. Slowly and quietly sobbing, she told him what had happened. She told him that she asked Revescu to continue, no matter what the cost, and however long it took. Then she cried for several minutes without saying anything, except to ask occasionally if Leonard was still there and thank him when he assured her that he was. She calmed down after a while and said she was sorry for doing this to him but she had nowhere else to turn, as Charles was in Europe and, anyway, she didn't want to burden him with her silly tears. And, after all, what were brothers for?

Leonard told Alexandra to hang on for a second. She heard voices in the background but couldn't make out anything being said. When he came back on the line, Leonard told her that he'd drive up to Montreal for the weekend – probably with Matt and with Clara. They'd all be together and they'd talk. Things couldn't be that bleak, she shouldn't feel so down. "Hang on for one day, Alsa – we'll see you on Saturday. We'll start very early. Maybe we'll take the sleeper. Yes, this way we could be there early in the morning. I'll call tomorrow."

She had cancelled her afternoon meeting with Jerome but, without thinking straight, had agreed to meet him the following day. She called the department in the morning to cancel that day's appointments also. In the evening, she felt slightly better and walked to the corner store. When she came back, she caught Leonard's call. He had been ringing for a while and was worried.

"I'm fine, Leonard, I'm fine." she said. "It's been rough, but I'll survive. There was nothing to eat in the house, so I crawled out to the corner store. I cancelled all the appointments I had today, and now there's the weekend and I'll see you and Matt and I'll be fine. And Clara, of course. It was awful the first twenty-four hours, but I'm better now. Dr. Time – the great healer – has been looking after me."

Chapter 18
June 1981 - January 1985

It had been Charles's idea to take a long trip that summer, five or six weeks in Europe. It would do wonders for her, he told Alexandra, he was sure. He was worried about her. "Lysiane also thought you were looking very sad the last time she saw you. She told me to amuse you, to take you away for a month or so. She cautioned me to find somewhere different, a place that will make you forget about things for a while."

Where, though? France, of course, but where else? And then Leonard, when Alexandra phoned him, suggested Istanbul.

"Yes, Istanbul. Go to France, by all means, but if you want something different, go to Istanbul. Unique, majestic. Constantinople, Byzantium, Istanbul. The Golden Horn, the Bosphorus – you won't regret it. And while you are in Istanbul, you might as well see if you can find anybody who remembers Aroso or his family. It would help me with my book. And it would be a distraction for you, all for a good cause. I meant to do it myself, return to Istanbul and see if I can find any traces of Aroso."

"Come with us."

"I'd like to, but I can't. I promised Matt a canoeing trip in Algonquin. Wilderness, loons, portages, beavers, deer flies. Civilized dangers. Clara is behind this – she does it every summer with a group of like-minded friends. You know the kind – bear wrestling, feed-the-mosquitoes devotees. She talked so much about it that Matt made me promise I'd do it this summer. All I know about canoeing is that water is involved. I have another suggestion, though, somewhere we could get together. Gottingen. I was planning to visit Gottingen – again for the book – for a couple of days after Algonquin. I'll join you in Gottingen if you make it part of your itinerary. You must visit Gottingen, Alexandra. Isn't it like a shrine for mathematicians?"

They were overwhelmed by Istanbul, but Charles's delight in the city was much more vocal. He acquired a pocket French-Turkish dictionary and learned how to pronounced the Turkish words. Soon they were sailing on Marmara Denizi (the Sea of Marmara), crossing the Bogazic (the Bosphorus), gazing across the Halic (the Golden Horn). They visited the Dolmabahce Sarayi (the Dolmabahce Palace), took the boat to Kizil Adalar (the Princes' Islands) from the Salacak Iskelesi (the Salacak Pier) on the Asian side. They strolled on the bridges – *koprusu* – across the Golden Horn and across the Bosphorus. They went to the Kapali Carsi (the Old Bazaar). They saw the Suleymaniye Camii (Suleyman's Mosque), the Blue Mosque, the Topkapi Sarayi, the Haghia Sophia. They took long walks, one time as far as the sombre citadel of Yedikule, where so many prisoners of the Sublime Porte languished for their remaining days. They walked the narrow streets and alleys of the older city, and Alexandra tried to find the street names Aroso had mentioned in his story. They crossed the bridge over the Golden Horn to Galata, climbed the hill to Beyoglu and as far as the Technical University, meandered through the *allées* of Yildiz Park. They took the ferry across the Bosphorus to the Asian shore of the city and the bus along the Bosphorus towards the Black Sea, through the little towns spread out along the water. They saw poor neighbourhoods, but the overall impression of the city was of overwhelming majesty and timelessness – on two continents, divided by the spectacular Bosphorus, overlooking one sea and almost reaching another. Charles loved to repeat the Turkish words he had learned. He claimed that they were pleasant-sounding, like the gentle ripples of the water when, late on a quiet night, they sipped a glass of *raki* in a small open-air tavern on the shore of the Bosphorus. As a tribute to Aroso, they ate fish freshly caught and fried on the spot, served up with black bread and raw onion from boats on the water. Charles was a bit doubtful, but Alexandra found the fish delicious. She also shed a few tears, and she wasn't sure whether it was the harshness of the onion or the recollection of Aroso.

Charles was restless, exhilarated, ablaze, and his enthusiasm rubbed off on Alexandra. But she found Istanbul melancholy, and she wondered whether it was the city itself or its association in her mind with Aroso. She recalled, or thought she did, that Aroso's eyes were often misty when he talked of Istanbul. When she first saw the Bosphorus, she greeted its dark blue waters with unexpected emotion. She thought she could see why Istanbul, a place in which Leonard had spent only a week, waiting to get to another place, had taken such a hold of him. She convinced herself that her nose detected the eternal mysteries of the Levant, and when she imparted this thought to Charles, he nodded happily, "Without a doubt, my dear, without a doubt." They rented a boat for a day-long ride along the Bosphorus, an extravagance they wondered if they could afford, and happily pretended that they were with young Asuero on the Dacostas' rented *kayik*.

They didn't worry too much about the research task Leonard had assigned to Alexandra. They were inept as trackers of Aroso's life – utterly, thoroughly, inept – but they did try, and Alexandra assured Charles, when he worried aloud that Leonard would be disappointed, that Leonard would understand. This was a vacation, not a working assignment.

"We haven't gone about it the right way," Charles said to her. "We shouldn't have come here without some solid letters of recommendation to people with enough connections or interest to help us dig into Aroso's past."

While they waited for answers to their questions and requests from puzzled clerks who seemed unsure of what was expected of them (and, even if they understood, doubted that they could help), they took long walks with a retired couple from Springfield, Massachusetts. Ed Tekin had taught history at some college in New England, and now that he was retired, he and his wife, Nancy, were spending much of their time in Istanbul. Ed had a passion for Suleyman the Magnificent and his period. Spry and full of energy, he spoke Turkish fluently (his father had emigrated from Turkey to America as a young man) and felt happy in Istanbul. He came as often as he could afford. Nancy did not mind. She cheerfully followed her husband everywhere, writing down his observations. Ed was writing a book about Suleyman. They had met the Tekins in the hotel's small breakfast room one early morning. One thing led to another, and Charles told them about their failed searches and that one of their last hopes was City Hall, where they had been promised they'd receive a message at the hotel if the staff there found something. "Come along with us, if you have nothing else to do," Ed said. "I'll go with you to City Hall. Who knows, it might speed matters up. We fellow researchers should help each other. I wouldn't get my hopes too high, if I were you, though. This is the Orient, things don't happen that fast. Hell, the bureaucrats back home aren't that fast either. It's unfortunate you can't stay longer. You should ask them to mail things to you if they find something after you've left. A bit of incentive money wouldn't hurt, although it doesn't grease the wheels as well as it used to. I'll show you how it's done. Meanwhile, join us. The more the merrier. I am sure Nancy would like to talk about other things besides Suleyman the Magnificent. Isn't that so, dear?"

Ed was happy to have a student of Charles's fervour, but one evening he confessed to them that lately he found the developments in Istanbul disturbing. The city was much noisier, more modern, more polluted than ever. The traffic was horrendous. The beautiful mosques and palaces were still there, but so were new apartments and hotels of strident incongruity.

The four of them took a helicopter tour, and from the air Istanbul looked as grand and magnificent as ever, the multitude of domes and half-domes had such stone-like hues and striations that Alexandra thought of giant prehistoric turtles petrified forever near a river. The next day they were caught in a sweltering traffic jam on the new suspension bridge across the Bosphorus, and for an hour they ingested exhaust fumes through the opened windows of their cab while the driver listened to a soccer game on the radio turned up to maximum volume. The Bogazici Bridge was slim and elegant from a distance, Ed had to admit that, but distressing as an idea. "You don't get to the continent of Asia by simply crossing a bridge," he complained. "It's like crossing the North Pole in a plane at thirty thousand feet on the way to Osaka. Big deal!" He felt that his disapproval was silly, but he couldn't help it. Nancy told him he was like the critics of the Eiffel Tower in *fin de siècle* Paris. "Snap out of it, Ed," she told him. "There is a new pulse to the city, and energy, and growth, and the people live better, and you are nothing but a fool, a prematurely old man disturbed by change and with no understanding of modern cities."

But the city is losing its enchantment," Ed replied, "its magic, its sorcery." He asked the driver to turn down the volume on the radio. In the relative silence that followed he turned to Nancy and said, "You might be right. It's I who have lost the ability to let myself be bewitched."

Alexandra and Charles went back to tracking Aroso, and they had a bit of luck, or so they thought. Alexandra remembered Aroso telling her that his family lived across the Golden Horn from the Old City, in a Jewish area of Istanbul. Ed told them that that was likely Haskoy, a bit further up the Horn, just before the Fatih Bridge. They took the boat to Haskoy. Up the steep hill from the wharf, they reached the Maalem Synagogue, where they were directed to the Jewish Old Age Home. Not far at all, they were assured, only a couple of minutes. "Well," Alexandra said to Charles, "this is the break we've been waiting for. We'll be able to talk to people of Aroso's generation. People who grew up with him. Same playgrounds, same schools, same stores. If they don't remember Aroso, no one will, and we might as well give up."

The home turned out to be a beautiful stone building. "It was once a school," they were told in very good English by a man in a well-cut suit who was pushing an old woman in a wheelchair. "It now looks after those at the other end of life. My mother attended school in this very place." The old woman had her eyes shut. Her head was tilted backwards and to the side, her face sunken and depleted. "She doesn't know I'm here," the man said.

He offered to help them. They found several old women – there were hardly any men about – who were quite willing to talk and reminisce.

One of them spoke French and acted as an interpreter, but nobody remembered the Arosos. They did remember the Dacostas, though. Yes, very, very rich family, good family, the best, but no, the Dacostas did not come to the nearby synagogue, good God, of course not, they went to a much larger and wealthier synagogue. It made them merry, and they laughed and chatted among themselves in what Alexandra assumed was Ladino for several minutes when she suggested that preposterous idea. They were all gone, the Dacostas, all gone, a long time ago. To America. To Israel. Alexandra asked where the synagogue was that the rich Dacostas attended. They gave her an address in Beyoglu, but they warned her that it was closed most days. Not enough rich Jews left, they said, and they laughed again. All gone abroad.

She asked them if they went to the Maalem Synagogue. Sometimes. Mostly for the main holidays. If they weren't too tired. It was hard at their age. Laughter. Charles asked if there were record books listing the members of their synagogue. There were. But the man who kept them was away for several weeks, and he was the only one who could show them to them. They weren't sure how far back they went, anyway. Why keep old lists? What for?

They were about to give up when one of the women, who had a four-legged walker beside her, suddenly came to life and, with a squeaky voice, claimed to remember the Arosos. But did she, really? She talked about two children, a girl and a boy. And she said that the mother was much taller than the father, and that created another bout of merriment and excitement. Alexandra asked if the boy went to study abroad. That led to a long pause, and Alexandra had the feeling she was influencing an already foggy witness. Prodded again, the old woman said that the boy indeed went to study abroad and had never returned. He became a doctor. A doctor? Alexandra was disappointed. Was she sure? A physician? Somebody who cured the sick? Yes, a physician, no doubt. A doctor. Whether he cured the sick or not, she could not say, since he had never come back to cure them. More merriment.

Ed Tekin went with them to City Hall. When he asked about the German *gymnasium*, they were met with blank stares until a man wearing thick dirty glasses and a blue tie with yellow donkeys on it said that there was indeed a German school in Istanbul. He wrote the address down after a few minutes of searching through a huge folder he removed from a drawer. The Deutsche Schule. Any cab would take them there.

The Tekins didn't go along – they were driving down the Aegean coast that morning, and they hurried back to the hotel. The school was in a nondescript building in Beyoglu, not far from the Galata Tower. They met the secretary to the school's director, who was there quite by accident; she had to pick up something for her boss. It was their good luck, she assured them in fair French. Otherwise, during the summer, it was hard to find anybody around. She was keen to talk about the history of the school. Founded in 1868. Yes, that long ago, and it had been educating young people ever since. Well, a few years of interruption after each of the world wars. When Alexandra told her about their interest in a former Jewish student who graduated in the twenties and later became a mathematician known through the whole world (Alexandra thought she could only gain by exaggerating Aroso's fame), the secretary shook her head. There were hardly any records from those days. She wished she could help. Then she brightened up. She was happy to tell them that the first student to graduate from the high school – it became a full high school in 1911 – had been a Jewish student. They thanked her and left, wondering how she knew this, given the lost records.

The small hotel was on Goetheallee, not far from the railway station. Leonard had arrived in Gottingen a couple of days before them and had made some inquiries already. There was some confusion, he told Alexandra and Charles the evening they arrived, as to how easy it would be to access records from more than fifty years earlier, but in the end the records were found. The university even provided him with help: a young student named Kurt, who spoke passable English and was keen on improving it. He made copies of all the pages in which he found Aroso's name and attached – in contorted English – brief descriptions of the context. Leonard hoped to get some help back home from somebody who knew German.

In the five days they stayed in Gottingen – a whole week for Leonard – they could not locate anybody who remembered Aroso. "It was to be expected," Charles said, seeing Leonard's obvious disappointment.

They took long walks in the streets of old Gottingen and along its walls, transformed at the end of the previous century into a pedestrian walkway. They found Munchansenstrasse and tried to guess which house had been Frau Huber's *pension*. They asked a couple of older people in the street, but no one could remember that far back. Leonard's helper, Kurt, eventually found it the next day by going through the city records, and they went back to Munchansenstrasse. It was a grey, three-storey townhouse, with tall windows, shutters, and ornamental balconies, attached on both sides to similar townhouses with different shades of grey. It was a dull day, with very low clouds and the menace of imminent rain, and they stared for half an hour at the building from across the street until Charles protested that he had had enough.

They strolled on Hilbert's street – Wilhelm Weber Strasse – under leafy linden trees and a warming noon sun, and passed several times by the yellow-brick house once inhabited by the Hilberts. They tried to figure out where the blackboard might have been mounted – Hilbert's outdoor office, as Aroso had called it – but couldn't. Anyway, why would the next occupant, or occupants, have kept it?

Did Hilbert ever talk to Aroso about Cantor? This was something she forgot to ask Aroso. A pity. Alexandra asked Leonard whether Cantor ever visited the Hilberts in the Wilhelm Weber Strasse. What did Hilbert really think of Cantor? Of Cantor as a person, not as a mathematician. Hilbert's opinion about Cantor the mathematician was well known. Didn't he call Cantor's work "the most admirable fruit of the mathematical mind, and one of the highest achievements of man's intellectual processes"? But as a person?

Leonard didn't know for a fact that Cantor had ever visited the Hilberts. But he held forth on Alexandra's questions – more loud musings than questions – while they "walked the wall" back to their hotel, gripping Alexandra's arm and then forcing them down into the soft leather armchairs in the small lobby, eager to talk. Cantor died in 1918. He was only seventeen years older than Hilbert. They must have met many times. What did Hilbert think of the strange Halle professor who believed his set theory inspired by God and who thought to battle materialism through the transfinite set theory? What did Hilbert think of this man whose mathematics had as much philosophy and religion as it had mathematics, who felt himself persecuted, who spent almost a quarter century trying to prove the continuum hypothesis, and gave up on mathematics for the last part of his life? What did he think of this man who suffered numerous nervous breakdowns and who died in a hospital for the mentally ill? (Was it a lunatic asylum that Cantor died in, or in a dignified mental hospital? Are there such things as dignified mental hospitals? Did they have mental hospitals in those days?) Cantor begged his wife – whom he adored – to come and take him home. What did Hilbert think of Cantor's efforts to prove that Joseph of Arimathea was the father of Christ? Or that Francis Bacon was the true author of Shakespeare's plays? He was an odd one, Georg Cantor, no doubt about it. What did a man like Hilbert – the acme of rationality and common sense – make of a mathematics professor who wrote in a letter to the German Ministry of Culture in Berlin, in a non-sequitur attempt to escape the University of Halle, that he had unique knowledge about the first kings of England "which will not fail to terrify the English government as soon as the matter is published?" Terribly tragic figure, Cantor's. Poincaré, the greatest mathematician of those days, had called him a charlatan, and Kronecker, from his lofty chair at the University of Berlin, had kept Cantor away and had undermined his theories at every opportunity. Was there anything worse than dying in a nuthouse? On the other hand, what would have happened if Cantor had lived long enough to catch Hitler's reign? Cantor was a Christian, a devout Christian, but his father had converted from Judaism to become a Protestant. His mother, a Catholic, came also from a converted family. Would Hitler have left him alone? Not likely. Besides, a theory of infinite sets was the kind of sick Jewish mathematics the Nazis had liked to index.

Kurt made a list of the names of the students who, with Aroso, seemed to have attended the same lectures. Leonard complained that trying to locate them would be a monstrous task, too lengthy and way too costly. Kurt turned out to be quite enterprising and said that he would try to match the names on the list with names on the current roster of active members of the Gottingen Alumni Society. And indeed, wonderful Kurt – enthusiastic, helpful, and quietly efficient – found a match, a certain

Egon Erhardt Zernst, a former math teacher now living in a retirement home in a small town between Frankfurt and Darmstadt. Leonard asked Kurt to try to contact Egon Zernst by phone and ask him if he remembered Aroso. They were in luck. Kurt had no difficulty contacting Egon Zernst, and Egon Zernst did remember Aroso, although, as it turned out, only vaguely, and when pressed for details he was prone to cheerful improvisation. Kurt and Leonard took the train from Gottingen – Leonard told Alexandra and Charles the story later – and met Egon Zernst in Langen, at a beer hall near the railway station. It was the early afternoon, and the large restaurant was fairly empty and quiet. Egon Zernst had had lunch there earlier, including a few beers. He had a touch of red on his cheeks and was quite expansive. With his round, almost bald head, small, smiling eyes, starch-white moustache, and tubby mid-section, Egon Zernst looked like a jovial, beer-loving seal. "Of course I remember Aroso. Who wouldn't? Exotic, smart, and arrogant, that's how I remember him. Very tall, too. All bones, not much flesh on him. Not like me, ha-ha. Good looking, in a sickly, romantic way. From Istanbul, right? A mathematical genius from Turkey. Well, it was quite rare in those days. Of course, he was a Jew, and that explains it. Oh yes, I remember him. We did not mingle, though. I remember he was always seen with the same young Russian mathematicians, whenever they were in Gottingen. And he made friends with one of Courant's protégés, another brilliant Jew, Levy, or something like that. Aroso only talked to the very, very smart students, and I wasn't one of them. Ha, ha. He had long discussions with professors and their assistants. Rumour had it that he even sat at the Hilberts' dinner table once or twice. Or was it Bernays's? No, hold it, Bernays was not married, couldn't be. No, at the Hilberts. Or the Landaus. He was very bright. Extraordinarily bright. During lectures, his questions and remarks betrayed an understanding that was beyond most of us. Arrogant, very full of himself. He even told Hilbert off, during one lecture. It was a famous incident, much commented upon among us, until we were told to keep quiet about it or Aroso's stay in Gottingen would come to an abrupt end. I don't remember exactly what he said, but he told him off. What happened to him? Where did he disappear to?"

On the whole, Leonard did not learn much about Aroso that he didn't already know. So he tried to steer Egon Zernst into talking about the atmosphere in Gottingen during those long-gone days.

On the morning of their last day, they went to the Mathematics Institute, the house that Courant built with the help of American money, a remarkable feat for those economically difficult days. Charles, who had been there already a couple of times warned them, "It's not worth it – quite an ugly building." It was south of the city wall, on Bunsenstrasse. Maybe not ugly, Alexandra thought, but large and unimpressive, a clear victim of a time when funds were scarce. It had a flat, grey, monotonous façade, with no adornment whatsoever. Two trapezoidal staircases, as plain as the rest of the building, led to entrances. They tried to get in, but it was Sunday and the doors were locked.

Leonard's monograph about Aroso was published in the summer of 1984 by Galileo House, a small publishing firm in Toronto that specialized in middlebrow science. In perennial financial crisis, Galileo House survived mainly through provincial subsidies and grants from federal agencies. Alexandra learned all this from Murray Walker, when she attended a one-day workshop at the University of Toronto. He had recommended Leonard's book to a neighbour of his, a retired chemistry professor who was on the editorial board of Galileo House.

"I liked your brother's book – the draft I've seen. There are not enough books like this around. Ought to be published. I told Leonard that his best chance was with Galileo House and that I'll talk to my neighbour. In the end, Galileo agreed. It took some persuasion, they summoned me to an ad-hoc editorial board to – how did they put it? – get a better feel."

When it eventually came out, after more than two years of ups and downs, the book about Aroso was published with three authors, and was thicker than the very slim volume that Leonard had initially envisaged. Leonard had asked Alexandra to contribute a piece about her former professor. She sent, very quickly, in two weeks, twenty pages of densely written math about Aroso's interests and contributions to mathematics. It was not an easy read, Leonard complained. Alexandra's pages were clearly written for specialists, and when he pointed that out to her, she added half a dozen pages of personal recollections about what it was like to have been a student of Aroso and what it was like to have worked with him. At Murray Walker's suggestion, Leonard insisted on having her name added as an author. At first, she wouldn't hear of it, but she consented when he explained that it would help with the publishing of the book. The third author was Sam Dorfmann, a German-speaking doctoral student of Murray Walker, who undertook to translate into English the manuscript Aroso had given Alexandra in the blue envelope proving the consistency of Cantor's continuum hypothesis. Sam Dorfmann also wrote a dozen introductory pages on the specifics of Aroso's paper, the history of the problem, and the idiosyncrasies of the German mathematical symbols used by Aroso. On this last topic, Sam Dorfmann had to do a lot of research, and Leonard felt that his name should also be added as an author. And, who knew, maybe the addition of a Canadian-born author would also help with the procrastinating crowd at Galileo House. The original German text of Aroso's manuscript was also included in the monograph.

Altogether, the book ended up being close to three hundred pages in length. The title of the book, on which Leonard had agonized for almost three years, was a compromise, and awkwardly long: *Asuero Aroso: The Continuum Hypothesis and the Discovery of an Astonishing Mathematician.* "The length of the title," Charles said cynically, "and its ambiguity, will give it credence among the academics."

The reviews, and there were only a few, since hardly anybody paid attention to the book, were mixed, but mainly dismissive and sarcastic. One review was particularly unkind. Leonard made a copy of it and sent it to Alexandra.

Mr. Jacobi has the annoying habit of unearthing mathematicians that were long forgotten (or not even that, because to be forgotten, you have to be known first) and trying to resurrect them into geniuses they never were. In the past he had delighted us by bringing Olinde Rodrigues out of a tomb which should have stayed un-desecrated. The long forgotten Rodrigues came back riding the ridiculous claim of having discovered quaternions before Hamilton. Therefore, Mr. Jacobi argued, it was Olinde Rodrigues and not Hamilton who deserved to be considered the father of modern abstract algebra.

This time Mr. Jacobi has written an entire book in order to shed light on another obscure mathematician, a Turkish-Jewish-Romanian mathematician who seems to have died ten years ago, a certain Asuero Aroso. Aroso, according to Mr. Jacobi, was a student of Hilbert and Bernays in Gottingen in the twenties. If true, this is Aroso's only claim to glory. But Mr. Jacobi builds some sort of mathematical melodrama from which nothing is missing. Indeed, one finds beautiful and whimsical women, passion, the tragedy of the Jews during the Second World War, exotic locations, square and neglecting fathers, deadly hesitations and fateful decisions, sacrifice and waste. Rather Hollywood and naïve. But this is not enough for Mr. Jacobi. Because, you see, during his humble career Asuero Aroso made a remarkable mathematical discovery. Mr. Jacobi claims that it was not Kurt Godel who proved for the first time – in the late thirties – the consistency of the continuum hypothesis, but – what do you know? – Asuero Aroso himself, who did it several years earlier. Mr. Jacobi has difficulty explaining why Asuero Aroso failed to inform the world that he had solved the most famous mathematical problem of the century. That's where the whole story collapses and becomes more ridiculous than ever.

To top it all, the writing is rigid, graceless, and obviously written by somebody whose mother tongue is not English. There is a transcript, in German, of a paper allegedly written by Asuero Aroso in the early thirties and never published, in which Aroso describes his discovery. There is an English translation of it also, but not being a mathematician myself, it was incomprehensible to me. I gave it to a friend of mine, a mathematician, who has assured me it is all gibberish.

The reader finds also twenty pages of dense symbols and formulae explaining the other mathematical contributions of the same Asuero Aroso. It is written by a well-known professor of mathematics at the University of Montreal, Ms. Alexandra Jacobi, who is a co-author. I wondered why Ms. Jacobi, who, my mathematician friend informs me, is quite a famous and respected mathematician, would stoop to write it? The same last name quickly explains the mystery.

There was no note from Leonard with the copy of the article. Alexandra got home quite late the day it arrived in the mail, and she read it while making tea. She rang him. He was glad to hear her voice, but seemed tired and listless.

"You don't sound like a famous author celebrating the publication of his book. Or is it that you're exhausted by too much celebration."

"Oh, Alsa, there isn't much to celebrate."

"Pay no attention to the reviewer. It's a wonderful accomplishment, Leonard."

"Maybe," he said, after a long pause. "I'm worn out for some reason. Now that the book's finally published, I feel too drained to think of it as an accomplishment. It is an accomplishment, isn't it, Alsa, whatever the critics say?"

"Of course it is. Charles loved it."

"The review I sent you is the worst. Clara thought it was quite funny. I presume, in time, I'll come to see the humour. I'm afraid that writing the thing and battling to get it published – while holding a full-time job and spending weekends with Matt – has exhausted me. I told myself that in a month or two I'd feel better. It's been a while, though, now, and I'm still not shouting whoopee. No, I don't feel elated, mainly aimless. I'm taking a break from writing about mathematics. To make it worse, work at the bank is giving me less and less satisfaction. I've been doing econometric models for a dozen years now. Younger people, who work longer hours and have opinions about everything, have been promoted above me. I've been telling myself that staying in a lower-level position gives me time to concentrate on my mathematical writing, but now that the book's done I'm beginning to have second thoughts. Maybe I should take a few courses in economics, get a better understanding of what I've been modelling and programming. Several colleagues and bosses have told me the same already. Maybe it's time to pay more attention to my career and future."

"But you love writing, Leonard. That's what you love, writing about mathematics."

"Maybe Monica was right. I'm thirty-nine years old, divorced, with a twelve-year-old son who I see only now and then and who thinks I'm odd and in need of strange signs of affection. I have hardly any friends and only a few acquaintances. I think about re-marrying from time to time, but it has remained only a thought. And in the meantime

I've managed to exasperate Clara to the point that she's booted me out of her life."

"When? What happened?"

"A couple of weeks ago. She'd had enough. Disgusted by my inability to make up my mind, she stopped seeing me. When I asked why, she told me she wanted a husband, not just a boyfriend to screw and have dinner with once a week. She said she needed somebody who enjoyed her friends and didn't grunt and get drunk at parties; somebody that was a permanent presence, a friend she could be with all the time; somebody she could talk to, for hours in a row if she needed to; somebody who would fix the deck and take the garbage out; somebody who would reassure her and tell her she was beautiful. And Andrew (that's Matt's friend) needed a father, a permanent presence. It was quite a list, Alsa. She told me I was unable to commit. 'I understand that,' she said, 'but it's enough waiting for me. You are a good man, Leonard, but somewhat flaky. You don't seem to be fully here. Frankly, I don't understand you. You have a drink or two and wax lyrically about Olinde Rodrigues and that Turkish mathematician – Aroso, or whatever his name was. Why can't you talk poetically about me? About us? Leonard, dear Leonard, it's more than just a dinner and a screw. You are a cripple in some way – stunted development.'"

"She didn't mince her words, did she?"

"I was quite taken aback, not by her decision, but by the harshness of her verdict. I told her that her criticism of me wasn't very consistent. Big mistake. She could barely control herself. 'Consistent? Consistent? That's all you have to say? Let Godel and that blasted Aroso worry about consistency. This is life, Leonard, not math. Life is anything but consistent. You're hopeless.' She was quite nettled by the consistency criticism, and she let me know about it, because she went after me with a vengeance. It was the commitment, again, but this time amplified. It wasn't just my unwillingness to commit to our relationship, but about commitment in general, in all aspects of my life. According to her I can't commit to my work at the bank because it's too boring and, anyway, math is my real interest. And I don't fully commit myself to math – even writing about math – because I also hold a job. This way, she charged me, I can't fail, because, either way, it's only a half-hearted, part-time attempt on my part. I'm an outsider in both. And I chose to be an outsider, I like it. There aren't many risks in being an outsider, a cool observer. I observe and make sarcastic remarks to myself – the kind of remarks I make, she knows, about her friends. The kind of remarks that betray, it seems, my sense of superiority, the overwhelming superiority of the serene observer. 'It's stifling around you,' she said. 'It must be hard to breathe in your outsider bubble.'"

Alexandra laughed. "Well, I have to hand it to her – she does speak her mind."

"I thought it was for the best when it happened – a couple of weeks ago – but I'm not sure anymore."

"You mean, you miss her?"

"I don't know. Do I miss Clara, or does my loneliness combined with this post-book depression make me think I miss her?"

"I liked Clara. I mean, the one time I met her, she seemed very nice. Cheerful. You need a cheerful woman in your life, Leonard. Are you going to call her – try to patch things up?"

"I don't know. I doubt it. I'm doing fine, Alsa, I'm doing fine."

"I'm coming to Toronto to see you. Next weekend. I'd do it earlier, but I have a few urgent things to do. Things pile up when you're away."

When she got to Toronto, she found Leonard in fine spirits, in spite of the cold, windy day. The landing at Pearson had been wobbly – the captain said, "Sorry, folks" – and as she walked out of the airport to hail a cab, it began to rain. In the evening, their walk to a nearby pub on Yonge Street became a struggle against the chilly horizontal rain. The pub was nearly empty, and they sat in a corner. Leonard told her the story behind his good mood.

"Not long after Clara threw me out of her life, I had dinner with Monica. She suggested it, out of the blue, one Sunday evening when I took Matt back to her house. Did Matt tell her that Clara wasn't in the picture anymore? I don't know. He claims he didn't, but nothing escapes the little fellow. Monica has had a few 'involvements' – that's her term for emotional entanglements – with other men. I knew about two of them, both fairly brief. My source was Matt, who was very well informed and matter-of-fact about it. He won't volunteer news about his mother, but supplies it when asked, and I always ask. With a bit of extrapolation and filling in of gaps, I've vaguely kept track of Monica's life. When she suggested we go out to dinner, she hadn't been 'involved' with anybody for, I would guess, a couple of years. Of course, we also see each other when we pick up or drop off Matt, but on these occasions the conversation is often minimal.

"When we sat down to dinner, Monica said she wasn't proposing a renewal of our relationship, but why not have a pleasant dinner and chat? 'After all,' she said, 'looking back, you were the nicest of the men in my life. By a long stretch. Don't be too smug, now.' We did have a pleasant dinner and chat, which ended, of course, in bed, and we've had a couple more of these trysts. We're taking it one day at a time and are very careful, very prudent. We're both wary of each other and of renewing any commitment – for Matt's sake, we tell ourselves. He views this new aspect of his parents' relationship with almost scientific curiosity. The first time he saw me coming out of his mother's bedroom one morning, he said, 'Hmm, interesting.' The second time, he remarked, with a sweet smile, 'I guess there were plenty of *fectionate* hugs in there, Dad.'"

Several months after the publication of the monograph, Alexandra sent Leonard a book about Cantor. Written by Joseph Dauben – who, according to the cover, taught history of science at the City University of New York – and published in 1979 by Princeton University Press, the book was a modern view of Cantor's life and achievement. She wrote a few words to Leonard with the book: "It would have been more useful to you several years earlier, as you were struggling through your book about Aroso, but it was only last week that somebody mentioned it to me. Let me know what you think about it. I'm sending it to you after only a quick browse through it. I wouldn't mind reading it myself once you've read it."

Leonard called her a couple of weeks later. "I just finished Dauben's book. Didn't understand much of the mathematics. So, that's the latest diagnosis on Cantor: manic-depressive, typical bipolar personality."

"It seems to be."

"Dauben is probably right, but how disappointing."

"Disappointing?"

"Unsatisfactory. I liked the old story better, that he went mad trying to prove the continuum hypothesis, looking, for all those years, for that final sign from the Almighty. Or battling the evil Kronecker."

"Oh, I see."

"To me – knowing that the continuum hypothesis could not be proven, knowing that his Sisyphean efforts were bound to fail – his madness used to have something heroic and affecting about it. There's a little poem in the book that Cantor wrote to his wife from the hospital a few months before he died. He awkwardly expresses his love for her in the poem, and his gratitude. A poem to a wife who didn't want to (or couldn't) take him back. It's a Cantor that is both heroic and human. Heart-wrenching. But now, with this modern diagnosis, all we are left with is a genetic disposition pre-stamped into Cantor by the vagaries of inheritance and random mutations. The whole thing becomes somewhat dull and uninspiring, wouldn't you say?"

"You're incorrigibly romantic."

"There's a parallel that Dauben draws between Cantor and Van Gogh, both manic-depressive, according to modern medical opinion; that is, both having bouts of madness, and, in-between, enjoying euphoric and creative periods. Well, so what, I told myself. But then I looked at Cantor's photographs in the book, especially the one taken in 1917, a few months before he died, and the resemblance to Van Gogh was striking. At first I thought that it was only a superficial resemblance – both of them, not surprisingly, showing suffering in their faces, the haggard, gaunt look of depression. But the likeness was uncanny. Maybe some shared genes from a common ancestor, a manic-depressive genius."

"Yes, you're right. I also thought of the odd resemblance."

"What kind of person devotes a lifetime to the study of infinities? Mathematical infinities, I grant you, but from Cantor's point of view it was the universal infinite, the infinite of philosophy and religion and of all things. What draws a man towards this kind of obsession, in spite of all professional abuses hurled at him?"

"A deeply religious man?"

"Beyond deeply religious, Alsa, because he thought that God was talking to him, like God talked to Moses on Mount Sinai. Ten commandments to Moses, a few dozen theorems to Georg Ferdinand Ludwig Philip Cantor. These are strange concepts and theorems that Cantor came up with. No wonder that he had this omnipotent feeling of being God's mouthpiece. Only the infinite is worthy of God's intervention in mathematics, he must have thought, and God chose him as his conduit.

"He probably stumbled into his fabulous idea of comparing sets by matching, or attempting to match, their elements one-to-one. Brilliantly simple, and it opened a cornucopia of new ideas and roads into the strange realm of infinite sets. All stemming from this definition of equivalent size sets. Once he got a few stunning results, he was hooked. There was no coming back. The infinite swallowed him. And inside the infinite, God was waiting. Was there a point when he decided that this is what he was going to do for the rest of his mathematical life? Oh, well, very likely he didn't have to decide anything. He just followed God's direction, because it was God who decided for him."

Chapter 19
October 1985 - February 1987

Ada died in the fall of 1985. It fell to Leonard to tell Alexandra of her daughter's death. In the months that followed, Alexandra slowly learned about Leonard's agony. He told her only later, and grudgingly, what he had gone through. And then Revescu, who for a while had avoided her, resurfaced and related to her the full sequence of events.

It began when Revescu rang Leonard from Montreal, wondering how he should break the terrible news to Alexandra. He didn't have many details, not yet. Ada had died of a sudden infection which, it seemed, could not be treated. He knew that she died in a hospital in Galati. He could not say, not yet, when exactly it had happened, but it could not have been more than a week earlier. He would do his best to find out when, and under what circumstances, but it might take a while.

Leonard knew from Alexandra that Ada had been working for the last two years in a chemical factory in Galati as an unskilled worker. She had not finish high school, got in some trouble with the police, and it was only Emil's connections that saved her from jail, with the condition that she would accept the job in Galati and mend her ways. Leonard remembered Galati. Comrade Nascuta had sent him there for a few days to gather some data he urgently needed shortly after he had joined the National Institute for Calculations. A dreary, polluted, industrial city on the Danube, just before the river made its bend towards the Black Sea. Leonard pictured Ada's death – the overcrowded, dirty hospital room, the lack of proper medication or medical attention, nobody around her, the dismal city – and he knew that Alexandra would do the same and that it would shatter her.

"Mr. Jacobi," Revescu went on, "there is something else. Ada had a child a month before she died. There is no father known. A girl. Her name is Alexa. It's very likely that Dr. Semeu and the current Mrs. Semeu will look after her. Mr. Jacobi, it would be best if your sister heard all this from you. You or M. Natraq. The last time I had some difficult news for your sister … it didn't go well at all. I'd botch the whole thing again, and your sister would be hurt more than she needs to be. Bad news is best handled by the immediate family. Yes, I know it's not a pleasant task. She would need all your support and the support of M. Natraq. I understand that M. Natraq is in Paris. Maybe you should discuss with him the best course to take."

Revescu had rung Leonard at about seven in the evening. Before he left for the airport to catch one of the late shuttle flights to Montreal, Leonard rang Charles in Paris, but there was no answer. He sent him a telegram letting him know about the appalling news and that he was flying to Montreal to tell Alexandra and be with her. As the plane took off, it crossed his mind that Charles might in fact be in Montreal.

It was as the plane took off that the full horror of it hit Leonard. Not only was he the originator of his sister's sorrows, of her estrangement from her daughter, but now he was the one bringing her the news of Ada's death. He was both the architect of his sister's unhappiness and the bearer of the tidings that would end all her hopes. He got three Scotches from a hesitant flight-attendant. Was he potential trouble? He told her he'd had a death in the family and that he knew of no other way to cope with the news. It worked. Leonard felt stupidly guilty about the half-truth and having to tell it to a perfect stranger. He lined the little bottles up on the folding tray – soldiers in the fight for some peace of mind. After the first bottle, he began to shake lightly and felt perspiration on his forehead. He felt nauseated and wondered whether it was the Scotch or a reaction of his body against what he had to do. Wild thoughts ran through his mind – cowardly thoughts. Maybe Alexandra was away, in

Paris with Charles, or on one of her many professional trips – lecturing at God only knows what university or institute. He quickly rejected the notion. He had talked to Alexandra only a few days earlier, and she hadn't mentioned any travel plans. He began thinking that if Charles wasn't there with Alexandra, it might be a good idea to call Charles's sister Lysiane, and her daughter, Charles's niece – what was her name? – Isabelle, yes, Isabelle. She and Alexandra had hit it off …

He told himself he was having a nightmare, the kind one always felt could be broken by just pushing oneself to wake up. Such things as this, he kept thinking, should not happen in real life.

For the entire flight, he couldn't escape the idea that, in a tortuous and inadvertent way, he was his niece's master executioner. First, master executioner, then designated bearer of the news, as a means of expiating what he had started. As retribution, as punishment.

At Dorval, he found Hugue Lortie's number in the telephone book (luckily, he remembered Lysiane's husband's name). There were three Hugue Lorties, though. The second number he dialled was the right one. It was Lysiane who answered. When Leonard told her why he had called, there was shocked silence at the other end. After a while, Lysiane asked what she should do. Should she meet him at her brother's house? No, she didn't know whether Alexandra was home. But she was definitely in Montreal and Charles was still in France.

Eventually, Leonard asked if she could find Isabelle and wait for his phone call in case Alexandra needed them. He wasn't sure, but he thought it best to be there with Alexandra by himself when he told her the news.

In the cab on the way to her house, he hoped that Alexandra would be out for the evening, that he would have another hour or two before the terrible moment. And when he saw the lights in her apartment, he took his time to pay the driver. He gave him a big tip and asked the driver to let him just sit for a few minutes.

When she answered the door and saw his face, she knew immediately that something was wrong. Something had happened in Toronto. He was depressed, had had another fight with Monica, had been fired. No, it was worse. Something had happened to Matt. Only when he said, "Let's go inside, Alsa," did she know that the bad news involved her. She thought of Charles, and then suddenly, at last, of Ada. She guessed the rest. All she could utter was a moan, a soft howl of animal pain.

Leonard put his arms around her, without saying anything. She sobbed quietly in his arms for several minutes, until Leonard gently steered her towards the sofa. They sat down together, his arms still around her. She noticed the large wet patch she had left on Leonard's shirt and wondered stupidly whether there was a limit to the amount of tears she could discharge.

"It was Revescu who rang me with the news," Leonard said.

She nodded.

"It happened several days ago, in Galati. A sudden infection that could not be checked. It was very fast and she didn't suffer at all. Revescu is trying to find out the details. It may take a while."

She nodded.

"I sent a telegram to Charles," he said.

She nodded. She said thanks, but no sound came out of her, only her lips moved.

"Lysiane and Isabelle –"

She put a finger on her lips and shook her had. She wanted to tell him that she had no strength for talk now, that words were pointless.

They sat there on the sofa for a long time, she wasn't sure for how long. Then Leonard got up and began to wander around the room.

"What is it?" she asked him.

"Is there anything to drink?"

"There's wine. There is a bottle of *poire* somewhere, I'm sure. Charles likes a sip now and then."

That's when Leonard told her about her granddaughter. He told her the story without looking at her. Only when he told her the name Ada had chosen did he stop and look at her. "She had chosen the name of Alexa for her. Ada did."

His eyes suddenly filled with tears. Him, too. What was it with their family? All so prone to emptying their tear ducts. Their mother, too, and their father, after the first stroke.

"I think the *poire* is in the kitchen," she told Leonard.

She went on, whispering mainly to herself, "I can't even properly mourn her. She's so far away, it's all so abstract. I don't even have a picture of her – I mean a picture of her now, before …"

Charles called the following day at noon, and it was Leonard who picked up the phone. Alexandra, who had not slept at all during the night, had just gone up to her bedroom telling Leonard that she was going to try to rest a bit, but she came out when she realized who the caller was. Charles said that he had been at Cambridge for a couple of days and had just returned. He would take the earliest available flight, but didn't think he would be home before the afternoon of the following day.

The next months were very difficult. Alexandra didn't teach for several weeks. Charles took a month off, too, and stayed with her. On the eve of his return to Europe, Alexandra heard him on the phone with Leonard, asking her brother to try to be with her as much as he could. For a while after Charles had gone, Leonard travelled to Montreal every weekend. A couple of times, he brought Matt with him. They took long walks without talking much. The only news she took any interest in was about Matt. Leonard caught on quickly, and Matt suddenly became the hero of many adventures and amusing tales. Some of them, she suspected, were sheer fiction. It didn't matter to her. When Leonard shook his head, unable to provide a new chapter in Matt's chronicles – that's what she began to call them – she would often say to Leonard, recalling one of the earlier stories, "Tell me about the disaster with the piano teacher," or "Tell me about the visit with his friends to the clairvoyant woman." She would gently correct Leonard, or ask for clarification, whenever a later rendition differed from the first version. At one point she said to him, "Many of these stories are invented, aren't they? Of course they are. How many things can happen to one thirteen-year-old?"

But most of the time their walks were quiet, those weekends Alexandra and Leonard were together after Ada's death. Quiet walks under grey skies. Alexandra was grateful for Leonard's company and his silence. It was often cold, but she didn't mind. She would sometimes take Leonard's arm. She often shivered, but not from cold. It wasn't the cold, she told Leonard, whenever he asked if she was all right. She liked walking in the fall, she liked the desolate sky, the leafless branches of the trees, the emptiness of the streets. She had even begun to like the cold. "I can connect with all this, Leonard. That's what real life is, at least to me. Sunny blue skies, the lush greens of summer, the screams of playing children – no, they're not for me. Poor Charles, he has to come on long walks like this with me, and now more than ever. He says he doesn't mind, but I'm not sure. He's puzzled by my desire for long walks. At least he's never cold – that's what he says. He jokes that Quebecers never feel the cold – natural selection."

There was another blow two months after Ada's death. Revescu, back from Romania, came to her house. He had had, he told her, an extraordinary stroke of luck. He found in Galati, at the hospital where Ada had been taken, a letter she wrote just before she died. The letter was for her, for Ada's mother. He handed her an envelope.

Alexandra thought she was in a bad melodrama.

"Are you sure it's from her?"

"Yes. This is not the original envelope – there was no envelope in fact. It was a nurse at the hospital, Maria Grija (a very appropriate name), who gave it to me. I paid hard currency for it – two hundred and fifty dollars. She wasn't happy about the transaction, Maria Grija, she had pangs of guilt, it seems, but as she said, circumstances forced her to do it. 'I have two children, M. Revescu,' she told me, 'and my husband died last year. The pay is too small. It was Mlle Ada who told me to sell the letter. I was very close to her. And I made sure that the little one ended up with Mr. Semeu.' It seems, Mme Jacobi, that after Ada wrote the letter she gave it to Sister Maria. She told her to wait for somebody from the West, somebody who might inquire about her, somebody who knew Alexandra Semeu, her daughter's grandmother. If such a person appeared, she was to give them the letter. Ada also told her that there could be good money in it for her, very good money. She advised her to sell the letter. And not cheap."

"And you can be sure it's really from her?" Alexandra asked again.

Revescu nodded. "I read it. I'm terribly sorry, but I had to. I couldn't part with so much money without reading it. I had to make sure it was not a fabrication. On the back of the page, you can see, she's written, 'For Alexandra Semeu, Alexa's grandmother.'"

She looked at the back first. Yes, her daughter couldn't bear to write, "For my mother."

It was a very short letter – only a few lines – with an abrupt start. *I've made up my mind about you a long time ago, and there is nothing you can do to change the way I think. My death, which I am told will come soon, will make forgiveness impossible. The dead do not answer pleas. My death will be your punishment. What you did to me is unpardonable. But I have no right to punish my daughter as well. I am a better mother than you were to me. I beseech you to come and get her. Get her out of this hell. The hell in which, eight years ago, you left me. Your granddaughter's name is Alexa.*

"It's hard to read, I know. But Mme Jacobi, there is a ray of hope in all this, and that's why I wanted to see you in person. You may want to fulfil your daughter's wishes and try to get Alexa out – of course, you'd have to adopt her. I know, I know, your former husband … Well, I took the liberty, without your go-ahead, of investigating the terrain. I asked M. Semeu again to see me, and this time he agreed. The little one, Alexa, was there. Very, very cute. A beautiful child, I assure you. I talked to M. Semeu. and he may be amenable to let it happen. Mme Semeu was very much in favour of it. It's the fourth child – they have three of their own – and the apartment is very crowded. I don't think that was the only reason why M. Semeu had a change of heart, though. I think Ada's death had shattered him. And when I showed him the letter Ada wrote to you, he had tears in his eyes. I need instructions from you, Mme Jacobi. Should I start working on it? It may cost a lot of money – besides the Romanian authorities, there is Mme Semeu, and she is a very greedy woman – but this time I think it's going to work."

A year later, Alexandra was the guest speaker at a small mathematical workshop on Lie algebras held at York University. Whenever in Toronto, she tried to stay with Leonard, and she had called a few days earlier to inquire if Matt's bedroom was free and if she was not inconveniencing him. She flew in on the eve of the workshop, and they went out for dinner to an expensive pizza place in mid-town Toronto. It had snowed the entire afternoon, and the evening traffic was almost at a standstill. The restaurant, when they finally got there, was small, crowded, and noisy.

"I don't understand this," Leonard said, while they waited for the waiter to take their order. "It's cold, it's snowing, the traffic is atrocious, barely moving – people in their right mind should be home blessing their central heating. Yet everybody seems to be out and in a good mood."

Alexandra wasn't hungry. She'd have a salad, she told the waiter, and she'd share some of Leonard's carpaccio and pizza. The waiter shook his head unhappily. She nibbled from the small lettuce salad and took her time with a narrow slice of the pizza. It was while Leonard was still working on the last slice of the pizza that Alexandra told him she was moving to the States at the end of the academic year. The Institute of Advanced Studies at Princeton had made her an offer that was very attractive. Not only were they almost doubling her current salary, but all she had to do was hold a seminar on a topic of her choice. She would have the rest of the time for her research. Of course, there'd be graduate students to supervise, but also providing helping with her research. She had a gigantic travel and conference budget allocation. Princeton, Leonard! Princeton! That's where Einstein and Godel ended up. She could not resist the temptation, and the flattery, of the offer.

"It feels good to be appreciated, Leonard. It feels good to be flattered and treated like a minor star. It's not too far from New York, I hear. The only thing that worries me is my English. I've not made much progress in Montreal. My accent remains a mystery to most of my listeners. I hope I won't turn into another Danczay. The only time I speak English is at conferences. It's a strange city, Montreal, divided by an invisible language barrier. You may cross it when you shop, and at parties. But I don't have much heart for parties, and most of our friends and acquaintances are French-speaking. So I rarely have the opportunity to speak English. When I do, I jump at it, to practise, which drives some of my friends and colleagues crazy. Many of them – maybe most of them – are PQ-supporters. Good God, Leonard, that's all I need, more politics, more causes, more indoctrination. I know, I know, there's no comparison, but it all sounds so childish, a prolonged, destructive sulk for things that happened so long ago. I'm sure I don't understand it. The whole thing, Leonard, makes me quite weary. I may be exaggerating, but I want a dull, ordinary life, without great causes, and without being told in what language to carry it out. Once bitten, twice shy. I like Montreal, I like the friends I've made, most of them Charles's old friends, but all this separation silliness made the Princeton offer so much easier to accept."

"I envy you, Alsa. The professional adulation, the fame."

"Of the two of us, you are the most likely to become famous. With your Aroso book, or the one you'll write next."

Leonard shook his head. "Clara, you remember Clara, don't you? Red hair, played the violin … You've met her once or twice, I'm quite sure …"

"The quartet lady. Clara. Of course."

"Yes, the quartet lady. In our parting scene – okay, the scene where she told me to get lost – Clara accused me of not trying to be a real mathematician because of fear of commitment, or of failure. I think I told you about it, didn't I? How did she put it? I don't remember exactly, but she called me something like a 'half-committed professional outsider – both in my private life and in my work.' She was wrong, wasn't she, Alsa? How could I have been afraid of failure in math when I was *already* a failure? I knew at nineteen or twenty that I was a failure. I'm all right, I got used to this a long time ago. How could she say this – a violin player, too? One does not become a great violin player just through commitment and hard work. You have it, or you don't. There are no late bloomers. Thirty-five-year-old David Oistrakhs don't just jump into the limelight. Sure, hard work is needed. Commitment goes a long way. But it's not – by any stretch – sufficient. Necessary, but not sufficient. What on earth did Clara expect me to do, to become a successful mathematician? Plagiarize papers? Attend conferences and workshops and pretend that I was something I was not, and couldn't ever be?"

She nodded a few times without answering. Then she took another unenthusiastic bite from her narrow slice of pizza.

"What's Charles saying about your move to Princeton?" Leonard asked after a while.

"Professionally, he's thrilled for me, of course. But he was rather taken aback by my decision, at the beginning. He's getting used to the idea and has moments when he doesn't mind it at all. He'll live in three places. Paris, Montreal, and Princeton. Not bad, if you can stand all the travel. That's what bothers him. He claims he already smells of airports. He says he'll never shake the stench of them if I move to Princeton. Charles is an angel. I keep saying that. He is my luck. For once, I made a good choice. A late, romantic choice."

She smiled. In spite of the good news, she had to force herself to be upbeat and positive about the change. She was aware that she had never had a quick and ready laugh, that she had always been rather serious, but now she was positively gloomy.

"Is Matt with Monica?" she asked. "Could I see him on Friday? Let's go out to a restaurant and a movie. How is he?"

"Well adjusted, in spite of our worries. Good at mathematics. Not that he works at it – it just comes easy to him. I love the little guy. Not so little anymore, come to think of it. He's going to be tall. Very sweet and funny. Yes, funny. He makes me laugh. And wise beyond his years. The way he looks at his parents, at Monica and me, and the advice he gives us, you'd think we were the silly children and he was the wise, protective parent who needed to encourage us, but not too obviously. Monica and I are seeing more and more of each other. Kind of dating. It's pleasant and convenient and comfortable. Quite civilized. Matt is very happy, and he's trying to get us to live together again. Without pushing it."

"Leonard, this is good news. Oh, you should have told me earlier."

"You never know, but it may happen. Matt is working his magic on us. Monica and I have finally attained the wisdom of trying to understand each other. Not necessarily agree with, but understand. Most people learn this very early in life. We've been a bit slow, it seems. Anyway, Monica has been unusually warm towards me lately. Unusually understanding."

"Go on, go on."

"It could be that I'm reading too much into one small incident. But no, I don't think so. I've been thinking, lately, of writing another book. Yes. At least do some background reading, some initial research. Slowly get going. Herman Gunther Grassmann and his theory of hypercomplex numbers. It came out only one year after Hamilton's quaternions, and yet it was a complete generalization of complex numbers and quaternions to any dimension."

Alexandra laughed. "Another one in your sequence of 'Lives of Undeservedly Obscure Mathematicians'?"

"In a way. That's exactly what Monica wondered, too. A few weeks ago, I was telling her a little bit about his life, about Grassmann's life. Unknown *gymnasium* teacher in Stettin (today it's Szcezcin, in Poland), around the middle of the last century. Took a late interest in mathematics, more interested in theology and church affairs, music and philology. Compiled a Sanskrit dictionary. His mathematical writings weren't easy to follow – almost incomprehensible, it seems – and his choice of notation added to the confusion. Which may explain why everybody ignored his work for so long. His contributions have been recognized only relatively recently. Anyway, I expected the usual sarcasm and disinterest from Monica. Sarcasm did come, in the form of the suavely phrased query as to whether it was another instalment in my series of mathematical injustices. And when, after some hesitation, I told her that, yes, it was, and it was the only thing I found worth doing, the only thing for which I had an interest, she didn't laugh or look at me with pity. No, instead, she said, 'Tell me more about Herman Gunther Grassmann. I might as well learn to like him.'"

"And you? In what way have you become more understanding?"

"It's not easy to confess, Alsa. I feel foolish. I went with them to a Saturday service. To the Synagogue, with Monica and Matt. The three of us. It was my initiative, too, although Matt had suggested it to me. As far as Monica knows, though, it was my idea, and I, shamelessly, took all the credit. It was tiresome, of course. I had just finished reading a book on Clifford algebra and the history behind its relative obscurity. Clifford, both a philosopher and a mathematician, had died very young, at the age of only thirty-four, before knowledge about his work was widespread. You may have heard of him. So, throughout the service, I thought of Herman Gunther Grassmann, of William Kingdon Clifford, who bored through the obscurity of Grassmann's text and created the geometric (or Clifford) algebra, and of Josiah Willard Gibbs, the Yale mathematician whose vector analysis, in hindsight, may have hindered the application of the best tools for mathematical physics. No, it wasn't too bad, Alsa.

Quite bearable. In fact, it was pleasingly restful to speculate, under the monotony of the religious babble surrounding me, whether having a tool properly handling the four-dimensional space would have created new insights among the physicists of the time, and Einstein's special relativity would have arrived earlier, only under another's name. Anyway. Now and then I turned and watched the two of them, Monica and Matt. Matt was sitting between us, and he kept winking at me. Then he would whisper in his mother's ear, and she would smile, look fondly at him, and nod in agreement. So, an hour and a half passed relatively quickly – well, add a trip to the washroom and a cigarette break outside. Yes, that's how Matt does it, the little magician – with a wink and a whisper. He may very well bring us back together."

"Leonard, try to make it happen. Work at it. Please. And, Leonard, ask Monica to join us tomorrow. For dinner at least. Please, Leonard, please. And, Leonard, promise me something. Promise that you'll visit me in Princeton as often as you can. And bring Matt. And Monica. Promise? I've never asked you for anything. I have a right to ask you for this."

She warmed to the subject. "Charles will be in Princeton with me the whole of June. Come, Leonard, and bring Monica and Matt. Oh, that would be lovely, the five of us."

"We could all take long walks – not that cold in June, though," Leonard said, smiling at her. "But we could look for desolate streets. I'm not sure about Princeton, but we should be able to find some in New York."

"No, we'll have a special program for visitors. We'll go to New York. We'll go to the theatre. Yes, walk a bit, but not much. You can take Matt to see a sports game. Boys like sports. They do sports in New York, don't they? Hockey? Basketball? Baseball? Do they have baseball in New York? We could climb the Empire State Building …"

When they got back to Leonard's apartment they watched the news on TV for a while. On CBC there was talk about renewed efforts to include Quebec more satisfactorily in the constitution. Brian Mulroney and his advisors were modestly confident of a possible agreement, sooner rather than later. There was talk about a first ministers' meeting at Meech Lake, not far from Ottawa.

"There's another thing I wanted to tell you," Alexandra said. "I need the money Princeton is offering. To get out Alexa. Yes, Revescu has finally arranged something. I can buy her out now. It's a lot of money, and this Princeton offer comes in handy."

She got up and fetched her purse from a small side table in the hallway. She took an envelope out of it. "I want to show you something. Revescu brought me this letter from Ada. She had left it with somebody at the hospital. Revescu got it when he went there to find out more details about Ada's death. It's a miracle it reached me. No doubt, it was meant to punish me fully for what I did. It's the final blow. The letter in which my own daughter curses me. I do sound melodramatic, don't I? And yet, in a way, I cherish this letter. Because she is also asking for help. From me. Not from her father. Not from anybody else. I got this letter two months after Ada died. I didn't tell you about it. I couldn't. It's too horrible. Because it's true. No, don't try to make me feel better. It's all true, Leonard, it's all true. You can read it now."

"Alsa, I don't have to read it."

"Please, I want you to."

Leonard read the letter and sighed. "Alsa, this was written when Ada was in the worst state of mind possible. To be young and to know you'll die is very difficult to accept. She was alone and bitter and angry. She had to find somebody to blame. She blamed you because you were the most important person in her life, because she loved you most. It's not reasonable to think that this is a true reflection of her actual feelings for you. After all, she gave her daughter your name."

On the screen, with a newsreel of Quebec premier Robert Bourassa running in the background, an expert was explaining Quebec's minimal conditions to join the constitutional agreement and of the need of approval by all the provincial premiers gathered at Meech Lake. She stood up and switched the TV off. "I spent a whole year agonizing before I made the decision to come here," she said. "I turned down an earlier invitation to a conference in Stockholm. It was the first time I was told I could travel outside Romania – about a year earlier than the congress in Rome. I was afraid I'd be tempted to stay in the West, and at the last minute I claimed I was sick and cancelled the trip. Charles was distressed, of course, but he never forced me one way or another. He had always let me know that while he wanted me to get out and live with him in the West, he understood perfectly my hesitations and was ready to accept whatever outcome. He left it to me – it was my decision. It was my decision, and in the end I let her down. I let Ada down, Leonard. I hurt her. I dismissed her. Oh, I know I did all that was humanly possible to get her out, to get her to join me here. But why is it, Leonard, why is it that among all the scenarios I run through my mind to consider the consequences of my decision not to return, the one in which I could not get her out, or make her come out, was never played?"

He wouldn't answer her. It was clear to her that he wouldn't, because he didn't want to add to her pain.

But she knew the answer. It has been incessantly ringing in her ears. "I subconsciously avoided it, Leonard, I dismissed it. Because, had I let myself be a good and loving mother, I would have been unable to leave."

She felt like a character in a Greek tragedy upon whom the Gods had turned their backs. And yet she was honoured, almost revered, professionally, and now, with this appointment at Princeton, she had reached the pinnacle of her profession. And Charles, ever caring, as much in love with her as ever, was doing his best to cheer her up. But she couldn't forgive herself. In her lowest moments, she viewed herself as a monster who had sacrificed her daughter. She said as much, once, to Charles. He said, "To most people, the efforts you made to get Ada out, the fact that life with Emil had become impossible, and yes, why not, your desire to get out of the stifling, repulsive, and, in the end, destructive world you had lived in, would be more than enough weight to tip the balance in favour of your decision. But not to you, who seem so logical about everything else."

No, not to her. She had abandoned her daughter, and her daughter had died. Like a boomerang, this thought always returned to her with nightmarish intensity. Watching Leonard biting with gusto into a large slice of pizza, she wondered whether she blamed him a bit, in some corner of her mind, for what had happened. Maybe "blame" was not the right word. But it was he who had triggered this chain of events. She remembered her disastrously prophetic words, that cold Sunday, in the snow-covered Cismigiu Garden, when he told her about his decision to run away. "Leonard, what's going to happen? This is the end for us."

She knew that she would always be torn by what she had done. She would forever try to convince herself that her decision to leave was the right one, or, at the very least, a reasonable, sensible one. That it had not been unreasonable for her to assume that Emil would follow her with Ada, or let Ada join her. It did not happen, and now, for the rest of her life, she would question herself without ever being able to answer, without ever reaching some peace of mind. There was no right answer, or unique answer, of course. It was like Cantor's search: either decision, either answer, was sound, cogent, convincing. It just led to a different outcome. There was no right choice; there was only the choice you made. You made the choice and you lived with it. Unlike mathematics, unfortunately. The wonderful luxury that mathematics offered. Today, tomorrow, this whole week, you could postulate that the continuum hypothesis was false, and then, calmly, you could sit down and think your way through it to see where it would lead. Next week, without much fretting, you could assume the exact opposite, you could assume that Cantor's conjecture was true. And you could see where this change of mind might take you. Both avenues, both worlds, were wide open.

Charles had told her many times that she was too hard on herself. That there was no point anymore in all this soul-searching, since the wrongs, if any were done, could not be corrected. Not now, anyway. His words always lightened her pain, comforted her, but only briefly. And she was grateful to him for even these short remittals. But in the end she would always return to the same thoughts. It was not as if she didn't know that there was no point, didn't know how hopeless her agonizing was, and, in the end, the harm it was doing.

"Alexandra," Leonard said, "don't do this to yourself. Please."

"It's much better now. For a while, after I was told that Ada had died, I thought I was going to snap. 'Mathematician in Mental Hospital' – it's probably not so rare, but, unlike Cantor's, it was only a trivial conjecture about life that was churning my mind. I couldn't make my conjecture work either – the one in which I would get my daughter out – however reasonable it seemed initially. Cantor was convinced, too, at the very beginning, that he would prove his conjecture easily, with hardly any effort. It seemed so reasonable, so logical. It was an excellent insight.

An excellent mathematical insight. What else could be lurking there, in the continuum, that he couldn't see? And yet, and yet ... Poor Cantor, he proved it several times, his continuum hypothesis, and every time, it turned out to be wrong. How could he have foreseen that there was more than one density to choose from the continuum. I feel a kinship with Cantor. Same endless efforts, same lack of definite answers. No wonder he got mushy in the head and turned to God. That's one way."

"Turning to God?"

"Was it in Dauben's book or in yours that I read how Cantor, towards the end of his life, began to claim that $2^{\aleph_0} = \aleph_1$ came directly from God. This way – presto! – there was no more need to prove his continuum conjecture. A neat way to unload the obsession of a lifetime. One doesn't have to prove God's rules. Maybe that's how I'll end up. I'll talk myself into believing that it was God's decision. Only, however hard I try, I can't convince myself that he is around and watching us."

They were quiet for a long time. It was close to midnight.

"Well, you know," Leonard said, "if you are a believer, and Cantor was very religious, saying that a formula comes from God is like saying that it is an axiom, which, in the end, it turned out to be. So he wasn't wrong, after all."

He stood up. "I changed the linen on Matt's bed. Good night, Alsa."

It snowed heavily through the night. She read for a while from a thin book she had noticed earlier near the TV set. It was a collection of short stories in English and – looking at the contents – she picked the shortest one, "Prue." She finished it quickly and put it aside. She liked it, but she didn't know why. Couldn't be the literary quality, her English was much too basic for her to judge. As to what it was about, she wasn't too sure – an accommodating woman, a self-absorbed, mindlessly hurtful man, a rather different way of marking life's little defeats.

She put the book down, and from her bag – a large, very practical bag, but chic somehow, a gift from Charles who never returned from France without something – she took out the folder with the address she was to give at the workshop the following day. She went through it again carefully, whispering the words. Her notes were more detailed than she would usually make in such cases – she had had an anxiety attack a couple of days earlier and decided to write most of it down. She was worried that she'd mangle the English words and sounds beyond comprehension. She had thought of several incidents in Sophus Lie's life – his late start in mathematics, his imprisonment at Fontainebleau, his bizarre clothes – as possible beginnings, but now she wasn't sure she was going to attempt it. No, with her shaky English it was better to plunge directly into the math.

She moved a chair – carefully, so as not to wake Leonard – to the large living room window and switched off the light. The street below was well lit. The cars parked at the curb had settled in for the night under heavy white blankets. There was no traffic now, and the snow had covered the tire tracks with delicate care, leaving only faint impressions, as if some underground beasts had burrowed their secret way along the street.

When she moved back to the sofa, she switched on the light and looked at her watch. It was close to three o'clock. She realized it was going to be another sleepless night. Resigned, she picked up the thin book again. She turned to the last story this time, the one that gave the collection its catchy name. A tense woman, a writer of some success, looked after her father, who had a defective heart valve and might or might not have surgery. She worried about her daughters – especially the older one, Nichola, who did not want to see her or talk to her. Alexandra's eyes filled with tears – although she was quite aware that any parallel with her own life was distant at best. But there she was, with tears. Anyway, Nichola wasn't dead, just temporarily unwilling to talk to her mother. And the woman in the story had the other daughter, the younger one. The author was a woman. She put the book down wondering whether all the stories were about women and all so melancholy.

She thought of Aroso, and the choice he had made, exactly opposite to hers. Driven by passion first, whatever that word meant, and then by a sense of duty cast on him by one of life's strange turns. Had Aroso, in the end, been happier than she, by choosing differently? He had never brimmed with happiness, as far as she knew. But he had appeared less overwhelmed by sadness. He had not seemed bitter, either, although that could have been the resignation of old age. Maybe we learned to hide our disappointments and regrets as we grew older. Or, maybe, the difficulties of day-to-day subsistence in the Communist regime had left Aroso with little time to feel sorry for himself.

She would never know. Aroso had a sense of irony that hid much, something she knew she did not have. Aroso had also reached some inner peace, the wisdom of demanding little, brought on perhaps by age. He believed that choices mattered very little, that they were like chipping away at the side of a rocky mountain. If we happen to chip in a felicitous way, and if we look long and hard enough at the result of our exertions, we may recognize a vague shape and we live the illusion that we carve, that we affect our future. Maybe Aroso had it right. He had understood that, like the continuum, our lives were imponderable, unfathomable. Our decisions altered our lives, but in what way we did not know. We thought we knew, we acted as if we knew, but we deluded ourselves.

Very early in the morning, when she heard Leonard rumble out of the bathroom back to his bedroom, she knocked and announced through the closed door that she was going to be in the bathroom for a while. She took a long shower, half an hour of luxuriating in the warm water. She dried her hair and decided on full makeup. Might as well look her best – shouldn't subject her audience to too much of an ordeal.

She heard Leonard shouting from the kitchen, "Tea and a slice of bread and jam, as usual? The traffic is going to be awful this morning. What time do you have to leave?"

She had plenty of time. Her address wasn't until ten o'clock. By then, the rush hour would be over. She stood near the large window of the living room and looked outside. It was still snowing, but not as hard as before, and the sky was light. Sunbeams were getting through the cloud cover somewhere, because the large flakes looked silvery. She felt suddenly better, but then it was always like that; she picked herself up in the morning.

Leonard brought in a tray and began to set the table.

"It's odd how one's mood is lifted by light," he said, as if reading her thoughts.

"When it's light, I can deal with it," Alexandra said. "I can be objective. I can blame others. I can blame the times. It's at night when it gets to me, Leonard. Do you remember those horrible pictures of Hiroshima victims? They were always being reprinted in the Communist newspapers. The horrible lesions, the tumours, and especially the wasted, vacant look on the faces of the victims. I don't know what Ada died of exactly, and I don't know how she died, but that's how I see her, night after night. I wander through my apartment in the middle of the night, and she follows me wherever I go. It kills me, Leonard. I get up and I pace and I cry myself to sleep. If I get my granddaughter, if I manage to get Alexa out, Princeton will offer a bit of a change. Not that the nightmares would end. Not that I would sleep better. But that, at the very least, I'd get up, walk to Alexa's room, and watch her sleep."

Marquis imprimeur inc.

Québec, Canada
2008